THE MOONBEAM LADY

As Ju-hai stood in the doorway of the study room, he had a feeling that someone was prowling in the shadows. But he could see no one.

Then the moonlight coming from the little window seemed to thicken and swirl. It drew into a cylinder of bluish light and began to take form. In another minute, a woman stood there, one who was beautiful and stately.

"What is—who are—what are you?" Ju-hai gasped.

She smiled and beckoned, as if inviting him to enter her own home.

"I am Mei-yu. And I'm an Immortal—one of the servants of the Moon Goddess."

Also by E. Hoffmann Price
Published by Ballantine Books:

THE DEVIL WIVES OF LI FONG

The Jade Enchantress

E. Hoffmann Price

A Del Rey Book

BALLANTINE BOOKS • NEW YORK

A Del Rey Book
Published by Ballantine Books

Library of Congress Catalog Card Number: 81–22887

ISBN 0–345–29835–7

Manufactured in the United States of America

First Edition: June 1982

Cover art by Laurence Schwinger

TO ROBERT SPENCER CARR

With whom I share happy memories of deceased friends, our neighbors in Chicago, 1927: Farnsworth Wright, editor of *Weird Tales*; William R. Sprenger, business manager; Hugh Rankin, illustrator; and Otis Adelbert Kline, outstanding contributor: a goodly fellowship called THE VARNISHED VULTURES.

Prologue

The Jade Emperor sighed. No matter how well the Celestial Bureaucracy ran Heaven, someone always had a complaint or wanted something changed. He tapped the petition his secretary had handed him and lifted one eyebrow inquiringly.

"Who and what is this Mei-yu?" he asked.

"Divine and Imperial Majesty," the secretary answered, "she was a Buddhist nun who was granted Immortality for her good works—the usual compassionate business. For the past thousand or so years, she's been a Jade Lady, working day and night to make jade out of moonbeams. She seeks permission to present her problem to Chang Wo, the Moon Goddess."

"And what's her problem?"

"Ah—Divine Majesty, she won't explain. It's something she—ah—has to discuss with another woman."

The Jade Emperor sighed again. "Permission granted," he said. Accordingly and in due time, Mei-yu appeared in the Lunar Palace of Chang Wo, dressed in her formal court robes. Her velvet hood was embroidered with pearls, as were her satin slippers; as a compliment to her hostess, her tunic was the gold of the full moon on the horizon and her long ear pendants were of moonstones, glowing as if from an inner light. Elegant and beautiful, she was truly Chinese, except for her nose, which was longer than standard and faintly curved—perhaps the heritage of a Turki ancestor.

There was no kowtowing; the Goddess loathed formal-

1

ity. Mei-yu permitted Chang Wo to seat her at a small table, well away from the stately area reserved for the Jade Emperor and his favorite concubine.

The Goddess poured tea, which had been set out by soundless attendants. "What's on your mind, Mei-yu, that's for the ears of women only?"

"Divinity—"

"Do forget that formal nonsense!"

"Ah—Chang Wo, this is awkward. You know, I was a Buddhist nun—"

"Some of my best friends were nuns." The Goddess sighed. "But that was thousands of years ago. So what *is* in your mind?"

Mei-yu squirmed, smoothing out her tunic. "It isn't just in my mind."

"Everything is mind. You must have learned that in the nunnery."

"I learned everything in the nunnery—except how to get a lover. I'm one thousand, two hundred and eight years, nine days, and eight hours old, and I've never had a lover. And I'm fed up with herding elemental jade spirits and listening to their chatter . . ."

The Goddess regarded her visitor shrewdly. "Just who is this man you've fallen in love with—another Immortal? Or is he human?"

Mei-yu's brows rose to pointed arches. "What difference does that make?"

"You're pure spiritual essence," the Goddess explained. "You have everything a human woman has, but not a bit of it is substantial enough for love with a solid mortal."

Mei-yu seemed suddenly on the verge of tears. "I never thought of that! He's a farmer's son, studying for the Imperial examinations. But he neglects his studies. He loves to work with jade. Kwan Ju-hai is an artist—a very sensitive artist . . . Couldn't I possibly get a physical body or something reasonably solid?"

"Difficult. But if he's sensitive enough to see your spiritual body—some humans are—you two might manage. *Yang* combining with *yin*—positive combining with negative to create zero; and that's total completeness; instead of nothing, it's really everything!"

Mei-yu looked dubious. "But those human girls—being solid and substantial gives them advantages no spiritual body has. There is nothing like that which I could offer him!"

"*Lingam* and *yoni* as spirit principles have amazing possibilities," Chang Wo assured her. "Try it. You might be surprised."

The Jade Lady sensed that she was listening to a woman who spoke from experience. Yet she sighed and shook her head. "If I'd started at the human level . . . But skipping the foundation course and the pillow book . . . I just can't quite . . ."

The Goddess patted Mei-yu's shoulder. "Perhaps a temporary substantial body could be constructed for you; but it's a complicated business with many obstacles. Some of the answers to the problem are likely to be impossible, others illegal or against public policy. Why don't you run along home, get yourself some nice things to wear, and then find out whether he can see you—talk without speaking? If he can—well, you can use your imagination. You might make some wonderful arrangements. And if you still have problems, you can see me at any time."

Chapter I

Kwan Ju-hai and his brother, Kwan Shou-chi, were glad it was a downgrade, and no doubt the overburdened pack horses shared that feeling as they came out of the wooded foothills of the Ta-pa Range, some three days march from Ch'ang-an, the capital city of the T'ang Emperor. Old Man Kwan's sons wore blue shirts reaching halfway to the knee, and flopping black pants, about knee length. Their shoes were heavy. This was rocky ground.

Despite cursing the pack animals and inspiring them with whip flicks to the rump, each brother had breath for gabbling and energy for lifting his mushroom-shaped straw hat to mop the sweat that cut channels through the dust that caked his sun-blasted face.

For a farmer, Old Man Kwan was well off, but he never forgot that three centuries had been eaten up to expand a couple of peasant shacks to a walled village. He gave his sons every chance to learn that Kwan Village had not been the result of tail-sitting.

The animals had it easier. They'd tail-switched buzzing flies and done nothing while the brothers plied axe and saw to cut a trainload of wood, some for sale, some for village use. That the animals had gone upgrade without a burden had been only because the Old Man didn't know what he could have had them carry on the outbound way.

Ju-hai, a head taller than his younger brother, was rangy, sharp-faced and, though he had the expression, he did not resemble father, brother, or any of the swarm of

5

Kwan cousins. These were square rigged, squarish of face, inclined to look fixed, stubborn, and somewhat grim. Ju-hai, some months past his eighteenth birthday, carried himself as if savoring the mountain air, relishing the breath of conifers, scenting and anticipating the distant, whether in time or space. His eyes covered the entire field, ever poised, ever alert. Eagerness, versatility, and self-assurance promised Ju-hai eventful years rather than longevity.

Ju-hai's vision reached from the range which tapered off from the snowcap of Tai Pai Shan, near Ch'ang-an, and reached westward toward Szechuan Province; it swooped up from the three-thousand-foot elevation of the cultivated plain of Shensi Province, cradle of the Chinese race. He looked through a golden haze of *loess* dust, windblown from waste areas which would before many years have to be cleared of rock and scrub. For too many years there had not been plague, war, or famine to keep the people from multiplying faster than the land could feed them.

Ju-hai looked through more than golden haze; his vision reached through the haze of time, and already instinct warned him against excessive optimism. Horse-flavored wind brought hoof-stirred dust to cake his mouth. He spat and said, "Younger Brother, this is a dog-fornicating mess —this is dung on our pancakes—for me, anyway."

"Elder Brother," Shou-chi dutifully responded, "it's not always honey or syrup, as the Old Man's always telling us."

"He happens to be right, most of the time," Ju-hai conceded. "You may wonder what I'm griping about."

"Since you mention it—*hai!*" He scooped up a rock, hurled it, and nicked an erring pack horse's rump. Be-latedly, Elder Brother cracked his whip and corrected the misguided animal.

"Horses are crazy," Ju-hai added. "That turtle-child is on his way home and still has to nibble at lilies and fern."

"Or the dry manure of better animals," Shou-chi cut in. "You were going to tell me how you like the idea of school in Ch'ang-an."

"With all respect to the Old Man, I don't want to be a

scholar. I don't want to be a bureaucrat. I don't want to start out as magistrate in some louse-bound town with people committing crimes for me to investigate or suing each other for imaginary wrongs and damages." He cracked the whip, drew a spurt of dust from a shaggy black rump, and resumed. "Dad does make sense. If one of us doesn't get into the Civil Service, other civil servants will eat us alive, rob us blind. So, I'll have to learn to be a gentleman."

"I'd rather be a farmer," Shou-chi admitted. "I see what you mean. But I'll do my best while you're at school and after you've got an official appointment."

Younger Brother didn't realize how dumb and plodding he was; he didn't suspect that his earnestness, his industry, and his dedication were not enough to cope with the ever-increasing rapacity of the Bureaucracy.

"I know you'll do your best, and I'll outwit my fellow bureaucrats whenever I can, sleep with their concubines, and keep you informed as to what their next trick is going to be. With you doing the work and the Old Man doing the thinking, we ought to hold our own. All I meant was that I don't like the idea of getting away from my own country and people, and from working with jade."

Mention of the jade-craft, the art which Elder Brother pursued whenever his studies at the Kwan Village school permitted, put Shou-chi in mind of another severance. "You were speaking of concubines, a minute ago," he finally said. "Our girl will miss you. Lan-yin, I mean," he hastily added.

Shou-chi was far from subtle; his afterthought expression was as good as stating that he, too, had become aware of another girl—of Hsi-feng, the little slave girl who had blossomed into womanhood.

"I know you had Lan-yin in mind, and maybe the Old Man would arrange for you to take my turns with her, once I'm gone to Ch'ang-an. That way, you'd go through her pillow book twice as quickly and be just that much better off when you took a wife."

Thus far, Hsi-feng was neither Ju-hai's, Shou-chi's, nor anyone else's girl. Each knew that if either seduced Hsi-feng—Little Phoenix—the Old Man would flog the offender half to death and thereafter sleep with the girl himself. Nevertheless, Ju-hai was sorely worried; leaving Phoenix was his principal reason for hating the thought of three or four years away from home while preparing for the Imperial Civil Service examinations.

Phoenix was a slave because of a contract which her parents, desperately short of money, had signed to make her a bond servant of the Kwan family, and the terms were honorable. When she reached marriageable age, the Kwans were bound by old custom and honor to arrange a decent marriage for her. If any of the Kwans had an illicit relationship with her, they could not sell her to any other family, nor could they make as good a marriage for her as they otherwise could.

Although Ju-hai had developed an obsessive craving for Phoenix, his sense of propriety kept him from trifling with the girl, or even trying to; and sharing Lan-yin with his brother kept his decent restraint from being too onerous.

This turtle-loving school in Ch'ang-an . . . He'd been brooding, day after day, week after week, as Hsi-feng became ever more aware of her ripening femaleness. *If Younger Brother doesn't get her, someone will marry her.*

The more he had of Lan-yin, the more he wondered how it would be with Little Phoenix as pictured on page such-and-such, of Lan-yin's pillow book. As he pondered all these facets of the disturbance stirred up by a slave girl suddenly become big enough and old enough, he was quite certain that Younger Brother and every other male within a hundred *li* was wallowing in comparable thoughts.

These woman-thinkings were interrupted as the pack train neared the yawning gateway of Kwan Village. Shou-chi pointed.

"Look at that big hulk of a Mongol!"

Ju-hai looked. "Must be a shaman. The old guy has his drum and rattles and stuff flopping all over him."

"What do you suppose he's doing out here?"

"I'll ask him."

The limping wanderer came from north of the Great Wall built centuries ago to exclude armies of Mongols,

Manchus, and other barbarians from the realm of the Son of Heaven. They were crude fellows—their daily life was so grim that warfare was a welcome relief from herding their flocks. They were so poverty-stricken that they had nothing to put on the altars of the Lord Buddha but the dried meat of sheep or the fermented milk of mares. Civilized folk, on the other hand, offered only fruit, nuts, grain, incense, or flowers—things which those dangerous blockheads never had except when they congregated around the western gate of Ch'ang-an, where a colony of the nomads lived in their *yurts*.

The brothers met the hobbling wanderer. Ju-hai waved his brother on with the pack train and paused. "You are tired. Why not go in and rest and eat?" he asked the man.

The big fellow eyed Ju-hai, and finger combed his forked beard. His ears reached out like fans. He leaned on his heavy staff. His sheepskin jacket was greasy-dirty, even for a Mongol. The rest of his clothing and his floppy-brimmed high-crowned hat were equally grimy.

"You're a shaman," Ju-hai said.

It was a statement, not a question. The little drum, rattle, and all the rest of the gear that those half-madmen used in their prophetic art or craft made questions needless. This man might be able to give Ju-hai a helpful answer to important questions.

Ju-hai dug into the sash which secured his short pants and found a piece of silver.

"How did you hurt your leg?"

"Tiger clawed and bit me." The stranger's Chinese was crude.

"What did you do—"

"I beat the bastard to death with my staff and cut out his liver and ate it, so I feel like a tiger, but my leg bothers me."

Ju-hai reckoned from this that the Mongol had come up from the southeast, and was heading in the general direction of Ch'ang-an.

"Man after my own heart." He offered the silver. "This isn't beggar-bait. It is a present."

The wanderer understood the great distinction between the two. He said something which Ju-hai no more than half understood.

"My father runs the village. Go in, get food, rest up, and later we'll talk."

"What you want?"

"Stick around and you'll find out."

The shaman made a grunting sound which might have been a word. "So you got troubles? Tax collector? Or who's going to get your girl when you go in the army?"

"How do you know I got troubles?" Ju-hai challenged.

The broad face became shrewd. He said, good humoredly, "Nobody talks to me except when he's in trouble up to his chin. All my life people tell me about troubles. So when I see a trouble-face, I know it."

"How long you been a shaman?"

"Born that way. Some got to study how, but I wonder why anyone is so crazy and wants to be one when he don't have to."

Ju-hai nodded. "I don't know a thing about shamanizing except what I've heard people say."

"Then both ears are full of manure. If you got a question, you can't ask me in this town."

"Why not?"

"My spirit friend takes my body and talks for me; I am somewhere else. Before I go into open-eye sleep, there is drumming and chanting and whanging and then my spirit friend roars like a crazy thunderstorm, and every bastard in town knows what is being said."

"Then why would anyone ask you questions?"

"Because they trust me."

Ju-hai didn't know whether to be skeptical or perplexed, and his face revealed the conflict.

The shaman explained, "When the spirit takes my body, I don't hear what you say, I don't hear what *it* says. So I can't tell you any lies, I can't make any mistakes."

"But your pet devil can tell me any kind of nonsense, and what can I do to him?"

The Mongolian chuckled. "You see what a lot of fellows don't. When they get worried enough, they'll believe anything. But a lot of times, my spirit-devil gives them good advice."

After a long silence, Ju-hai said, "You're on your way to Ch'ang-an." A grunt, a nod, and then Ju-hai resumed, "At the Moon Festival, I'm going to Ch'ang-an with my Old Man's wagon train. You wait and give your leg a chance. I'll see you get food, and you can ride one of the wagons. I'm Ju-hai. My father is the Kwan."

"I'm Yatu and I don't know who my father was."

Yatu made for the cooked-food stall near the inn, and Ju-hai went to his apartment in the Kwan quarter of the village.

Chapter II

Ju-hai's crowded life was quite too diversified to permit monotony: with an early morning start as a farmer, he put in more than half a day, sometimes working, sometimes overseeing; then, three or four hours were spent at the Kwan Village school, where he was becoming a *literate countryman*, a status by no means rare, yet, a step upward. After evening rice came the diversities—calligraphy, reading of classics, or several hours of pursuing his avocation, the working of jade.

One of the bedrooms of the apartment had been converted into a workshop dedicated to what had been a dominant passion until Hsi-Feng's ripening femaleness became a distraction, a competitor, at least and thus far, on the emotional level.

Details of his patterned life-style varied according to circumstance. He might eat with the family on holidays and birthdays, and certainly would join in all festivals. There were conferences with the Old Man, in his office, where Ju-hai was briefed on the season's prospects and how to offset tax collectors, the Bureaucracy, recruiting officers, and every other plague. Finally, there were occasional discussions on neighboring landowners, one of whose daughters it might be advantageous to marry. As an additional safeguard against the Government, the looter and the spoiler, each marital alliance with a worthwhile family made for greater security when influence and bribery were required, whether for survival or for advancement.

Aside from the Kwan dwelling, which occupied a quarter of the entire walled enclosure, the rest of the village consisted of the inn, the cooked-food stall, a few shops, and the plaza, on which the dwellings of tenants and neighboring landowners fronted. When disbanded soldiers or bandits—the distinction between the two was purely academic—prowled the fringes of Shensi Province, the farmers manned the wall and repelled the would-be looters with flights of arrows and rockets.

Ju-hai had scarcely bathed and changed when the slave girl brought a tray crowded with spicy-sour soup, "pot stickers," a smoked duck, steamed, and a miniature tub shaped from wooden staves; steam still escaped from the rice which the cover protected. Finally, there was a jug of *shao-hsing*, the yellow wine which tasted as if it had set out to be dry sack but had taken a few detours to a destination all its own.

Once Phoenix put the meal on the worktable with its clutter of books, brushes, brush holder, sticks of ink, and the slab for grinding ink, she fired up the charcoal brazier to heat water for after-supper tea.

Despite farm work, school, and enough time with Lan-yin, the joint concubine of the Kwan brothers, Ju-hai found Hsi-feng ever more disturbing. Her jacket, a hand-me-down from one of the Kwan women, was becoming a bit more snug, and the wearer a little more luxurious, yet short of opulent—an exciting understatement. And when not-so-little Phoenix bent over the table, meticulously careful in setting dishes out in a harmonious pattern, Ju-hai was quite too appreciative of her three-dimensional geometry to extemporize a verse. Leave that to Li Po! The devastation began when Phoenix half straightened up, slanted her glance, and moved the *shao-hsing*. Then, as if he had given her the final approval, she shifted it ever so slightly and contentedly wagged her head of ultimately black hair. She had done it exactly as it should have been done . . . the positioning of the rice wine, of course.

But the stray lock which sneaked almost to her left eyebrow, while the remainder of her bangs almost grazed her right, and the slantwise glance of amazingly luminous dark eyes . . . ! The nice thing about it all was that Hsi-feng was very innocently being female. Only a female bungler or a supreme artist would have risked Hsi-feng's instinctively perfect baiting.

Her eyelids were almost tangent to the pupil; and while she'd be eye-catching in any position, the angle was perfect and made the utmost of dainty features and fine facial contours. She was a lady, a very young one, but time would tend to that by refining and maturing an elegant beginning. From cheekbone to jaw was a smooth, squarish contour, tapering to a fine little chin.

Dimples lurked, and she almost smiled and then remembered the proprieties—

Ju-hai silently cursed his stupidity when, on the way from woodcutting, he'd told his brother, "I've got to work on those earrings for the Old Man's Number One Lady—you take care of Lan-yin tonight."

The most dangerous creature on earth was the human female, fully aware of her femaleness, and burning with the urge to try it out, to fascinate, devastate—

Quite aside from the Old Man's views and warnings, Ju-hai's own integrity and the Confucian ethics he'd been studying had kept him from approaching Phoenix. But for this accursed business of going to the capital to prepare for the Imperial Civil Service examinations, there was no reason why he should not have her; even though her family's poverty and consequent unimportance made such a marriage useless as an alliance against the Government, hers was a good family, and the early Kwans had done well enough without any important alliances.

But a student was quite too busy to be handicapped by a

wife; and by the time Ju-hai passed the examinations, Hsi-feng should be properly married. And if she lost her virginity, the Old Man could not arrange a marriage as good as he had agreed to.

He told himself that tomorrow night Lan-yin's insatiable desires would make virtue quite easy. The fact was that when he was with the concubine of the Kwan sons, he'd begun to close his eyes and imagine that he was making love with Hsi-feng; and when Lan-yin had left him comfortably depleted, he still had a mental craving for Hsi-feng.

"Old Master, when you've eaten—shall I come back to brew your tea? Or may I serve your meal?"

"I don't know what would be nicer—" He made a vague gesture to indicate papers and books. "Thank you, maybe tomorrow."

Ju-hai was learning why the daughters of aristocratic families were guarded day and night until marriage.

Each regarded the other. He knew that she had seen through him; she knew that she had not been rejected. Not this night, not tomorrow, but she'd be back, and he'd eventually let Phoenix serve evening rice and stay until he gave permission for her to leave. And she'd not beg permission to depart; she'd wait for him to speak the words. Her eyes, dark and magnificent as never before, predicted and promised.

After a moment longer than propriety permitted, she modestly lowered her glance; with his permission, she left.

Ju-hai savored his final glimpse of the girl's elegant backside. *If Younger Brother weren't so dumb, he could pass the examinations and I'd be a happy farmer*, he thought.

Though he ate heartily, the skill of the Szechuanese cook was wasted. He didn't know whether he ate smoked duck or sorghum stalks. Abruptly, he got up and made for the jade shop adjoining the bedroom.

The shop centered about a workbench made of wood smoothly squared with an adze. Two X-frames, a couple of feet apart, fitted snugly into cuts in the bench edges. A horizontal bamboo shaft rested in the vee of the X-frames.

A foot length of bamboo was covered with rawhide which, after being soaked to make it flexible, had been tightly wrapped about the central portion of the shaft, one end of which was fitted with a bamboo drill. This was spun back and forth by belts drawn tightly over the hide-covered portion of the shaft. At floor level was a foot treadle which moved the belts.

Beneath the end of the drill was a small dish of kitchen grease mixed with ruby dust or emery powder. There were also polishing discs and blades of bamboo, as well as saw frames with blades of soft iron or copper wire. These implements got their cutting, grinding, and polishing surfaces from the same mixture which gave the drills their bite. Jade was not, properly speaking, carved; it was abraded.

By the light of an oil lamp, Ju-hai looked at the flat piece he had sawed from a chunk of jade. He reached for the bow with which he would spin the drill to pierce holes which would give the abrasive-loaded wire a starting point in sawing the floral scroll design which he had sketched. Perplexed, he backed away. He blinked, shook his head, and picked up the thin plaque of jade. He turned it over, cocked his head, and squinted at the blemish near the edge—a flaw he had noticed the previous work session.

This was the same piece of jade. The color striations, deep green, the paler tint, the nearly colorless shadings—it was the very piece he had cut from the chunk. But the design he had inked was gone; in its place was a new one drawn by a hand more skillful than his own. He went back to the study room, where he examined the ink slab and the brushes in the holder. Whoever had changed his design had carefully cleaned the writing gear.

Reciting a *mantra* undoubtedly would drive away the devils who had played this silly trick, but that would not give him the meaning of what had happened. Extinguishing the light, he sat by the ash-veiled coals of the brazier. Because of the towering Ta-pa Range, sunset and darkness came earlier to the eastern slope which cuddled the Kwan lands. He stepped into the little courtyard to watch the moon rise from where the distant Wei River joined the

Huang-Ho. Ju-hai had problems enough without devils meddling in his avocation, the work he loved.

Something had kept him from wiping the new design from the plaque. That he had not done so puzzled him. And then he admitted ungrudgingly that the beauty of the endless knot and the phoenix had checked him. He couldn't obliterate it. But he could saw another plaque, draw his original design, and perhaps improve it.

And then, though he heard no sound, something urged Ju-hai to quit moon-watching and go back to the study room, grind some ink, and make a new sketch.

Someone was prowling in the shadows! She was about of Hsi-feng's build and making herself very much at home. The faint glow of the coals made her seem translucent as jade, a fascinating illusion. She beckoned as if inviting him into her own home. As he stepped toward the threshold, she retreated, beckoning again.

Although moving from brilliant moonlight into shadow thinned only by the ash-filtered glow, Ju-hai saw that she was not a village girl. From gilt-embroidered shoes to velvet hood and silver-twinkling foliate figures which gave her headgear the appearance of a coronet, she was stately; stately, although a head shorter than Ju-hai.

Her graciously welcoming him as if to her own home took him aback. Even without the benefit of a tunic worthy of an imperial concubine, the stranger would have had presence. Long pendants reached from her earlobes almost to her shoulders. She had ears small and close to her head and a fine nose a shade longer and narrower than most women of her race, with nostrils not quite as flaring; nor were her lips quite as full.

"Ju-hai, you're right. I'm not of pure blood. One of my ancestors was a barbarian from the City of Jade."

"Ah . . . Ho'tien?"

"Is there any other City of Jade? Though many ignore the Son of Heaven and still call it Khotan."

She gestured toward the shop. As if reading his thought, she forestalled his unspoken objection. "Never mind the lamp, we won't be long."

To say the least, this person not only knew what she was doing, she likewise knew what Ju-hai proposed doing, and before he himself did. He pulled up abruptly. He had just realized that neither he nor his visitor had been articulating. As the moon path shifted, he could see the whiteness of teeth and the carmine of skillfully made-up lips, lips which moved to smile but not to speak.

"You've not been mouth-making words either, Ju-hai. Don't look so amazed—when you talk to people in dreams, you don't mouth-shape your words, except when you actually talk in your sleep, and that wakes you up."

"You mean, I am dreaming now?"

"Ju-hai, children have to ask questions, but a grown man keeps his mouth shut, and simply observes facts instead of wanting other peoples' answers. My time is short —and don't ask me *why!* Either listen to me, or I'll leave right this instant!"

Her bewitching smile took the sting from her direct communication. "Mouth-talking makes stupid mistakes."

Things did not shape up in elegant Chinese, but the exchange was undeniably clear.

From one of the main corridors came the slip-slop-shuffle of felt boots, and a murmur of two voices.

"Your brother and Lan-yin would have to come in if they heard us or saw lights."

The footfalls and voices faded.

"I forgot to tell you I'm Mei-yu. Yes, I rubbed out your inked sketch. It's lovely but I had a better idea."

Mei-yu—this meant true, precious, superlative jade. It also implied not-other-precious gems, such as were included in mere *yu*, jewels of all sorts, all of which were inferior to jade. If she had called herself Tai-yu, it would have been about the same as Mei-yu, but a bit on the grandiloquent side.

"*Aiieeyah!* You do know jade talk." She was delighted and she gestured magnificently, all the more so because of sleeves which trailed to her knees when she spread her arms. He'd never seen a garment with such Imperial sleeves.

Mei-yu continued, "You had the darlingest design, and it was clever the way you got two earring blanks out of one small cutting of jade. The color veins contrast and at the same time harmonize, so the pendants will be mates but not duplicates—if you'd made ear pendants for your father to give his Number One Lady, you'd have embarrassed him and yourself—before you could shape a second pair, she and his other concubine would be enemies. And the Old Man has enough problems already."

The Old Man's one and only wife, Ju-hai's mother, had died a good many years ago.

Mei-yu turned, and as if she had been blocking the moonlight, he clearly saw the lines sketched on the jade plaque.

"This is a single piece—it would make a beautiful pectoral, but the situation would be no different from a pair of ear pendants. You started a wine cup for your father—finish it, and when the plaque I designed is done, save it for a girl who doesn't have a sister concubine to hate for being Number One."

Mei-yu came nearer and for the first time he was aware of her perfume. Though the sweetness left him as if dizzy-drunk, he couldn't help but wonder how he got the scent of this fascinating girl when he could not hear her voice.

"Old Master, that's spirit-bouquet, and nose smelling has nothing to do with it. With all the problems you have for thinking about, why have wonderings about friend or lover? Do you have to understand me all at once—"

This was a declaration; it was as if she had parted curtains which concealed a realm of wonder.

Moonlight shifted from the workbench, leaving Ju-hai and Mei-yu in cozy darkness. Her warmth and the tantalizing touch of her body were a promise rather than a fact, an *almost* touching, from knee to breast and mouth to mouth, a moonbeam's breadth short of completeness.

She gasped. "Don't squeeze me—" Her dismay checked him. "I'm all moon-misty—kiss me a not-quite touch—" Her tongue traced the width of his mouth, and then, swaying half the distance that separated them, Mei-yu shaped

the kiss. Ju-hai forgot her warning, but she evaded his
arms, leaving him with an embrace of emptiness.

His exclamation made her recoil.

"I'm awfully sorry—I didn't mean to tease you—it was
a crazy impulse—I couldn't help it, really, I couldn't—I
should have known you'd sense my wantings."

"*O mi to fu!* What is—who are—what are you?*"

"I don't know what to tell you—" She came toward
him, then checked herself; she opened and closed her
hands, clutching air. "*Aiieeyah!* I'm crazy!"

Ju-hai outgrew his dismay and confusion when she
wavered, on the verge of tears. "If you're crazy, then what
am I?"

She drew a deep breath. "I'm an Immortal—one of the
servants of the Moon Goddess, Lady Chang Wo. She
could not spare the time to see the Kwan Village Moon
Festival last year, so she sent me to have a look and tell
her all about it—and I got a sensing of you and how you
love jade—I saw your work."

Details bewildered Ju-hai, but a shade of sanity came to
help.

"I met a man in a Taoist monastery—they said he was a
hundred and eighty-one years old, but he looked about my
age. When he sat on a cushion, it bulged from his weight.
Everyone in the neighborhood knew he wasn't a fraud—
grandfathers remembered him."

Mei-yu brightened. "Then you do understand enough to
hear more. I'm not a Goddess like Lady Chang Wo, and
I'm not solid like your *tao-shih*—there are different sorts
of Immortals—from saints that still wear human bodies to
the *Pah Hsien*, and Tien Hou, and Lady Hsi Wang Mu—
well, I used to be a Buddhist nun."

"So that's why I shouldn't kiss you. But your hair isn't
cut—your hood doesn't hide it all. Why don't you sit
down?" He pointed to the bench. "You've let your hair
grow."

The cushion did not sink when she seated herself.

"Ju-hai, you're precious! You're fabulous! Keeping your
wits about you that way! Of course the cushion doesn't

sink; I really have little weight; and in your world, I don't have any." She patted her hip. "Looks good, but simply not solid enough. None of me. Well, not yet."

"But you changed my inked lines on the jade and you drew new lines."

"You're impossible! If I did have a solid body, you'd not love me to death, you'd question me out of existence! So I'll tell you all about it. I was a nun and I did so much good work, as they call it, that the Emperor of Heaven made me an Immortal, and I went to work for Lady Chang Wo—jade is made of moonbeams, you know."

"You make all the jade—"

"No, I race around wherever jade is found in the entire world and I see to it that the elemental spirits who turn moonbeams into jade do their work properly—and—and—" Mei-yu rose to her feet and laid a hand on his wrist. Her eyes were misty, glowing, a luminous, dark wonder. "I was a virgin when I became an Immortal; I've never had a lover—and you're wondering just how—"

"With a Buddhist nun, *o mi to ful* But with a Goddess—"

"Ju-hai, I'm not a nun, haven't been for years, and I've never been a Goddess. I'm simply a woman, only not as solid as Lan-yin."

"But I'm not an Immortal—do I have to—"

She swayed toward him. "We're going to meet again; and next time, you won't have to wonder how to become as frail as I am now."

Mei-yu retreated to the court. He stood for moments before he could accept the fact that somewhere short of the shadows of a bamboo she had become entirely moon glamour enveloped by darkness.

Chapter III

As usual, Lan-yin and her husband, Chen Lao-yeh, were haggling some well-worn subject. That evening the topic was their son, Chen Yin-chu, recently conscripted because of trouble in Turkistan. The Chens were speculating on how lavish was the bribe which Old Man Kwan had offered the captain to make sure that neither Ju-hai nor Younger Brother, Shou-chi, would be taken into the army.

The brothers had been in the next higher foothills of the Tai Pai Shan, cutting firewood, as everyone knew. The debate centered on how it had happened that the Kwan sons were away just when the recruiting officer made his rounds.

Each villager, male or female, slave or free, was listed on the census rolls. Law required that on the door of every house there must be a list of the dwellers. The captain, after declaring that he'd pick up the missing on his way back and en route to Ch'ang-an, had not returned. There were many approved solutions which helped the military stave off madness because of the Bureaucracy. Any officer worthy of his rank would have sense enough to pay the jailer of the nearest city a reasonable sum, whereupon every prisoner, regardless of offense, would become a soldier. The jailer split the *cumshaw* with the magistrate. The officer was reimbursed for expenses in getting the recruits missing the first time around, and all balanced out.

Chen Lao-yeh had automatic responses which made it seem that he was listening to his wife, who was busy in an adjoining room. Although Master Chen, who was nudging his fortieth year, wore the dark blue jacket and knee length pants of the Shensi farmer, there was something about his easy, graceful posture, his long slender hands, and his thin, sensitive face which gave the overall impression that this man normally wore the robe and cap of scholar and for some unspecified reason was disguising himself. The few lines of his smooth face were about the eyes, and largely sun squint. His expression was benevolent, serene, and his attention, like his gaze, was far away from the little farmhouse with its rammed earth floor and whitewashed walls.

The Chens had done nicely; he and his late father had put undeveloped farmland into production, starting as had the Kwans, though three centuries later. And a good deal still depended on his temporarily soldiering son.

Lan-yin was busy. Between dipping a finger into the pot of water heating over the coals of the hearth, then dipping strings of *cash* from a more or less secret wall niche, slapping them on the table, and all the while declaring herself to her husband, the mistress of the house was fully occupied.

Now that the crypt was emptied, the strings of *cash* were heaped, and the water sufficiently hot, Lan-yin grabbed the pot and, without skipping a beat, headed for the adjoining room. There she outvoiced her splashings in the little tub until at last she paused in the tirade. His Honor, Chen, who was unaware that she had changed the subject several times, felt that it was time to say something.

"You're going to be with one of the Kwan sons this evening?"

"If you'd been listening to what I was saying, you'd know that Ju-hai is going to Ch'ang-an to study for the examinations and the Old Man wants him to sleep with that little snip of a slave girl, that Hsi-feng, so he'll get used to doing it with a *lady*—mind you, a lady slave girl!"

While she was laughing that one off, Chen prepared his retort. "And since when," he asked with elaborate smoothness, "has Old Man Kwan begun telling you his plans? When he finally got you knocked up and you spewed out that son of yours, he had his fill of you."

"Your *Excellency*, Master Chen, in the first place the Kwan sons are more fun than he ever was, and in the second place, his Number Two Concubine told me all about the plans for Ju-hai to go to the capital to study for the Imperial Civil Service."

Every once in a while Chen won a round, so he pursued his opportunity. "And of course the concubine knew all about Hsi-feng? Mmmm . . . She is getting to be luscious and I bet Ju-hai is drooling. The change will do him good."

"You'd never get as much as a look, much less a smell of that!" Lan-yin mocked. "And so you think I was waiting for concubine chatter? The other night Ju-hai woke up and still more than half asleep, he called me Hsi-feng; and then, when he was fully awake, he felt awkward and told me all about the girl and how he was going to persuade his father to send her to Ch'ang-an to keep house for him."

Chen snorted. "Anyone persuading Old Man Kwan to do anything has his life's work cut out for him."

"Whether he can or can't talk his father into line, I'll not be collecting as many strings of *cash* for you to buy silver in Ch'ang-an."

Lan-yin could buy silver in the village market, but that would tell the entire village how much she was hoarding. The total which she had amassed since the Kwan boys had been interested in women was buried where only Lan-yin knew. The arrangement, having become a tradition, was hallowed, accepted by the villagers as entirely respectable. This, of course, was because of their politely pretending to ignore Lan-yin's being a polyandrous concubine.

Trying to estimate the effects of Ju-hai's leaving the village and going to the capital alone to study, and then to repeat the calculation, after taking into account Hsi-feng's entering the Kwan heir's life, kept Chen too busy to get more than scraps of what his wife was saying.

And there was another factor which for some while had contributed to Chen's cogitations: it was an outright nuisance, keeping his concubine in a neighboring village—it was not so much the distance as simply the principle of the thing. He'd gain face if ever he moved his Number Two Lady into the Kwan Village. The house was large enough. The only obstacle was Lan-yin.

Then he realized that she was and had been saying things.

"You splash so much I missed something. What did you say?"

"I said you're missing the point of everything! Don't argue with me, shut up and get the facts! Once Ju-hai gets accustomed to a lady, he'll realize that it takes three of her to equal one of me!"

Chen was about to dispute that estimate, but his Number One Lady interrupted. "Once he's passed the examinations—"

Chen triumphantly shouted her down. "He can't even take them for another two or three years."

That was more than a patient woman could endure. Lan-yin pounced from the bathing room, towel in one hand, fresh garments in the other. "If Ju-hai makes it and gets an official position, we won't have a chance to get anywhere—the Kwans will gobble up more and more land!"

"They can't take what we have; and, with that buried silver, we can get a red certificate for uncleared land."

"What makes you so sure?" she challenged, flipping the towel into a corner and sorting an undergarment from the outer jacket and trousers draped over the crook of her elbow.

They had wrangled so many years that her unusually attractive body didn't interest him. Whereas the years made haggard wrecks of so many women, there was a significant proportion of ageless ones with timeproof bodies and unblemished chinlines; when these favored ones nudged fifty and more, their smooth skins were finer of texture than any female teen-age barbarian. And Lan-yin was one of these. Farm work had left her legs elegant, without knots.

Aside from a few fine, white stretch lines, she was as unblemished as she'd been a good nineteen or twenty years previously.

"What makes me so sure?" Chen echoed. "Just a rough estimate."

"We could buy twice as much land if you'd not squandered so much on part-time, unwashed village whores! You're so used to wenches carrying honey buckets to the fields till they're too tired to wash up, the minute I take a bath you think I'm sleeping with one of the Kwan boys.

"And before I forget it—when you go marketing in Ch'ang-an, I'm going along to make sure you don't let that Colonel Tsao talk you into something stupid. He was getting impatient, last time he came to see us."

Lan-yin referred to the retired Colonel Tsao's talk with them at their farm, some distance from the walled village. To have him come to their home would have been fatally conspicuous.

"I don't see where we come in on his impatience. We're not selling property. He ought to know that; he must know by now. He's after a chunk of Kwan land."

Lan-yin sighed, praying for patience. "Chen Lao-yeh, before he finds out that Ju-hai is going to school in Ch'ang-an, you and I are going to let him in on something important, if he gives us a commission. Knowing about the plans for Ju-hai ought to be worth a hundred *taels* of silver."

Chen admitted that it would take a lot of sleeping with Ju-hai and Shou-chi to total a hundred ounces. Certainly it was an important sum, but it really led nowhere.

"It will be a lot more than just silver," Lan-yin persisted. "If Colonel Tsao knows enough about where Ju-hai's going to school, he can figure things so Ju-hai won't qualify for the examinations. He—I mean Ju-hai—he is smart, he's quick-witted, but he's ignorant about big cities. Get him started drinking and playing around with singsong girls and gambling—whatever he becomes, he won't be an official; and if he did make it, Colonel Tsao could get the bureaucrats to transfer him beyond the Great Wall.

Once he gets into trouble, Shou-chi will be the Number One favorite. Shou-chi's a nice youngster, not really dumb, but he's easy to deal with."

"Dealing with Old Man Kwan never was easy work," Chen objected.

"You're right," Lan-yin agreed. "But Colonel Tsao knows a lot of generals and civil officials. Suppose the Old Man is nabbed by a conscription officer rounding up another draft of recruits."

"He's too old."

"If Tsao can't take care of a few military details, then he is too dumb to manage the Kwan lands. He'll have to have some farmer to help him—a general overseer or steward. You begin to see where we can take a hand— if Ju-hai goes crazy, the way youngsters do when they quit the farm and get among high-stepping city people, and runs up debts. The Old Man will borrow money—"

Chen began to get the point. "And Tsao buys the note? *Tai-tai*, sometimes I think you're brighter than I gave you credit for being."

"*Ta jen*, I'm not so bright. I've just been thinking for months and months . . . did you see that shaman hobbling about the plaza?"

"With the funniest hat with a crown as high as from my knuckles to my elbow, and not much bigger around than my forearm? And a forked beard? Yes, at the cooked-food stand, he was eating garlic sausages—what about him?"

"Ever since I saw him, I thought maybe I should get some advice. Those shamans give good answers. How much should I pay him?"

"Let him take it out in trade!"

Lan-yin made a mocking face. "*You'd* have a grand time with his mother. I bet she's greasier than he is—or your farm girls."

When, half an hour later, Lan-yin set out for the village inn, she wore a turquoise tunic slit halfway up her thigh and a brocaded jacket, gay with gold. Two jade pins secured her gleaming black hair, and white coral pendants tinkled from her ears. Her makeup, though on the dramatic side, was not glaring; it gave her style.

"*Aiieeyah, tai-tai*" Chen sounded off, and genuine admiration colored his voice. "If you weren't such a contentious little bitch, I'd really love you."

She glanced over her shoulder, gave herself a resounding slap on her silk-shimmering behind. "You don't know what you're missing."

"If only the rest of you were that nice!" he retorted.

He was thinking that, if the disposition of his concubine sequestered in a nearby village could be combined with Lan-yin's elegant body, he'd have the superior woman.

Lan-yin did not have to inquire at the inn, the Kwan Village information center. By the smoky flame of an oil lamp, she saw the shaman. He was eating pot stickers and gulping hot *shao-hsing*.

"I don't know your name," Lan-yin said, "but they tell me you're a shaman."

"Name is Yatu. For once, the dog-turd fools, they told you right." He plopped a second pot sticker into his mouth. "What's troubling you?" Yatu tossed off a cup of *shao-hsing*. "Speak up, woman! Take your thumb out! I'm busy."

She glanced at the cooked-food man. He said, "I'm too deaf to hear what customers say, and I'm too dumb to understand them if I could hear."

Lan-yin addressed the Mongol. "Distinguished sir, I need advice. Is this a lucky time for me to speculate in real estate?"

"You must have sold a farm to buy those clothes and that stuff." He grabbed another pot sticker and gestured for another jug of wine. "You don't seem to know a thing about shamanizing."

"If I knew, I'd not be asking you, would I?"

He sniffed the breeze. "You smell funny."

"I could say a thing or two on that subject myself," she retorted.

"But you're just ignorant," Yatu elaborated, explaining that the drumming, the rattles, the whanging of cymbals, and the bellowings of his familiar spirit would draw a crowd. Even if she whispered her question, the answer would sound like a cavalry charge in a thunderstorm. Yatu concluded, "I live in the Mongol camp outside the wall of

Ch'ang-an, west of the Jin Guan Men." He paused and eyed her, a section at a time. "If you're in a hurry, round up a couple of musicians to chant and sound off until I'm in a trance. We can go out into the hills four or five *li* so nobody would hear."

"Thank you, Old Master, but I'm not dressed for moonlight walking in the Ta-pa Range. Do you have many female customers?"

He refilled his cup and wagged his head. "One of the best whores in Ch'ang-an consults me regularly. She started out as a street slut and now she's the darling of a prince. Haiii! Don't get discouraged, maybe I could do something for you."

Yatu didn't understand enough Chinese to know what Lan-yin called him, but he smiled and said, "Well, so are you." Then, to the cooked-food man, he confided, "That flossy bitch is up to some kind of dirty work or she wouldn't be so shy about asking me a question."

Chapter IV

Before Ju-hai could begin to convince himself that Mei-yu and her promises were other than hallucinations, or the whimsical doings of a devil or a fox-woman to kill an idle hour, he was called before his father instead of going to the village school; and before the talk began, he expected bad news. Nothing short of major disaster would justify cutting a class.

The Old Man, a blocky man well over forty, always looked grim unless he decided that pleasantry would not be unharmonious. His wind-burned, sun-blasted, squarish face was deeply seamed. He was half a head shorter than his eighteen-year-old son, but he stood two heads above the tallest man in the settlement, because he never had to remind even a towering Manchu that Kwan Yu-tsun was in command.

"The Old Man should have been a war lord," was Ju-hai's summing up—an exaggeration, yet far from absurd.

Quizzical, almost smiling, the Old Man appraised the boy.

"Son," he began, "you're doing well, but things have to speed up. The way it is in Ch'ang-an and the whole dung-eating Empire, I want you to take the examinations sooner than when I mentioned the matter. Do you understand?"

"You want me to get three or four years of study done in two years."

With his short, solid neck and his head hunched forward, Kwan Yu-tsun seemed a bit hump-shouldered. "All I ever ask for is the unreasonable! My great grandfather told me that that was how the Ancestor did it. That's why we're not coolies today."

"Sir, if I knew more about your long term aims, I'd know better how to go about all this. What I do and how I do it has to fit into things as you see them. I ought to see where I'm going."

The Old Man wagged his head. "When my father was about your age, a man could take a few risks during the fall of one kingdom and the building up of the next. With good luck and quick wit, he had a chance of keeping what he had and adding something to it, doubling it maybe. But the great days are gone, and you'll never get it as good as I did; and I never had it as good as great-great-great grandfather Kwan did. The good soldier—today he's turtle-dung."

Father and son bowed in memory of the man so many generations closer to the Ancestor Kwan whose name was carved on the wooden slab of the family shrine. Then the Old Man resumed, "The Son of Heaven remembers how many Emperors were finished by good soldiers. So, instead of getting better ministers to run the country right, he lets the Civil Service Bureaucracy get stronger every day, getting all the loot, all the face. A handful of generals can't possibly rob us the way a million bureaucrats are doing. Bastards who've never marched arse deep in water or ridden in the teeth of snow, never got more arrows between their teeth than they could spit aside—that's the Bureaucracy. They grab the goodies, tax us to death, and the mother-lovers never got plough handle calluses on their fine hands—they don't even get calluses on their lard bottoms. And soldiers and farmers get dung on their pancakes instead of honey, largely because they're too dumb to tell the difference between the two."

"Sir—Honorable Father—"

"Shut up and listen! So these battle-dodging, work-dodging sons of diseased whores get the high positions. Shut up and don't interrupt me! The reason I want you to be a scholar is so we can have a bureaucrat bastard in the family. You'll be a magistrate—then a prefect—finally governor of a province. Get enough graft, without being oppressive, mind you—just enough honest *cumshaw* to buy another two or three or four pieces of land, or clear and improve wooded lands—now listen with both ears—and keep the other bureaucrats from robbing us with taxation."

"Yes, Honorable Father."

"That slave girl, Hsi-feng—remember? Well, good family, but not important enough, so what happened? Tough luck, so twenty *taels* bought her. If the Kwan Family hadn't had enough land, I might have had to sell your sisters and either you or your brother, just to keep the family topside.

"Family is one of the safeguards against government. Particularly when the bureaucrats crap on the army that keeps the barbarians from Tibet and Mongolia and Manchuria and Turkistan from taking over. Farmers and armies made T'ang great—bureaucrats are ruining it. So I want you to stack up status, and your brother will marry into a worthwhile local landowner family."

"Sir, Younger Brother fits into your specifications for a bureaucrat—"

"Manure! He's a good farmer, but he's too dumb to pass

an exam, even if you gave him a book of approved solutions."

"Well, Honorable Father, I'm not so bright."

"No, you're not, but he is dumber. I'm smart enough to know it's time we got off the dung heap and did things."

"Sir, when do I go to Ch'ang-an?"

Having got his son conditioned, the Old Man smiled. "Don't pull such a long face. I'll tell you when, and meanwhile, read *The Book of Rites*, or is it *Odes*? Learn how to be a gentleman. Pour me another cup!"

Ju-hai grabbed the jug and poured wine.

"Yes, revered Father?"

"No more Lan-yin for you. Is that clear?"

"Am I going to a school or to a Buddhist monastery—I tremble and I obey—but—"

The Old Man laughed heartily. "Don't holler before you're hurt! Why, in a year of thirteen moons, do you suppose I bought Hsi-feng?"

Kwan Yu-tsun fist-thumped the table. Ju-hai knocked over a wine cup trying to check the one his father had set rolling.

"Between now and the time you go to Ch'ang-an, you're going to be sleeping with her to find out what it's like with a girl of good family, instead of with a farm woman."

Shock left Ju-hai groping. He was wondering whether Mei-yu would drop him like a honey bucket or cling to him and harm Hsi-feng. After some gulping, he said, "I hear, with fear and trembling."

He meant exactly what he said.

The moment amorous and ardent Hsi-feng crawled into bed with him, he'd have a case of cold horrors from wondering whether Mei-yu would materialize. Or even if she did not appear at the very worst possible moment, he could not help but be apprehensive. Even if she never came to the apartment, the horrible possibility would haunt him, nag him, and he'd be helpless, useless, emasculated without surgery. He'd qualify as a eunuch in the Imperial palace.

After a long silence, the Old Man said, "You look as if the magistrate just told you that you'd be getting the death of a thousand slow cuts. If you can't do anything else, just imagine she's Lan-yin until you get used to her.

"Listen, son, a lady of good family is built the same as any other, or that's what they tell me; I never tried one—I saved her for you."

"Revered Father—I'm not worthy—you made a sacrifice—"

"Well, all right, maybe, but it's for the Kwan Family or you'd never got this chance. Son, what's gnawing at you?" And then the great illumination came to Kwan Yu-tsun. He slapped Ju-hai on the shoulder. "You've heard too much nonsense about virgins; no wonder the idea worries you."

The Old Man's dissertation on virgins was in line with the standard books on anatomy, gynecology, and folklore. He concluded, "That sing-song girl in Ch'ang-an, the one they said was a virgin, she was a swindle. Every farm boy this side of the Ta-pa Range had her before you came to town. She'd been the house virgin for years. Well, now you'll know Hsi-feng is the real article."

And finally, inspiration came to Ju-hai.

"Sir, how long can you keep Little Phoenix from moving in—I mean, without insulting her?" The Old Man looked so perplexed that Ju-hai ended his groping by continuing, "It is this way—first of all, I've never let her clean up around here; women always get things into an awfully confused mess."

"Uh—well—you've learned something—and so?"

"There's more to it than just that. Everyone knows I've been sleeping with Lan-yin. Even so, I want to go over everything, just in case she's left an ear pendant or hairpin or anklet socks or—um—uh—"

Kwan Yu-tsun wagged his head. "Son, you are right, but you can't win. Seven magistrates and their bailiffs could follow each other, looking for souvenirs of Lan-yin, and any half-witted girl would spot something at first glance." He got up. "When your Little Phoenix finds a Lan-yin souvenir, tell her so many women have scattered their stuff around that you couldn't guess whom it belonged to."

Ju-hai bowed a perfect ninety degrees. Once the Old
Man was on his way, Ju-hai fired up nine joss sticks at his
personal shrine. He needed gods, Buddhas, and Immortals
on his side.

Chapter V

Ju-hai pondered ever more on his unusual
facility at jade-craft. Looking back, Mei-yu's appearance
and his apparent instinct for jade set him thinking. There
had been a farm boy, not even moderately bright, who
could not remember when he was not able to loose an
arrow and bring down a partridge in flight. And the Ancestor had handed down the story of a comrade conscripted
into military service, a clown with no more sword experience than a pig had with chopsticks; yet in his first
battle, he came out a master manslayer.

"They learned those things in earlier incarnations," Ju-
hai summed up. "Maybe I got the knack of jade working a
couple lives ago."

Again nearing her fullness, the moon caught Ju-hai off
guard, perhaps because he had become muddled by the
prospect of Hsi-feng's living with him, if only for a little
while.

After a few nibbles of supper, he said, "Hsi-feng, these
books—" He gestured. "No shop work tonight—"

As soon as she left, he drew window curtains and set to
work, giving that pectoral the final touches. When it was
perfect, he'd give it to Hsi-feng. He had to get her out of
sight and beyond smelling, before he and she talked each
other into bed. This was a critical period.

He was busy amending the arc of a curve, flattening the

roundness of an over-sharp foliate stem, and working on the bird figure, the Phoenix which Mei-yu had outlined, in place of the lotus blossom—that and the endless knot which she had inked in for the background.

The watchman's calling the hour warned him that it was well past bedtime. He put out the light. There was barely a glow of coals in the brazier. He groped his way to the curtained bed in the alcove.

Although sure he'd not slept a wink, the voice of the watchman assured him that he'd been drowsing and had missed one call entirely. A sudden and intense awareness had aroused him—the watchman's voice was an incidental. He was no longer alone—he sensed a presence.

Then he saw her, smelled her fragrance, and heard the tinkle of ear pendants and bracelets. Moonglow bouncing from the whitewash of courtyard walls thinned the gloom of the all-purpose room. Silk shimmered, and her hair mirrored the lurking half light.

This time, her coiffure was informal—nothing stately about it.

"So, sleepy head . . ." She was fondly mocking as she came toward him. "I'll go back home to the Moon."

This brought him to his feet. He reached with both arms, but drew back before he touched her. Mei-yu laughed softly. "Didn't I promise I'd get a body solid enough for everything we'll do. Of course I'm real! Kiss me and find out."

When finally they let go of each other, her breathing had an exciting cadence, and it took him moments before he remembered to breathe again. He ran a caressing hand along her back and drew her closer. This was no hallucination, and that wasn't an apparition's hip-illusion.

"I'm really real, and isn't it nice?"

"How'd you manage?"

"I pleaded with Chang Wo. The *karma* was good—"

"*O mi to fu!* But how—my *karma* or yours?"

"As long as you like it, what do we care?"

Mei-yu seated herself on the edge of the bed and extended her legs. "From here, you can't make any mistakes."

He knew all about Lan-yin's undressings, but whatever a lady would have beneath a long tunic—

"*Aiieeyah!* What if you do fumble? It will be fun and I'll love it! All my life, I have had to undress myself."

"All your *life?* But you're a moon spirit, an Immortal!"

"Lady Chang Wo was human before she became a Goddess. Me, I was a Buddhist nun. Ju-hai, Ju-hai, what you were doing was quite all right, I'm not a nun any more!"

He took off her gilt brocaded shoes and the anklet socks. Then he made a hopeless muddle of ungirdling the simplest garments known to civilized folk. She got to her feet.

"I've never been undressed by a man—" She caught his hands. "*I'm* not a bit shaky! Of course you're going to undress me! I spent a long lifetime doing good works, serving mankind in all ways but the most important, and now I'm going to be waited on—look at the merit you'll get, Ju-hai! What a tangle—start right here, and don't fumble—go ahead, fumble all you want."

Not even an Immortal could guide Ju-hai's jade-skillful but farmer-clumsy paws. After groping for the little oblong buttons that slipped into loops of cloth and getting his hands full of woman all the way from collarbone to waist, Ju-hai felt foolish when she said, "At your age, you ought to know that a woman's dresses fasten on the left."

"All right! I'll get a light!"

"Don't! Please—I forgot to tell you—"

That she was upset helped him to regain his poise. "So, it's all right undressing an ex-nun, but I mustn't peek? Not even a glimpse, not even accidentally—"

"*Ta jen*—superior person—" This was cold-haughty. "A body made of moonlight can't endure even lamplight." She wriggled out of the long tunic and flung the garment aside. She stood there in something white, her innermost garment. "*Ta jen*, you're fun, you're nice!"

Though this was fastened up the front, it was thin, close-fitting, and in its own way baffling, with many small fasteners. When Mei-yu was clear of her foundation garment, she sighed.

"If I'd worn a harness instead of buttons and loops, you'd have had me bare in a wink!" Then she laughed. "We had to get acquainted, didn't we?" Mei-yu half-turned and drew the curtains together. When she faced him again, she snuggled up and said, "Lover, you've been used to a woman who's given birth several times. I was a virgin when I entered the nunnery."

When Ju-hai awakened, a bit before dawn, Mei-yu was not beside him. He'd never before slept so restfully. When he got a taper fired up before Hsi-feng brought his tea and *congee* for breakfast, he yawned mightily, and recalled flashes and fragments of the hours not long ended . . .

Instead of attending the class for Literate Countrymen, Ju-hai settled down to searching for evidence of Mei-yu's visit. Of this, he found nothing, not a stray hair on the bed nor on any of his own garments, and not a trace of anything to sustain the Old Man's dissertation on virgins and virginity.

The situation was much better than he had hoped. Mei-yu had reassured him that he need never be apprehensive about her spying on him and Hsi-feng. She had stressed the uncertainty of her next visit. "Lover, I can't promise anything—live your life—"

Much of her occult talk had been perplexing: her telling him that shaping a female body out of moonbeams by lunar magic was no more difficult than making jade out of moonlight; and her talk about *karma* and winning merit was a confusing mess, which she frankly admitted.

"Your world's logic doesn't always make sense on my level," Mei-yu told him. "About the only way you can make sense of what I've said is to keep on doing your duty as well as you can—carrying on with what you really are—going with the law of your nature—not necessarily what 'they' say you should do—*o mi to fu!* Don't ask me how you can learn what you really are, what your nature is—I can't put it into words, either! You'll finally learn through experience. And I'll be doing the same in my place in my world.

"I'll go to see Lady Chang Wo and beg her to help. I'll kowtow nine times. I'll work those elemental spirits overtime till their tails drag in the dust. See how difficult it is! I was thinking like a nasty tyrant so you and I can meet again. And reckoning that way may cost us weeks, even months—"

Puzzling, confusing—but her words rang true.

Ju-hai made the most of his day and cleaned up the apartment. As he searched for souvenirs of Lan-yin's days, he was wondering how Hsi-feng and Mei-yu would get along, if ever they did meet. There was no reason why they couldn't be sworn sisters, as wife and concubine so often were in classical novels.

When he told the Old Man that the house cleaning was done, his father chuckled and said, "Son, you're getting sense. Everybody in the village knew what was shaping up. Everyone but you. You killed all afternoon crawling around, looking for hairpins, so you don't have to show up in the fields tomorrow."

Chapter VI

"*Find out what it's like with a lady—*" The Old Man's words left Ju-hai in a muddle of qualms and self-doubt as distressing as his earlier worryings lest Mei-yu materialize at an embarrassing moment. It never occurred to him that a man twice his age, in like circumstance, could be in a similar emotional fumble.

That Hsi-feng stood by to serve the meal was purely ceremonial. His elbow comfortably planted, Ju-hai dipped chopsticks into every dish, gesticulated with them, picked a morsel of this, a bit of that, and paused for a nip of *shao-hsing*. Finally she moved, refilled the cup, and again became a Kwan-yin image of serene femaleness.

Ju-hai slapped his chopsticks across a bowl of fried *to-fu* and black mushrooms. He might as well have been trying to eat buffalo hide. She poured a cup of wine. He gulped it.

"Little Phoenix, sit down—I've done eating."

"Yes, Old Master," she agreed and got a chair. "Where do I sit, *ta jen?*"

The "great man" pointed to a spot improperly near. "Bring—find—one of those teacups will do—yes, for wine. Or do you want tea?"

She set out teacups and poured wine for two. He had as good as commanded her to drink with him, and she was the perfect slave girl. Ju-hai wished he could be as serene, as poised, as elegant as Hsi-feng. All the devils in Shensi were reminding him that he was not a gentleman; he was a *padi* field clod, commanded to undress a lady.

Ju-hai grabbed for the refilled cup. He swallowed down the wrong throat and began coughing and choking, convinced he'd never be able to stop. Before he checked the spasm with a gulp of tea, he remembered how simple it had been, that time Lan-yin had brought in his supper. She'd announced that his father had ordered her to explain a few things to him. "It will be a lot simpler for both of us and you'll like it better if I just show you."

Taking him by the hand, she'd led him to his bedroom, undressing as they went. He had already had a pretty sound guess as to what was on the agenda, having had an uncommanded initiation by one of the older housemaids. Then, as she was unfastening the loops of her innermost garment, Lan-yin remembered that she'd forgotten to bathe. She set water to heat and sat on the bed, cozily bare, explaining details which he was sure would be more exciting than it had been with her predecessor.

One tub of water was enough for two, turn about, if the first one didn't splash too much. By the time each washed the other, it was the most natural thing on earth to couple up closely.

Memory and a gulp of wine down the right throat helped him forget his apprehensions and his qualms. Then he said, "Hsi-feng, when the Moon Festival is over, I'm going to Ch'ang-an to study for the examinations."

The perfect slave girl started as if a hot iron had

touched a sensitive spot. Then her fine features were again composed. "Yes, Old Master, you are going to Ch'ang-an. This clumsy wench will—will—be—awfully—sad."

She vainly tried to rearrange her face again. In a flash, she was on her knees. She knocked her forehead twice against the floor before he could sink to one knee and raise Hsi-feng to her feet. Unwittingly and innocently, perfect *yin* had shackled fumbling *yang*. He didn't suspect that he'd been meshed in seven nets of witchery.

Having touched her hands, he could not let go. She spilled tears so lavishly that the mouth to mouth kiss was a salty, wet business and a feast for starved souls. He couldn't let go until he had sense enough to fumble with her jacket and get a handful of woman. Meanwhile, she was at work with the loops of an inner garment.

It culminated in a tangle of each other's hands.

"Old Master, I've wanted you, months and months and months."

"It's all been such a crazy muddle—"

"All the jade and ploughing and studies . . . and now you're going away . . ."

He didn't know whether Hsi-feng smelled like Mei-yu, or whether the Immortal had a Phoenix bouquet, and he couldn't care less, when an armful of girl left no time for metaphysics.

Sunrise awakened the lovers. After they'd broken their fast with supper's leftover noodles and reheated wine, Ju-hai got the jade pectoral. Having no chain for it, he found a string of twisted hemp. "This will do till I find a chain. Or you find a cord."

"And all the times I watched you working on this—I never imagined—*aiieeyah!* How lovely—it looks different, now that it's for me!"

"And I never imagined it would be a first night present —this was going to be a leave-taking gift. But maybe the jade phoenix will bring luck to my Phoenix."

"I won't call it leave-taking," she declared. "I like the other name. We have from now to Harvest Moon and the Moon Goddess Festival, and I'll save my crying until after you're on the road to Ch'ang-an."

Chapter VII

    The full moon of autumn by no means indicated that all the crops had been brought in. The tall *kaoliang* stalks, green with splashes of red, had come in and so had the maize, but there were the later harvestings, the threshing, the winnowing, and the storing. Much work had yet to be done, but it was time for fun and for paying respect to Chang Wo, the Moon Goddess who ruled all living things and all growth, from the sprouting of seed to the ovum quickening in the womb, whether animal or human. Without lunar *yin*, solar *yang* was formless, useless, and had nowhere to go.

Already, the plaza was crowded. Talent from neighboring settlements teamed up with the Kwan folk. Acrobats, jugglers, and lion dancers were lashing lengths of bamboo together to make a stage. Musicians tuned up their new fangled *pi-pas* from Persia, and made their moon fiddles wail and sing and sometimes screech horribly. Performers raced about to join huddles of others getting their pageant costumes shaken out and unwrinkled for wearing. And voices joined all the plaza's crowd into a happy madness.

Fires blazed, embers glowed, and spicy fumes drifted from grilles and from kettles.

There were travelers and porters from the salt wells south of the Kin-Ling mountains. The latter worked their way to whatever space they could find. Each had to help another release his burden, for each was bent double by the enormous block of salt he carried; he could rest only by fixing a cross staff to his harness and leaning against it. And among the unburdened travelers, the Mongol shaman, still limping, made his way among the faster moving

Chinese whose heads came little above his shoulders. Ju-hai, circulating through the crowd, followed him to an angle of a buttress of the village wall. He began, "So many things to tend to before I start out for the big city tomorrow, I can't take time for a bit of food and wine with you."

The Mongol wagged his head, grinned, and made an obscene gesture to indicate that Ju-hai would be engrossed with a woman.

"I see your leg is troubling you."

"Not too much."

"If you get drunk tonight, sleep by the wagons so you'll wake up and ride with us. Eat with me on the road." He handed the Mongol a piece of silver. "Just to make sure you don't go to sleep sober."

"No harm, once in a while," Yatu conceded, "as long as you don't make a habit of it." He made for the food-and-drink stand.

From the stumpy little tower near the gatehouse, a drum rolled, and its voice finally swelled into thunder. A gong clanged—the sound persisted, lingering, sighing, and whispering itself into silence. Light bearers circulated about to plant the staves of their torches. Hubbub took charge again. Drums again, gongs, flutes, and moon fiddles sounded, and lion dancers emerged from nowhere.

Each lion was of cloth, with an enormous head shaped of paper pulp and cloth, gaudily painted, gilded for good measure. Two mummers kept the beast pouncing about, rampant on his two feet, with his forepaws clawing; all the while, the two-man lion roared magnificently, darting about, climbing, bounding over the stage which awaited players and acrobats. And then, it all climaxed in a lion fight.

The shaman had a bowl of noodles and a moon-cake. The latter was large enough to fill the palm of the hand and was three fingers thick. The pastry shell contained the yolk of an egg, minced ham, minced fruits no barbarian had ever heard of, and minced odds and ends—everything but minced moonbeams. Among humans, all Chinese and an occasional barbarian could survive the eating of one or two moon-cakes. As for a Mongolian—he survived, being considered not human; however, a jug of *shao-hsing* did promote digestion.

Ju-hai caught all this in flashes as he hurried to the stairs leading to the pavilion which topped the gatehouse. Built two centuries ago by an ancestor, it was a miniaturized version of the gatehouse of Kaifeng, too pretentious for a farm village; but the original had impressed that ancestor. When an error endured sufficiently long, it became a hallowed tradition—as Lan-yin had become in her busy lifetime.

Ju-hai went to pay respects to his father and to bow to the handful of family guests. Already, he had permission to set up a three-leaf screen, well away from the visitors, where he and Hsi-feng could share their final hours.

Presently approaching by an inner stairway, she joined him, bringing a tray from the kitchen. Happy Springtime, another slave girl, came up with a brazier of glowing charcoal and a wine jug. She said to Ju-hai, "Old Master, I'll have a fire made in your apartment."

In their screened privacy, the lovers did their best to watch the folk play in which a divine messenger offered the Emperor the potion of Immortality. The Son of Heaven, setting the gift on the table, went with the messenger to the door. Chang Wo, an Imperial concubine, snatched and gulped the potion. Now an Immortal, she became Moon Goddess.

They watched and they plied their chopsticks; and Ju-hai groped, pursuing in circles those thoughts which were such depressing company. Before he could pass the examinations, Hsi-feng would be past the optimum age for marriage. The Old Man might get her married off, to make sure that having Hsi-feng on the brain wouldn't interfere with Ju-hai's studies. And if the Old Man did not do so, her parents might demand that he live up to the terms of the contract.

Kwan Village, being in a sheltering fold of the Tsin-ling Range, got early sunset shadows and darkness. Thus, the pageant was well under way when the most magnificent moon of the year came up, red-golden, like a brazen gong, rising from where the Kwei River joined the great Huang-Ho. The lovers stood silently for long moments; then, having seen wonder and beauty, they turned their backs on the festival.

Picking their way through the Kwan Family complex, a village within a walled village, going from moon patches to black shadows cast by the lacquered columns which supported the canopies over the walkways, they came finally to Ju-hai's court, with miniature mountains, a pool with a bridge, and clumps of bamboo against whitewashed walls.

The wavering light of a single taper and the glow of charcoal reached from the apartment and into the deep shadow cast by the drum tower. "Our last night—" Ju-hai sighed, fumbled with the fine silver chain about her neck, and drew from the warm depths of her jacket the pectoral he had given her before their first breakfast together. He fingered the Phoenix and the endless knot. "This was for finding each other. Now—now it's for rememberings. It will tell how I've always wanted you. If I could stay here and be a farmer, we'd marry—but it's my family, my duty—"

She caught him in both arms with a cry, and words blurred into sobbing. ". . . Remembrance and good-bye—you would if you could—if they allowed you—*Aiieeyah!* The happier the rememberings, the more the grief!" She gasped. Her fingers sank into his shoulders. "*O mi to ful* What's that over there?"

Ju-hai twisted about. He saw what Hsi-feng saw—a spindle of luminescence forming instant by instant until, in the further gloom, a shapely woman became ever more solid seeming. Mei-yu had returned. He thrust Hsi-feng back and stood in front of her to face whatever the apparition brought him.

Smilingly, Mei-yu mocked him. "Foolish farm boy! Why worry so much about my jealousy? Little Phoenix, step out so I can talk to you. If you can't get mind-words, he'll tell you later—I'm awfully busy! Anyway, you nice silly lovers, I did better than have Lady Chang Wo build me a body—Hsi-feng, Little Phoenix, I borrowed your beautiful body, and it had everything. In the dark, Master

Ju-hai thought I was as fascinating as he's thought you were, ever since—*Aiieeyah!* So you do get thought direct?"

Whether she laughed aloud, or whether it was an unheard, spirit laugh, mind to mind, neither Ju-hai nor Hsi-feng could be sure. But it was friendly mockery, affectionate and whimsical. "Ju-hai, Ju-hai, don't look so surprised —you, Little Phoenix, you're entitled to your wonderings. How many times in all history has one male lout with one stroke taken the virginity of two women?"

The shape of moon-mist was thinning, but Mei-yu's words were clear. "Thank you for the loan of that lovely body, and I wish you many a year of enjoying it as I did."

Chapter VIII

Whenever Ju-hai got down to the yellowish alluvial flats of the Wei River valley, he would look up, and up, and further up, back at the snowcap of Tai Pai Shan, towering thirteen thousand five hundred feet above sea level, a ten-thousand-foot swoop from the network of irrigation canals to the peak which commanded the valley. Always, he would draw a deep breath and shake his head; and he was happy that he lived among the lower folds of the Tsin-ling, the tapering off of the tremendous Kun-lun which reached eastward out of Tibet and Turkistan. Long shadows moved northeast as the autumn days shortened.

Like his brother, Ju-hai rode a blocky, durable pony and carried a lance. At his saddle he had a cavalry bow, reflex curved, of horn and bamboo, the deadly weapon of the nomad horsemen from beyond the Great Wall. Some of the villagers, Chen Lao-yeh among them, tramped along, each with a donkey-drawn wagon or two, while another drove until his turn came to walk. A few, like the Kwan boys, rode horses. Each farmer was armed after his taste and fashion.

Ju-hai pulled up abreast of Shou-chi, who was heavier of face and frame and half a head shorter. "Younger Brother, ride up yonder—" He pointed. "Get a good look while the light is right. I'm going up to the next crest. You keep an eye on me, just in case I see something I don't like."

"Trouble?"

"Too much silver in the party."

Shou-chi dipped his bow from its case and strung it. Unless a bandit wore rather good armor, a shaft from that Mongol bow would stick out from his back half an arrow's length.

Ju-hai, riding forward, paused for a word with each teamster. With the train a good mile behind him, he reined in, well short of the crest. From this elevation he got a better view of the verdant flats where farmers would be planting winter wheat or harvesting maize, *kao-liang*, barley. Dismounting, he picked his way through the brush. Looking back, he saw that his brother had dismounted. Ju-hai drew his sword and mirrored the low sun. Drawing his blade, Shou-chi twisted and turned the steel until it bounced an answering flash.

The everlasting wind blew *loess* dust, the fertile yellow topsoil of the valley bottom. Despite the golden haze, Ju-hai could see the walled city six miles square, and girdled by green suburbs reaching to the Wei River, a dozen miles north of Ch'ang-an.

He could just distinguish the tiles and gilded eaves of towering pagodas, tall temples, and the dome of a mosque.

The road ahead looked good. Nearing the crest, he squatted in the brush and looked down toward the camping spot he knew from early childhood, when the Old Man drove his own wagon and took his turn tramping in the dust. There were no flights of birds to indicate disturbances in the wooded area around the campsite. This suggested that there was no freshly dropped horse dung nor lurkers whose scraps of food would attract birds. Ju-hai signaled the leading wagon. As it came abreast, he waved and halted the party. After a few words from their new wagon boss, a dozen archers ran ahead to crouch in the brush. When they were posted and had strung their bows, he rode recklessly over the crest and downgrade, a fool barging headlong into trouble.

This apparent folly drew no one from cover. He circled the campsite and found no traces of recent activity. The shadows were now long and the sun half below the horizon when the final cart came over the crest and down into the camping area. Dusk was closing in before the animals were watered and picketed in the circle of wagons. One third of a watch later, the moon rose. Fires blazed; wood smoke and cookery scented the air.

Presently, the shaman limped toward Ju-hai.

"Your leg, it is not well yet?" Ju-hai asked.

"Yes, it is not well."

"You are not eating with my wagon comrades?"

"Yes, I do not eat with your helpers." There was a jingle of metal, coin probably, to keep Ju-hai's gift of silver from feeling lonesome. "I have parched corn, parched beans, dried mutton. Tomorrow, I ride in another wagon."

Not waiting for further talk, he went to sit well apart from the fires, with his back against a high wheel of Chen Lao-yeh's second wagon.

Ju-hai sat with his brother and the Kwan donkey drivers. There were questions about the shaman. Ju-hai reported, "He eats his own food. He rides in one man's wagon, then he rides in another man's wagon. One man's silver jingles in his pouch. I don't know whether it jingles against the silver of one other man, or of many other men."

"Or women, Elder Brother?"

"Or women, Younger Brother."

The entire party knew that Lan-yin had ridden in one of the Chen wagons. Whether she had come along to shop or to keep Chen Lao-yeh from squandering too much silver on the expensive sing-song girls of the great city was a question not worth debating. Her husband remained bland and serene as ever.

Ju-hai plied his chopsticks; his bowl contained rice,

pickled leeks, bean curd in millet spirits, and scrawny little
apples dried after having been preserved in syrup. He said
nothing, having many thoughts. The towering snowcap of
Tai Pai Shan no longer elevated his soul. He was not
homesick; having become accustomed to Hsi-feng, he was
lonesome.

When the villagers neared Ch'ang-an in late afternoon
of the following day, the train passed through the Ming
De Gate, and up Red Bird Street, which divided the city
into eastern and western halves. Some of the carters swung
left, following Ju-hai; others, turning right, went toward
the Chun Ming Gate and the eastern market. As Chen Lao-
yeh's first wagon led off in that direction, Yatu, the taci-
turn shaman, crawled from the vehicle which had carried
him since sunrise and hobbled in the opposite direction.
He overtook Ju-hai's wagons as they swung left, making
for the inns which faced the southern wall of the market
area.

Ju-hai said, "Have evening rice with us and give a hand
watching the animals and wagons."

Yatu gestured to include Kansu Province, Koko Nor
and much of the Gobi. "Among the *yurts*, outside—"

"Yes, there are friends you have not seen for a long
time. But the city gates will be closed before we eat. Find
your friends tomorrow."

The travelers' quarters of House of Auspicious Rest
were L-shaped. Wagon park and space for animals occupied the other two sides of the enclosure. In each room
was a *kang*, a long bench of brick through which ran air
ducts from the central fire that warmed each solid bed
during cold weather. The food, Ju-hai knew from previous
experience, consisted of watery mutton broth, millet por-
ridge, and sometimes coarse maize bread.

Accordingly, Ju-hai reminded Yatu that he had spoken
of Maqsoud's place. The Mongol led off to the restaurant.
In the center of each low table was a fire pot charged with
glowing charcoal over which was an iron grid. Diners got
strips of mutton and leathery wheat cakes from Maqsoud,
a beak-nosed Uighur. The air was smoky from grease dripping to the fires, and it was enlivened by the savor of bread

heating on the griddle and of the spicy sauces into which grilled meat was dipped before the diner wrapped it in the split-half of a wheat cake.

All this fragrance blended with the bouquet of sheepskin jackets, manure-enriched boots, and the reek of travelers.

When they were back in the courtyard of the inn, Ju-hai decided that dry manure and waste fodder would be more comfortable than the *kang* which he'd share with a half dozen road companions.

In the morning, Yatu said, "I go home now. When you have nothing to do, see me and I tell you what the spirits say about this town. Anyone can tell you where my *yurt* is."

Chapter IX

When Chen Lao-yeh and Lan-yin emerged from the bathhouse and made for the red and gilt sedan chairs which had been waiting, they were dressed as they never were in Kwan Village. Each wore clothes hoarded for this day.

He wore a turquoise silk tunic, an embroidered girdle with an embroidered purse, a sedate jacket, and a cap with an ambiguous button. Chen, though not in any detail impersonating a scholar, had the manner and bearing of a "literate countryman"; he did indeed look literate, but without the appearance of a countryman.

His glance surveyed Lan-yin, from brocaded shoes to pearl-trimmed satin hood, sedate yet with a touch of style deriving from the way she carried herself. Her trim figure and her just-right makeup, seen through a flirtation veil, made her seem no more than half her actual age. If she weren't such a quarrelsome bitch, he would be fond of her.

The more Chen cogitated, the more acceptable it was that she had made a point of accompanying him, to be sure that he'd not overlook things less trivial than he might suppose them to be. In addition to presence, Lan-yin had keen wits. Like her husband, she made no pretense of being something which she was not. She simply did not appear to be one who lived the rural life.

She could pass almost anywhere as the concubine of a moderately well-off merchant, was Chen's summing up as he got into his chair and the bearers set out for the home of a certain Colonel Tsao, whose failing fortunes and gathering years had pushed him back into active duty.

Problems developing in Turkistan offered a chance of command and *cumshaw,* plus whatever loot Colonel Tsao could keep off the record and divert to himself. This and some good agricultural land would give him a comfortable retirement. Despite a good military record, his reward had been skimpy. He was making his final bid. All this the Chens had got from hearsay or had inferred from the man's oblique approach.

The Chens did not have to do much guessing; many a career officer had learned, too late in life, that the great T'ang Dynasty, great because of its conquering armies and outstanding generals, was squelching the military and giving the Civil Service Bureaucracy ever more influence. General after general had been promoted to stations where he could not raise revolt. But for being engrossed in satisfying their own craving for more land, the Chens might have been sorry for Colonel Tsao.

Tsao lived not far from the Pagoda of the Classics, in one of the hundred and ten walled quarters of the Outer City, enclosed by the walls of Ch'ang-an. In the entire world, including that of the western barbarians, there was no other city to equal Ch'ang-an for magnificence, culture, public services, and a high standard of living. Three centuries previously, Rome, that great city of the West, had fallen into the hands of the ultimate barbarians, because Roman armies were not what they had been in its golden days.

Chen said to the doorkeeper, "Tell Colonel Tsao that I have arrived." He handed the man a card. "He is expecting me."

When the man returned, Chen and Lan-yin followed him across a court, skirted a garden, and were led into a small reception room. After only a few minutes, a houseboy came to announce that Colonel Tsao would see his visitors at once.

The man who got up from his worktable and set aside his brush was on the tall side, well fed, affable, and kindly seeming; but the lines at the corners of his broad mouth— a generous mouth which nature had designed for smiling —had been shaped by overlong compression.

The narrow, penetrating eyes were restless. It was as if Tsao had lost too many years of his more than half a century in seeking without ever finding what he sought. And then charm brightened his smooth face. His bow was as low as Chen's. Before he spoke, gesture and amiable demeanor made it clear that informality should prevail. He indicated seats and brushed aside all the conventional pretenses of declining whatever passed for the position of honor.

Tsao accepted Lan-yin's presence as if everyone who visited him on business was accompanied by a woman.

"You arrived this midafternoon? You must be deathly tired—and you lost no time seeing me!"

Chitchat about the trip led to queries about the weather, suspicious characters, and prowling gangs of disbanded soldiers—a cumbersome term which meant bandits. Then Tsao sat back; and without his speaking a word, his visitors knew that the interview was in their hands.

Lan-yin went saucer-eyed to suggest that she was too deeply impressed by the great man to remember she had femaleness to turn on and she contrived also to flash Chen a silent reminder, without ever cracking the awed-woman portrait. Farm life had seemingly engulfed one who, but for the quirks of *karma*, might have been a high grade sing-song girl.

"Kwan's older son," Master Chen began, "is in the city, as I told you he'd be, to study with Doctor Wu, for Imperial Civil Service. The Old Man borrowed enough to finance the entire three or four years it will take—just in case he should die before the boy completes his studies."

"Who loaned him the money?"

"Your Excellency, I'll try to find out."

"The tax office knows," Tsao remarked, as if that detail were irrelevant. "Don't bother. You can do more important things for me."

Lan-yin cut into the lengthening, thoughtful silence.

"Your Excellency, just recently soldiers were drafted, and my son was taken. Neither of the Kwan brothers went. They were out in the second range cutting wood. They're always away when an officer comes to make illegal demands for more soldiers."

"What's that got to do with our business?" Chen snapped at her.

Tsao's attention remained fixed on Lan-yin.

"They can't always be cutting wood!"

He nodded as if to thank her for a helpful hint. Then he asked Chen, "This woodcutting—do the villagers ever sell wood—I mean, is it a business with them?"

"Not at all, sir, but if anyone wants a few wagon loads or a pack train load, the brothers get busy and keep at it till they have all that's needed."

"Tell me about this Kwan Ju-hai—what sort of a lad is he? We didn't have time to go into that when we started discussing the situation that time at the village."

A talk anywhere on the Chen acres would be conspicuous if it went further than what appeared to be a stranger's asking direction to some distant settlement. "What would make him neglect his studies?" Tsao continued. "Does he drink much?"

"He's crazy about women," Chen answered, and his wife added, "He's awfully interested in jade-craft—no, he doesn't even get sociably drunk."

Tsao's upward slanting brows flattened slightly and he leaned forward, his eyes focusing on the Chens, first on Chen, then on Lan-yin. "Do any of the villagers use *afiyoun?*"

They exchanged glances. It was clear that neither had ever heard the word before.

"No matter! If I can find a girl who is interested in jade, there'd be no problem getting him off the track. A fascinating sing-song girl ought to keep him up too late for a student."

Tsao reached for a brush and wrote an order. He clapped his hands; when a servant appeared, he handed him the paper, after first putting his chop—his seal—on it. "Put the silver in a stout bag. And serve tea." Then he turned to the Chens. "You've given me something to think about. If you learn anything interesting, I'll have more silver for you."

"If I came to see you or sent anyone from the village with a message—"

Tsao gestured to dispose of that suggestion. "I'll send someone to see you. A peddler, for instance, who'll hand you a note."

They drank their tea, and the Chens took leave, to head for the bath where they'd left their traveling clothes. Tsao sent for a sedan chair. He directed the bearers to Professor Wu's address and told the sons of turtles to stretch their legs.

They did so; and half an hour later Colonel Tsao was facing the elderly scholar, a frail little man with sensitive features.

"Master Wu," the Colonel began, after respects, "your many years as an outstanding teacher moves me to impose on your kindness."

"Be pleased to clarify. I am at your service."

"A comrade of the old days—we were fighting in Mongolia—had a charming daughter. Unhappily, she is now a widow and living with her in-laws. During our final campaign together, he must have had a premonition. His daughter was then quite young, and he asked me to be her guardian in the event of my outliving him. This I did. And

I arranged a good marriage for her when she reached
that age. But no arrangement is ever good when a woman
is a widow and living with her late husband's kinfolk."

"Deplorable," Doctor Wu admitted. "One of life's sad-
nesses."

"So many students come to you for instruction," Tsao
resumed. "Talented young gentlemen, but young, and
sometimes from agricultural regions. Unsophisticated
young men. Each needs a housekeeper. Possibly you could
recommend her to a certain Kwan Ju-hai. His father,
Kwan Yu-tsun, commended him to my care, after saying
that he is to be one of your pupils. He's a bit wilful, the
young man, and he'd pay far more heed to your august
self than to me. You might be so kind as suggest a suitable
place to live? Adequate, yet not too expensive."

After a long moment of serious pondering, the old man
said, "There's a certain Hui Kai-shek—he has vacancies in
this house on Old Pagoda Street, right in the adjacent
quarter. As for your deceased comrade's daughter, why
not send her to Master Hui? She can get to work readying
the rooms and doing a bit of shopping to stock the place."

From his sleeve, Colonel Tsao took a red envelope inscribed in gilt. Holding this with both hands, he bowed
three times.

"Doctor Wu, if you give this trifling gift to the poor,
you will gain a small measure of merit. I earnestly hope
that it brings you luck."

As he took leave, Tsao was certain that Doctor Wu
would consider himself to be one of the underprivileged;
and then there would be a present from Master Hui and,
finally, from the widowed daughter of the Colonel's deceased comrade.

The coolies took him to a quarter where lights, song,
and music brightened the night. Elaborate chairs and
palanquins, lacquered and gilded, were leaving and arriving. A few were preceded by footmen with staves and
whips to clear the way. One had an escort of halberdiers
—almost certainly the palanquin of a patron, as few ladies
of that quarter rated any such distinction.

Tsao's inconspicuous equipage halted at a quiet place,

one with the minimum of lights; the gatekeeper affected no livery, though his jacket was faultless and freshly laundered. He admitted Tsao at once. And *tai-tai*, the Supreme Lady, received him without delay.

She was an elegant, small person, white-haired, imperial in bearing and manner. Her tunic was of black silk. Her only adornments other than jade hairpins were a necklace of emerald jade and bracelets of mutton fat jade.

On each side, the greeting was stately. Lady Meilan was a personage; she could not be called a booking agent of elite sing-song girls, and much less the keeper of a superlatively fine whorehouse. Insofar as she could be classified, one might say that Lady Meilan supplied temporary concubines for officials setting out, for instance, on tours of provincial inspection. Nothing was standard except supremely high quality. Each arrangement was by special negotiation.

"Colonel, you're concerned about something. Do sit down and get it off your mind. When that's done, I'll send for wine."

He sighed. "Mind reader! Well, yes, I am concerned. How is Orchid Cluster doing?"

"She's doing very nicely." Meilan flicked her silken fan. "I hope you're not thinking of buying her contract?"

"I'm hoping no one has a claim now or . . . well, it won't be too long, but. . . ."

"Suppose," Lady Meilan proposed, "that I send for Orchid Cluster and we'll hear what you have in mind."

Tsao brightened. "I feel better all ready! This is something special, and I can't imagine anyone I'd trust further than Orchid Cluster! Such a grand background."

Chapter X

After standing for a moment, pondering the departing Mongol's suggestion, Ju-hai turned to Shou-chi. "Younger Brother, I may have to consult a shaman before I'm through with all this school business. Anyway, you take charge—sell what's to be sold, buy what's to be bought, and don't take too much of anyone's advice. That includes mine! I'm going to be busy from now on—getting some clothes, paying respects to Master Wu, finding a place to live."

"You think you ought to see the shaman? I won't know what to do or say—I'll make nothing but mistakes."

"You'll not catch up with me! Do I know how to be a student or live in a city? Did the Old Man ever tell you about the burglar whose health was failing, and how his son learned to be a burglar?"

"He never tells me stories."

"You'll get your fill, now that you're taking my place. Listen with both ears:

"The old burglar and his Number One Son went to the house they were going to rob. The man handed the boy a thing to bore through the rammed earth wall, hole after hole, with no noise. When the boy made enough holes, he took out the piece of wall.

"He followed his father into a room where no people slept. In the room were chests of camphor wood and chests of cedar. The smells told him where to start. He opened the door of a tall closet—not built in; it was sitting against the wall. The father said, 'Very good, go in, pick good things. Feel, smell, heft, and make no noise.'

"The son stepped in. His father closed and secured the

door from the outside and got out of the house. Being in a bad position, the son wasted no time cursing or crying. He began to scratch, making a sound like mice or rats. This awakened the servants. One of the slave girls opened the cabinet. The young burglar gave her a shove, sending her tumbling. She screamed. The whole household turned out to chase the housebreaker. To make it worse, a bright moon was rising. But he got through the hole in the wall; he ran and he ran. But with so many chasing him, one of the crowd always headed him off. Then, while he still had a lead, he saw a well, an old well, and he ran toward it till he got to the coping around the well. He flopped to the ground, but it looked as if he'd thrown himself into the well. Lying in dark shadow, he picked a stone from the coping and dropped it into the well. Being close, the people heard the loud splash and the yell. They figured he'd drowned himself rather than get beaten to death, so they went home.

"And the boy also went home. The old man said, 'Son, do not speak unfilial words. You are now a journeyman burglar, and I bow three times. You are now head of the house.' "

Having thus encouraged Younger Brother, Ju-hai cleaned up at a bathhouse and made the rounds of clothing stores. Finally, he had himself fitted out in a dark gray tunic, proper felt boots, and the right sort of cap with the correct button. Ju-hai looked better than he felt. Ch'ang-an was impressive, and oppressive.

He made a detour to the street of jade workers, watched the artists at work, and looked at their finished belt buckles, pendants, hairpins, and statuettes. Finally, he left with a better opinion of the pectoral he had made for Hsi-feng and picked his way toward the home of Master Wu.

The teacher lived on one of the less affluent blocks of one of the less affluent streets. A scholar who did not reach the better official grades could always make a living, but little more than just that. One revered a teacher as one step short of a parent—but who'd want to be one!

Ju-hai managed to make one kowtow before Master Wu checked him.

"This person—Ju-hai, surname Kwan—" He dug a paper from his sleeve and offered it with both hands. "—is the son of a farmer."

"I remember your distinguished father. Please sit with me—I am honored—"

When they had gone through the routine, with inquiries regarding the health of each other's families for three generations back, Master Wu at last got to new business. "And where will you be living?"

Ju-hai said that he could not have been so sottishly stupid and ill-mannered as to pick a spot without first getting the jade opinion of his distinguished preceptor. After frownings and beard combings with slender, well kept fingers, the learned man admitted that he knew of an unworthy hovel. "Just vacated by one of my students—a few blocks south and a block off Red Bird Street. Not at all uncomfortable. It happens that I know of a cow-clumsy servant, cook, laundress, and clean-up wench who would keep house for you."

"When would it be permissible for me to move my ragged possessions into the luxurious dwelling your Honor has been pleased to recommend?"

"Whenever it is your pleasure, but better that you ask Hui Kai-shek, the manager of the building."

Minor details and leave-taking attended to, Ju-hai set out for an interview less exacting. Looking back, he was sure that he had committed no social errors; he had followed the book. And despite his dedication to Hsi-feng and jade, he began to feel that his new status was not as loathsome as he had anticipated. By their robes, he recognized fellow students, candidates for examination, and graduated scholars of three or more grades, each stately in his gown of proper color and cut. Ju-hai patterned his carriage and manner to accord with these veterans, not suspecting that some of the new arrivals were accepting him as a model.

At his destination, Ju-hai learned from the doorkeeper that his auspicious arrival had been anticipated. However, it was not the manager who welcomed him; nor was the woman who received him Mistress Hui. She wore a black jacket, little more than waist length, and black trousers, and her hairdo was in accord. A good looking servant, quite attractive. "I'm Orchid Cluster," she announced. "I hope you've not brought servants with you. If you have, I'll be out of a job, even before I've started. How did we hear of you so quickly? The fact is, Master Wu always sends new students to us and we're happy to welcome them."

Female servants had never been formal with Ju-hai. Although he liked it that way and accepted Orchid's self-assurance as an indication of competence in knowing her way around the enormous city, he took special notice and he wondered. Her eyes and her bearing made him feel that she had always been accustomed to supervising, managing, and directing—which would be good, if it didn't go too far.

He followed Orchid to an inner court from which she stepped into a small reception and utility room; there were also two bedrooms and servant's quarters, as well as a bath cubicle and a kitchen annex.

"I can save some of my time for other tenants, or you can have my full time—shopping, cleaning up, and fixing all your meals; you'll have nothing to interfere with your studies. If you like the place, you may leave a deposit, and, when your things arrive, I'll tell the porters to arrange your belongings the way you tell me. There's Master Hui now. Wait, I'll tell him."

Chapter XI

When the Ming De Gate opened at dawn, Ju-hai told Shou-chi, "I went with you when we combed the western market, but the Old Man should know that I didn't tell you what to do or how to do it. When you say this to him, say that I told you to speak for me."

Shou-chi bowed, then straightened up, grinning. "Elder Brother, I'll also say that I didn't tell you how to pass the examinations."

It was Ju-hai's turn to bow.

The drivers were looking to Shou-chi for the go-ahead. He said, "Mustn't be robbed the first time I'm in charge."

"In this dung-eating city," Ju-hai retorted, "I stand a better chance of being held up than you do." Lowering his voice, he added, "It's all yours!"

Shou-chi raised his arm. "Lead off!" he shouted; he reined in, pausing long enough to say, "Good luck, Elder Brother."

Ju-hai raised his arm in farewell. He wheeled his pony and rode to the rear until, with a start, he realized that he was near the Jin Guan Gate, beyond which was the Mongol colony. Retracing his course, he rode to his new home.

Doctor Wu allowed new students several days in which to become accustomed to their new environment before he assigned studies. During this interval, Ju-hai had divided his time between the Kwan villagers and touring the shops to get additional town clothes and to buy books, brushes, ink slabs, and all the other accessories of scholarship, which his teacher had suggested in a longer talk the day following their meeting.

As he flipped the reins to the doorkeeper, Ju-hai realized how right the old scholar had been in allowing time for acclimatization. He still groped, off balance in the way of a man prowling about the house, one shoe off, one shoe on.

When he stepped in, Orchid said, "I knew you'd be back soon. Everywhere else is still strange."

Now that his fellow villagers were on their way home, this was the least strange corner of Ch'ang-an. From the reception room, his glance shifted to the study room. Orchid had arranged all the things he'd been buying and dumping on the table.

"Old Master," she said, following him, "you forgot to

get a brush-holder, so I got one when I bought kitchen supplies and a few utensils." She beckoned, and he stepped into the kitchen, where he noted other purchases: jugs of *shao-hsing*, and some *shao-hsing hsueh chiew*, something he'd never heard of. There was *kao-liang*, *san shu*, and *ng ka pai*. The last named was considered a tonic because of the many herbs which the potent stuff contained; that made it popular with orthodox Buddhists, since it wasn't an intoxicant, but was a medicine.

"You probably won't care for all of these," Orchid continued. "But you'll be making friends—students always do—they'd go crazy, otherwise, in a strange city. And they do have a range of tastes. There is even *araq*—I can't say that word right, it's Arabic. Anyway, there are a few camel jockeys among the students; they come from Khotan."

"You think of everything!"

"I've lived here all my life. I know you must be hungry, since you left before sunrise. What would you like?"

"After road cookery and the stuff at Maqsoud's, I'd go for anything. Use your imagination. Come to think of it, I didn't get to the inn at the west market until my brother's wagon train was all ready to roll, so I didn't have breakfast."

He stepped into the study room and reached for Li Po's latest collection of poems. He stretched out the accordion-pleated pages compressed by hard covers and glanced down column after column of elegant calligraphy, but nothing suited his mood until, finally, there was one which fitted the mood set by the day:

Here I must leave and float away
On river flood or soaring cloud.
Our days are gone, our nights are done . . .

Farewells—the keynote of the Civil Service. Fellow students, graduated, serving in the same prefecture several years of their youth, meeting again many years later and a thousand miles from the start . . . another encounter, perhaps after retirement. Ju-hai had had his first sample.

The great city was not the loathsome place he had anticipated. After several days of rest and recuperation, he showed up in midforenoon at his teacher's home to begin the study of classics and to practice calligraphy. The following day, he appeared soon after breakfast, but promptness tapered off. Each time he was late, he apologized with charm and entire sincerity. Master Wu, after mild reproof, urged him to devote more time to sleep. In the long run, late study was not productive.

Ju-hai attributed his comfortable lethargy to letdown, after years of farm hours plus overtime, to change of climate, and to change of diet. There could be no doubt that Orchid's kitchencraft was outstanding. She worked on impulse. Whatever she offered, it was exactly what he would have asked for, if ever he had bothered to wonder whether his next meal would be a tray of snacks—*dim sum* in or out of season—or a nine course meal.

And here she was, bringing a bowl of spicy meat balls floating in *congee*—this in lieu of soup; duck feet, smoked, steamed, and each garnished with a ribbon of red roast pork; a plate of dumplings stuffed with minced meat and vegetables; and a small earthenware casserole, a farm-style, one-dish meal of duck, mushrooms, diced pork, and dried oysters miraculously brought back to fresh size and texture. For good measure, clusters of tree fungus floated in the gravy.

Always, Orchid stood by, ready to refill his wine cup; this ceremonial touch gave him a feeling of magnificence. Master Wu, the teacher, was indeed understanding. It did take a while to become accustomed to his new life.

Courtyard walls blocked out the cries of street hawkers. He could not recall when he'd ever been more content with life and the world, except for missing Hsi-feng.

Ju-hai sighed. Yawn followed sigh. It became ever more fascinating to watch Orchid's stately pacings from the table side to the kitchen annex for more wine, and finally, for tea of a flavor different from any that he'd ever tasted before. He'd been speculating, not so much as to what Orchid's contributions to his welfare were to include, as to when she'd be getting around to *that*.

"Nice, really nice . . . kind of exciting, in her quiet way."

A deeper sigh, another yawn . . . the Orchid query would keep until he set his books aside, tonight, but right now . . .

Ju-hai decided he'd lounge in the garden, loll around, and compose verses to capture the autumn spirit; but at the door opening into the court with its miniature lake, miniature bridge, and pavilion not large enough for three persons, he paused. He'd eaten too much . . . *o mi to ful* . . . what a cook . . . what wine!

Before he was halfway to the bedroom he was sleepwalking from golden pleasance into a cozy blur of shimmering shadow and darkness, a confusion of times, places, and people . . . a borderland wherein dream and waking merged, each borrowing from the other, until finally he could not guess whether he was in both or in neither.

Eventually he became aware of certainty; someone, during one of his waves of more than half oblivion had slipped into bed with him—a shapely girl, none the less alluring because her warmth was filtered through the filmiest fabric imaginable.

That *shao-hsing hsueh chiew*—dark, syrupy, sweetish, with a mouth filling flavor . . . oddly enough, he knew that something had stimulated his imagination and he wondered at this, as if he stood outside himself, studying his moods and whimsies. Maybe he was becoming a poet . . . Master Wu would be pleased . . . *mouth filling* flavor of that dark wine . . . how ideas associated . . . Hsi-feng's two outstanding attractions, dainty and . . . Speaking of Little Orchid—no, Little Phoenix—what would happen if she and Mei-yu and Orchid merged to become a one-woman composite . . . with a dash of Lan-yin essence—

In his stumbling drowsiness, Ju-hai had not drawn the bedcurtains; but moonlight reaching in, after contending with all the obstacles of the courtyard, cast a glamor which was more deceptive than revealing. The girl in the fragile garment ought to be either Hsi-feng or Mei-yu—and why not Orchid? The light was too tricky but he'd outwit that bit of lunar witchery.

He closed his eyes firmly. With the most subtle caress, a scarcely touching stroke, he traced her curves and paused at times to appraise the fastenings and the confusing loops.

Despite tightly closed eyes, he could see her exquisite body, a bit at a time . . . Careful now . . . mustn't wake her; that would be discourteous. The further he progressed the more he became confused as to her identity—

"Going to school hasn't done a thing for you," she murmured. "If I'd worn harness, you'd have had me undressed in a flash. I'm not your housekeeper—"

"Mei-yu!"

Before his awareness could find voice, she gave him no further chance for word or gesture. "I've been going wild, day after day after day." She sat up. "Let me get out of this thing."

This she did, with a body twist and arm flash, whisking away the fragile garment, a wisp of mist swallowed by darkness.

Finesse ignored, the pillow book forgotten, for some while the lovers had no thought for Orchid, whose elegant body had pleased many a high official when he needed a traveling concubine during an inspection tour of a remote province.

Finally, Mei-yu sighed and went comfortably limp and relaxed. Like Ju-hai, she was ready for gossip, retrospect, and for words relating to their future.

"Lady Chang Wo's light is shifting. Let's hitch over and stay in the dark. You can imagine this is all-me; some time, maybe, if I can talk the Goddess into it, I'll be all-me, in a body all my own! Then you'd know, really *know—*"

"Jade Lady, I'd not live through it."

"Of course you would!"

"If I didn't, I'd die happy."

"I was desperate that night I appeared long enough to give you and Hsi-feng my blessing. I didn't want to spoil your farewell night, though." She sat up, twisted about, and caught him by his shoulders. "Lover, I know all the stories and things about what bitches women are when another woman is concerned—but really, I wouldn't have borrowed her body. I was an idiot ever to start this escapade. I'm miserable whenever we're not together, though I'm happy we've shared as much as we have. You've got to become an Immortal yourself, so I can make up for my lost thousand years."

It was night in Ch'ang-an, three thousand feet above sea level, and the harvest moon was past her fullness.

"It's getting chilly," Ju-hai said.

Mei-yu groped till she found and drew covers about them. "It would be awfully bad *karma* if you and Orchid got pneumonia, which is something an ethereal Immortal can't get—*aiieeyah!*" She shuddered. "What nasty *karma* we'd get!"

"We must have good *karma*," Ju-hai objected. "Or I'd never have met you or Hsi-feng."

She snuggled up and clung desperately tight. "Lover, you've never had me in a body that's all-mine." Mei-yu shuddered. "I've been worried about you."

"I've had my worryings. Getting Hsi-feng the last minute, just to make it as sad as possible—just when I had to leave."

Mei-yu sat up straight. "The sadder you are at parting, the more you should know that it or she was so awfully good for a while. If you just have to be sure you'll never be sad, avoid everyone that's fine and wonderful. You'll have none of the pains the Lord Gautama the Buddha talked about."

"You mean no attachments, no loving anyone, no wanting anything, no wanting anyone, then no grief?"

"That's right," Mei-yu replied. "That's the Great Law of the Cosmos. Whatever you get, you pay for, in one coin or another. Once you accept the Great Law, know its rightness, you don't suffer any more. It is written and it has been said, '*He who knows how to suffer, that one suffers never again.*'"

It took Ju-hai moments to digest that one, and it ended by giving him spiritual indigestion. He said, bitterly, "That *is* simple, isn't it?" He made a snarling sound, deep in his throat, as if a far-off tiger had bared its teeth. "I'll accept the grief it takes to pay for the good I—we—have had."

"Really mean that?" Mei-yu asked, very softly.

"Yes."

"You've challenged the Great Law. All you have to do now is to accept the Great Law, *karma*, and at the same time go beyond that law—do the impossible and win." She drew a deep breath and shook her head. "Sometimes, I look into the future, and I see grief for you. I can't see details. I'm awfully uneasy about you. I had a talk with Chang Wo, but a Goddess can't go more than so far. Things are closing in on you. My *dharma*, the personal law that rules me, the law of *that-which-I-really-am*, often makes me leave you when I want to be with you, when I could do more than crawl into bed with you—"

"Jade Lady," he cut in, "I'm still *people*, and a thousand years ago, you were *people*. And people manage to carry on. How long can you stay in Orchid's body?"

"If I keep her body too long, there's the risk that she could die."

Ju-hai frowned. "That would be a left-handed way of killing her?"

"It's not that simple, but you're not far off! That would be bad—awfully bad—for you and me—and there's the law of what I am. No one and nothing makes that law—it *is*, just because I *am*."

"Meaning?"

"I'll be with you here as long as I can and I'll be with you somewhere else when I can. I promise."

Each caught the other and, mouth-to-mouth, they found the deepest darkness, beyond the moon's reach.

Chapter XII

Ju-hai was so early for school that Master Wu was both amazed and happy. This was neither ambition nor filial piety; Ju-hai had much thinking to do, and school was his only escape from the mental and emotional turmoil stirred up when, awakening a little after sunrise, he found himself alone.

Then Orchid scratched on the drawn curtains of the alcove, and said, "Old Master, time for breakfast."

As he soup-spooned *congee* with meat balls floating in it, he sensed that something was puzzling Orchid; before he'd finished his rice-gruel, he was sure that Mei-yu had quit Orchid's body. This left him wondering when she'd return.

The nice thing about calligraphy was that he could two-track, digesting his experience with Mei-yu in Orchid's body and at the same time getting the brush strokes to make perfect triangles, perfect wide lines ending squarely, and strokes that would taper into barely visible but unbroken hairlines which swept on and on, to swell again and become massive. There was also something intoxicating about the camphor bouquet which came up from the slab whenever he ground ink.

No doubt about it, he was woman-intoxicated. But he was wondering which woman?

Although Master Wu applauded Ju-hai's amazing performance that morning and all that afternoon, the old man was puzzled. And when, after a long day of classics and calligraphy, Ju-hai begged permission to quit his teacher's august presence, each wondered about the other. School was not loathsome; and Ju-hai was not a trifler with an engaging personality, but . . .

When Ju-hai got his daily exercise by walking from Master Wu's home to his own cozy refuge, Orchid's welcome enriched the day.

"I've been out shopping, thinking up surprises for you," Orchid began, with a glow in her splendid eyes that set him wondering whether her thoughts were shifting from evening rice to the broad mattress behind the alcove curtains. "You'll never guess what I found!"

If she'd allowed him another instant, he'd have blurted out, "The frailest silken shift. It must've been woven of moonbeams."

But she chattered him down, most happily. "Sit down, and I'll show you. I was prowling the market—" Orchid raised her voice so that he could hear her from the kitchen annex. "—and there was a very special duck roasting, but I talked the man out of it—he had time to do another for his promised customer.

"But first you've got to have some *ng ka pai*. You need a tonic after all day at school."

Orchid danced into view with a small tureen on one upraised hand; on the other, she had a wine heater in which an onion-shaped jug barely raised its neck out of the hot water. Pot-lifters protected each hand against its steaming burden.

All on edge, Ju-hai bounced to his feet and sidestepped, ready to dodge when everything smashed to the floor.

Nothing dropped.

"Fooled you, didn't I?" Triumphantly, the question came an instant after she got the little tureen to the table and slid the wine heater into place beside it. "Neat, wasn't it?"

Ju-hai let out a long, quavering breath. "How'd a Buddhist nun learn a trick like that—"

Perplexed, Orchid blinked; then, instead of eying him, she picked it up, smoothly. "Master Wu got you more than you counted on! And you guessed wrong—*ng ka pai*'s really a tonic, and it's good for you, and it's not just for pure-awfully-pure Buddhists who want a high-powered drink without going against their religion. *Aiieeyah!* Maybe there is ginseng in it, but you need something to pick you up after a long day at school."

Ju-hai began to suspect that his housekeeper knew that something had happened to her the previous night, and that she was still puzzled, groping for the answer; and he was asking himself how much tonic she had gulped while awaiting his return. Although let down because Mei-yu had been called away by the laws of her being, her *dharma*, his curiosity regarding Orchid-as-Orchid had a good chance of being satisfied.

And some day, there'd be Mei-yu in a body all her own.

Then Orchid brought him back to Ch'ang-an. "While you're busy with duck soup, I'll get the big event!"

The soup, made of the fowl's bones and spare parts, was not the ninth or thirteenth heaven of Chinese gastronomy —not in the way of a tree fungus, or bird's nest or shark's fin soup—but it had body and flavor which a farmer could appreciate, as did all the non-elite Chinese soups.

And then Orchid brought what had become a not-surprise.

She uncovered a platter heaped with thin slices of fowl, a stack of *pao-ping*—paper-thin *crêpes*, almost as thin as the Mei-yu-plus-Orchid gown—thread-fine, slivered leeks and scallions, and a little dish of plum sauce.

Before he quit blinking, Orchid was busy with ivory chopsticks, the nastiest, the most treacherous, and the most elegant of eating gear, except, perhaps, for jade.

First, she set out the crisp skin of the duck—square flakes of it. That Ju-hai could have done, and so could any Chinese person, even half asleep and dead-drunk. Next Orchid plucked a *pao-ping* and set it on his plate. She arranged sliver-thin strips of duck and laid thread thin lengths of leek and scallion over the plum sauce she'd spooned on the supreme duck.

Then Ju-hai learned that he was a farmer!

Daintily, with supreme *legerdemain*, Orchid plied the

chopsticks and quickly had the *pao-ping* rolled, enclosing the filling.

Mo-shu pork—any clown could roll that one—but this—!

"*Tai-tai*, you're too formal—too stately. Sit down and roll yourself one, so I can watch closely."

Wide eyed, she regarded him. "Old Master—really—you don't mean it—"

"Of course I mean it! Why not sit and eat with me. I've been wondering why you waste time as a student's housekeeper."

Watching the flicker of chopsticks and listening to her answer kept Ju-hai busy. Her explanation, that she had begun by taking the job to oblige a friend who had not been able to accept at the time required, was entirely convincing.

"So, it was to be temporary, until Mou-lan could take over—"

"Temporary? We'll go into *that* later!"

He gestured and she got a chair for herself.

Ju-hai knew that he couldn't have rolled that *crêpe* with chopsticks, but he picked up *pao-ping* and contents, biting off a bit at a time without letting it fall apart or spill its filling.

"You could cook duck like this?"

"I'm not too sure."

She poured *ng ka pai*.

"You're all the tonic I need."

"*And I'm not rolling the next pao-ping—not with you watching!*

"*Tai-tai*, I'll watch you and learn how!"

Addressing her as *tai-tai* was a gross social error, or else a declaration, a proposal, or a proposition—but whatever it might be, it was not the appropriate honorific for a temporary housekeeper.

Orchid neither accepted nor declined promotion to Supreme Number One Lady, with connotation of affection and great respect. Meanwhile, it was amazing what she could do with those chopsticks—

Twinkle-flick-flip—

The *crêpe* was rolled, duck, leek, onion, and sauce inside.

"Simple, isn't it?" She answered her own rhetorical question affirmatively and waited.

"Of course," Ju-hai said. "Slowly, now, real slowly, roll one for yourself and let me watch."

One thing was sure: she'd not learned the trick in any cooked-food stall.

The especially fed and especially roasted duck, and Ju-hai's inviting Orchid to eat with him . . .

They'd been reading each other's minds and moods, until neither could separate what had been sensed from what had been spoken. "Old Master—I've been puzzled silly—all day—about things—I can't put it into words—"

"Another surprise in the kitchen? Let's wait for that and you tell me what's on your mind."

"You've been so gracious—I'm frightfully presumptuous, asking for explanations—" Orchid got to her feet, and blurted it out: "When I made up your alcove—*aiieeyah!* I'll show you!"

Orchid caught his hand, and he followed her. The bed had not been made up. She plucked a long strand of hair, almost black and with the faintest wave, like her own. And then, from the far corner, she picked up a garment of fragile silk. "It's mine. I'll show you others like it . . . I must have been sleepwalking."

Orchid, who always thought of everything and knew every answer had met more than she could handle. "I must have been wearing this, and that's what's so puzzling—this isn't what I would have worn. It would have been a robe."

She explained with a gesture; a robe would part, flip wide open, with nothing to be flung into a corner.

"Was I—but of course I was—"

"You were, and of course I asked you to eat with me tonight. You mean, you didn't know?"

Each moved to the other. He added, "This time, you'll know."

He stepped back into the study room just long enough to pinch out the taper flame.

Chapter XIII

Orchid sighed, stretched, and relaxed in total contentment.

"Now I know what I missed last night. Imagine, sleep-walking and not knowing what I was doing! *Aiieeyah!* I did know something nice had happened. What was I like?"

"That's not easy to answer—I was kind of surprised—"

"Afraid I'd wake and run away and hide in the garden?"

"Mmmm . . . You weren't the way you were after our duck dinner. Of course you're more wonderful when you know what's happening—I can't really explain. You and your questions!"

"Ju-hai, you're *awful!* Suppose things had been the other—"

"You'd have screamed and hid in the garden."

She ignored the interruption and resumed. "If you'd been asleep and I'd been awake, wouldn't you be asking questions?"

"Let's try it and find out." And then his face lengthened. "But you might not stay long enough—you told me—"

"About my friend, the one I promised to fill in for? Temporarily? I can't break away, not when I've been so crazy about you that I began prowling in my sleep—"

"So you were loving me in your sleep?"

"Now who's asking questions?"

"While we're discussing that—" He caught her hand and got his feet on the floor mat. "Let's finish the duck. Or maybe you've got another surprise—in the kitchen, I mean."

"Let's have a drink first?"

71

"If I said no to either idea—"

"I'd know I was dreaming!" Orchid, however, did have reserves in the kitchen, thanks to the Malay barbarians who kept themselves busy with piracy, collecting the edible nests of sea swallows from the Borneo coast; and when neither man-slaying nor bird-robbing, they boiled and dried *tripang*, a sea creature shaped like a cucumber. All this she explained from the kitchen, where she was heating the sauce. She continued as she came back, "You'll love the sauce, very delicate, and black mushrooms and tree fungus—"

Though Orchid was ahead of him in some respects, his prowlings in the markets near the Chun Ming Men gave him a chance to keep up.

"Mmmm . . . the barbarians, the Allah-lunatics, they call them *zebb-al-bahr*."

She eyed him as he knew she would. "That's a crazy language."

"What do you expect of Allah-idiots?"

"What does it mean?"

Having arrived at cozy informality, it was easy to translate graphic but obscene Arabic into poetic Chinese. Orchid quipped about the time required for the real or imaginary aphrodisiac powers of *tripang* to take effect and how long it lasted.

Other dishes, other drinks . . .

The quarter patrol, passing by, called the hour.

"Evening's barely begun!" Ju-hai declared triumphantly.

"I know it's early," Orchid admitted, "but I was busy shopping while you were busy getting tired at school—let's snuggle up and have a little nap and then we'll see."

As he followed her to the alcove, he conceded that gourmet surprises had left him drowsy—more so than he'd realized. He awakened once from sound sleep to see her returning from a prowl in the kitchen. She was saying something about covering the fire so there would be live coals in the morning. Then, slipping between the sheets, she murmured a sleepier afterthought. ". . . and you get some rest, lover . . ."

When the voice of the patrol awakened Ju-hai, he knew

that he had slept several hours. And Orchid, restless, sat bolt upright.

"That's odd, he'd never awakened me before—"

"Forgot to draw the curtains," Ju-hai said. "Moonlight makes me wakeful, and sometimes I don't know whether I'm asleep or awake."

Orchid was now on her feet. "I'll get us a nightcap! With so much happening to us, it's no wonder we're this way. Then we'll be all bright and good as new in the morning, and it will be fun going out to the lake. You've never been there."

She went to the kitchen and came back with a tray on which were two jade cups, one a clear, almost transparent ghost of green and the other translucent, dark green.

They drank and she said, "Good night, Old Master. We'll have something nice for breakfast . . . but now, we do need sleep."

It was not the gray of daybreak which awakened Ju-hai. His was an arousing which startled him. All befuddled, he was tense, alarmed without cause, on the verge of panic, and, for some reason, groping in the darkness, looking for Orchid—

That was the strangest of all: reaching for her, instead of looking for the trouble—

Then he saw a thread of phosphorescence which lengthened and expanded. Mei-yu was taking shape, and he began to catch her direct thought, without sound. It must have been Mei-yu who had aroused him from deep sleep. It was as if she screamed. "Get up! Get a light—that bitch doped you with *afiyoun!*"

He lost moments trying to stay on his feet. In the study room, he fumbled with flint and steel. Mei-yu was soundlessly saying, "She doped your nightcap, she had it ready. When she dozed, I took her body and poured the drinks into teacups and then switched the opium-heavy drink into the white one, and turn about—"

Carrying a lighted taper, Ju-hai bounced into the alcove. Orchid's lips were bluish. Her breathing was labored and slow. She had a faint pulse, so feeble that he could scarcely feel it.

"Get to the herb doctor next door. For you, she mixed enough opium for a man who'd eaten a lot of food. You got the light one, just enough for easy sleeping for a woman her size. I was in a hurry—I didn't stop to think she'd get an overdose—

"If it kills her, get out of town. If she lives, get out—get out—" There was a long pause, as if for breath. Her power was tapering off. But he made out her final words. "I burned myself out trying to wake you. I'm—I can't stay—I'll see—"

The luminous thread faded.

Ju-hai got into his robe and raced to the home of the herbalist. By dint of pounding and shouting, he aroused the medical man. Doctor Hong followed him, took one look at the patient, and diagnosed her pulse almost as quickly. They bundled her in a robe.

"Keep her on her feet—walk her about. Heat some water —or left over tea. I'll be back right away!"

By the time the physician returned, Ju-hai was sweating like a hard-ridden horse. Between effort and anxiety, he was ready to drop.

"Get her into that chair!" Doctor Hong opened his acupuncture kit and selected a needle. "Make fresh tea. Heat more water—"

Before Ju-hai got fairly started with his task, the doctor exclaimed, "Haaa! Good!"

Orchid had vomited all over herself; needling the right nerve had turned her inside out and left her choking and coughing.

"Good again, young lady! Swallow some more. You, young man, get her on her feet, keep her moving!"

Orchid blinked, mumbled, and drooled, totally confused by everything. Ju-hai set aside the bellows and diluted an herbal infusion with fairly warm water. He pumped the bellows some more and poured boiling water into the teapot. They chafed Orchid's arms and legs and moved her near the brazier. Another gulp of medication, and this she took readily. Her color was improving. The edges of her ears were no longer bluish, and her lips had a warmer color.

"Shouldn't have let her take so much *afiyoun!*" the old man reproached. "Lucky you didn't get an overdose yourself."

"*Afiyoun?*" Ju-hai echoed. "What's that? I didn't give her anything."

"That's stuff Arab traders bring in from Persia. Some of the people can't manage that barbarian Arabic, they say *opium*, but no matter how you say it, it's bad stuff. Some people can gulp it like steamed buns and they have fun. Others take a little bit, and it kills them. Some of the stuff is full strength, some is adulterated, and some is just naturally weaker—it's a marvelous medicine, but it's nothing to play with! You mean that you never heard of it?"

"I'm a student, I'm from Tsin-ling Shan."

The doctor snorted. "You young idiots and the palanquin coolies buy most of what's imported! You must be a new one." He shrugged, then smiled. "A student doesn't have to be a pure fool, but it does seem to help if he is one! Now, your young lady—I don't say she wouldn't have lived through it without treatment, but it would have been awkward if it had killed her." He included Orchid in his remarks. "Keep on with strong tea. Keep walking. Take some of this in hot water." He gave Ju-hai a powder in a twist of paper. "You'll live!"

Ju-hai dipped into a muddle of garments and drew out his belt and purse. He found a few *cash* and a couple of *taels* of silver. After glancing about, he found a red envelope.

"Learned doctor—please wait—this isn't sufficient."

"You are too lavish," the physician protested, but he stood fast.

Ju-hai thrust the envelope into his hands. "I'll get more." He turned to the far corner of the room, to move the tile beneath which he had concealed all but his shopping money. The tile however had already been flung aside.

The physician pulled a long face. "There's more to this than there seemed." He took a *tael* of silver from the envelope and offered it to Ju-hai. "This will buy rice until your father sends more money."

Moving like a marionette, Ju-hai accepted the silver. He followed his benefactor to the gatehouse.

"Learned and honorable doctor, I am embarrassed."

"If you wish to offer me a gift when your family sends funds, I would call it gracious and right-minded."

"I don't know the customs of this Imperial city. I am deeply indebted—I hate to think of the possibilities—a stranger with a dead housekeeper—"

The old healer smiled thinly. "The magistrates of Ch'ang-an are incorruptible, and the law is just. If she had died, it would have cost your family all they had and more."

Ju-hai bowed deeply. Feet dragging, he turned back to his own court. He'd sit there awhile, giving Orchid a chance to get herself reorganized. She'd be feeling sick for some while.

The unfired brick of the courtyard wall told Ju-hai a thing or two. It was a reminder of his telling Younger Brother about the young fellow who had watched his elderly father drill holes through the wall of a house to make an opening for an apprentice burglar.

Before him was an example of such craftsmanship. And then his muddled wits collected themselves. The chunk of wall was *inside* the court, and so were the borings.

He went indoors and to the kitchen annex. There he looked sharply at the stores, the groceries, the wines, and the spirits. On the counter was a jug of highly alcoholic *kao-liang* spirits and a teacup on the bottom of which were the dregs of a brownish liquid. The millet whiskey was normally water-clear. This still exhaled the reek of strong liquor, but there was a foreign smell.

Nearby was a small earthenware pot of dark, pasty stuff from which quantities had been taken out, probably with the point of a knife, judging by the shape of the numerous depressions.

There was a single mark, apart from the others, which was by far the deepest. The surface was still moist. A big dose . . . He covered the little pot and put it into his belt purse. Then he went into the bedroom. Orchid looked bleak, grayish, and miserable, but without doubt she'd survive.

She'd been taking hot tea and the herb potion.

Ju-hai said, "I'm going to the market. The doctor told me you'd be all right. It's lucky something woke me up in time. If I ever touch any more of that dark sticky-sweet *shao-hsing*, you can chop my head off and throw it to the dogs."

Orchid grimaced ruefully. "I should have known better; I'd heard that *shao-hsing hsueh chiew* did go a long way . . ." She closed her eyes and shook her head. "If there's any of it left, I'll give it to the poor!" She contrived a smile, bleak, yet a smile.

Ju-hai did a neat job of pretending to be a fool. He started with facial maneuvers and inarticulate sounds; and then he said, "I'm still dizzy and I've got a headache. I'm going to pick up some stuff that will really fix us up. Anything I can get you?" She shook her head. He patted her cheek. "You're still cold, you better bundle up and keep warm."

Gently, he closed the door behind him and tiptoed to his own bedroom. There he spread out a tunic, buttoned it to the collar, and used the garment as a bag into which he stuffed spare clothes and then, in the study room, as much of his student gear as he could ram home. Shouldering his bundle, he got out of the quarter, stretching his legs until he met two coolies with a vacant sedan chair.

Chapter XIV

Once he had the Jin Guan Gate behind him, Ju-hai felt better.

Students, he began to suspect, were fair game—and, like himself, largely simpletons burdened with overwhelming knowledge and devoid of experience. Scholars such as his teacher, on the whole, innocent persons, would be an honest lot, making it easy for a conniving slut and her pimp to develop a thriving industry; and with students arriving in droves each year, it would be a profitable business.

At the West Gate market, he had sold the clothes and other things he'd salvaged. Mei-yu was right. He had to get out of the city.

On leaving the market, he wore a dark blue jacket and black trousers stuffed into felt boots. All this was second hand. And despite his having taken a loss because he had had no time for dickering, he still had sufficient silver for immediate needs. Happily, he had paid in advance for the care of his horse, which was with the animals of the shaman's friends.

Ju-hai found the shaman in the *yurt* of a friend. This mobile home on a wagon bed was a tent of heavy felt, supported by latticework. It was warm from the burning wick which floated in a bowl of rancid butter. A teapot sat near a fire pot fueled with dried buffalo dung. Firewood was conserved for some indefinite northward trek into Mongolia.

Yatu mumbled a Chinese greeting, and poured a cup of tea, with parched barley meal and yak butter to thicken it.

After drinking the unpalatable mess, Ju-hai said, "There has been trouble in the city."

"I thought so. You don't look like a student."

He poured tea.

Ju-hai offered a *tael* of silver. "This is not a payment. This is a present."

"When Chinese offer presents, it is because you have done a favor or because you are going to do one. You have done me much kindness. But I can't refuse a present. What do you want?"

"Advice. What happened last night—"

"Don't say it. I don't give advice. Spirits give it. If it is good, then I am glad. If it is not good, it is not my fault. Argue with the spirits. Don't quarrel with me. What you want?"

"Advice from a spirit-devil. If all is wrong, it's not your fault. Am I crazy to start quarreling with devils?"

Yatu leaned to one side; from the shadows, he picked

his drums, cymbals, and flute. He got to his feet and gestured for Ju-hai to come with him. Once on the ground, he spoke to a boy lounging with other lads and went toward a larger *yurt*. The lad raced to somewhere in the encampment, for a purpose which Ju-hai could not guess.

The *yurt* which Yatu and his client entered appeared to be a compact temple on wheels. At the far end was a small altar on which butter-fueled lamps burned. Yatu fired up joss sticks which he put into a sand-filled bowl in front of a gilded image of Gautama the Buddha. That done, he seated himself on the floor, cross-legged, with his back to the shrine.

Having completed his errand, the small boy stood by the entrance, alternately glancing back and squinting to discover what he could see in the dimness of the *yurt*. Presently he pointed and stepped aside.

Two lean and weathered men entered the *yurt*. One took the shaman's drum. The other took the cymbals. Each seated himself on the floor. Yatu gestured, and Ju-hai seated himself. After a few minutes of silence, the musicians set to work.

Clanging brass and the thundering drum shook the *yurt*. The flames of butter lamps cast dancing light on the ceiling. Though the shaman's face was in shadow, Ju-hai could see that the man's eyes were closed. He muttered and made gargling sounds, deep in his throat, until he emitted a tremendous blast like the long trumpets of Tibetan lamas. He began chanting in a voice utterly different from that of his ordinary speech. Whether this was illusion or because of muscular tension, the flat, squarish face rearranged its features until the shape seemed more triangular, and the ears no longer flapped out so widely from his head.

Abruptly, the chanting stopped, and with it the cymbal clash and pounding drum. The deeply tanned face froze into a fixed expression. As if this were a signal, the cymbalist picked up the flute and played softly, a remote, wailing sound as from a great distance.

Staring as if from beyond the limits of world after world, the shaman shouted in a voice which terrified Ju-hai,

"Who fed opium to Orchid? Stole your money? Don't sit like a fool. What you want to know?"

"Will Father beat me to death. Shall I face him? Shall I run and not come back? What do—"

The dreadful voice shouted him down. "Father has more trouble than you have, idiot boy! Find him—there is war, and he has gone."

Abruptly, there was silence. Drooling, the shaman sat there, swaying from the waist. He almost toppled. The drummer caught him by the shoulder. The shaman's face was relaxing, gradually rearranging itself into normal lines. Presently Yatu blinked and wiped his mouth with his greasy sleeve. "Did he tell you something helpful?"

"I was going to find out if my father would beat me to death for losing silver for three years' schooling—whether I ought to face him or run and never come back. He shouted me down and said my father needs me to help him—he has gone to war. What do you make of all that?"

"You make something out of it. I don't. When the spirit-devil borrows my body, I'm away, I don't know where, but away some place else." He noted Ju-hai's change of expression, his leaning forward, making as if to speak when he quit gulping. The Mongol shrugged and went on. "My devil-spirit, he won't borrow my body unless he is invited with song and music. Other people's devil-spirits take a body without being asked. Different spirits, different bodies, but all I know is how it works with me.

"No—no use asking again. No telling what you'll hear. One poor fellow gave me three horses, two skins of *koumiss*, and some silver, and nagged away until I called my devil to say more. I was wrong—he was wrong—"

"The devil-spirit did him . . . uh—harm?"

"Yes, gave him a clearer sounding answer. The man followed the answer. All was nice until he was killed in the trap the spirit had fixed. Nasty streak. Teaches people to listen the first time, not to be a dung-eating pest."

Ju-hai eyed the musicians. "You heard what he said."

"When we are making music, we go somewhat away ourselves," the cymbalist said. The drummer advised, "You told us he said your Old Man has troubles about a war. Going to help your father is always right. If you get killed, then you die doing what is right."

The shaman added a bit of wisdom. "You don't make sense out of what you heard. Can you make better sense if you hear more?"

Bemused, Ju-hai began speaking as much to himself as to the three he faced. "He asked if I wanted to know who stole my money. I didn't mention any of that. Then he scared me out of my wits, yelling at me and then I asked my question. The old man will go wild at my being such a fool. I didn't show her where the money was hid, but I wasn't careful. After all, she'd been recommended by the teacher—but I didn't use sense. All I wanted to know was whether to go home or hide for the rest of my life."

There was a long silence. Then Yatu nodded. "The devil-spirit knew someone took your silver." After considering for some moments, Yatu brightened. "He was right on two points you didn't tell, and he may be right on what you did ask. Suppose he *is* wrong on two other things, and your father is *not* in trouble, is *not* mixed up in war—my spirit-devil is still smarter than you were; you were wrong all the time."

Coping with Mongolian logic and Mongolian spirits was becoming a nonprofit enterprise. Ju-hai said, "A man can't be wrong all the time. Pretty soon, I'll be right, maybe once. So I'm going home and find out about the Old Man. If he has enough trouble, he won't beat me."

He bowed to the trio and hurried away to get his horse.

Chapter XV

When Ju-hai came within half a day's ride of Kwan Village, he left the wagon track and picked his way up and along the wooded slopes of the second range of foothills until he could look down on the wide expanse of cultivated ground and into the walled enclosure. He was in no hurry to blunder into trouble. For his horse, he had barley; for himself, parched corn and dried mutton. Dismounting, he followed obscure trails and ways he had learned when woodcutting.

Finally he climbed a tree which offered a good observation post. Work in the field was going on as it should go. As much as he could see of the village appeared normal. From high spots along the way he had watched, without seeing parties of riders or men on foot. He did not wish to blunder into a recruiting party; like tax collectors, they went abroad for second and third collections, according to the whims of Bureaucracy.

He was convinced that something was wrong in the village. But while pausing to chat with wayfarers along the road, he had been told by someone that the spirit which took possession of a shaman when he was in one of his trances would often speak words which should not be taken literally.

Shadows were lengthening. Farmers unhitched their buffaloes and made for home. Ju-hai could almost smell the savor of cooking fires. He mounted up and followed the familiar trail.

When Ju-hai rode into the plaza, neighbors came racing from every house. They surrounded him so tightly that he could not dismount. A few concluded that he had passed the examinations, and was now an official. It was not until his brother wormed through the pack and took the bridle that Ju-hai's gesture for silence got attention. "Tell me— ask me after you've eaten your rice." He grinned, patted his belly. "I'm hungry—so is my horse."

One of the older serving women brought evening rice to Shou-chi's apartment. Coordinating chopsticks and words took neat work.

"How did you know—when did you hear?" Shou-chi began.

Ju-hai countered, "Hear what?"

"If you didn't hear, what are you doing back home?"

Ju-hai persisted in his fishing. "You might tell me what

all the excitement's about. School studies were interrupted. Another bureaucratic foul-up." When Shou-chi accepted this as the perfect answer, Ju-hai's thought, *O mi to ful The bastards actually can be useful!* He said, "Anyway, I'm back for a quick look-see. What's all the excitement? One quick-witted fellow thought I'd passed the exams and was an official. I bet others thought I flunked out, but were too tactful to ask me."

Shou-chi said, "A conscription party caught us flat-footed. In every household with three grown men, one was grabbed for the army. You were gone, and I and cousin Quong Ah Wan were cutting wood. A pack train load—took us and Cousin Quong Ah Sam a couple of days to fill the order, and we slept and ate on the job."

"That's luck for you! And for them."

"Well, it wasn't for the Old Man. That turtle-turd officer got sore. We'd given him a story like that the last time. He said to the Old Man—I heard this later, of course—'You go in place of one of your sons—I'm getting sick of that tired old yarn.' By the time I came home, it was all over."

"Where's the war?"

"Hasn't begun yet. Troops are concentrating for a move against some barbarian bastards—maybe in Tibet, maybe Khotan—maybe Turfan. How come you're not studying with Professor Wu?"

"I heard enough in Ch'ang-an to get worried. Too much talk about a big draft. I figured that if they got you, I'd be here with the Old Man and never mind school—or he'd decide which of us ought to go. He's too old for a campaign—It will kill him."

"Now they haven't got either of us!"

"Which is what makes it bad for me, Younger Brother."

"Why especially for you?"

"I've got to take the Old Man's place. It's my fault they picked him up."

"It's just as much my fault—I was away."

"You were chopping wood; that's business."

"School was just as much business. The Old Man made that clear."

Ju-hai shook his head. "I was sitting on my tail, living

like a gentleman. I cost Dad all the silver he had buried. So I'm going to find him and take his place. With enough silver I can buy my way through the bureaucrats and find out where he is."

Shou-chi was quick enough this time. "He might be on the march to one of the spots you mention, while you are prowling a concentration center. The bureaucrats don't give anything but misinformation, excepting by accident. Someone's likely to behead you for a spy, if you go asking where is the Great Man from Kwan Village."

"We'll talk about that later." Ju-hai slapped chopsticks across his bowl. "While I'm still awake enough to know what I'm talking about, let's go to the Old Man's office and see what we can find out."

"About what?"

"About the property you're going to operate until the Old Man comes back. If I don't get him out of this mess pretty quick, he won't live to come back. I was talking to traders, caravan men, in Ch'ang-an, men who've been to all the spots I mentioned, and to Kashgar and Boukhara, even further. Desert marches will kill anyone his age, even if he never meets the enemy."

Kwan Yu-tsun's accounting room was a muddle of papers, as if the Old Man had been interrupted before he could complete a statement of what he owed and what he expected to collect. Although his health had seemed sound, the Senior Kwan had led a rugged life; and with Number One Son to be away three or four years, it would have been a sound idea to leave a statement for Shou-chi.

"I know I'd want some such notes," Ju-hai summed up. "And it would not hurt you, now that you're stuck with it till he comes back."

They did not find what they had hoped. What little they found was bad news. Their father had borrowed heavily on the Kwan lands. Although the name on the *kei wai*— the deed end—was the Old Man's, it was his only because he was head of the family. Every male Kwan had a share and could demand an accounting from the others. There was also the moral obligation, beyond mere legality. Old custom stared Kwan Ju-hai in the face. The money which his father had borrowed had been only a little more than what Ju-hai had lost in Ch'ang-an. The Old Man or his successor could tender payment at any time within thirty years and regain full title. Meanwhile, whoever had made the loan could, in default of interest, take possession.

"Who loaned him the money?" Shou-chi demanded.

"We'll know, if we are lucky—or if we are so unlucky as to be caught short, and the lender makes his claim. He can sell it anytime, at a discount or at a mark-up. Whoever has the red certificate has a claim on everything we own."

Shou-chi said, "This isn't as bad as it looks. You've not had time to spend more than a handful."

"Younger Brother, it's not that simple. Swear with me that you won't tell anyone the bad news."

Shou-chi said, "In the presence of gods, devils, and spirits, as if Elder Brother and I had mixed the blood of a white fowl, the blood of a dog, and a bowl of wine—I swear as you have asked."

"I knew I could trust you without, but swearing leaves a mark on you. You'll not talk on impulse or make slips."

"What's gone wrong?"

"A housebreaker got the silver the Old Man gave me for school expenses. I sold my fancy clothes and got out of town."

"That wasn't your fault—"

"We're not interested in blame. The burglar figured I did everything just right."

"When will you take off to find the Old Man?"

"In the morning. How much silver do you have around the house?"

The brothers could have talked until sunrise but, with what loomed up ahead of Ju-hai, they knew better than to waste sleeping time. At Shou-chi's court, he detained Ju-hai.

"Elder Brother, we moved Hsi-feng to your old apartment. She's pregnant."

"That makes one more bit for me to think about. If Father and I don't find our way back, the family council can't sell her and can't marry her off. See to my horse and wake me early. I'll have a bowl of *congee* with you. Be sure there's sausages in it."

So Ju-hai went to the playmate who had become a firmly established member of the family.

Hsi-feng wore one of the tunics he'd bought for her in Ch'ang-an; the silk was not quite apricot and not dark enough for persimmon. Whatever the color, it enhanced the jade pectoral he had fashioned for her.

"Did they tell you about me?"

"They wouldn't have to. I'd have known at first look."

"But I can't be showing, not yet."

"Silly! It shows all over—you're more beautiful than you ever were before getting yourself that way!" He caught her by the shoulders, back her off an arm's length, and eyed her from toes to jade hairpins. "And now you've written a new contract—told Younger Brother that we can't even give you away!"

"*Aiieeyah!* And now you're wondering—maybe you should have married me off to some nice farmer before it was too late?"

While the wine was heating, he told her that he had to ride in the morning, and why.

She filled the cups; and then, as if having forgotten someone or something very important, she got a third and filled it.

"*O mi to fu!*" Ju-hai exclaimed. "I might've thought of that myself!"

His glance had shifted to her waistline.

"Now who's silly? Penalty, five cups. Don't tell me it was a wine game that got me this way. This one is too young for wine."

"I won't pay the penalties till you give me the right answer."

"I'm filling the third one for the Jade Lady—to drink and to pass on—and not to borrow what I've been saving for you and me."

Chapter XVI

　　At the Mongol encampment in Ch'ang-an, Ju-hai said to the shaman, "Your spirit-devil said my father has more trouble than I have. That is true. I've got to find him, but I'm not asking where he is. A true answer now is no good tomorrow—things move too fast."

Ju-hai left horse, bow, and lance with the Mongols, and went into the Imperial City—the official section which stood between residential-business-market Ch'ang-an and the Palace City in which the Son of Heaven lived.

As the son of a landowner, Ju-hai had learned enough of the official world's pattern for him not to need a guide. There was the Metropolitan Division of the Bureaucracy, and a Provincial Division. The former was divided into six ministries: Civil Offices, Revenue, Rites, Punishment, Public Works, and War, which was his goal.

The doings of these ministries were surveyed by a Censorate, a board interested in public welfare, morals, ritual, social proprieties, and adherence to old custom. The Censorate reported its observations to the Emperor, who was the link between Heaven and Earth—that is, between Gods and Mankind. As to the latter, the scholar was the aristocrat, regardless of his origin; after him, the farmer; then the military caste which had made the Dynasty great, and which was being degraded as a matter of policy, a fact which was giving the barbarians dreams of conquest, or at least of profitable looting. Lowest of all were merchants and businessmen, no matter how wealthy; yet the sons of even such as they, if those lads could pass the Civil Service Examinations, could become officials, aristocrats.

Accordingly, for Ju-hai to enter the Imperial City afoot

and dressed as a farmer was entirely natural and proper. Each spring the Son of Heaven ploughed a furrow to indicate the respect with which Heaven regarded the tiller of the soil, though some suggested that this was simply ceremonial magic to foster good crops.

Patiently, Ju-hai bribed his way from doorkeeper to doorkeeper of each of the offices to which a previous officeholder had told him that he should go to find the information he required. Each day his purse of silver became less of a burden as he worked his way through the maze of passages, corridors, and courts, until at last he saw that he had bribed his way back to the start. No one had heard of any regiment manned by farmers from the Tsin-ling Range, much less of Kwan Village, or of Kwan Yu-tsun. And this finally moved Ju-hai to forget the courtesy which was the essence of Chinese life. He had asked and had got permission to depart. He had bowed each time he took a short pace backward. But as he completed his third bow, he shouted words not on the list approved by the Board of Rites. And his voice was louder than custom permitted.

"A present for every doorkeeper in this dog-dung confusion has got me back to the start! You can all take turns buggering each other—I'm saving my final silver to get a hearing by the Board of Censors!" He turned, head down, but shouted over his shoulder, "And may pigs defecate on your graves!" Belatedly, he realized that in losing his poise, he had lost face; he had committed a social error; in the simplest of terms, he had screwed things up hopelessly.

Head down, shoulders hunched, he barged into the corridor to get out and on the way to the Mongol camp to consult the shaman. But instead of bashing his head against a column, or cracking it against a wall eight feet thick, he nearly floored a stately old man who had not been watching traffic. The cut of his tunic, the drape of his sleeves, and the button on his cap indicated that knocking such a one off his course was the worst error within Ju-hai's reach. Anyone of loftier status would have been hemmed in by an escort.

Shocked beyond fright, Ju-hai kowtowed.

The old man said, "Once is more than enough—get up! What's this about seeing the Board of Censors?"

This official seemed surprised and interested—so much so that he hadn't got around to indignation.

"Sir—your Excellency—I want to join the army—I mean, when the recruiters came—I wasn't at home."

"What kind of nonsense is this? Who ever heard of anyone wanting to join an army?" The man's long finger-nails made his gesture impressive. "You mean they wouldn't let you join?"

"Sir, I was asking about my father."

"What's he got to do with all this?"

"Your Excellency, he's in the army."

"You just told me you were trying to enlist."

"I was—my father's too old—I want to take his place."

"Filial piety! The Board of Censors *ought* to hear about this. Going to fight in Turkistan! Half the outfit won't live to see the enemy—the desert's the real enemy." He backed off, stood there with his fingers combing his white beard, and regarded Ju-hai. "Don't look like that. You come along with me!"

This was right in the Censorate's field. In addition to checking the doings of the Bureaucracy—vainly, of course —the Censors called to the attention of the Son of Heaven such evidences of outstanding virtue as of one living for three years in a tent pitched beside the grave of a parent, or of a widow refusing food until she perished of malnutrition. Ju-hai's combination of patriotism with filial devotion—this was a natural!

On returning to the Mongol camp, Ju-hai said to Yatu, "With the Censorate on their tails, those bastards will find out where my Old Man is, what regiment, what company, and what squad, just as easily as they locate a man delinquent in taxes."

This proved to be the understatement of a short lifetime.

The following forenoon, six riders, two heralds, and a yellow sedan chair carried by eight bearers came to the camp. A guide led the procession to Yatu's *yurt* and invited Ju-hai to come out to get an Imperial communication.

The Number One herald opened the sedan chair and

took from it a tray on which sat a cylindrical case which was covered with brocade of that vermillion color which only the Son of Heaven used or wore.

Ju-hai kowtowed nine times and remained kneeling.

The assistant herald opened the case and took out a scroll of vermillion damask, inscribed in red. This he handed to the Number One herald, then took cymbals from his belt. These he clashed nine times.

The Number One herald read the text: the Son of Heaven was pleased to recognize the merit of Kwan Ju-hai, and would facilitate Ju-hai's finding his father.

The proclamation scroll was returned to its case and put back into the sedan chair. It would go into the Imperial Archives. The assistant herald handed a document to the Number One herald, who read the text and handed it to Ju-hai. Finally, there was a purse of silver which weighed considerably more than what Ju-hai had spent for bribery. After Ju-hai gave each of the party a proper gift, there remained somewhat more than required for expenses to his destination, the assembly and training area of the Hsien Ming regiment, now stationed at Tun Huang, twenty-five miles from Kara Nor.

When the embassy departed, Ju-hai studied the document carefully. It was chopped by one of the assistants of the Minister of War and it was issued in the name and at the command of the Son of Heaven; hence, *obey with fear and trembling*. It commended Ju-hai to every commander from Ch'ang-an to Khotan and back to Ch'ang-an to facilitate the herein named Kwan Ju-hai's meeting his father, Kwan Yu-tsun; and Kwan Ju-hai, upon overtaking his father's regiment, was to assume his father's duties and serve in his stead, until the regiment returned to its point of origin.

Somewhere in the western portion of Kansu Province, the Silk Road divided into three branches. The northern-most was improbable—but the central and the southern routes to Khotan, the center of revolt, were a standoff. Each offered advantages which were offset by grave handicaps.

Yatu said, by way of leave-taking, "If you want to make the best time, sell or eat your horse and go afoot—a man can walk further and, in the long term, overtake a horse. A good man, I mean. Going it alone, you can march all day and much of the night, which a regiment can't do. It's easy, as long as you don't get robbed or killed."

"Yatu, I was born lucky or I'd not be here now. Your familiar spirit-devil was right. The High Dignitary who helped me instead of having me flogged said the desert's deadlier than the enemy. It would finish my Old Man."

The Mongol grunted something unintelligible. Ju-hai however had to speak his mind. "I'll tell the Old Man to see you on his way home. The Kwans owe you a lot."

"Manure! The Kwans don't owe me nothing."

"I'll talk that out after we capture Khotan. Or if we have to occupy the city for a while till there's real peace, I'll write you."

"I'll find someone who reads Chinese. Good luck and be careful who you sleep with."

Chapter XVII

Ju-hai soon learned how right Yatu had been in their talk the eve of his departure: "You militia farmers learn how to handle weapons, but not one of you knows how it goes on the march. No army can move faster than the supply wagons, and a regiment can't do much better. A company of footmen—well, yes, good for thirty miles, but not for many days in a row. A good man going it alone can do forty miles or more and keep it up."

And this Ju-hai verified long before he got into the chill, the silence, the thin air, and the awful loneliness of high mountains. He was out of his own world and he turned inward, making himself one with rememberings of those from whom he was isolated as never before. He kept each evening's cooking fire small and well off the wagon track.

As ash film veiled the coals and his hobbled horse scented neither strange animals nor humans, Ju-hai backed away and found himself a spot in the shelter of a storm-uprooted tree. Sword ready, he'd be the hunter if anyone heard the horse and approached.

The dying little fire gave more smell than glow.

Though Ju-hai had not been expecting Mei-yu, he was not surprised when she took shape and came near him. "You've been thinking of me all your way through these mountains," she began. "I've got to build up my energy so I'll have enough to help you. You're going into trouble; there are bad things ahead of you. But I had to be with you a few breaths and blinks so you'd know I'm never too far away."

"And you're worried now? What's coming up?"

She shook her head. "I can't predict. The best I can do is sense the forces of Nature as they change. Each creature responds according to—well—to his own individual nature."

"You mean, his *dharma*—you were telling me about that, our night in Ch'ang-an."

"You're learning! What you're doing to get your father out of the army is an expression of what you are. So was the way you kept your hands off Hsi-feng. She was a darling, setting out a cup of wine for me, when you went back home. And you were so concerned about your father's trouble that you couldn't hate Orchid—what he'd lost was more important than what she had done to you."

Mei-yu gave him a moment to digest the substance, and then said, "*What you get is what you are*—your own substance brings you grief or good. And I'm no better off than you are. You and I—by increasing what we are, going the way you've been going—I can't promise, but we may have our day, even if we have to wait till you're an Immortal. Now I'm running out of power. Do what it is your nature to do, and go on into new danger. When things are at their awfully awful worst, I'll see you, if I can—"

Then, as never before, Ju-hai was alone.

In An-hsi he sold horse and gear and continued afoot, with a bag of parched barley, a jug of cooking oil, and a skin of water. His lance was a staff. He wore a three-ply buffalo hide corselet covered with overlapping discs of metal and a light helmet. In his pack, with rations, he had a heavy cape and spare shoes.

In Tun Huang, he verified the information he'd got in Ch'ang-an: the Hsien Ming Regiment had passed through and was making for the central of the three branches of the Silk Road.

Not long past midday, after he knew not how many days on the road, he reached the assembly area. His travel order got fast action. And then Ju-hai fought collapse when he learned that the Hsien Ming Regiment was there, and awaiting orders. As his legs threatened to go limp as well cooked octopus tentacles or the noodles with which they were served, he knew why a man could outmarch a horse. No horse had to redeem himself for losing borrowed money.

At regimental headquarters he thrust his document at a clerk.

"Don't try to memorize it. Look at the chop. I'm supposed to report to the commanding officer the minute I get here and I've been standing too long already."

A few moments later, the clerk called him to Colonel Tsao's presence. The smooth-faced, elderly officer glanced at the order and noted the date. As he returned the paper, he remarked, "You didn't take much time getting here."

"Sir, this soldier marched after dark and set out before daylight."

"Very good!" Then he ordered a noncom, "Sergeant, tell Captain Li that Private Kwan Yu-tsun is relieved from duty until tomorrow morning. His son has come to take his place. Kwan Ju-hai, the Son of Heaven and the Minister of War have recognized your filial piety and your patriotism. What need I add? Dismissed!"

When the paper work was done, Ju-hai followed the noncom to Tao Lung Company. The chop of the Minister of War was still working its magic. Presently, Ju-hai and his father stopped at the prepared food cart, somewhat beyond the regimental area, where soldiers were getting pieces of pork in spicy sauce, garlic flavored sausages, and steamed buns filled with minced meat. And there were dried *lichis*, salted and spiced plums, salted ginger root, and small apples—very small—which had been stewed in sugar syrup and dried.

Ju-hai, washed and rested, was far from relaxed. Like his father, he was still dazed. Neither had said a word since leaving camp. Before getting their passes, there had been disconnected scraps of speech. Ju-hai was waiting for the Old Man to lead off; and the Old Man did not know what to say.

They'd eaten their bowls of rice gruel and dried shrimp before Yu-tsun asked, "Son, why aren't you at school?"

"A shaman, the one who rode in one of our carts—"

"The one that beat the brains out of a tiger. I remember. What did he tell you?"

"That there was a war, and that you were in trouble. So I went home and Younger Brother told me about you. I came to take your place."

"So, I am no good for war?"

"It's my duty. Anyway—" And he went into details of his bout with the bureaucrats. "And two days after I nearly knocked that official off his feet, I got my travel order."

The Old Man actually smiled a little. "So it took rioting in Khotan, and killing the *amban*—the Board of Censors— and the Minister of War—everything and everyone working for you so you'd not have to go to school!"

"Sir—" Ju-hai gulped, swallowing air. "It just happened that way."

"You've been up to some fool caper. Did your teacher say you were too dumb for him to fool with?"

Ju-hai blurted it out. "I was robbed. Every piece of silver except what I had in my purse."

The Old Man's face tightened into its fixed pattern, the one which came just before he went into action to cope with disaster. Ju-hai broke out in a sweat.

"Laying up with a sing-song girl—yes?"

"It was my housekeeper. My teacher recommended her."

"Probably a virgin, and her mother was going to sell her to a whoremonger, and your compassionate teacher got her a job and then found you."

Though far from cheerful, the Old Man's face did not indicate beheading or flogging to death. Encouraged, Ju-hai told all. "That bitch," he concluded, "had been doping me with *afiyoun*—it's a sort of drug from Persia—it's just beginning to come into the country." He dug the jar from his pack. "Each little knife point dig was just enough to keep me drowsy and late for school; and then there was one deep dig. When I saw your money was gone, I got out in a hurry. She was working for someone who looked important, or Master Wu wouldn't have recommended her. Someone he felt beholden to."

"And that someone fixed it up so her helper gave her an overdose and you and the herb doctor saved her life? Mmm . . . you were smart to get out." The Old Man clapped him on the shoulder. "Eat some more of those pork rib nubbins and quit acting as if you came all this distance afoot to get a beating."

The Old Man laboriously got to his feet, went to the food stand, and picked up a jug of hot wine. "You need a couple more drinks. Marching this far left me creaky."

Ju-hai didn't know whether to laugh or cry, so he did both. Then he blurted out the ultimate bad news, which he had for the moment forgot. "Younger Brother and I went through your papers in the office. You borrowed all that money I lost."

"Son, that's nothing to what the Government's been robbing us of all my life. Sure, I did borrow that money, but I had more than that buried." He grinned, enjoying his son's gaping perplexity. "I did not want poor relatives to think I could fork over three years' expense money for you —they'd all have closed in and taken me for even more than the Government does. But claiming you're in debt doesn't help you any with the tax collector. The son of a bitch always tells you you're owing just a bit more.

"Students from well-to-do families would depend on drafts from home. A farmer's son can't bet on any year's crop. The wrong people must have found out you had a pot of silver buried somewhere."

Ju-hai's wits began to sharpen, now that meeting his father had not been the disaster it had threatened to be. "As you said a minute ago, my teacher is honest. Whoever Orchid was working with must have doped her and run off with the loot. She'll figure he tried to kill her with an overdose so I'd be blamed. She'll try to level things off. If we can find her, we'll get him, maybe."

"Drink up, son!" The Old Man reached for the jug. "All you have to do when you get back to Ch'ang-an is to get her to help you settle that fellow quietly."

"Kill him?"

"Get the money back first. When you do that, there's no need of killing."

"Sir, I'm taking your place in this five-*cash* war, and you can tend to Orchid Cluster—you're smarter than I am. And when we've looted Khotan and driven out the barbarians, I'll have enough plunder to make good what I lost. And you'll run our land better than Younger Brother."

"And get so rich I can buy you that Orchid. If you sleep with her long enough, she'll learn how to be a lady. A nice concubine."

The head of the Kwans and his heir settled down to drinking *shao-hsing* and getting acquainted, each trying to outpoint the other in the reassignment of duties.

The following afternoon, when Kwan Yu-tsun's pass expired, he went with his son to speak to the regimental commander.

"Sir," Ju-hai began. He tendered his travel order. "This soldier has found his father, but he has not yet been assigned to duty in his father's place."

His third-person address put him a step ahead of any other rural militia man or conscript. His long solitary hours and the hundreds of miles on the road had given him a touch of the professional. Having been his own commander had marked him.

Colonel Tsao considered for a moment. His smooth, benevolent face predicted the tone of the words he was about to speak. "Filial piety—patriotism—they are akin, but I honor each, separately. Your sense of duty is commendable. You will report to the commander of Tao Lung Company. Private Kwan Yu-tsun, you will report to your present company commander for orders. Dismissed."

They waited only a few minutes for a clerk to brush an order confirming the Colonel's words. They lost no time reporting to the clerk of Tao Lung Company: and they got an immediate hearing. Ju-hai repeated his statements, and in his best military manner.

He was thinking, as Captain Li glanced at the Minister's order, *Soldiering with this nasty bastard will be no treat.* He did not know what was wrong with the Captain's taut, seamed face, but he sensed that this was a man who had encountered much of life and hated most of what he had met. *I don't have to go to Khotan—I'm facing the enemy already.*

And then came the instructions to the clerk: "Private Kwan Ju-hai will take Private Kwan Yu-tsun's place and perform his duties. Private Kwan Yu-tsun is transferred to the Transport Company."

The clerk's brush had scarcely begun to flick its way down the right side of the paper when Ju-hai protested, "Sir, I came to take my father's place, to relieve him of duty. He is—"

Ju-hai did not get a chance to finish.

Captain Li was on his feet. He stood for a moment, eying the presumptuous rookie. He slashed with his riding whip, a wrist flick too swift to be evaded. It was beautifully controlled, stinging cruelly, but stopping short of damage.

"Now that I have your attention," he began calmly, "I remind you that his Excellency the War Minister's order commends you to all unit commanders, and instructs them to facilitate your taking your father's place. You have taken your father's place.

"There is nothing in this order about your father's being discharged from the service. Each will be hostage for the other's good behavior." His twisted almost-smile was mocking. "Considering your father's age, desertion together would not be practicable. Dismissed!"

The Old Man went to the platoon shelter to get his gear. Ju-hai, after leaving his pack and equipment at the sleeping space vacated by his father, got the noncom's permission to leave at once to give the Old Man a hand. As they set out, Ju-hai said, "Sure you could carry this stuff alone. I want to know the way. We've got a lot left to talk about when we're off duty."

Chapter XVIII

Before going to Transport Company for some talk with his father, Ju-hai would gossip with comrades after evening rice. Most of his company was from Kwan Village and neighboring settlements. Having marched fifteen hundred miles or more from their start, the troops knew by now what and whom to hate and watch and which officer or thing was not the soldiers' enemy. Much of the lore was fanciful. Some, however, had a foundation.

Aside from being a congenital son of a bitch, Captain Li was an unknown quantity. Ju-hai's account of meeting Li merely confirmed an established opinion. Colonel Tsao, on the other hand, was by no means disliked, and he was not entirely a mystery. It was known that he had an outstanding record as a soldier, and that behind his bland face and equanimity lurked the bitterness of a man too often disappointed. The clerk at headquarters had heard Tsao say such and such to his adjutant. The clerk had passed it along to a noncom in the cavalry advance guard, and the last named had leaked the facts to someone in Tao Lung Company.

". . . a bitter fellow . . . good soldier, good enough to be denied promotions because, with another couple of steps up, he'd command enough troops to give him notions about plotting revolt, or taking over a province. So he gets put in command of two regiments of infantry, a squadron of horse, and enough sappers to breach the walls of Khotan, wipe out the rebels, and hold the city until the inhabitants venture out of the hills and come back to town. . . . Quite an assignment for a soldier with a record, and not even a promotion to accord with his command. Scholars, intellectuals running the country . . . the farmers, plodding in mud and manure, they resent military service and resent the army but for which brigands would loot their granaries, burn their homes, rape their women, turn things inside out. . . ."

Before Ju-hai had fairly summed up the Colonel's thoughts on government, he reached the Transport Company. One of the outfit hailed him and said, "Your Old Man is on picket line guard. He's just come off post and he's eating."

"Guarding horses, donkeys, and camels, uh?"

"What do you expect, elephants?"

Neither the guard fire nor the mess wagon was a good place to discuss camels, a subject which had become ever more important.

Whimsically, but with an intent look in his eyes, Ju-hai said, "Dad, you had better learn to ride those stinking devils. In case you get tired marching."

"I'll study on that . . . Maybe you could learn about camels." The Old Man returned the probing look. "You can start three nights from now, if you're not on duty, and help me gather camel droppings and dead brush for the cooking fire."

"No horse turds, Dad?"

"Those are at headquarters. How do you like Tao Lung Company?"

"It's like being back home, except that the loud-mouths are making it awkward for me, beginning about my second or third evening."

"What are they doing?"

"They're showing Chen Yin-chu a nasty time of it, all left-handed. He pretends he doesn't catch on, but I can see it is eating at him—"

"I still don't see how that's anything to you."

"You mean, in all of the time you and Lan-yin's son have been on the march with Tao Lung Company, there was no left-handed fun about Lan-yin being the Kwan concubine?"

The Old Man grimaced. "You saying it started a couple or three days after you got here?"

"Just right! Quips about how, if Younger Brother had been caught by the conscripting party that got you and Yin-chu, Lan-yin would die of heartbreak. No, it's not put that directly; it's kind of accidental, growing out of group chatter. Unless I could give you the exact words and voice and all that has been said, you wouldn't get it."

"I know what you mean." Kwan Yu-tsun cursed bitterly. "Making dirt and trouble where there never was any before." He shook his head, snarled deep in his throat, and spat. "It all started with her and Master Chen not getting along and fighting too loud. She and Chen quit being so noisy, once we—uh—you and your brother got friendly with her, or she with you, whichever way you want to put it. It wasn't according to the Book of Rites, but it worked nicely and naturally. Everybody figured it a grand answer; and once a thing is accepted, it becomes a tradition. But Tao Lung Company has a lot of outside neighbors and outright strangers, and that's what is making it bad for Lan-yin's son. It would have made it bad for Chen, if he'd got caught in this draft."

"And it's making it bad for me," Ju-hai caught the Old Man's querying expression, and explained. "Because someone started this thing as if on a signal. It didn't grow up naturally. None of the home folks would have done it. It would never have occurred to them. There is a purpose; someone has planned this, and he didn't lose much time."

As he walked back toward Tao Lung Company's area, Ju-hai reviewed his expeditionary experience. The Old Man's prospects were worse than his own, and these were none too good. Already, Ju-hai was one of a silent minority, each of whom had in his quiver one arrow marked with the name of Captain Li, to be used during the looting of Khotan.

The moon had not yet risen; but though he was well within the limits of the regimental area, with units staggered alternately on the northern and southern sides of the road, the spaces between companies gave hints of the desert's treachery. The wind played tricks, as if mimicking voices and the stirring of animals. Tamarisks and wild poplars made obscure shapes. There were hints of distant music and of human voices.

What brought him up sharply was that, for the second time, he was sure he had heard his name called. Ju-hai was not inclined to accept what he had heard of malicious presences, spirits, and devils, beguiling travelers from the trail. Only the most stupid of spirits would waste his time in such a corner of good-for-nothing desolation.

On the other hand, the peculiar echoes, resonances, boomings, and whinings of the wind, the patter of wind-driven sand, and the murmur-whisper-hiss of dunes changing shape would bedevil their way if he and the Old Man stole camels and deserted, as he was sure that they would have to.

From time to time he paused to observe the stars. Such and such constellation and a star that was near it, or part of it, was what he'd face when his direction was westerly; and when his right shoulder pointed in that direction, he'd be looking south. These short walks were important.

Shadow swallowed Ju-hai, shadow so dense that starlight became comparatively bright. There was not much farther to go. This tamarisk cluster was a landmark he'd picked before dusk.

Then he sensed a presence, though he could neither see nor hear, other than the desert's illusions. Despite wood smoke, the scent of draft and pack animals, and the smell of sweat, leather, and manure, he caught a familiar sweet-

ness, the spirit bouquet that Mei-yu exhaled when she was
near and in a mood; but there was no luminescence.

And then came direct communication: *Lover, be awfully careful—and the more so, the nearer you get to the
oasis—resting area for the army—most danger there—
several days— if I don't borrow someone's body soon, I'll
go quietly crazy—I have to save power—we'll meet . . .
when . . .*

Communication failed. Ju-hai's black loneliness assured
him that, for a moment, he had not been alone.

Piecing together Mei-yu's patchwork of messages would
keep Ju-hai busy until the army came to a rest halt—the
first time he'd heard that military matters ever took resting
into account—but what she said of danger, that was all
too clear!

Chapter XIX

Desert lay beyond desert beyond desert, a
road without end, leading somewhat south of west, with
tremendous snowcaps to the north, and nothing to break
the monotony except watchtowers which differed only in
height. Ju-hai, however, was intensely interested; he was
learning to sense what was behind him without appearing
apprehensive when he went about camp at the end of each
day's march. He was also watching to see how the Old
Man was enduring the difference between long days behind the plough and days just as long in the camel train.

The latter should have been the easier, but the lines of
Yu-tsun's face and the droop of his shoulders showed that
such was not the case. He stoutly denied his weariness. Ju-
hai, however, got the answer; the Old Man was carrying
the Kwan acres on his back.

Ju-hai also had his invisible problem; the commanding

officer's gross injustice, the Captain's viciousness, and Lanyin's son, Yin-chu, had become elements of an entirety, although this came out of nothing more tangible than inference and sensing.

Someone was keeping the polyandrous concubine an amusing topic of whimsy. Whoever that was had been working neatly; the jesters were always new. Apparently each had been primed in a casual way, privately, so that he didn't realize how he was being used. "Our Girl," the darling of the Kwans, should have become dull and should have made way for some other campfire jest. Sometimes she seemed forgotten, but this never lasted long.

Yin-chu was too skillful to be quite convincing in his apparent stupidity. He overcorrected. And this was what warned Ju-hai. Eventually Yin-chu would try to assassinate Ju-hai—after all, the wearisome "in" jest had not begun until Ju-hai's appearance.

Captain Li's reaction to a protest which was neither disrespectful nor insubordinate, though it might have been a breach of military etiquette, had been extreme; if not unlawful, at least it was a violation of every principle of soldiering in the field. He could reasonably expect stealthy vengeance—a soldier could resort to no other kind. As a matter of ordinary common sense, Captain Li had to strike first and either secretly, using a catspaw, or openly by trumped up charges and a drumhead court-martial.

Ju-hai settled down to attempt baiting the prospective assassin, if in fact there were such a person. The best procedure was to tempt him to strike, be ready for the attack, and get him first, once he'd committed himself.

However much camp and watchtower talk usually contradicted each other and varied from day to day, all agreed that before the column reached the confluence of the Khotan and the Tarim rivers there would be a halt for men and animals to rest and for shoes, rations, and equipment to be inspected. For Ju-hai, this would be the place of decision. A halt, a temporary lapse of discipline, and relaxation at an oasis settlement quite near the road—if anywhere, it was here that the enemy would strike. Mei-yu's warning became very real now, and urgent.

Finally, the road did skirt a puny oasis, and then Ju-hai saw at last the place which had been described at many a tower station. There were clusters of wild poplar and stands of tamarisk, some planted as a wind break, others growing haphazard. The settlement—it might have been called a village—a quarter of a mile off the southern side of the road was a clutter of cubical houses. If their walls of sun-dried brick had been whitewashed, the settlement might have been mistaken for dice cast among the dunes by a gigantic gamester. When the wind subsided momen-tarily before raising its voice again—a cycle which made sleep difficult for newcomers—the wail of pipes, the thump-thump-thump of drums, and the voices of singers reached into camp. This was unlike any music which Ju-hai had heard. This was Turkistan, alien, alluring, dan-gerous—warning and invitation.

The troops had heard all about the whores and sing-song girls and the wines made of grapes growing in Turfan, far to the north; there was a lot of speculation.

"What have these Uighur girls got that you can't get back home?" was demanded, and the rhetorical question got military answers: "some new diseases . . . them Uighurs are right here, and home is a nasty two thousand miles east."

Then individual analysts contributed bits:

"They're the most beautiful women in the world. And they put it out for fun, don't charge even one *cash*."

"Manure!"

"Why do you suppose there's always been war with the Turkistans?"

"They're thieving bastards."

"You're not a thieving one, but you're ignorant. It's because they got the most beautiful women and the finest horses; and whenever we whipped the Uighurs in a war, the Son of Heaven made them hand out women and horses."

"Fat lot of good that did the troops!"

"Those down there—" There was a gesture toward the 'dobe houses. "Not good enough for the Son of Heaven."

"What do you know about women?"

"Why do you think the palace is jammed up with eunuchs if they weren't hot stuff?"

"Li Po's mother was an Uighur princess—"

"You don't have to have a beautiful mother to be a poet."

Ju-hai faced the driving sand; the wind had begun to whoop it up. "Quickest way to find out is to go over and see—and get the Old Man a jug of that grape wine for a breakfast appetizer."

"Don't get lost—them devils mumbling—"

He grinned. His glance shifted from face to face, and included Yin-chu, who at times looked somewhat like his father, except that the facial structure was coarser; his resemblance to Lan-yin was more in mannerisms and quirks of expression.

"I'll pick landmarks before dark," Ju-hai said, "and once I make it to the camel jockeys and back to camp, I'll stick to it. Don't you worry about having to go out and hunt me."

He'd already decided how he would go. The moon was somewhat past full. The watchtower was all the landmark he needed until he got back into the tamarisks and poplars between the wagon parks and the camel drivers' area. With moonrise three-quarters of an hour later each night, the light would be just about right, if the assassin snapped at the bait. And if Captain Li was pulling the strings, he'd be sure to prompt the executioner. The most likely spot would be between the fun-oriented settlement and the caravan park. Dunes cut off observation and distorted sound.

"Handy for him," Ju-hai mused. "Handy for me . . ."

As he had surmised, the local garrison's watchtower, from which heliograph, smoke, and fire signals were sent to the next one along the Silk Road, was never out of sight.

Having eaten evening rice, the Old Man had walked over to gossip with fellow villagers in Tao Lung Company. Seeing his son approach, he got up from his huddle with three cronies and went to meet Ju-hai, who raised his voice.

"Here's your wine! Some like it before meals, some like it during meals, some like it after a meal—"

The Old Man sounded off, giving a family gagline: "And a sensible man likes it all the time!"

They turned to retrace Yu-tsun's course to the Transport Company area. Ju-hai raised his voice enough to make sure that his comrades of Tao Lung Company would hear. "So I'll be bringing you a bottle every night—bearing on the tower—I'll not get lost—"

Once beyond that company's area, Ju-hai cut his running fire of comment on how the villagers regarded the army; in a low voice, he gave his father details of what he had planned. He also handed him the little pot of gum opium. "Don't take more than a small knife point dab for each man. And dope just one bottle, the second bottle the guard is going to get. Drink with them from the first one and then beg off; say you're too old to drink with young fellows."

"If we're going to desert anyway," Yu-tsun wondered, "why wait to bait Lan-yin's son, or whoever you figure is out to finish you?"

"Dad, it's this way. During this rest and refit for the final dash, someone will see a nice chance—Captain Li and whoever he is egging on, or Colonel Tsao, that nice smooth officer. Maybe there is no one out to take our hides—you're right, so far—but with all our figuring, you and I don't know that we can grab two camels and get away; in case we have to stay with this army, we've got to defend ourselves! Tsao didn't act as a good officer should, and his history shows he was a good officer. Li was a nasty son of a bitch, in a way that does not make sense, not for a career officer. My being doped and robbed—and that irregular second conscription that caught you . . . And there was no point in keeping you, when I came to take your place . . ."

"Son, I begin to see it your way."

"I might be stuck with guard duty out of turn. You might get something like that, some duty to foul things up. My plan won't interfere with your getting a couple of camels."

They were near the Transport Company area when they halted.

"Dad, I'll bring you a jug tomorrow night . . . maybe better two jugs . . . it's a long march up a riverbed that might be dry."

Chapter XX

Ju-hai risked dallying another day to get the best hour of moonrise. Now he had the oasis settlement behind him, as he took the route which wound among low dunes. He was poised between material fact and intangible fancies. He and his people made no such a sharp distinction between material and the invisible aspects of Nature as did the barbarians of the west. Living closer to the borderland which separates the world of devils and spirits from that of solid substance came naturally to the Chinese and many other Asiatics—so much so that their awareness of this difference between them and foreign devils was scarcely conscious. Instinct made them at home in that zone wherein two worlds merged, an overlapping rather than a sharp division.

This boundary could well be compared to that between mortals and Immortals, between Immortals and Gods and Buddhas—or between animals and mankind. These were all of a single family—a fact which was beyond the comprehension of foreign devils and barbarians, who considered themselves separate from Nature and separate also from gods, of which the sottish fellows had only one. An insane and incomprehensible pack!

And Ju-hai was further into that Borderland than he realized. His senses were more sharply tuned than normal. Accordingly, he coped with the ticklish business of being receptive without trying to be such—this was like the Cha'an masters' lessons on the futility of *trying* to relax, to let go. But, as he neared the critical zone, his breathing became ever more natural, and his pulse subsided.

"Now I've done it—"

The mere thought of having let go and become receptive had undone all; but he regained control, and began to do nothing. Doing nothing consisted of stumbling, footfumbling in the sand, floundering and diverging bit by bit from the path which he had so carefully established for anyone who might have been observing him. He had at last ceased wondering whether the assassin, if there was one, would elect the lurking place which Ju-hai had picked as the best one for assassinating a victim.

If truly fine-tuned, Ju-hai would respond no matter where the archer lurked. It would have to be an archer. Neither lance, mace, nor sword were appropriate to the terrain. But now Ju-hai was poised so that, if the lurker snatched a star from its heavenly bed and hurled it, he could dodge it readily enough.

He had watched mounted archers demonstrate their practiced skills.

A bowstring twanged.

Ju-hai lurched, clawing sand. The arrow struck an instant after he heard the bowstring's voice. To say that he had reacted quickly would be the plausible talk of ignorance, of logic. He had begun diving into sand before the archer loosed the arrow. A logical person would say, *That motion in moonlight made the archer let go!"* This, in Chinese, would be nonsense. The arrow sank into sand, not into the man who writhed, clawed, struggled, made sounds—and jerked the arrow from the sand, getting it between his upper arm and ribs.

This motion baited the archer from cover. He was hurrying in; he had to make sure.

Ju-hai got the haft of his blade—he'd help the man make sure of the outcome which Ju-hai had planned.

There came another sound, one which Ju-hai had not anticipated, another was coming, kicking up sand. There was a choked yell. Ju-hai rolled and his sword whipped out. His assailant's dagger dug deep into sand. Then the two were knocked breathless by the late mover who had gone into action.

"Son—did he—get you?"

It was the Old Man. Ju-hai rolled and knocked aside the dagger. "Don't kill him—see who—"

Yu-tsun, still the head man of the Kwans, struck with the pommel of the haft, silencing the assailant.

Ju-hai sat up. He was not surprised to see that the archer was Yin-chu. The Old Man licked his lips and fingered his blade.

"What's this—"

In the cold moonlight each saw the other, clearly, sharply.

Ju-hai choked. "Dad—he's a neighbor—I can't kill her son."

"I hope you know what you're doing."

Yin-chu was stirring. The dagger pommel had done no real damage. Ju-hai snatched the jug of spirits he'd dropped. He grabbed the archer by the shoulder. "Dad, give him a nip of *kao liang!* I'll watch him here, while you get the camels."

The fierce pungent millet whiskey made Yin-chu choke. Lan-yin's son eyed his captors. He was too shocked to resist or plead.

"Dad, Yin-chu and I, we'll be waiting up there." He pointed to the clump of tamarisks which had sheltered the assassin. "Can you make it right away?"

"It's almost made, son—that's why I was standing by."

As the Old Man went to get the animals, Ju-hai spoke to the still dazed archer. "They were showing disrespect to your mother." His voice was warm, compassionate; he was doing better than he had expected, for it was as if Mei-yu were at hand, using his voice. He stroked Yin-chu's battered head. "You didn't really want to kill me. And I don't want to cut your throat, not unless I have to. Don't believe them. It was a nasty thing, mocking you, trying to make you lose face. We've always loved her; she's a lovely lady

—whoever told you to do this is no friend of yours . . . If you resist, we'll have to bury you in the sand dune . . . no rites, nothing . . ."

Ju-hai sighed and fingered the blade of his dagger. "I'll always be sorry—don't know how I'll tell your mother."

Then it burst forth. "The Colonel put me up to it. He's been at the village. Don't let him know I told you. It was really the Captain who told me I'd gain face if I shot you; Tsao told Li . . . they were mocking me so much . . ."

Ju-hai's voice was commanding, devoid of compassion, when he said, "On your feet!" His blade hissed as it whipped from the scabbard into bitter moonlight. "Dad's coming with two camels, water, and rations. If you'd killed me, the Captain would have had to finish you to make sure you wouldn't squawk! One sound out of you, and I'll save Captain Li the trouble. I'll take your head with us, and dump it in the river."

And then the Old Man came, leading two loaded camels from the darkness of the tamarisks.

Ju-hai and Yin-chu rode the cargo panniers of the two-humped Bactrian which carried the supplies. Kwan Yu-tsun's experience as a camel jockey made him caravan leader. He set a course by the stars which Ju-hai had indicated during their fuel-hunting talks. This took them south from the Silk Road until, well away from it, they paralleled that ancient highway.

Although he didn't say so, Yin-chu looked as if he felt that he'd bought his life at an unreasonably high ransom. He was uneasy about his fellow rider. After a silent hour, the captive-comrade asked, "Which way is the road?"

Ju-hai pointed. "That way, over yonder."

Hour after hour, the Dipper's wheeling told how the night was wearing away. And as the moon slipped halfway to the horizon, they came to stark trunks and scattered branches of poplar, deadwood white as bones against the sand. The Old Man called a halt, to bivouac near trees which had been killed by shifting sand.

Once the camels were hobbled, Ju-hai set a pot of rice to steam over a bed of coals. The animals could go to the confluence of the Khotan and the Tarim without drinking.

When sunrise awakened the deserters, a backsight on the rising sun reassured them.

"We're not far from the Silk Road," Ju-hai told his companions.

They ate, they mounted up, and they rode. All day, heading westward, they watched for smoke signals. Toward sunset, Yu-tsun declared, "They've not missed us, not yet, or no one cares. Maybe the outfit is still resting in camp."

Ju-hai said to Yin-chu, "See why we're taking this nasty way? Smoke or mirror signal by day, or fire by night, and the guard at the tower would grab us. And the Khotan River comes from the Kun-lun—" He gestured. "If we ride far enough west, we're bound to hit the river."

He wanted to keep Yin-chu happy, and there was a good chance of doing this. The prisoner-companion missed the chatter of fellow conscripts. Next to hearing his own voice, he liked to hear the voices of others. Bit by bit, he talked more than he might otherwise have done. After having talked his way from an impending death sentence and execution, he now talked his way to life.

The Kwans learned a good deal about their village. Neither father nor son had suspected how much subterranean life had eluded their attention. Yin-chu's version of things, however distorted, was worth hearing. That he still distrusted his captors and was keeping them interested by improvising and elaborating would have to be discounted. To Yin-chu, it seemed necessary to insure survival by constant promise of further information.

Regardless of scrambled details and improbabilities, a pattern was developing. The disgruntled officer wanted to become a landlord and needed not only land but someone who could farm for him. Since he had not enough silver to buy the acres which a retired officer of his rank would require, there had to be some trickery, such as buying up from some money lender the document which would give the holder the right to take the property if the interest were ever delinquent.

Chen Lao-yeh and Lan-yin, anxious for more acreage, had responded to Colonel Tsao's inquiries.

The thing fitted nicely. And with Ju-hai and his father liquidated, Younger Brother would be all too likely to succumb to pressure and conniving, until he lost all the Kwan lands.

Two deserters would have no chance against a usurper of Tsao's status. Escaping with their lives was all which remained to Ju-hai and his father; and if they succeeded in that difficult enterprise, their only prospect was outlawry.

Finally the fugitives came to the willows and poplars which flourished along the banks of the Khotan River—a lonely land, yet paradise compared to the Takla Makan. Ju-hai's suspicions had been justified. If Yin-chu had fumbled too long, a drumhead court-martial on any trumped up charge would have disposed of the troublesome Kwans.

The present, however, was luxury—riverside bivouac, silence, a broiled duck which Ju-hai had shot, and a jug of millet spirits. They laced their tea with the fiery stuff.

In this desolation, there was no need of watching by night.

Sunrise and bird chatter awakened Ju-hai. After moments of taking it easy, he yawned. He blinked and stretched. He wondered what was missing. Presently it came to him. He did not hear the grumbling, mumbling, and coughing of camels, those revolting clods of the desert. He sat up. The Old Man still slept, which was good. It was the first real night's rest since quitting Tun Huang.

Silence was lovely, but there was too much of it. He got to his feet. No camels! Windblown sand smoothed the depression which Yin-chu had made in bedding down. Ju-hai looked about him. He looked upstream. He looked downstream. He looked west and finally to the rising sun.

The camel pad prints from the east were blurred, barely visible in the slanting light. Those leading northward along the river were much sharper.

And now the Old Man was on his feet. He stood for moments, looking about.

"No camels!" Ju-hai told him. "It's my fault. You wanted to kill that bastard!"

Kwan Yu-tsun smiled sourly. "Take it easy. You can shoot game in a way I never could. So I won't flog the hide off of you till we get back home. He was so careful sneaking out, he left us all we'll need—we slept under arms."

"What do you figure he's trying?"

"The stupidest lout can follow a river downstream. He's going back, with a good story. He saved two camels for the army."

"If he can find his way downstream, we can walk upstream. A man can outwalk cavalry, in the long term. No problem."

They ate cold duck and cold rice, then set out.

Chapter XXI

Kwan Yu-tsun made a gallant fight of it. Whenever he had breath to spare, he repeated, optimistically, "Nothing to do but follow the river and rest whenever you're out bagging a duck or a partridge."

The deserters wore jackets over their corselets, and carried helmets in their packs. Each had a skullcap with scarf wrapped around to keep sweat from trickling into sun-strained eyes. However cold the desert nights, the sun's teeth were sharp.

The Son of Heaven ruled every village along the river, but the natives had not learned to love Chinese strangers, least of all armed strangers. Ju-hai and the Old Man began to approach a settlement near dusk, to wait in willow clusters near the river until they caught the scent of Chinese cooking. There were civilians, craftsmen, and farmers, long accepted by the natives. And when there was no evidence of fellow countrymen, the deserters made a wide sweep into the desert, to return by dark to the river.

One night they sat with Fong, a villager who looked as

if he had spent the past century cultivating his plot of ground. He knew more about raising vegetables than did any of the natives. He was one of them. And there was the old lady, agile though bent double, welcoming them with a toothless smile.

Ju-hai offered two ducks he'd shot that morning. The truck gardener offered rice and homemade wine. It was good to take a joss stick from the tiny shrine with a gilt Buddha and eight little ceramic Immortals, light it, and bow to these and the Ancestral tablet. It warmed the hearts of the old people to see this. "The Gods and the Ancestors are unhappy when no one offers incense."

When they had done eating, the old lady packed up parched barley, millet, and dried octopus tentacle steamed with vegetables. Finally, she added a parcel of advice.

"The trouble in Khotan—the *amban* they killed—he was a nice man—nobody hated him. Hotheads made a riot, stirred up the city."

Her husband cut in, "A courier brought news to Khotan by the short way." He referred to the southernmost branch of the Silk Road. "Go by night. Men have been riding the river to see when the army comes this way. Get rid of all soldier stuff before you are near Khotan."

"Riders along the river? Which way?"

"Both ways."

The Kwans exchanged glances. It seemed that scouting parties had been busy. "How soon does the army reach this place?"

"Was three day's march this way, from the Tarim River."

Once clear of the settlement, the deserters got well off the caravan trail. Between cavalry reconnaissance patrols and scouts from Khotan, there would be increasing traffic and ever more risk of being turned in by natives. Whatever favor the folk could win from the advance guard was worth getting.

In the late afternoon, as the deserters dragged weary feet, they saw a village well ahead and across the river. On their left, the level sands and then the shifting dunes of the Takla Makan stretched endlessly. Standing out from the scrub-dotted flats and not more than a quarter of a mile from the bank was a ruined house, half buried by drifting sand. Dead poplars reached up, their bleached branches ruddy in light which lanced between the scattering of trees lining both banks of the Khotan Darya.

Ju-hai pointed. "Let's camp over yonder. My tail's dragging the dust. It's been a bitch of a hike today."

The Old Man was too tired to say that he could hoof it for another couple of hours and bivouac in an unsettled stretch. Ju-hai was not as weary as he pretended, though he was far from fresh.

The Old Man would walk himself to death, otherwise, he cogitated. *Women have better sense—but a man who won't keep going till he drops is no good. He's no man, he's not yang. No more good than a female creature who won't go the way of yin.*

Darkness took charge before they reached the half-buried house. Its whitewashed brick and the poplar skeletons guided the deserters through the gloom. A few lights from the village winked across the river.

Ju-hai would have taken the two canteens to the Khotan Darya, but pounding hooves and the shout of a rider checked him. The Old Man cursed bitterly. As the pace slacked off, they heard the creak of leather and the jingle of accoutrements. Unless the desert raised its voice, sound traveled far.

A torch flared. Squinting between poplar trunks, the lurkers guessed that there were no more than three troopers coming downstream. Whether enemy scouts or messengers for Tsao's little army, the deserters did not care to encounter either.

The riders might stay for the night or they might change horses and gallop on.

"Of all the stinking luck," Ju-hai grumbled. And then he forced himself to say cheerfully, "We can rest our feet until we know what those bastards are going to do."

They chewed parched barley, bits of dried melon, and scraps of sun-dried duck. The Old Man quipped, "That Orchid bitch of yours, she dished out better chow than this."

"Sir," Number One Son began, as if addressing a learned audience or the Board of Censors. "When I told you about Orchid *niang*, I touched somewhat lightly on a few salient details. And I may as well tell you frankly that I omitted several details totally, and without reference to their existence."

Kwan Yu-tsun snorted. "The way you said *niang*, you made a nice word sound like slut or human garbage. She must have been good, and you figured if you told me, I'd feel left out and be jealous."

This brightened Ju-hai. The Old Man was not too worn out to be snotty and sarcastic. Number One Son said, "Yin-chu's yarns changed the scene a lot. When I talked to you before I learned that you were not going to get out of the service just because I busted myself to overtake the regiment, I told you what I figured would be useful and helpful. I didn't know that you and I were going to start a desert march that we'd not live long enough to finish."

The Old Man dug up his latest creation in Chinese obscenity, then said, "When you fall on your face, you still finish the march—that's the one thing you can't ever *not* finish. Go ahead, son, I won't flog you till we get home."

"Well, I told you that while I was in the war, you could find Orchid and tell her that her partner tried to give her an overdose of opium to kill her, so I'd be blamed and he'd get to keep all the silver. But now we know that Tsao had fixed the deal, and our chances of getting back to Ch'ang-an aren't too good.

"So I'll tell you what really happened—"

Ju-hai gave his father the entire story of Mei-yu and how she had switched the drinks, drugging Orchid. He concluded, "You still don't believe me!"

The Old Man retorted, "What I believe makes no difference. We got plenty of facts to keep us too busy for beliefs."

And for that, Ju-hai had a response. "Later on, I'll sneak closer to the village to see if the patrol is out of town. You stay here. In case I screw things up, we won't both be caught."

He saw a moving light. There was still too much activity.

Finally, there came from the settlement the sound of a single-stringed fiddle, that instrument which Chinese wanderers have carried to the uttermost east, to far off Java and beyond, and into the barbarian west. The music varied from screeching, which only the player could love, to eerie and heart-snaring beauty. And here some homesick exile was making a single string sigh and quaver, wail and plead, imploring the friendship of spirits, the blessing of gods.

The sound would guide Ju-hai to a Chinese home, perhaps the only one in the village.

At the riverbank, he wasted no time looking for a ford. The water was not quite knee deep. And by now he was sure that the village was asleep, keeping farmer's hours—all but the homesick musician.

Whoever quit China would be homesick; no matter how he fared, wherever he settled, he would not live long enough to feel that his new home was as good as what he had quit. Ju-hai, facing a life of outlawry and exile, forgot the dangers of a strange village, at best troubled, and probably hostile. And then the voice of welcome went silent, leaving Ju-hai with no more than a general idea as to the direction of the house.

He skirted the river, keeping close to the trees. His prowl was not as long as he had expected. Presently, Ju-hai caught the bouquet of a joss stick, the savor of ginger, and the smell of dried cuttlefish and dried shrimp.

No light came from within. Low voiced, someone was reciting a *sutra*. Ju-hai scratched at the door. The recital ceased. He spoke a greeting to the house. A man answered in the speech of Shensi Province and then spoke to someone within.

A woman answered, but Ju-hai could not understand what she said. Her voice indicated that, like the man, she was quite old. A bolt slid aside. The door opened on darkness.

"Come in."

When the door closed behind Ju-hai, someone blew on tinder and fired a taper.

This was a dwelling and small shop. Aside from dried

vegetables, garlic, *lichis*, melon, and mushrooms, the flame concealed more than it exposed. Ju-hai bowed to the old man, to the old woman, and to the family shrine. The old woman set aside the kitchen chopper she had picked up just in case. She set it beside the shrine in the corner of the shop section; this contained an image of the fiercely frowning General Kwan Kung, the guardian of the shop. If the great patriot happened to be engaged elsewhere, the chopper would take the place of the Immortal's protection.

"The riders—soldiers? Chinese or Turki? Where are they?"

"These are troubled times," the old man said.

"If the riders are in the village, I leave right away." He drew a string of *cash* from his pouch. "Father is waiting for me. I came to get food ready to eat—parched barley, maize, anything. Food we can cook and tea, for when we can make a fire."

The woman set to work stuffing things into Ju-hai's haversack. He said to both, "No matter who is or is not in the village, I leave right away."

"You came in darkness. Leave in darkness."

The woman said something in Turki, and from a back room, a woman answered. The first woman explained to Ju-hai. "Férideh—an orphan from the war—I forget how long ago—not a slave. She helps us. This is her home. You can trust her."

A question from Férideh produced a terse answer.

The man noticed water dripping from Ju-hai's pants and shoes.

"Yes, Grandfather, I crossed the river. My father waits on the other side. We stay off the road."

The woman had done packing victuals into Ju-hai's haversack. When he took *cash* from the string, she said, "Férideh is heating soup. She'll put it in a gourd. No pay for that, not from a hungry traveler. Keep the gourd, we have plenty."

Ju-hai's glance shifted to the door. The man said, "Go out by the back. Cross the river and go up stream a way. Férideh speaks Chinese. She'll show you the way. You mustn't look as if you don't know where you're going."

Férideh stood in the doorway opening to the rear. A Chinese jacket and trousers emphasized her solid build. An almost aquiline and most un-Chinese nose commanded her squarish face. A taper's feeble flame picked glints from the ruddy-golden hair which was too plentiful to be confined by her dark red and well-worn cap; its embroidery, once gilt, had tarnished almost to black.

She had a gourd sawed off not far from the neck, making a deep bowl. It was nested in hemp cords which had once secured a bale of goods. Steam rose from the container.

"Smells good. I like octopus and vegetables."

"Better than soldier soup!" she smiled, and her determined features became quite attractive. Férideh gestured, pinched out the taper, and caught his sleeve. "Easy now, don't stumble, don't spill your soup."

He followed her through the darkness of a passageway and across a small court. At the wall, she drew the bolt of a solid door.

"This isn't the way we usually deal with travelers. I'll go with you a little way."

They stepped into an alley wide enough for walking side by side. Presently, they cleared the houses which fronted on the river road. There were a few houses further upstream, widely spaced, their whitewash making them just visible in the darkness.

"You can find the ford. There's a clear space, no trees." Then she caught his hand. "I'll show you."

They glanced upstream, downstream, and listened. All seemed clear. They crossed to the riverbank and slowly went upstream, keeping to the darkest stretches, until they came to the ford. For moments they stood close together, until finally she said, "I wish you didn't have to leave so soon. You're camping far from the other side?"

"That ruin, reaching up out of drifted sand."

"I used to play there, when I was too small to do much housework." Suddenly, impulsively, she kissed him. "Good luck—Allah be with you!"

She turned, and darkness swallowed her. Loneliness crossed the shallow stream with Ju-hai. And when he was halfway to the ruin, the voice of a single-stringed fiddle bade him farewell.

Ju-hai found the Old Man, asleep but sitting with his back against the wall, not far from the doorway, but well out of the wind. He did not wake up until Ju-hai said, "They are good people, that old couple. They sold me stuff for the road but gave me a gourd of soup. Couldn't risk asking me to sit and eat. Sure, I filled both water jugs. With a Chinese army heading up the river—"

"I know how they'd feel, in a Turki town. How about making a pot of tea?"

"They put out the light before they opened the door for me. I got out as quick as I could."

"Any questions?"

"None asked me, and I asked none. I was a soldier and my shoes were wet. No matter what they said, it might cause them trouble or make trouble for us. Things move too fast. It was, *'Here's your victuals and get going'*—even before I got into the house, that idea was so strong they didn't have to say it. But the soup was Chinese-friendly, and I loved the old folks."

He remembered the cooked rice the old woman had put into his pack, after he'd paid for the groceries. When Ju-hai and the Old Man finished the cooked food, he got up.

"I'll bed down in the angle outside. And I'll take the first watch."

"I got a good sleep. It was just my feet hurting me."

Ju-hai didn't tell the Old Man that nobody could have slept long between departure and return of the foraging party. Instead, he remembered his beautiful housekeeper in Ch'ang-an. "Take a light dab of Orchid's opium, and your feet won't keep you awake."

He dissolved a bit of the drug in a dollop of *kao-liang* spirit.

From force of habit, Ju-hai remained awake and on guard. He could have slept without risk, since only an all-out, organized search would make a point of crossing the river to go through a sand-buried ruin. Ju-hai, however tired, was far from sleepy. Turki and Chinese alike were on edge from the thought of the approach of a punitive expedition. The tension of that little settlement had left him keyed up and thinking, pondering on the dangers of the road ahead of them.

He considered sleeping by day and walking in darkness until he realized that finding hiding places by night would be leaving entirely too much to chance.

Férideh as a child had played in this ruin. But ruins weren't distributed evenly enough for deserters' hideouts. He considered getting rid of arms and armor and trusting to his wits. This idea died shortly after birth; if being a fugitive was bad, being an unarmed one was far worse.

Looking up, he observed the Dipper's pivoting about the Pole Star and being all too deliberate about it.

Apprehension would keep him wakeful, painfully alert until it was time to give the Old Man enough of a guard tour to make him feel that he was carrying his share of the burden. Or so he thought, until he started, drew his sword, gathered himself, and realized that he had been busy with more than dozing. His thinking in circles had tricked him, so that in sleep he fancied himself awake and pursuing the same old plan, over and over and over.

Chapter XXII

Darkness had thinned a little. Behind Ju-hai, the scrap of a waning moon would be rising. From his shadowed angle, he saw a shape moving toward the ruin, easily, and without stealth. What began as darkness against a lesser darkness was now outlined, bit-by-bit, by faintly glowing haze, so faint that it was perceptible only because of dark garments, a hip-length jacket, and a cap. That was the shape of Férideh, shoulders as squarish as her face, returning to her childhood play spot. He slipped his sword back into its scabbard.

The figure changed course as if guided by the whisper of steel. The glow became brighter.

Ju-hai got up out of his dark corner. He would have caught her in his arms, and then he remembered—the voice was Mei-yu's, and only the body was Férideh's. She clung to him, and needlessly said, "I'm as solid as that Turki girl—"

This was stating the obvious.

"She was in a mood," Mei-yu went on, "and it was easy to borrow her body. I didn't even have to wait till she was totally asleep. And I have some of her money. Where's your father?"

Ju-hai gestured. "His feet were killing him. I gave him a bit of opium."

Mei-yu led into the room where the deserters had eaten; from there she picked her way through an adjoining room and into one beyond that. Through holes in the roof, he saw stars and a shred of rising moon.

Mei-yu shivered. "Stay here. I'll get some dead wood. A tiny fire—nobody but the stars can see it. No, lover, I'm not going to make a pot of tea, but I can't let a borrowed body shiver—"

Flint, steel, and a bit of tinder got the long dried poplar wood burning, and there might have been tamarisk needles, well dried.

"I picked it all from the sand; it was easy," she explained. She broke a length of poplar over her knee and fed the pieces to the burning splinters. "Something's worrying you, lover. You were so awfully, lecherously happy, and now when I come back with fuel. Ju-hai, if you're let down, just imagine I'm Férideh, close your eyes and it will be easy."

"Mei-yu, Jade Lady—maybe it's the odd light—but you're still Férideh. Well, those old folks are such *good* people! They knew I was a deserter—Férideh isn't their daughter, but—"

"Suppose she were their daughter?"

Mei-yu's soft voice was a challenge.

Ju-hai answered, "I'd feel awful about it all—and I don't feel right about this."

"And I've been slowly going crazy."

"I was wishing she'd go with me to this place and I was glad she did not, and then I sat here, feeling like a fool because I didn't ask her. Of course she was exciting—I knew she was in a mood—"

"You felt foolish because you hadn't asked her to wade the river with you, but when I walk her from bed to a soldier's cloak spread on an indoor carpet of sand, you lose your appetite! Ju-hai, she's nicer than three of that Orchid!"

"I didn't know Orchid was a thieving bitch," he mumbled hopelessly, helplessly, miserably. "I did know that whatever she and I did, it made no difference; it would just be fun for two and no harm."

"The first time for you and Orchid, it was really you and me."

"If you hadn't borrowed her body, she'd have slid into bed on her own account."

Mei-yu sighed and shook her head. "I thought I was slowly going crazy, but you've gone a couple lengths ahead of me! Ju-hai, I'm puzzled into knots. I know you want me so bad—"

"So bad I can taste you, so bad I could eat you raw without seasoning!"

"Only, no appetite! Lover, suppose I moved out and made way for Férideh to get into her body—" Mei-yu peeled out of her jacket; after a few finger-twinkling tricks, the red-bronze hair tumbled about bare shoulders and all else was bare to the hips, smooth white and untouched by sun. He'd never seen such clear skin, and the eyes were grayish-green. Mei-yu resumed, "She wouldn't be alarmed; she wouldn't kick and scream. She wanted to go with you."

"You don't—you don't understand. Those old people were so worried they put out the light before they opened the door so nobody would see whom they'd let in. They kept their voices down. They didn't take profit on the food they sold. The soup was for the Old Man; that was a gift."

"I know all that, Ju-hai. You're afraid you might get her pregnant. That wouldn't harm her or them; she's never given birth but she hasn't been a virgin for years. I'll make way for her, and when she's all happy and asleep, I'll take over long enough—well, yes, and walk her home before daylight."

Ju-hai had nothing to say.

Mei-yu read his unspoken thought while he still groped for the expression of what he really meant.

She arranged her hair, adjusted the worn cap of ribbed red fabric, and got her inner garment up where it belonged. She got to her feet and brushed sand from jacket and trousers.

Ju-hai was sure he'd never seen a woman as glowingly beautiful as this momentary blend of Mei-yu and Férideh. She said in a voice neither quite her own nor the Turkistani girl's, "Ju-hai, I've lost my appetite, too. Seeing you turn down what I/she offered, well, it did something to me, or for me—maybe, for us—no, I'll not explain that last, not now!

"But hear this, and don't forget! Once I leave you, I'll go quietly wild and curse you, and curse myself and curse the Gods and the Buddhas, but right now, I'll tell you something.

"You and your father get out of here so you'll be two hours on the road by sunrise. When you get to the river that joins the Khotan Darya, follow it. It's dry now, most of the year, the Kara Kash. Keep going till you get into the foothills. There's a town called Yotkan—stay out of Yotkan and keep going till you reach a monastery, well upstream, in wooded country.

"The abbot is a Taoist, a *tao-shih*, not quite a magician, not quite an Immortal, but he works at those achievements and other things. You'll be safe there, and out of trouble."

"You'll see me there?"

He was at once doubtful and hopeful.

"I'm too befuddled to promise anything! Maybe this is my *karma*, maybe in some life I said no to a lover. Yes, there's one thing I'll try to do, though I shouldn't promise."

"What's that?"

"If I find a lone women old enough not to be a sort of daughter to elderly people, I'll borrow her body. It's time you learned that working downward from the collarbone, the body of a so-called old lady is often amazingly smooth and awfully exciting, and—"

She swayed. The kiss she shaped was a grazing touch. "Don't you dare lay as much of a finger on me or I'll do something wild! I'll be seeing you, somewhere along the Kara Kash, or at least at the monastery, if I have to fight Gods and devils!"

Chapter XXIII

When they finally came to the Kara Kash, they learned the difference between a river and a watercourse; the latter would be a river if there were any water flowing in it.

Ju-hai said, "Just what we need. We can walk by day and no one will see us."

On the face of it, he was right.

When they wanted water, they dug for it. A helmet was a good scoop. It also was a good cooking pot. Half a helmet full of water, a handful of millet, some slices of dried melon—it was almost as much fun as those early childhood rides to Ch'ang-an.

"Ducks can't dig for water, so we don't find duck to eat. Getting into a dry river is our first bit of luck. Sleeping with one eye open was whipping us down."

"Right now," Yu-tsun told his son, "is when we'll divide the night into watches. I'll take the first and third, you take the second and fourth; that way I'll be all rested up and not dragging my feet when we start out. With short watches, if there's any trouble, each of us will have had a bit of sleep."

"If you'd started earlier, you'd be a general now." After a long silence, Ju-hai said, "Dad, next time you're in the mood to slice a man's head off, slice mine first if I talk out of turn."

"That has been worrying you?"

"Yes, it has."

"Having that young son of a bitch come back with the camels is good. He'll claim he killed us in our sleep, and that will make him a hero and cover our tracks. Better than if we'd buried him near camp. The Colonel would hope we were dead but he'd always be on the lookout, instead of reporting us missing or killed in action and forgetting us."

"I never thought of it that way, or any way at all."

The Old Man shook his head. "A man twice your age might have acted that way." He counted on his fingers. "Having Lan-yin four or five years, how could you not be fond of her, in a way? How else do you figure so few wives are strangled, beaten to death, or sold to a slave trader?"

Ju-hai sighed. "I guess I've not started thinking yet."

"It was natural and you weren't an idiot. You did a neat job of baiting him into talking to save his life."

"He was an idiot, taking it for granted he could kill me."

"*You* were the idiot, betting you could drop at the twang of a bowstring."

Ju-hai chuckled. "You didn't notice I wore armor under my jacket."

"If you pass the examinations and get to be an official, you'll be rich in no time!"

The reconnaissance patrol was as surprised as Yu-tsun was when he heard the crunch of gravel and the creak of saddle leather. The Old Man was squatting beside a tiny fire over which he had propped his helmet on three small rocks. Helmet, sword, and corselet identified him as military; and he was far from the route of the expedition.

Ju-hai heard the sounds, the words of challenge, and the Old Man's answer: "I'm a scout. Same business you're in, but no horse."

Ju-hai, who had dug where vegetation indicated surface water, needed no look. He was out of sight and unseen. He dumped the water from his helmet, donned it, and drew an arrow from his quiver.

"We'll take you to headquarters—"

Ju-hai stepped clear of the natural buttress. The first sound was the twang of his bowstring. He caught the leader neatly in the throat. The horse bolted. The rider pitched to the ground, clawing gravel. He choked and coughed blood.

Ju-hai's yell and their leader's fall startled the two troopers. The Old Man whipped out his sword. The nearer soldier wheeled, drawing his blade. The farmer dropped his weapon and straight-armed the helmet. Water near boiling drenched rider and mount. The beast squealed and pivoted, knocking the animal on his offside a good yard out of line. Ju-hai loosed a second arrow as the rider of that horse nocked a shaft. The impact of horse against horse made the rider's arrow go wild. Ju-hai caught the dappled bay, drilling him just fore of the saddle. The shaft sank nearly to the feather. As the horse fell kicking, Ju-hai's straight blade got into action. He slashed at the neck of the mount that had been spooked by boiling water.

The Old Man had been busy dodging clear of the confusion. For lack of a better object at the moment, he hamstrung the spooked horse. Landing clear of his crippled mount, the trooper confronted Ju-hai, who shouted to the Old Man, "Get that other bastard!"

Steel clashed on steel.

The Old Man wheeled. His footing failed him; the rocky bottom was tricky. He lurched, clawing sand and rocks. In the dogfight confusion, Ju-hai's opponent made a futile slash and Old Man Kwan got a long, raking cut, purely by accident and because of lost balance. Ju-hai got in a good one—a neck cut which settled his man.

Ju-hai wheeled, a wasted move. The remaining unhorsed trooper recovered the sword he had dropped and bounced to his feet. This was Old Man Kwan's moment of triumph. The enemy who was intent on menacing Ju-hai shifted and left his rear unguarded.

Kwan struck, and the head rolled off, trunk toppling and leaving Ju-hai's blade with nowhere to go.

The one uninjured mount had panicked; wheeling, banging against the steep bank, throwing itself, rolling, the animal raced crazy-blind after a gravel scattering recovery, knocking the older Kwan end for end. Ju-hai gave his father a hand. There were no broken bones, but having been bowled half the width of the riverbed had left him shaky and sprained. His every move was painful. He grinned, though with considerable effort, and said, "An officer told us at militia training how infantry can face càvalry."

He hobbled to the horse he'd hamstrung. One slash to the throat stilled the wounded animal. Turning, he looked at the first casualty, the one who had died from an arrow to the throat.

"Nice work. Half a finger width off and the mail coif would had fouled your shot."

Ju-hai stepped over for a good look. "That is Persian mail and helmet! It's good enough for the Son of Heaven."

Kwan Yu-tsun was looking skyward. "I wish we had that horse that went crazy."

Ju-hai shrugged. "After what happened to cavalry that met farmers—"

"Look up, you turtle-child! Look up!"

Ju-hai looked up. A vulture circled, a tiny dot of black. Two other observers of warfare joined them. The dot became larger.

"I see them."

"You still don't get it! No matter how far away the next patrol is, they'll see the vultures and know there was a killing. The birds will eat, but we won't have time."

He hobbled to the nearest carcass, and set to work with his sword, butchering a horse. "But we'll eat later—what are you up to?"

"I'm taking that armor and scimitar—if I have to fight, I'll be well dressed, just for once."

"That stuff is heavy; I'll bet it weighs six-seven *catties*."

"I'll wear it and carry enough horsemeat to get us to the

monastery. We'll fight our way, if need be. We're a good combat team, our average is killing one and a half men apiece. When we get home and we find Tsao has grabbed our land, as Yin-chu said, we'll take him by surprise."

When father and son set out, Ju-hai wore a tunic of scarlet silk, a plumed helmet, and a scimitar with Persian characters in gold inlay. For luck, he had a purse of gold coins minted by Persian, Roman, or other barbarians. A piece of dead poplar made a carrying pole for his burden of horsemeat.

The vultures were circling.

Kwan Yu-tsun grumbled, "Something worries those gobblers. They ought to be settling, now that we're quite a piece away." He gasped, then grimaced. "Well, they're shy; they have to have someone else do their killing, like those bureaucrats."

"If I'd only killed the men and saved us a couple horses," Ju-hai grumbled. "But that's partly your fault."

"Son, get used to always doing the wrong thing. I've spent my whole life that way."

Ju-hai rigged a deadwood crutch to keep most of the weight off the old man's slashed and sprained side. After a laborious mile, they sword-chopped the thing down to a more useful cane. When the vultures finally settled, the deserters relaxed until Kwan shared another thought with his son. "That patrol knew what they were looking for; they didn't just blunder up a dry riverbed. I'm not blaming the girl who told you to go up to Kara Kash. Someone else might have seen you go to the shop and talked."

There was a long silence; then he added, "Something else. An officer's horse going back to the other horses stirs things up."

"Dad, you make it sound better every *li*. First thing I know, you'll be bringing in wine and sing-song girls."

"Don't forget the opium," Kwan Yu-tsung mocked, "and one girl who's really good."

He was getting used to being half crippled. Constant motion and the whip of impending danger kept him from stiffening. But he finally hewed his chunk of horsemeat in two and let Ju-hai carry half. They stumbled, they staggered, they wove, and they pitched through darkness, always a step short of collapse.

Finally, they made a dry bivouac. They chewed bits of horsemeat, a few raisins, and some parched barley. Ju-hai still had the little pot of opium which had done so nicely in doping the camel guards.

"A little, just a little," Ju-hai suggested. "It won't dope you, and it will smooth out the aches."

"You taking some?"

"Not until you get me a good housekeeper."

"I'm not taking any either."

But Ju-hai talked the Old Man into taking a pill of the stuff.

"I've got no aches; I feel fine. You rest well and you'll hike better in the morning. We'll start three hours before sunrise, if you're able to hobble along."

Chapter XXIV

Mei-yu's years in a Buddhist nunnery had centered on the most effective way of winning liberation from the griefs and frustrations of life—being bound to that which one does not want, and being separated from that which is desired. There were neither Gods to worship nor doctrines required to be believed; the teaching was simply an operational method for gaining freedom from the eternal round of birth, of growth, of deterioration, and finally of death.

There were many other ways, but these required hundreds, perhaps thousands, of incarnations more than did the Way of the Buddha.

For a long time, it had all seemed so reasonable and self-evident to Mei-yu—but now the operational method was not working.

A shortcut to Nirvana would have been well lost for the loan of that Turkistani girl's body; but it was not that the loan had not been negotiated. Such failure, Mei-yu could have accepted—if not serenely, then at least with good grace and patience.

What hurt, what infuriated, had been and still was Ju-hai's rejection of their first opportunity in ages and ages.

When Mei-yu had cursed everyone and everything except Ju-hai, she paused and drew a deep breath. She would need a fresh start before she damned him. The Férideh letdown left Mei-yu wavering between perplexity and shreds of half-understanding.

Helpless from having expended all her power in desire, frustration, and rage, she saw Ju-hai and the Old Man trapped in the bed of the dry river, the branch to which she had directed them. So burned out that she could not warn Ju-hai, she watched them go into action.

It seemed as if several lifetimes elapsed before the victors set out afoot, one dragging along, wounded and bruised, the other carrying a load of horsemeat and helping his father get used to moving in spite of injuries.

Only one resource remained. Mei-yu rode the wind from Turkistan to the palace of Chang Wo, the Mood Goddess. Traveling as fast as thought and perhaps faster, she arrived unwearied and without a travel stain or a wrinkle in her gown.

There was no kowtowing. The sisterly kiss of Goddess and Immortal had in it none of the malice common in terrestrial families.

"I'm so glad you could get away for a little while." Chang Wo noticed her visitor's weariness, her tense posture, the nervous motions of her hands. She could almost guess the answer before she posed her question: "And how did it turn out? I've wondered at times, about you and that talented young man, the jade artist we discussed?"

"Divinity—"

"Please forget that divinity nonsense!" The Goddess

poured tea. "Mei-yu, something's troubling you—you're so twitchy you'll disintegrate any moment!"

"I wish I could! I'm in an awful muddle. I told him I was slowly going crazy—I was all wrong—I'm going crazy faster than I can take it." She bent over, cradled her face in the crook of her elbow, and narrowly missed upsetting her cup of tea. "I was ready to tell him to get himself half a dozen farm girl concubines and two or three whores and be happy with wenches who'd not stir up any conscientious scruples or whatever made him turn down that lovely creature—that Turkistani girl—whose body I borrowed— but I knew—I shouldn't get out of patience—"

The remainder was a pattern of sobbing and incoherent words.

The Goddess patted a twitching shoulder. She clapped her hands. Two Moon Maidens appeared, heard a few words, and hurried away. One returned with a tray of refreshments and left before Mei-yu was sitting up, blinking, gulping, and composing herself. Chang Wo picked up the decanter by its short neck and poured a nip of spirits into a tiny cup.

"Try a bit of this. You'll feel better."

Mei-yu did so. And she told everything. She concluded, "I should have taken your advice about that romance. Do I have to keep on being an Immortal? I've never had a chance to be really mortal! I've been going wild. I wanted to cut out his heart and feed it to the dogs, I wanted to be a human woman and live with him on a farm—"

Mei-yu swallowed, brushed a trailing sleeve past her eyes, and hopelessly smeared what remained of her makeup. She sniffled, took a nip of something akin to *ng ka pai*, but much more fragrant and somewhat stronger.

Chang Wo smiled. "And you're frightfully set back because Ju-hai didn't start glowing when you half undressed Férideh?"

Disconsolate, Mei-yu nodded. "Even if he'd seen all of her, it would have meant nothing."

The Goddess said, "You are luckier than you realize."

Mei-yu sat bolt upright and gaped, blinking like a teen-age wench who's had a well deserved slap in the face.

Chang Wo smiled amiably, and sighed as if her own many memories were coming to life and making her a sister of this sorrowful Immortal.

"First, you borrowed Hsi-feng's body and she lost her virginity. Happily enough, Old Man Kwan had intended her for Ju-hai, and now that she's pregnant, she's one of the family. And Ju-hai wasn't the standard male imbecile when he found that someone—apparently—had got at his dream girl before he did. Before he got the facts and understood what had happened, he accepted her and loved her as he always had.

"Younger Sister, if he'd been the usual fool, he'd have flared up and rejected her. And you with your itchy-twitchy cravings would have been responsible for grief she didn't deserve. If she'd got the usual package of hard luck, you'd have some nasty *karma* dumped on you. No thanks to you, you're probably in the clear."

"I guess I was lucky," Mei-yu admitted.

"Then it was dangerous meddling when you borrowed Orchid—"

"Divinity, she is a whore—after all."

"Mei-yu, Mei-yu! Like most nice women, you have a lot of morals and no sense at all! You're almost like those western barbarians who have one God who is also three Gods, and a saint who imagined that love making for the joy of living is sinful. What Gautama the Buddha taught was something entirely different. It makes no difference whom you sleep with as long as you don't harm your lover or any other person; of course, your sleepings-with do set up obligations and attachments which may keep you from attaining Nirvana for hundreds of incarnations—"

"Orchid is a travel concubine, a very high-class whore."

Chang Wo drew a long breath, exhaled, and shook her head. An Imperial concubine who survived long enough to become an Immortal did so only because she had greater wisdom than other women.

"The worst that could have happened to your farm boy jade artist was that he'd be doped and robbed, and he'd have learned a lot at little cost," Chang Wo resumed. "But with your meddling, and in spite of your good intentions, switching those drinks could have killed Orchid; a husky farm boy, stuffed with a lot of food would have overslept, but with no harm. She got his drink—a dainty package of woman, all on edge from planning a bit of thievery, and eating very little—"

"I give you credit! You just about burned yourself out to awaken and warn Ju-hai; and between him and the doctor, she lived."

"I never thought of that."

"Again, you were lucky! Immortals can and do build up the kind of *karma* that gives them many miseries."

Mei-yu went saucer-eyed. "Maybe that's what I'm getting now."

Chang Wo shook her head. "You're here because you advised Ju-hai into a trap."

"That's right. I've been shying away from that; that's what's so awful."

"What you told him was sound, wise, and reasonable— so, quit feeling guilty! Neither gods nor men could predict that a nobleman who was a guest of the army would take a notion to ride ahead of the advance guard—a whim, pure impulse. Now you're pacing the floor, feeling guilty, and that's the worst mistake you could make—"

"Mei-yu, you and I and the rest of our kind are simply people who don't have material bodies. Otherwise, we're what every earth-level human is. You don't have the problems you imagine you do!"

Mei-yu regarded the Goddess. "No problem?"

"Whether you can get yourself a body of your own, the kind you'd need for terrestrial honeymooning, is an open question. Maybe the Jade Emperor might arrange a special dispensation; maybe you would build one out of moonbeams—there's always a first time; and then there's the simple approach—"

Eagerly, Mei-yu sat up straight. "What would that be, Divinity?"

"A girl as seductive as you are might bait Ju-hai into becoming an Immortal."

Mei-yu went through a spectrum of changes, but before she reached self-doubt and dismay, the Moon Goddess resumed, "Ju-hai and the Old Man—each step brings them nearer to falling apart—but, being very much *yang*, they'll keep moving. Jade is all *yang* and it is not bare female flesh that makes a lump of jade glow—it's the intangible *yin* spirit presence—and you're as totally *yin* as moonlight. Every Earth-moment you waste feeling remorseful—"

But Chang Wo was speaking to vacancy. She smiled contentedly. "Silly girl, she did catch on, finally, and didn't even wait for permission to depart."

Chapter XXV

Ju-hai was too tired to wonder how much longer he could drag himself along and keep his father moving. The combination of wound, weariness, skimpy rations, and little water kept the Old Man muttering and mumbling, except when he sang or talked to villagers Ju-hai had never heard of. Sometimes he talked to Lan-yin . . . he must have had her before she married Chen Lao-yeh . . . or was it after . . . or more likely, both?

Desert sun and air had dried the strips of horsemeat which Ju-hai had cut from the bones. Hewn to pieces and simmered in a helmet, the bones had made good soup. But anxiety was an enemy deadlier than hardship; if the circling of the vultures attracted the attention of an advance guard patrol to the spot where three riders and two horses had lost their lives, pursuit was all too likely to follow. And the deserters had long passed the stage at which men afoot could outdistance horsemen.

"Dad, you hobble alone just a bit, while I shift this carrying pole. The drier the meat gets and the more we eat, the heavier it gets."

"What happened to all those women?"

"You ought to know—you were talking to Lan-yin and some I never heard of—"

The Old Man stumbled and fell. Ju-hai knelt beside him.

"Did you hurt yourself?"

"I stumbled and busted my cane—that deadwood's brittle. No harm. We're just about out of water, so when you fill up the canteens, you can cut me a piece of green wood."

At this season, so little mountain snow melted that the Kara Kash was a seepage beneath the gravel bottom. Whatever surface growth survived did so only if it was so near that its roots could tap the underground source.

Laboriously, Ju-hai clambered up the bank, and got to the surface. He shaded his eyes and squinted upstream.

"You see anything?"

Ju-hai answered, "There's a willow clump maybe a couple of *li* and beyond that I see a poplar or two."

He turned to scramble down the bank, but the Old Man stopped him. "I can crawl over to the bank. You stay where you can see when you get to the trees."

This made sense, but Ju-hai did not like the idea of needless exposure in barren country and by the slanting light of a lowering sun. However, his legs were unsteady; to descend, only to climb up again to cut a walking stick, would be too much. But for what would ordinarily have been a trivial mishap, they could have walked on, and he'd have no backtracking—a minor nuisance, after all those days of handicapped flight, had become a disaster.

Far overhead, a vulture circled. The sun, almost touching the Tien Shan—the Mountains of Heaven—emblazoned the bird. The sight of the scavenger reminded Ju-hai that there might be pursuers on the trail, and that each delay could be critical.

He and the Old Man were neither starved nor dehydrated, though chow and water had been skimpy. Apprehension was whipping him down, and having the Old Man out of his head quite often did not help.

That sword cut was not in bad shape, but it was not healing as it should.

The shadow of the Tien Shan was lengthening rapidly.

Finally, Ju-hai came to the desert willow and sword-slashed a branch which would make a cane. That done, he slid down the bank and into half dusk. He circled only a little before he saw a clump of weeds and a sandy patch still marked by the foot prints of birds.

Ju-hai set to work scooping with the helmet he'd kept as a cooking pot.

Two vultures now circled.

"Maybe they know the Old Man has had it."

Dusk was falling in the riverbed, but a golden sun spot-lighted the vultures. A third had joined them.

Finally, sufficient water had accumulated for him to scoop it out and fill a canteen. One would be enough. In the morning, there'd be some for the birds; after shooting a few of them, he'd fill the second canteen. But for the vultures, he would now see that fresh fowl in the morning was the reward for his extra stint on the hoof.

Two *li*—about two thirds of an English mile—

He had been doing well until the Old Man stumbled. The break in cadence, in sustained purpose, had left Ju-hai disorganized, shaky, almost crippled. For the first time he realized that he had been carrying on by force of will rather than bodily reserves. And the ultimate shock came from the question, *Then how's the Old Man going to make it?* Ju-hai tried to tell himself that his father was the most superhumanly stubborn, persistent, and unwavering man in all Shensi Province or all China.

He looked up. The vultures were no longer circling. After cursing them, he concluded, "So you corpse eaters keep farmer's hours! Screw yourselves and eat your own droppings!"

He felt better already.

Ju-hai rounded a rocky buttress.

The Old Man sat with his back against the eastern wall. He had got out of his buffalo hide corselet. Good sense, but unusual. Kwan Yu-tsun had declared that getting out of and back into armor burned up too much energy, so he'd sleep in it, like a soldier. If those dung-eaters overtook them, he'd be dressed for battle.

The Old Man sat with drawn sword.

Someone—something—there was no sound—spoke to Kwan Yu-tsun and Kwan Ju-hai also got it: *It is not your right! Your son would not be free of you. You old fool, he'd bury you, go on alone, and carry you on the shoulders of his soul, all his life—and you'd carry your stupidity on your back, many lives to come—*

Ju-hai got all that. The Old Man stirred, made a move with the sword. Ju-hai yelled, making a cracked sound—and then he saw Mei-yu, so dense that he could not see the riverbank through her form.

Resolved to give his son a chance of survival, the Old Man had been startled from his purpose by Mei-yu's thought and visible presence.

Ju-hai ran.

He stumbled, lurched, and clawed gravel. Getting to his knees, he snatched the sword and flung it aside. He caught the Old Man by the shoulders and screamed, "It's my fault that you're in a fix worse than army or battle—"

He broke down, crying.

The Old Man looked foolish and embarrassed.

Mei-yu said, *Young idiot—you've won. Why throw it away?*

Ju-hai demanded, "Is this the woman you saw back there when you were talking about women to yourself and to Chen Lao-yeh—"

"This is opium dreaming. She talks and her mouth don't move."

"This is the Jade Lady I told you about. You said I was crazy."

"I didn't say you were crazy—all I said was that you had women on the brain!"

"You ever have anything better on *your* brain?"

Kwan Yu-tsun, Mei-yu screamed, *listen to me—I'm a thousand years older than you—*

"She's lost her wits—"

"Dad, she's right."

Mei-yu cut in, *Make a fire and cook up some horsemeat. And you, you put that silly sword away.*

Kwan Yu-tsun blinked and licked his dust-caked lips.

"Sounds like my grandmother, ordering my father all over and around the place."

For a virgin until so very recently, Mei-yu looked like a woman who had realized her total worth. Her smile was sweet, a bit complacent. *Put that sword away in the scabbard, not into yourself. Listen to me, each of you, and you'll have a chance of getting out of this awful desert.*

Ju-hai busied himself collecting scraps of deadwood washed from the hills when the summer sun melted high mountain ice and there was water in the Kara Kash. He was glad that the Old Man could understand direct talk, and that he could also see Mei-yu. And a glimmer of wisdom infiltrated: *That sweet, gentle Hsi-feng would word-lash the skin from me and the rest of us, the minute she's Number One Lady.*

Kneeling, he coaxed tinder and chips to flame, and cursed the lack of bellows. A vagrant whiff of wind offered the draught he needed. From close beside him, Mei-yu said, *Before I forget it, you were right about Férideh. For a little while, my mind was where yours is almost all the time. And you're right about sweet little Hsi-feng . . . but keep on loving her.*

Dried horsemeat, bits of dried shrimp from some village far down the river, octopus tentacle and grains of parched maize simmered in a helmet half filled with water—the cooking helmet, not the gold inlaid Persian headgear.

When they thinned the last bit of gravy with water and drank it as soup, Mei-yu said, *I don't eat material food, and I don't need sleep, so I'll watch until you've rested up. I'll guide you through darkness, and think-talk you by day, though you'll not see me. Being visible by daylight costs me too much power.*

Yu-tsun blinked and glanced about.

Mei-yu said, *Father, we won't need privacy till I get a solid body—which Earth Women don't appreciate as much as they ought to.*

Later, when the Old Man was in the dead tired phase of sleep, she snuggled up with Ju-hai. *I don't need your cape, and your armor doesn't bother me a bit . . . No, I'm not sleepy, but you'd better be . . .*

"Your nearness feeds me strength."

I was hoping it would, but I couldn't tell till I tried. And now you're wondering why I don't give strength to the Old Man.

"Mmm . . . well . . . yes. He needs it worse than I do."

You don't know whether that's true, neither do I. But one thing is sure—he knows now that he's not holding you back. He can rest, and so can you. And he'll not try any more foolish tricks with that sword.

Chapter XXVI

Now that Mei-yu watched by night, the odds favored the deserters. And presently they came to pools of water; as they gained elevation, the stream—whether still the Kara Kash, or one of its tributaries, Ju-hai did not know—became continuous. The fugitives, however, were not aware of this until they were halfway up to their knees in icy water. Climbing, slipping, each dragging the other back, they fought their way to the rim and collapsed.

When the Old Man sat up and began to remember that the poplar and tamarisk dotted sands of the Takla Makan were below and behind him, he glanced about and frowned.

"Where's Mei-yu? I don't get her thinkings."

"Dad, you must have missed it when she said she'd leave us for a while, now that we'd got well into the foothills."

"Where's she gone, what's she doing when she gets there?"

"I forgot most of it, and scrambled the rest, but the nearest I can come to it is that if we just keep going upstream, we'll know when to stop."

They still had scraps of dried meat, and there were pine nuts to be knocked out of fallen cones. There probably was game and there was no longer need of keeping strict watch by night.

Kwan Yu-tsun still frowned and muttered after hearing Ju-hai's remarks on foraging for food. "Well, I guess that proves she is real and not hallucination."

"That's what I been trying to tell you, long before you even saw or heard her. Now you're finally convinced?"

"You can make sense out of mirages, opium dreams, and hallucinations, but women still don't make sense."

"Dad, if you want to split hairs about it all, she helped us a lot and maybe we'd have made it and maybe not, if she hadn't given us a chance to rest each night. And twice she got me a shot at a partridge."

Each avoided the subject of the Old Man's attempt at suicide, but each remembered it; and father and son made a new appraisal, each of the other. Revision of Yu-tsun's fixed opinions about female creatures, however, was not so easy. The Old Man still felt that Mei-yu was an erratic and unpredictable wench.

There might be game, but eyes too long accustomed to the endless desert were thus far useless in wooded country. There were sounds aplenty, and stirrings, but never a living creature in view until the Old Man caught Ju-hai's arm.

"Over yonder—other side of the clearing. Pheasant—"

In a little clearing some yards upstream a bird paced majestically, all golden and scarlet, with patterns of buff, and a fine crest, high and gracefully trailing. But that wasn't a pheasant. The creature's body-feathers were jewelled and outlined with fine lines of gold, like the inlay on a Persian scimitar fashioned for a prince.

There was no music to be heard, yet Ju-hai was sure that the splendid bird paced to an unheard harmony. He couldn't hear it, yet he knew that it must be the music of a seven-stringed *cheng*. Presently the strings would make sound-notes to the same beat, except that the ear could then hear them.

"*Of course it's not a pheasant,*" his teacher back home

was saying. *"It's a Dancing Phoenix. See if you can brush the four characters with one stroke, never taking brush from paper."*

"So, you have Hsi-feng on the brain," the Old Man mocked, making a play on the slave girl's name.

"So, you have Lan-yin on the brain," Ju-hai retorted, and Yu-tsun laughed with delight. Ju-hai continued, "Dancing Phoenix . . . I never saw Hsi-feng dancing."

A great shadow reached into the clearing, cutting off the sunlight and leaving only the Phoenix head and imperial crest in daylight glow. "That's not a vulture shadow, so we can't be dead, but we ought to be."

Then the Old Man muttered, "Dragon—"

Ju-hai remembered: *Soaring Dragon, Dancing Phoenix,* four ideograms and a single continuous stroke, never lifting brush from paper. All you needed was years of experience, and the finest of brushes.

Far up . . . mighty wings . . . glittering scales . . . five-toed claws . . . and in the clearing, the Phoenix pirouetted, elegant as a sing-song girl. Ju-hai caught his father's elbow. "We have to get moving."

They walked when they should have collapsed. The Phoenix made chirping music-fragment sounds, looked back, and circled rather than stand still for them to catch up. The chirpings were like quail talk.

Beneath the Dragon's shadow, springtime warmed the air. A creaking little waterwheel irrigated the highest terrace. The overflow went from level to level. Well away from the clearing at the end of a gently sloping path, a wall of masonry reached to the front of a small monastery whose entrance was amiably ajar. The Phoenix spread splendid wing and took off, following the Dragon.

The power went with them. Ju-hai caught the Old Man to keep him from collapsing. Then, as they recovered and would have hobbled toward the entrance, they saw a man wearing a deep blue robe and a Taoist hat shaped like a tent, set crosswise on his head instead of having the ridge fore-and-aft. The woman standing beside him was Mei-yu. In the shadow, she was faintly luminous, and not transparent.

When Ju-hai would have kowtowed, the Abbot checked him. "This is the monastery of the Dancing Phoenix. I'm Lung Tzu. Leave the stately nonsense to Confucius!"

"Your Reverence—Master Lung—Old Dragon—Lord Abbot—"

"With not a monk, and only one novice, how call me Abbot?" His smooth face and quizzical smile made him look almost as young as Ju-hai. "The Divine Jade Lady came to prepare a place for you. Your father has a high fever. His wound needs attention. Please follow."

Mei-yu's thought reached through her smile. *I had to let you men of iron make it alone. Otherwise Master Lung and his novice would have come to help you those final few miles.*

They followed the Abbot from the first court to the second. There they paused. "This place is bigger than it looks. There's a jade shop used by a monk no longer with me. Much room, guest rooms—Abbot's quarters—study— kitchen. While a bath is heating, I'll get soup."

When Ju-hai awakened he was not surprised to learn that as soon as he had gulped a bowl of bean soup, he had crumpled and toppled from table to floor, there to sleep well into the following afternoon. The Old Man still slept.

Ju-hai passed his hand over his head, wondering what had happened to his helmet. Glancing about, he saw it and his shirt of mail. Venerable Abbot Lung Tzu smiled and said, "You took off your armor, complained about the condition of your shoes, and bathed before you would eat." He gestured. "Your father, he must rest. That sword slash begins to heal. I have a room for you where you won't disturb him. You will share it with Mei-yu when she has time for you."

Ju-hai picked up armor and pack, to follow the *tao-shih* to the second court. In the northeastern angle there was a suite of rooms. "Here is the library. You'll make your bed—you'll find books—" A gesture. "Use whatever brushes and paper you find. Go as you please, when you please, except in there, which is my meditation room. When you smell cooking, come and eat with me. If you're hungry and don't smell cooking, do without or eat what you find. Once you've rested, you will work in the garden and sweep courts and passageways. It's simple. Imagine you are six novices, ten lay brothers and several ordained doctors of the Tao."

Ju-hai grinned. This dish-faced, placid *tao-shih* was not as young as he looked. He did not take himself or anything else as seriously as most young persons did. "In my spare time, may I walk the Chamber of Horrors and learn which of the ten hells I'm bound for? I might leave a larger departure gift."

"No Chamber of Horrors. When fellow Taoists came to help me build this place a little more than ninety years ago, I told them that there would be no such nonsense."

"Ninety years ago and more, your Immortality?"

"I was then older than your father now is. The last few years, I've begun to wonder whether limited or unlimited Immortality is worth while. Master Ko Hung wrote an interesting book on Immortality. But until a man dies, he can't ever be sure whether or not he is an Immortal."

Ju-hai tried to cope with that one.

The *tao-shih* relished his perplexity. "They usually do fumble that one. But you have something else on your mind."

"I got interested in . . . ah . . . the idea of humans becoming Immortals, but . . . " He brightened and beamed. "But I'd have to be an awful simpleton to have opinions on the matter until I'd tried it and found out."

There was appreciation in that ironic smile and those ancient eyes which were much older than the smooth, bland face. Then came the words which the smile had foreshadowed: "And that would take quite too long for impatient youth?"

For no reason which he could point out to himself, Ju-hai felt like a natural-born fool, in spite of having spoken truth.

The Abbot resumed, "Since I am a healer, you were too polite to ask whether I could do anything for your father. The outcome depends upon what he wishes."

Chapter XXVII

Ju-hai's patience was nearing the breaking point when the Abbot accosted him in the Great Book room. "You'll see your father as soon as he's recuperated enough to endure an old soldier's boasting and drinking bout! He still needs rest and silence, and so do you. Now listen to this: I forbid you to work in the vegetable patch or what we call the field. You'll not sweep courtyards."

"Your Reverence, I'm as good as new and I know my obligations."

"On the contrary, you are a good-hearted ignoramus and you have not the faintest idea of what your obligations are or how to go about them! You remember that I mentioned the jade shop that's been gathering dust and cobwebs ever since the death of my good friend and assistant, Venerable Zeng. You may complete some of his unfinished pieces. Traders passing through used to buy his work. They'll buy yours and that will help the monastery a lot more than sweeping or garden work.

"You're still pretty well burned out. Practice calligraphy until your perfect circle tells me that you really are yourself again. Read for Imperial Civil Service examinations. Study magic and learn how to kill Captain Li—"

"Sir—Lord Abbot—what—"

Master Lung Tzu explained, "While you were lying like one of the dead, you muttered and mumbled. Sometimes you spoke clearly of the Captain, and of Colonel Tsao—your eloquence was impressive! And there was Lan-yin, and your giddiness about Mei-yu, a female whose occasional presence has honored the Monastery of the Dancing Phoenix. Losing her virginity has helped her a great deal!

And you didn't lose too much time talking about Hsi-feng, the Little Phoenix. There were words of plans for strangling a whore named Orchid Cluster. Your aspirations, affections and hatreds would keep half a dozen men busy for several incarnations—that, and worrying about your father, and Kwan acres. But for now, try to get yourself in order and take a few things at a time. The fact is, your Old Man isn't in half the mess you are!"

Ju-hai blinked, licked his lips, and tried not to look too foolish. "Immortal Sir, jade work for the monastery—I knock my forehead on the tiles! But the everyday chores have to be done, and my father and I—"

"I'm expecting another novice from Yotkan, that dinky town not many *li* from Khotan," Lung Tzu patiently explained. "I do respect your right mindedness—it is a credit to you and the Old Man—and there is more to the Stone of Heaven than you may realize. One of the pieces of jade has lain in the shop for many years. It has a peculiar quality. Venerable Master Zeng never worked it."

"Peculiar, Lord Abbot? Rare, precious? I might ruin it."

"It is precious but not in the way you mean. I'm as ignorant as you are in many things—you probably know more about jade than I do. My friend believed it had magical qualities. And it might help you drive your enemy from the Kwan Family land."

"Old Master—your Reverence—which piece of jade—"

"I don't know. Read Zeng's book. Let Mei-yu help you." The self-made Immortal walked out.

Ju-hai began to understand what Confucius had meant when he wrote, *If I give a man one corner of a problem, and he can not grasp the other three, I waste no time with him.*

Ju-hai turned to Master Ko Hung's great writings. Each volume was a long strip of paper, folded in pleats in the manners of an accordion, and secured between board covers faced with brocade. It would take a lifetime to read what the great *tao-shih*, that outstanding doctor of Taoist basics, had written on medicine, magic, alchemy, and perhaps, how moonbeams are changed into jade.

He might even explain how the Jade Emperor attained Immortality by copulating with a thousand girls, and how Hsi-wang Mu had become the Earth Goddess by draining the male essence and the life from a thousand young lovers. What Ju-hai had heard concerning these enterprises discouraged him. On the other hand, if there were a method whereby he and Hsi-feng could simultaneously attain Immortality, and she could accept Mei-yu as Number Two Lady, it would be worth a good deal of study.

Ju-hai sat down to the writing table, poured water into the depression at one end of the slab, and set to work grinding ink. The camphor smell was fragrance and happiness. It reminded him of his study room at home, where ink smell and Hsi-feng bouquet blended, and sometimes left him wondering whether it was Hsi-feng or Mei-yu he followed to bed.

He reached for a brush. He'd write Hsi-feng that he and the Old Man were in a secluded spot favored by Immortals, and then a line to Yatu, to tell the crusty Mongol how neatly two farmers had coped with three cavalrymen. And at once, he decided against any such boasting. If the shaman ran true to form he'd retort, *Only Chinamen—if you'd met three Mongols, you and your Old Man would have had your dung-clawing hands full.*

He jerked his brush from the pool of ink, sat back, and grimaced ruefully. However much food and sleep had done for him, his mind was still a comfortable confusion. The Abbot was right. Ju-hai had forgot the siege of Khotan and he realized, belatedly, that the isolation of the Monastery of the Dancing Phoenix would make it difficult to get a letter into the hands of a caravan man.

Shadows crept across the second court. Finally the moon came up over the ridge and topped the trees. Ju-hai sat and digested his first lesson in Taoism. It was nonsense as long as he tested it with logic, but once he kept his meddling mind out of it—*Do nothing, and there is nothing you can not do* became wisdom.

The smell of ink reminded him that he'd intended to write letters. His gropings were interrupted by a familiar sweetness and the tinkle of bracelets.

He'd never learn to judge from the sound of jade what the color of that jade was . . . Mei-yu had told him that only a simpleton would ask how you learned the trick . . . all you needed was experience . . . *if you have to ask, you'll never know.* A female speaking Taoist axioms was the ultimate mystery . . . if only Mei-yu had a solid body, all her own.

A spindle of bluish white formed in the deeper shadows. He had asked why the color never varied. She'd mocked him, advising him to consult an astrologer.

And there she was, fresh and smiling, tantalizingly solid-looking. As she came toward him, she observed, "Comfortable, but still muddled. No wonder, after what you've been through. Mind moving that rug? Over about here—that's just right."

The inner border was of tiny medallions against a ground of old gold; on a field of apricot-persimmon red, a central medallion of blue, flanked by smaller ones on each side, ran the length of the rug.

"Just right." Mei-yu seated herself. She looked solid, but the deep nape was not depressed. "It will be some while before you should risk letters."

Ju-hai had been regarding her. He asked sharply, "Now you mouth-talk?"

She shook her head. "Not really. You and I have got so used to each other's direct-think-talk that our faces move with our thoughts. I'm still too frail, or you're too dense. More and more, I know that borrowing a body is dangerous meddling. We've been lucky so far. One bad mistake could put us hopelessly far apart, with never any future—not for aeons and aeons."

For moments, each eyed the other. Finally Ju-hai said, "We can get used to anything—well, so I hope."

Mei-yu answered, "We're going to be awfully busy. After this, I won't make the gradual appearance. As long as it's after sunset, I'll look natural. Don't be so dismayed-heroic—we are in a most fortunate spot. I can't see a chance of becoming more dense, but there's nowhere that could offer you a better home for becoming—well—less dense. We can gain ground by tending to our work and learning what we can from the Abbot."

"We? Where do *you* come in on *learning?*"

"Ju-hai, Ju-hai, can't you ever get it through your head that the Goddess and I are only people with bodies not solid enough to die? We have a lot to learn, just as you have—and—" She paused groping. "Your substance has been changing just as her substance and mine changed ages ago. The way you went to get your father out of the army; the way you carried on ever since; that Turkistani girl for instance—you were right, I was so wrong—"

"It just wouldn't have been right. Those old folks were nice."

"And if you'd taken her, as herself or with me borrowing her body, it could have touched off a lot of trouble. Getting her all aroused and then leaving her to herself—as you'd have had to—she'd have taken up with the first soldier who looked a bit like you and become a camp follower, all the way to Khotan, and then—"

"I didn't think of that."

"Neither did I. And don't look puzzled—it's the way you respond when desires and urges are strong—they do change your substance."

Whimsically, ruefully, he said, "If I keep it up, I might be an Immortal in a million years, and you'd still be young and beautiful and we'd be the same density, and—"

"That's not as funny as you think. Anyway, you're going to work in the jade shop. There'll be a new novice to do the chores. When the Old Man recuperates a bit more, he'll tell you your next duty."

"I can just about guess."

"Let me hear your guessing," Mei-yu challenged.

"Dad and I are deserters and outlaws. I didn't tell you how Lan-yin's son thought we were going to kill him. Well, he talked a lot to save his life, and told us all about how his mother and father had connived with Colonel Tsao to get control of all the Kwan land.

"Tsao won't hurt Shou-chi," he continued. "Younger Brother is a good farmer and the people will work better for him than for anyone else—better than for any manager Tsao could find elsewhere. So, Tsao can take his time to get title to the lands. That will give me and the Old Man our chance to work against him. But where does the jade come in?"

"Didn't the Abbot tell you?"

"He told me enough to leave me nicely muddled. He gave me a couple of books to study, and he said you'd help me."

Mei-yu pondered a moment. "We'll have to work together. You'll have to make an image, a small one—" She held her palms about two hands-breadths apart. "This size, of your father confronting Colonel Tsao, hating him."

Ju-hai frowned and shook his head dubiously. "I do pretty good designs, but a portrait sculpture—"

"Back home," Mei-yu reminded him, "your work improved so rapidly that you were puzzled. You were learning what you had always known. And this is another step."

Although encouraged, he remained perplexed. "Two images, the Old Man facing his enemy, helpless against armed authority. Then what?"

"You and I, we'll put life into the jade, life and the Old Man's wrath, and yours." She read his latent question and answered before he could shape it. "No, not a physical life; for that, I don't have the substance; but there's spirit life, and that can finish your enemy. Don't try to figure it out; you'll learn as you work at things you do understand."

"Make a joss and put a devil-life in it. You'll have to be the Jade Enchantress; all I can do is the cutting and grinding and the polishing—and lucky if I can do that well enough—"

"Lover, don't look so dismayed! I don't know which of us has the harder problem—your doing your duty to the Kwan Family, or my getting a solid body for us. But it isn't hopeless as you think. My problem is worse than yours."

"How could that be?"

"I want everything possible for you and me; I want us to spend a thousand years honeymooning to make up for lost time, and I must not do anything to keep you and

Hsi-feng from having every possible good." She got to her feet. Her soundless voice went to a pitch higher than any scream. "I can't wish against her. Digest every book— grind and saw and polish—and when you know which has the harder problem, you'll know the answers!"

For moments after Mei-yu's departure, he stood looking at the rug and at the space she had quit. Finally he took a taper and crossed the court to go to the jade shop.

Chapter XXVIII

During the half-moon following Mei-yu's departure, Ju-hai was turned back whenever he asked the Abbot's permission to see the Old Man. The hours between morning gruel and evening rice were spent in the Great Book room. There he read, among many other things on jade, what many had dismissed as nonsense.

On nights of the full moon, girls would gather along river banks, strip down to bare skin, and wade, little more than knee deep, upstream a way and downstream again. Since jade was *yang*, masculine, and solar, and the girls were *yin*, feminine and lunar, the Stone of Heaven would glow from excitement when a parcel of femaleness passed by. Thus a girl could distinguish between an ordinary stone and a lump of jade coated by the mineral from which it had been washed by summer floods and carried downstream until it came to rest among all manner of geological rubbish.

Ju-hai speculated: *If jade glows from glimpses of a girl's most precious possession, she ought to finish a night's prospecting in quite a mood, being exposed to yang so long.*

After another quarter moon of study, Ju-hai found his first useful hint: thought, will, desire force, vitality could be impressed on jade. If there were harmony between the thought and the Stone of Heaven, if the spirit and the form were harmonious, that is, if *yang* and *yin* forces were compatible, the jade could exhale the power it had absorbed. The argument put him in mind of a signal bomb: its ingredients were *yang* and *yin*, and when ignited, there was a blast.

Shell and contents vanished.

Yang plus *yin*, positive plus negative, equaled zero.

Ju-hai and *yang*, Mei-yu and *yin* . . .

She'd have a lot of explaining and demonstrating ahead of her when she returned from wherever she was, but however fragile it sounded when put into words, Ju-hai felt that the combination could settle Colonel Tsao, and perhaps include Captain Li in the blast.

But first they must shape the portrait sculptures and infuse them with spirit.

Ju-hai set Zeng's monograph aside and got back to Ko Hung, the supreme *tao-shih*. Unfortunately, there was so much on magic that only an Immortal would live long enough to learn which of the many pages applied to the problem at hand.

Mantra . . . *dharani* . . . plain incantations and enchantments. Magic was far more than intellectual knowledge. It was a discipline of uttermost severity.

Turning at last from the books, Ju-hai went to eat evening rice with the Abbot. He noted two changes: first, that the new novice, a wrinkled, stoop-shouldered little man in his sixties or older, had arrived; and second, that he was a good cook.

There was birds' nest soup; *bêche de mer* with black mushrooms; smoked duck; a sweet dish made of tree fungus; and finally, syrup-cured apples soaked in *kao-liang* spirit and set afire.

After a lifetime as a petty merchant in Yotkan, Ah Yen had retired to the monastery, and the meal was made up of some of the gifts he had brought to his superior, the Abbot.

When they had done eating, the Abbot said, "This becomes as crowded as it used to be a century ago."

Once the meal was served, Ah Yen joined the Abbot, Ju-hai, and the senior novice.

"Lord Abbot," Ju-hai began, "I beg permission to ask your new colleague a question."

"Please do! He's all of an itch to tell you about the siege of Khotan. I told him you'd be interested."

Ah Yen began, "You missed nothing but trouble. While the punitive expedition was getting ready to besiege the city, Tu Fan tribesmen came down out of Tibet and caught the army all off guard. The army had too much thought of looting Khotan and no attention to their rear.

"Colonel Tsao was caught flat-footed but he prevented disaster. He organized a rearguard action and fought well. Instead of the massacre the barbarians expected, the Imperial forces escaped. And what helped them was strange."

He paused and chuckled. "When the garrison of Khotan saw that the Tu Fan were well in pursuit, they sallied out and caught the tribesmen from the rear. They figured that the Tu Fan would be back and would use the abandoned siege engines to take the city. So the Imperial task force escaped, but it was in no shape to rally and get back at the siege."

Ju-hai had little time for comment. "Ah Yen, I've been waiting for news. Thank you. Lord Abbot, may I see my father?"

"Yes, it is time. He has made up his mind."

"Sir, it was made up before he got here."

Master Lung Tzu smiled cryptically, and then said, "You leave with my permission."

Ju-hai found his father in what had been the quarters of the Abbot's associate, the late Master Zeng. The Old Man looked as good as new. Ju-hai sank to his knees to kowtow, but his father caught him by the hands.

"None of that nonsense, not after what we've been through—and with what's ahead of you."

"That's what I came to tell you about."

"Grab that jug and sit down. Master Lung told me how the siege turned out, and you're all excited, looking for more trouble."

The jug sitting near the charcoal brazier was warm

enough. After filling the cups, Ju-hai outlined what Mei-yu had told him, and what he had been studying. He concluded, "Making a portrait sculpture of you and Tsao is going to take time, and more than just time."

The Old Man grimaced sourly. "Being outlaws, we're in no hurry to leave a comfortable, out-of-the-way spot. Any idea when your spirit girl, Jade Lady, is coming back?"

"She left here nearly a moon ago, and, till she's back, I can't start the jade work. So I am going to write Yatu—remember that shaman?—and find out what's going on back home."

"That will keep. Let me get something else straight. While you are shaping and grinding that sculpture thing, Mei-yu's going to breath life into it, and that's going to make it bad *joss* for Tsao. Then you have to know enough jade magic to start it breathing out to finish him. Sounds good in words, but getting close enough to Tsao may not be too easy."

"All the more reason for getting information from Yatu. The more we know about what's going on back home, the better you and I and Mei-yu can figure this out."

"Son, whatever is going to be done, you're doing it. I am not going back to the Village. I am staying right here. Master Lung Tzu is my *guru*. Whatever Mei-yu is, a ghost or a fox-woman or an Immortal, I'm taking her on faith."

Ju-hai sat there, chewing air and looking dumb.

The Old Man went on, "I am glad Tsao and Captain Li did not let me go home when you came to take my place."

"Please explain. Number One Son is stupid."

"You and I were strangers until you joined the regiment. When you and I soldiered together and got to know each other, it meant a lot. And the further we went, the more it meant. It was good for the soul."

The Old Man paused to relish his memories. These gained a new savor each time he recited them. He refilled the cups and went on, "Sitting here with Master Lung Tzu, being doctored back to life, and for the first time having a chance to think on life and the world, has been good.

"Change never stops, never pauses for breath. *Heaven does not speak, but the four seasons come and go.* I don't know which of the Great Men of old said that, but it's true. Something has been shaping up. You can go with it, or you can stand in the way and get crushed flat.

"You're not as tired as I am. You get to work. I'm staying here. Drink up, and refill the cups."

"You're quitting the Red Earth and working to become an Immortal?"

Kwan Yu-tsun chuckled. "That spirit girl of yours has been talking to you a lot. Master Lung's gone a long way toward being an Immortal; but as far as you and I are concerned, better we should keep our minds on Kwan Village. It's been there three centuries, and your chore is to start it off for another three." After a long pause, he said abruptly, "What do you think of Hsi-feng? And for once, I am not referring to fun and wine games."

"Sir, you once told me about how a clod of a farmer could get ... um ... a cultural polish by finding out what it's like sleeping with a lady of good family. Seems to me there ought to be a marriage contract according to old custom; otherwise I'd not be treating her like a lady of good family. So I ask permission—"

"Son, listen with both ears. Since I have quit the Red Earth, you are head of the family. I have renounced the right and duty of flogging you. You do not ask permission. You give permission or you do not give it."

Moving like a puppet show figure, Ju-hai knelt and knocked his forehead three times against the floor.

"Get up and sit!" the Old Man commanded. "I am pouring a drink for the Number One Man of the Kwans."

The Old Man filled the cups. With both hands, he offered wine to Kwan Ju-hai. "Don't sit there like a dummy! Take it—this is the first and last time I am paying you respects."

They drank.

"Son, I feel years younger."

"Dad, I feel years older."

From time to time, the Abbot brought in a tray of rice and vegetables, of bamboo shoots and mushrooms, quail eggs, raisins, and dried melon slices. Each time he refused to eat and drink with the Kwans. "My presence," he would say, "could not improve this meeting. Enjoy your rice."

They said the old things over again, speculating on the seemingly casual encounters and apparently minor personalities which had become critically important.

"Orchid Cluster, whore-turned-housekeeper . . . limping shaman's familiar spirit, sending me home . . . Lan-yin's greed, or resentment, or ambition, conspiring with Colonel Tsao who was also land hungry . . ."

They sat, dozing, like sentries off post, resting by a guard fire. Sometimes, they stretched out on the *kang*. But after each rest, they fed the brazier some charcoal, brewed tea, or heated wine, picked over the morsels of a snack tray, and resumed reliving their adventure, their Kwan Village years . . . and then, the Old Man's memories of deceased kinsmen and neighbors . . . Ju-hai's mother . . . and a concubine . . . and Lan-yin, whose first venture as part-time concubine began through an amicable arrangement between Chen Lao-yeh and Kwan Yu-tsun. Each repetition of saying the old things over brought with it new bits dredged from the long forgotten past.

Food and wine and tea—the Abbot tended to these, and neither father nor son counted the hours or the days, not even when the venerable Master said, "Your father is tired. Perhaps he will be pleased to give you permission to return to your rooms? And each can dream new ways of saying old things?"

Ju-hai begged for and got permission to withdraw.

This was completeness. This was good. The two had a total understanding of all but the details of Ju-hai's doing his duty. Whether each had come to an understanding of the other's whims, notions, aberrations, and inconsistencies was immaterial; neither required reason or justification or understanding where the other's acts had been concerned.

Ju-hai was almost steady on his feet, though he was not sure that those feet always touched the flagstones. Least of all could he decide whether being head of the house was a burden or a stimulant. Probably some of each. And having this reciprocity, each accepting the other and without reservation, Ju-hai had become a grown man, to live up to his own standards, rather than to another's.

Chapter XXIX

Although the jade shop in which the Venerable Zeng Tze-Lin had worked was larger than Ju-hai's room back home, the grinder and implements were similar. On shelves and in corners, the artist had left an accumulation of crude lumps still coated with the mineral "skin" through which, in spots, the jade could be seen. There was a cabinet containing partially completed artifacts. Some were roughly outlined; others were completed, except for polishing.

It took Ju-hai little time to sense that the deceased *tao-shih* would be his teacher. Zeng's guidelines on nuggets from which the skin had been removed indicated his response to shape, to the swirls and patterns, and to variations from the barely perceptible greenish to the deeper shades. Ju-hai saw why the master had outlined a Fu-dog on this chunk and a teapot on that. And there were pieces which puzzled him until, turning to almost completed work, he began to understand how the master had perceived the image hidden in the heart of a crude lump.

Presently, Abbot Lung Tzu stepped into the shop. "When you've become what you really are, you will learn much from setting to work on those unfinished bits. And polishing the completed ones will teach you much, simply from watching your progress."

"Your Reverence has suggestions?"

"Jade Lady tells me that she became interested in you when she saw that you had an instinct for jade, a response to it, and that this told her about your inner image—that invisible image that speaks the way the hidden image of jade speaks to the artist."

Ju-hai frowned. "There's nothing about that chunk that looks from the outside like a Fu-dog, but he sensed it was there; if he'd lived longer, he would have worn it away and abraded all the waste and the rubbish, leaving what was there from the beginning."

Abbot Lung Tzu nodded. "A good way of saying it. You don't outwardly look like a jade artist." He chuckled. "Just how is an artist supposed to look? Matter of fact, Zeng didn't look any too bright; and there are sensitive, spiritual looking people who are gross clods!"

"Lord Abbot, thank you for instruction—it has made my work a lot more difficult than I realized.'"

"And maybe a bit better, too." The Abbot turned, then paused long enough to add, "It is the Stone of Heaven— and Heaven speaks to him who listens—provided that the listener can also hear."

Clearly, the Lord Abbot did not believe in generating unwarranted optimism.

Once alone again, Ju-hai went to work polishing an incense burner. Instead of the usual bowl, it was a lotus blossom somewhat short of being fully open; in the center were holes drilled to make a holder for nine joss sticks.

He worked until the smell of cookery called him to evening rice. Now that Ah Yen's ceremonial gift delicacies had been eaten, the monastery was back to its normal fare: a bowl of vegetables, cubes of soy curd, and octopus tentacle soaked and boiled until it was almost as tender as buffalo hide armor.

When he crossed his chopsticks, Ju-hai said, "Your Reverence, my predecessor in jade-craft is a hard man to follow."

"Keep at it and live to be his age; then he'd probably say the same of you, if he looked at your later work. You had a profitable day?"

"Sir, having done nothing, there is nothing that I did not do."

This perversion of a basic Taoist axiom evoked a

chuckle. "The truth is not as sour as your face makes it. If you didn't have so many women and other enterprises, you'd be a fine novice."

"Lord Abbot, I beg leave to depart and resume doing nothing."

Ju-hai went to the Great Book room. He had scarcely entered when he sensed Mei-yu's presence. *And high time!*

He had barely shaped that thought when the lady stepped from behind a three-leaf screen. The ivory, the mother of pearl inlay, and the gilt which gave life to the dark wood did not show through her glowing form.

"Yes I'm back, and I am not as solid as I look. I'll be appearing this way, the way a mortal would, and I promise you, if ever you're entertaining any of those jade-hunting wenches working the big river . . . " She sighed. "I'd not blame you, either." She gestured. "Master Zeng wrote a lot about jade."

"Divinity—"

"Call me that once more and I'll scream! Ju-hai, Ju-hai, I am as muddled as you are. I neglected my work horribly, and whatever you did or didn't, it was better than I did. What I started to say was that a lot of Master Zeng's writings have nothing to do with art or craftsmanship."

"Then what does he have for me?"

"I can't read books the way I read you."

"I wasn't such good reading, evidently."

"I was in a dark mood already and you'd done nothing to improve it. But if we combined our moods, we'd get brightness."

"That's the last word in female logic!"

"That's not female, it is pure Tao, which is neither *yang* nor *yin*, but both."

Ju-hai gulped and blinked. "Let me in on it."

"If you had your mind on the *Book of Changes* instead of me in a borrowed body, you'd remember that when anything is total *yin*, it changes and becomes *yang*, and of course, the same for total *yang*. So, you and I, totally dark and muddled, being together, will make totally total darkness, and brightness has to appear. Let's go to the jade shop and look around."

She would have caught his hand if she'd been sufficiently dense, but the almost-contact had force enough to get him going. Cicada chirpings blended with chanting in the meditation hall. "No, we won't need a light. The moon's high enough and it will reflect from the wall."

While waiting for his eyes to become accustomed to indoor dimness, Mei-yu said, "Take those jade nuggets out of the corners and scatter them on the floor, just any way. Never mind the pieces that are cut or have the skin taken off. Only the crude ones."

He set to work.

When he had done making an obstacle course of the room, Mei-yu said, "Now get out of my way and watch."

"Watch what?"

"Just watch!"

When she peeled out of tunic and undergarment, Ju-hai was on the point of saying, "I can watch but I'll do little enough seeing till the moon shifts some more." Then he suspected that his first reaction had been in error. Mei-yu picked her way among the jade lumps. At the far end of the shop, she turned and picked a course so near the first one that at times she stepped over pieces she had once crossed.

Jade hunting, but no river, no water, and it's all jade here, he told himself. *So it begins to make no sense after all.*

Once more, at the far end, she turned and came toward him. And then, when she was halfway to the entrance of the shop, he shouted, "It's true! Right where you are! Stop!"

He stumbled, then recovered; he bounded and knelt at her feet. He reached for the glowing chunk of jade. He had scarcely touched the rough surface when the phosphorescence blinked out.

"Pick it up—that's the one!"

It was bigger than any of the pieces he had previously handled and much heavier than he expected. After fumblings, he got it with both hands. When he regained his feet, Mei-yu was dressed.

Ju-hai followed her to the Great Book room.

"You were bare enough, but none of the other chunks
—do you mean to tell me that they're not jade? The Abbot
said—"

"They're jade, but I'm not a solid human woman.
They're not sensitive enough to respond to my level of *yin*.
But you do, that's why you could see me, understand my
wordless talking. Very few people can. Your father saw
and understood—he was so far free and loose from his
physical body that he could see and understand. And he
won't lose the power. Being so near death for so long
changed his substance.

"Anyway," she continued, "this is the special nugget
that the old sage found—maybe during his final months of
living between the spirit world and the material world.
Live with this, read its heart."

Ju-hai stood facing her, clutching the heavy chunk. He
glanced about him, looking for some place to set it, some
surface which it would not mar.

"*Aiieeyah!*" Mei-yu laughed softly, contentment and
happiness in her voice. "You can study here all you need,
but as long as I'm here, we'll sleep in your quarters, where
the old *tao-shih*, Master Zeng, spent the final months of
his many years at the monastery. This special jade, the one
he picked out, will be sleeping with us, and if Ah Yen
brings us a meal, we'll have our jade at the table with
us."

He led the way to his quarters. He remembered that for
nearly a century, Mei-yu and Master Lung Tzu had been
friends, and the Monastery of the Dancing Phoenix had
won a spot in her heart.

"Lover, remember in the bitter cold of the desert, I
didn't mind the sand, the rocks, and your chain mail; I
didn't need even a corner of your cloak. We were very
close when you were sound asleep, mortally, dead-weary
asleep."

He regarded her for a long moment. "That explains
some things."

"My sleep isn't like mortal sleep. The special jade-sleep

is likewise different. But during your sleepings, you and I and jade will be very close, and we'll understand each other more and more."

Chapter XXX

Ju-hai wrote a studiedly rambling letter addressed to *Yatu, the Shaman, Mongol Colony, near Jin Guan Men, Ch'ang-an*. Since he knew only a few words of the Mongolian language, he used Chinese. Not knowing who could translate for Yatu, Ju-hai identified himself by references to the tiger which the shaman had clubbed to death after the beast had clawed his leg and half crippled him. *I don't know when I'll be in town*, he continued, *but maybe your spirit will tell me where to find the bitch who put opium in my wine. Our commander fought a noble rearguard action. I was gravely wounded, left for dead. An old merchant helped me back to life. No doubt I have been posted as a deserter. I can't risk coming home till I find out how I stand with the authorities. No one witnessed me being wounded.*

The caravan man bringing this letter is an Arab. I had to have him write his name in his language. I paid him to deliver this, and likewise to give you twenty taels of silver. I heard our great commander was going to retire to a farm in the foothills when the campaign was over. The silver is for you to pay an identification artist to sketch that commander. Let no one know you have word of me. The commander is good, but my captain is a son of a bitch. I hope you and I meet again at the season of moon cakes. I bow three times. I forgot to say, send pictures and write me at merchant Zeng Ah Lin's store, Yotkan.

Mei-yu, the Lord Abbot, the Old Man, and the new

novice read the letter. After suggesting a few minor changes, they agreed that the new operator of the business in Yotkan, which the novice had turned over to his nephew, could not be endangered by receiving a reply to the letter.

That much accomplished, Ju-hai asked Ah Yen, the new novice, to buy a big chunk of vegetable wax when he went to Yotkan to get supplies and also to leave the letter with his nephew. There it would stay until a reliable caravan man would pick it up.

"You model in wax instead of abrading jade?" Abbot Lung Tzu queried. "Impatient as always?"

"Sir, Taoist doctrine: when the ultimate doing-nothing has been reached, it is like a *changing line* and becomes intense activity."

Lung Tzu chuckled appreciatively. He said to the Old Man, "Your son is not yet my *guru* but he does new things with old axioms." Then he said to Ju-hai, "I accept your thought. But don't wait for Ah Yen to go shopping. Melted votive candles will give you a block of wax."

Once Ju-hai closed the door of their apartment behind them, Mei-yu asked, "Do you think the Lord Abbot knew your real reason for wanting wax?"

Ju-hai regarded her somberly. "*You* know, or you'd not ask me such a question. And Master Lung Tzu must have known or he'd not have agreed so smoothly."

"How about the Old Man?"

"He and I think alike a good deal, but each also puzzles the other sometimes. But if he suspected my real reason, he wouldn't care."

"You want a quick portrait sculpture before he dies? Jade work of that kind—I hate to think how long it would take!"

"Jade Lady, when he made me head of the Kwan Family, I was prepared for whatever may happen, and so was he."

After a moment of cogitation, Mei-yu said, "Peel that jade and, as soon as you see what's in its heart, saw it where it needs to be cut. As you become more acquainted, you and the Stone of Heaven, rough out your father's

portion and Colonel Tsao's portion, to clear the little battlefield between them.

"When you are making the wax model, for best possible
likeness always have our jade with us—yes, I should see
Kwan Yu-tsun whenever he sits for that portrait."

She turned and gestured toward the sleeping alcove. On
the floor beside the bed was the Yarkand rug which Mei-
yu had asked him to bring from the Great Book room.
"When you get our jade, find some nice little mat to set it
on—or maybe a cushion."

Ju-hai closed his eyes, shook his head, and then looked
at her. Mei-yu read the questions and his confused sens-
ings; he was groping, reading but not understanding. She
said, "Yes, all things are living. People know animal life
and plant life—you are beginning to suspect that there is
mineral life, and that leaves you perplexed. You always
responded to jade, but this piece is different from others,
in the same sense that you are different from most
humans."

Ju-hai pondered and filled in the long pause. "Being that
way used to make me feel lonesome and groping."

Mei-yu resumed, "The painters, the landscape artists of
the Great Days—one of them would sit, day after day,
until after six months or more, doing nothing but look at a
scene, become part of it, and absorb much of its life. Then
he'd set to work and in a few hours have the finished
picture. He had no more need to see the actual landscape;
he had looked into the heart of the scene—it was part of
him—his inner image directed the brush strokes—

"You have a more difficult task. You have to look into
your subject, and also into the jade; the painter never had
to look into his paints or his brushes."

They took the rough-trimmed jade with them when Ju-
hai went to the Old Man's quarters with a block of vegetable wax. He made no attempt to shape more than the
posture of the Old Man, crouched as if to lunge, a man
willing to die for the luxury of killing his enemy—and
Tsao, at the beginning, remained a shapeless columnar
mass, without indication of head or limbs. Even that sym-
bol had its force.

Seeing what would depict the man conspiring to seize Kwan lands, the Old Man's face tightened. Ju-hai plied his tools, all the while speaking of what had happened before as well as after his joining the regiment. Each stroke which rough-shaped the face made the image ever more lifelike. Bit by bit, the features became more angular, the lips drawn back against the teeth, the corners of the mouth expressing the fury of knowing that before he could close in, his head would roll in the dust, his life be spilled before the other's was endangered.

The sun was low when Ju-hai said, "Sir, this jade has been drinking your feelings, but the spirit needs a substance for it to animate. After I've rested from hating with you, we'll be back to work on details."

The Old Man sighed. "Almost, I wish I could go with you when you go to liberate the Kwan lands. But desert crossings and high summits aren't for old farmers. You say you need a rest from this—so do I!"

Mei-yu cut in with her thought projection. "If you find this jade good company at times, we'll leave it with you."

Kwan Yu-tsun's eyes narrowed. "When you have the Great Commander's face rough-shaped, I'll have more penetrating thoughts. Go, enjoy your rice!"

Once back in their apartment, Mei-yu said, "He spoke of our enjoying our rice, but he let his guard down, and I got what he was not saying."

Ju-hai drew a deep breath and exhaled slowly. "He still doesn't believe you're too fragile. He's midway between being sorry for me and thinking I'm a dung-eating liar, for no reason whatever."

Where before jade-craft had been an avocation deriving from love of jade and of beauty, it was now work. To make it more onerous, Ju-hai had to be his own taskmaster. With wire saw and bamboo drill dipped in a mixture of kitchen grease and ruby dust, he roughed out the pedestal and the masses in which he would find figures and faces which had always been there.

It would take months for Ju-hai's letter to reach the crusty shaman. Guessing how long it would be until Yatu got the identification sketches, the kind which the police used for tracing fugitives in flight from justice, was futility beyond one even as patient as Ju-hai. He tried, but failed to suppress the thought that Yatu might be on one of his wandering spells, going into Szechuan Province, or into Mongolia. The shaman, half madman, half sage, was a tortured soul.

Late one afternoon Mei-yu said, "Lover, you're fighting heroically, but impatience is wearing you thin."

Wearily, he sighed. "Jade Lady, sometimes I forget what we'd be doing if you had a body all your own."

"I'd refresh your memory! But why don't you work on Tsao's portion of the wax? Try to model from memory and see if your father reaches a higher pitch of destruction-craving."

And after evening rice, Mei-yu said, "During our walking up the dry river, did you ever see my *aura?*"

"Mmm . . . I was so near the border line, I couldn't be sure whether I saw or just imagined." He closed his eyes, then opened them. "Well, one night . . . when the fire was dead except for a few coals peeping through ashes, I saw a kind of wavering, cloudy glow spreading out from you, reaching out a couple of feet or more in every direction . . . kind of egg-shaped and thinning out as it spread further away from your shape the way I see it usually."

"What color was it?"

"It was mixed. Crimson-rose, against dark gray, and changing—more bright rose, then more gray. I didn't know which it would be."

Mei-yu nodded. "You saw truly—darling, you're really special! I was awfully depressed and I was too worried to have the shade of man-craving red I had when I stripped the Turkistani girl to the hips and asked how you liked her. What color do you see now?"

"I'm not near enough to the dead-tiredness I had then. For ordinary people like me to see the unseen, we have to be worn nearly to death, or *afiyoun*-drugged, or somehow overtaxed."

Mei-yu nodded. "You're sensitive, but you need more training to be able to see when you are normal, and not half-dead from weariness."

"Does it make any difference," he asked, "whether I see your color? I mean, your *aura*-color?"

Mei-yu exhaled a long breath. "I was wondering how close you and I could be without each of us getting a red-passion *aura*. From the first meeting, we've had a craving for each other."

Ju-hai frowned. "There's no point in teasing games. Walking up the dry river was one thing, and lying around this monastery of the Dancing Phoenix, well fed and comfortable, that's something else."

"Ju-hai, Ju-hai! I don't want it to be teasing games! Whatever *that* would do to you, it would do twice as much to me! Make room for me—maybe it would help if we were close together, and maybe we wouldn't drive each other wild from craving what we couldn't have.

"It's this way—mortal lovers share bodies and *auras*, and sometimes the wrong *aura* can be harmful, dangerous. But if you and I could be close without getting a disturbing color, I could experience your memories, and you'd get intuitions from my life. And if we had our jade close to us, its mineral soul could help us—*maybe*! I don't know—I never tried it—"

"You weren't a bit exciting in the dry river, the way you were in the ruined house, with a borrowed body. In the dry river—well—I just loved you and it was good you were close by. Let's try."

Chapter XXXI

The awakening of Ju-hai and Mei-yu was abrupt and simultaneous, without any half-waking, half-dream stage. Before he could wonder whether in his sleep he had inadvertently pawed and fondled her fragile astral body, she asked, "Was it too much of an ordeal?"

"It was too strange to be troublesome. Being careful not to get too close to you, and not wanting to be far from you—it was awfully confusing until I turned my back and you snuggled up; it was just right, once I had my doubts and got rid of them."

"And then?"

"Ever walk on a woolly rug on a cold morning," he began, fumbling for words. "And reach out and touch the brass drawer pull of a cabinet? You'd feel a tingling and there'd be a blue or purple spray from your fingers before you got near enough to touch the metal—"

Mei-yu shuddered. "The nunnery wasn't far from Yarkand, a thousand years ago, and way up above the oasis level—yes, shuffling feet on wool. They said it happened with silk. But what's that to do with my getting too close to you?"

"I didn't mean *too* close; but for a little while I felt all of you—" He made a gesture to indicate breast, navel, and the swell of her thighs. "A tingling like I told you; it was a peculiar excitement. The first thing I knew, I'd been asleep for I don't know how long and it was good, your being so close."

"Did you dream at all?"

"Lot of the time, I didn't know whether I was awake or asleep. There were thinkings about our jade. And I know where to start cutting."

"*Aiieeyah!* We're wonderful! We kept our minds above our navels. If we could get used to sleeping that way, it could be awfully good."

With saw cuts, Ju-hai took away the waste which concealed the portion that contained the figure of the Old Man. Shorter cuts left planes which enclosed the head and shoulders. The remainder he left untouched. The nearer he came to the head shape and facial contours, the slower his work, and the stronger, ever stronger, his feeling of urgency.

Finally, Ju-hai had the Old Man come to the shop and sit at his ease, none too disturbed because of having been taken from his Taoist studies and meditation. As abrasion progressed, with grinder and with knife-shaped bamboo loaded with ruby dust gradually uncovering facial features, Mei-yu got the bedroom rug and sat watching sculptor and subject. The Old Man's expressions varied from cold killing wrath to thoughtfulness and moments of whimsy.

"Life's funny, or maybe it's people," he said as if speaking to himself. "I'd happily slice Tsao for the full thousand cuts if I could make it last so long and I'd eat his liver . . . but it comes to me that if he had let you take my place, you and I and Mei-yu would have lost a great experience in not going up the dry river. I'd ask you to compose a poem of thanks to Tsao for giving me a chance to know my son as a man to respect."

When weariness told Ju-hai that he'd reached a dead end, he laid aside the taskmaster's whip and practiced *tai-chi* figures, dance postures equally useful for training to kill with bare hands or with lance, mace, or halberd. And when the elegance of *tai-chi* became mechanical, he practiced other martial arts. Ultimately, those went stale and jade-craft became fresh again, each rest from work finally becoming work.

Abstract art—imaginative art—was far less demanding than this attempt to shape a face which in one fixed aspect gave the essence of the Old Man's character: whimsy, humor, stubbornness, wrath, serene deadliness, unwavering resolution—beyond pity, passion, or prejudice. The Old Man, Ju-hai was learning, was not a simple formula; and Mei-yu was a bewildering complexity. In two borrowed bodies, she had used each to express her own contagious sensuality—and in her spirit form, she had been no less devastating.

Something had happened to Mei-yu, that night he had rejected Férideh and the subsequent nights of her guiding him and his father to the monastery. Sleeping with her and a piece of partially finished jade had not been the ordeal he had expected.

Mei-yu's presence, her closeness, had become an emotional and a spiritual nourishment. However little sense this made, the fact could not be denied. He finally resolved the riddle by telling himself, "She's been changing and so have I; and if we're both crazy, I'm in good company."

Trying to put life into a chunk of jade which had a life of its own finally became either a way of life or simply an obsession; Ju-hai could not decide which.

There were weeks during which he quit in despair and turned to concentrate, moon after moon, on completing the unfinished work of the Abbot's deceased friend, Venerable Zeng.

A trader, one of those who followed obscure trails instead of taking the Silk Road, stopped one night at the monastery. This was one of several who had in times past bought jade. Ju-hai wondered what this buyer would decide when he appraised new pieces started by the Old Master. Though pleased beyond measure, Ju-hai was not amazed when he learned that the buyer had paid almost as much for these as he had for Venerable Zeng's work.

And finally, after months which had piled up, one after another, there came a message from Yatu, the shaman who had beaten a tiger to death.

Yatu wrote: *The town is so full of whores I can't waste time asking my spirit who put opium in the wine. If she was good, why complain? Maybe you will like the pictures. When you come to town you owe me one* tael *fifty* cash; *he overcharged me. So did the camel messenger. I was walking toward Szechuan and stopped where I used to get moon-cakes. They got a guard company, with a captain bastard and a colonel promoted to general for losing a battle. I didn't talk to nobody at all. If somebody gave her true facts, she would look happy. That is dung in the noodles. She got to look sad, and a happy one don't look that way. When you come to town, see me at my yurt or somebody else's . . ."*

As Ju-hai saw the situation, Tsao, now a general, had moved into Kwan Village to protect it and the lands against raiders. Having bought the notes which the Old Man had signed, Tsao had a legitimate interest. It would be impossible for Younger Brother, Kwan Shou-chi, to protest having a company of soldiers which, on the face of things, guarded him.

When Ju-hai had done translating the shaman's into its clear Chinese meaning, the Old Man said, "That descendant of nine generations of dung-eaters has tricked us to a finish. What thoughts do you have?"

"Tackling a company of infantry is too much for one or even two persons. Mei-yu's jade magic and whatever Taoist tricks the Lord Abbot might teach us are the only approach."

The Old Man frowned. "Time also enters the matter."

Ju-hai agreed. "It takes time for Tsao to feel comfortable, quite sure of himself—and it takes time for studying the many ways of going at whatever mode I use and figuring ways of surviving."

"If you don't outlive Tsao, that hardworking farmer, your Younger Brother, will be left helpless. You can depend on him as long as you're leading. How will you use this jade work?"

"Mei-yu hasn't been clear about it—the best way I can put it is to say that your image is going to be bad *joss* for Tsao, and it's going to breathe fumes that will disable him permanently. Seems it isn't a simple business of sending it to him—I'll have to be near at hand to start the jade breathing. But I begin to feel that he might not recognize me, so I wouldn't have to risk using a disguise."

The Old Man frowned and shook his head.

"Each time, trimming my beard," Ju-hai said, "I'm confused by the face that looks from the mirror. I thought I saw strangeness before I began growing a beard."

"That was when I told you that you were Number One Kwan."

"Head of the family, sir. A beard is essential, all the more so for my being too young for that position. I think I have become, not so much older, but simply different looking. Is it my imagination?"

The Old Man pondered as he eyed his son. "That walk upstream you and I took would mark anyone, and not just lines that would smooth out when you gained lost weight. Killing an armored prince with nothing but an arrow to keep him from getting closer—no, that doesn't put lines in your face, but things of that kind make it a different face. The eyes are different."

Ju-hai shook his head. "Old Uncle Hong looks like a

sweet little Grandmother, bland and smiling and gentle. And he can't remember how many men he's killed—like the time bandits tried to rush the village—you saw him—"

"A lot of us were with him, and we expected it. The raiders fell into a trap; butchering them was fun, like a festival. With you in the dry river—"

"Sir, that was no festival."

"Anyway, you have changed a lot. You've been chanting *sutras*, reciting *mantras* and making *mudres*. I don't say Mei-yu is a fox-woman, but sleeping with one of those ladies does change a man's expression. Being Number One Man of the family does something."

"When I get to Ch'ang-an," Ju-hai decided, "I'll talk to people I used to buy from, or those I used to see when I went with you."

Chapter XXXII

Mei-yu's departures from the monastery were as unpredictable as were her returns; and having gone as far with the Tsao likeness as he could that afternoon, Ju-hai got up from the grinder whose pedal he'd been pumping most of the day and set aside the image group.

"I'm beginning to think we had better wait till Mei-yu comes back. Maybe she can read our memories and see if what we've been telling each other is really what we used to see."

The Old Man nodded. "Meaning we may have built up something in our imagination that never existed anywhere else?"

"Something like that. It looks like Tsao; I'm sure it does. It's good work. If he had ordered it, he'd have no complaint. Only it does not have any *life*." Ju-hai pondered, frowning, looking beyond the walls of the jade shop. Finally he said, "Speaking of life, how's that Immortality discipline going?"

"I'm beginning to have my wonderings."

"Mmmm . . . dull business, you mean?"

Very solemnly, Kwan Yu-tsun declared, "Truth is, some of the disciplines sound fascinating. A man could make a life's work of it."

Ju-hai suspected that he was being built up for a surprise quip, and decided that he'd beat the Old Man to it. "You mean, the one about starting with one thousand young girls, and—"

Kwan Yu-tsun cut in, "There's not room enough even for five hundred girls, and I'm not the Jade Emperor; he was about your age when he began that discipline. But since you brought up the subject, being an Immortal is just right for the Abbot. Look what he's done for us. And he's helped other people get themselves renewed, rebuilt. But a world jammed up with Immortals would be a confusing mess, like an army with nothing but generals. If it weren't for helping people like us, an Immortal would be sitting around on his rump, doing nothing, or worse yet, trying to help other Immortals who don't need help."

"So it is not your wish?"

"Let a man do his work, live his life, and when he's comfortably worn out, it's better to die before Heaven draws back the welcoming hand. It's better to leave too soon than to stay too long when you're the guest in a good friend's house. So with life. Don't wear out your welcome.

"Death and life, each is like what is cast in the metal of a coin, a name and a date. The reality is what lies between the inscribings. Death is getting ready for a new body and a new life—and birth is the start of an interesting way of wearing out, with death the final experiment before you need a rest."

"That's what we've always believed," Ju-hai protested, "but look at Master Lung Tzu and all the experience he's been gathering for almost two hundred years now."

The Old Man grinned and wagged his head. "Your jade girl has been an Immortal the past thousand and some years. She meets a farm boy and now she's neglecting her work and she keeps her mind and yours in the same spot, which was also Lan-yin's center of interest, till Hsi-feng took over."

The Old Man snapped to his feet. Though a head shorter than his son, Kwan Yu-tsun towered majestically. "The more experience we get, the more we bog down. We get involved with each experience; we get grand new ideas; but the entire past is a swamp, a quicksand, and what we've learned is useless." He grinned and winked. "A new incarnation is what a man needs—to be a new kind of horse's arse and make new mistakes. While you and I empty that jug, let Tsao get himself just that much more involved in the Kwan lands."

Before the Kwans had got fairly started in the day's new direction, the Lord Abbot stepped into the shop.

"Ju-hai," he began, after greetings, "you hadn't been here more than a few months when you asked me whether I knew of anyone who could change the color of your mail and helmet."

"Your Immortality, I did ask. Jade Lady hadn't picked that special nugget that Father and I have been shaping. Possibly you asked Ah Yen if he knows a good armorer in Yotkan or Khotan?"

The Abbot shook his head. "What put me in mind of it was that three horse traders arrived last night—and they have one horse worth meeting. Now, your armor—only a magician, an expert armorer, or an idiot would attempt heat-treating to change the color. But a Taoist student of alchemy—that's another approach. It would be like a singsong girl's makeup, except a bit more durable. Nothing under the surface would be changed. And I have chemicals. Are you losing confidence in Mei-yu's magic?"

"Immortal Abbot, our enemy has a company of soldiers to protect his interests, and I'd feel better for having disguised armor."

The Old Man cut in, "You'd look funny, without a horse!"

"Since the Lord Abbot thinks I should meet a horse, I

beg permission—" He bowed to each. "—to quit your presences."

Ju-hai found the traders and their animals in the first courtyard. One of the trio got up from the cooking fire. Like decent Moslems, they could not, except in ultimate necessity, eat the unclean food prepared by infidel Chinese; so, without personal disrespect to the Abbot, they cooked their own meal.

After an exchange of greeting, the tall man with the long hennaed beard identified himself as Gul Mast Khudayar. The foreigner could haggle a few words of Chinese, and Ju-hai had picked up scraps of Turki, Farsi, and Arabic each time he'd gone to West Market in Ch'angan. They lost little time in cooking up a compact and serviceable *urdu*, or camp language.

Ju-hai's stumbling Arabic plus his thanks for food made for good public relations. Moreover, having swallowed their food, a morsel of mutton and a scrap of bread only a bit larger than his thumbnail, he was their guest. However they might defraud him, no decent Moslem would kill or forcibly rob a guest until at least three days had elapsed. But more to the point, even a barbarian who would not eat pork or drink wine was easier to deal with after a show of liking his food.

As a cavalryman, Ju-hai rated a low zero. However, he had ridden horses and had seen horses all his life, though he did know a lot more about buffalo and camels.

The trader paraded three Ferghana stallions—the tallest horses either Chinese or Mongol had ever seen, mighty chargers for heavily armed men, such as those who wore Persian steel-link mail and accoutrements to match.

Ju-hai looked, and looked, and squinted. He pulled a long sour face and finally wondered about one of the camels, the one with a vicious eye and a breath which kept even enemies at a distance. That the creature had come from as far west as Boukhara or even Samarquand and still looked fit was a good indication.

Ju-hai made a noncommittal grimace and gesture. As an

afterthought, he pointed to a small horse. "Maybe nice for polo," he said in a rising tone. "Or, for a one-man plough?"

He turned back to the camels and eyed a more benevolent face, that of one even more stupid than the first. Three times he bade the trio an elaborately courteous goodnight, and headed for guest quarters. His final move toward departure was accompanied by a gesture and hand sign, conspicuously obscene, implying that not far away was a woman who was restless, impatient, and in no mood for spiritual contemplation.

If a trader tried to go the limit in overcharging a man thus involved, he would surely walk out on negotiations and devote himself to important matters. Accordingly, the Iranis split the difference between what was asked and bid. Ju-hai led into the second court one benevolent looking but vicious Bactrian two-humped clod, and one small horse with a dappled bay coat which would gleam with good grooming like the upper portion of Mei-yu's tunic, when she drew a deep breath. Small muzzled, the stallion could drink out of a pint pot; he had a tremendous chest, elegant head, small ears, flaring nostrils, and slender legs— like the hooves, as durable as iron. Perhaps he had a blot or a blank in his pedigree, but that was of no matter. Ju-hai liked him and had confidence in him. With saddle and gear included, Ju-hai hadn't paid more than fifty percent above what Wind Drinker would have cost a buyer who did not have a sleeping engagement with an important lady.

This was a horse for which Ju-hai would have paid twice as much, if need be, and ridden away smiling. A farmer who respected this horse could become a superlative rider. And mounted by a rider he respected, Wind Drinker would face a tiger, and slash him to pieces with his hooves, unless the rider got home with a lance first.

Chapter XXXIII

Ju-hai rode Wind Drinker into Yotkan, where he bought several lances and enough tent pegs to fill a saddlebag. He gossipped in the bazaars about the state of the country, the caravan traffic, and the prevalence of banditry. He learned much from Ah Yen's nephew, who operated the store the old uncle had quit, heard gossip from Ch'ang-an and Shensi Province, and left a letter for Yatu:

I don't know whether with arrows from ambush or jade magic, and least of all, I don't know when, but one way or another, or maybe several ways or others, I'll see you, and you can guide me on my way home. And I bow three times . . .

In the bazaars, he bought raisins, red dates, and a jug of liquor which in the Turki languages was called *araq*— which meant distilled spirits, distilled from anything whatsoever which would ferment. Not until it was too late did it occur to Ju-hai that he should have sampled the stuff.

But the voices of even dinky Yotkan had distracted him: the wail of flutes, the thumping of little drums and larger drums, the screeching Arab fiddles, and the fascinating *pi-pa* which had come from India only a few centuries ago—a newcomer rapidly becoming Chinese.

Ju-hai rode on; and that the Old Man was changing his mind about retiring from the world and becoming an Immortal made ever more sense. But what was more difficult to understand was his own response to the minor festivities of Yotkan. Sleeping with a female shadow shape and a chunk of jade, he found his only explanation of his turning his back on the little market town far from convincing.

177

"Must be something contagious about Mei-yu . . ."

Or maybe it was something she had said, or something the Old Man had said.

On his way back to the monastery, Ju-hai followed circuitous mountain trails to return downgrade from an elevation higher than his home, which the Monastery of the Dancing Phoenix had become. There was no reason for elementary strategy—but befuddling observers or pursuers had become part of his instinct pattern.

In the course of this prowl, he found a small upland valley, too rocky for cultivation, small yet more than long enough for his purpose and sufficiently wide.

Ju-hai proposed to win the confidence of his horse and to practice riding and weaponry. After having driven tent pegs into the earth, he rode, weaving and twisting among the boulders, picking the pegs from the earth with his lance point.

He splintered one lance, after chewing up a good deal of virgin turf, without ever touching a peg. He glanced at the sun and said very seriously, "Wind Drinker, have patience. Even a farmer can learn."

It was nearly sunset when he had done grooming his horse. Then he went to the Old Man's apartment.

Kwan Yu-tsun nodded approval. "You do know how to treat a fighting man's horse. You smell of sweat, but I'll bet he does not. Where did you learn? Not with the army and hardly with your teacher in Ch'ang-an. Or did Orchid insist on being groomed after a brisk jaunt?"

"Sir, in the Lord Abbot's library I read of that Immortal cavalryman who took care of the horses before he found bivouac for his men, took care of the men before he showed concern for the officers, and considered the officers before he had thought for himself. Each soldier, each officer, no doubt took care of his own camp follower."

"Son, I hope you have as ready an answer when your head depends on it."

"Thank you. I call that your blessing for this day," Ju-hai said. "I'm glad that the officer's horse escaped that morning."

The Old Man poured wine. "I know now that you bought a good horse. And the Lord Abbot was right?"

"For a man wearing a prince's armor to ride as if he were a mongol would be good and more than good. But not to ride like a carter. Mei-yu can tell us all we ought to know about jade magic. I'm going to be busy learning how to handle myself easily when I am wearing a shirt of mail that weighs seven or eight *catties*."

He told of his private arena.

The Old Man said, "I'll go with you and watch."

Ju-hai answered, "Only when a life is at stake does such a horse carry two. He could, but it would not be proper."

"I'll walk."

"That would be improper, unless I walk with you."

So the Kwans trudged two hours upgrade and an hour downstream again, day after day. At times Ju-hai rode at the tent pegs; again, he charged at deadwood figures with straw-ball heads, half a dozen at intervals to his right, and as many at his left; and these he slashed as Wind Drinker leaped over a hip-high boulder. Sometimes he felt that he was living up to his mount. Much more frequently, he fumbled and hoped that he had not lost the respect of his horse.

One day the Old Man said, "Don't forget that you're a good archer. Don't ever forget the rider who never got near enough that morning to touch you with that fine sword you inherited."

So there was mounted archery with the deadly Mongol bow, as Wind Drinker, guided by an increasingly competent rider, wove his way among the boulders.

Halberd and mace had to be ignored.

One day, as they walked homeward, letting Wind Drinker cool before grooming, Kwan Yu-Tsun said, "Son, it's been good, these walkings. It's good to sit in our private valley, eating the stuff Ah Yen fixes up for us, and saying the old things over again."

The Old Man sighed, and his gaze shifted to far away.

Ju-hai broke the silence: "Dad, I'm glad you finally got around to telling me a bit about my mother."

"She was a lady of good family," the Old Man said. "But she did not live long enough for me to get really used to her." He sighed again and shook his head. "The more I see of your practice, the more I know that I was young enough to be a good camel-man, and too old to be a soldier.

"I'll stay home after this, and give your horse a chance to talk to you."

And so, according to what had become old custom, Ju-hai continued walking to and from his private valley. This went on and on, until the day, after grooming Wind Drinker, when Ju-hai headed toward the Old Man's quarters for the usual appetitizer snack tray and jug of *shao-hsing*, the Lord Abbot intercepted him. Master Lung Tzu's face told the story. Ju-hai was surprised; at the same time, he wondered why he had not known, ever since the Old Man had announced that he would no longer attend martial arts practice, that this moment had been awaiting its time.

Ju-hai clasped his hands and bowed to shape an exact right angle. "The Old Man?"

"Yes, the Old Man. He was sitting." The Abbot gestured to the apartment door. "As if asleep. I had talked to him only an hour previously. We'd had a few drinks and a snack."

"Immortal Master, I should have been expecting this, and I was, but still—"

The Lord Abbot inclined his head. "You feel years older, as you did when Kwan Yu-tsun abdicated. But now there is a difference."

"Sir, there *is* a difference." He smiled bleakly, and looked as old as he felt. "My late father was skeptical about magic and Taoism. He put more trust in horse and sword, lance and bow." He felt a flash of sad whimsy. "Since I am an outlaw and the son of an outlaw, should the prescribed three years of mourning keep me from practicing martial arts? My horse would not be the worse for age, but he'd lose what little respect he's had for me."

"Perhaps you remember what the almost-divine Chuan Tzu said when neighbors reproached him for drinking, beating a drum, and singing with drunken neighbors the day his truly beloved wife died?"

"Who has not read this? Old custom never dies. But I think that my Old Man and Chuan Tzu would have seen each other eye to eye, except for the thousand years between the birth of one and the birth of the other.

"Lord Dragon, I have this day become Older Generation, but in your presence, it is ridiculous to speak of old or older. There are no neighbors to be scandalized if my mourning is not according to the *Book of Rites*. You have suggestions?"

"*The four seasons come and they go, but Heaven does not speak*," the Abbot recited. "Ah Yen and Ah Lin have built a coffin. They are busy gravedigging. Take care of yourself—I'll call you in the morning."

"Lord Abbot, the newly dead do not go far away from the body. If there are any candles left, I'll sit this night and keep the Old Man company. We may think of things still unsaid."

Chapter XXXIV

A jade buyer and five pilgrims stopped at the monastery before the Abbot and Ju-hai could take the first steps toward funeral rites for Kwan Yu-tsun. Thus, unsought, there were mourners, pall bearers, and musicians. *Dew on the Garlic Leaf* was the only dirge which each of the group could sing. Customarily, this was reserved for the burial of kings and princes. The banquet came from what Ju-hai, riding Wind Drinker, could bring from the bazaar of Yotkan. He welcomed going alone, to digest thoughts which he and the Old Man had exchanged.

The Abbot played a peculiar instrument heard only at

funerals: it was of brass, shaped like a small frying pan, except that around the edge was a circle of metal, in the manner of a halo. The Abbot had a rod on the end of which was a wooden ball somewhat smaller than a dried *lichi*. By flicking this flexible rod against the bottom of the frying pan, he evoked rattlings, tinklings, whirrings and rustlings of peculiar timbre.

The mourners filed past the coffin, each bowing to the deceased and then to Ju-hai, turning leftward to face him. As *feng shui* man, the Abbot had declared that the burial site was agreeable to the air, the wind, the earth, and the water spirits. Thus assured of a harmonious burial, Yu-tsun, once head of the Kwans, went to his grave.

Then there was rice, broiled mutton, and hot wine, which the Buddhists drank because of the occasion and because they liked wine, and the Taoists, because they went with Nature, and their nature was to eat whatever would not eat them and to drink whatever was available.

Ju-hai gave to each funeral guest a small red envelope inscribed in gilt, with thanks and good wishes. Each envelope contained a piece of "lucky money." Although a single *cash* would have sufficed, Ju-hai put a *tael* of silver into each.

"A sacrifice," he explained. "Offered by one of my father's enemies. His life cost me only one arrow, and in his purse I found money."

This was poetry to the strangers, justice and truth.

Then Ju-hai gave the mourners permission to depart, which they did, going to the appointed guest rooms. Ju-hai followed Lung Tzu to the Abbot's quarters. There the latter said, "There is this to explain—that there was nothing that your father ate or drank, and he did himself no harm. He was one of those who learned that a man can step out of his body because he is tired, or because he has done all that was set forth for him to do. He told me that he would die after he had spoken to you and he had made you head of the house."

"Sometimes I wondered at his words, and at times I was dark and a little troubled, but I didn't suspect. Now I wonder how I could have failed to know. What else do you have for me?"

"He knew that you could do all that duty and honor called for. Still and all, having once been your age, he knew that youth sees tomorrow as better than any day at hand, and often to his regret in later years. But if he died soon after he made you head of the family, you would be bound to liberate the Kwan lands, to kill those it was your duty to kill, and to reward those who had dealt justly.

"He would not burden you or hinder you in your outlaw life, and he knew that the hours you and he shared here would prod you day and night."

Ju-hai smiled somberly. "I couldn't imagine anything except that he was tired, and that it would be good to stay here to study the Tao, perhaps to become an Immortal."

"That was true and reasonable," Lung Tzu agreed. "I told him I'd help him along the Way. He knew he was welcome. He had great capacities. There was manure on his boots, but none in his mind."

"And he said?"

"Better for a man to do his work, live his life, and take leave before Nature withdraws her welcoming hand. Death is getting ready for a new body and a starting over. That was his testament and his thinking.

"Before I forget, you are not commanded to be a scholar. As head of the Kwans, you will study and pass the examinations if it is possible and proper—or you will forget the entire business. I told him that you were welcome to study here. When the time comes for you to outlive charges of desertion, and compound matters with the relatives of the man whose armor you took—perhaps you could convince them that you killed him by mistake—then you could stop in Ch'ang-an and try for the Civil Service. That order commending you for filial piety and patriotism might win you a good appointment after you've qualified for office."

"You and the Old Man settled my future rather generously!"

The *tao-shih* pulled a long face. "My imagination tells

me that the further you go from here, the more you'll meet
what he and I did not cover. No doubt you have a lot to
do before you start homeward."

"Much thinking on the past, and on becoming the Older
Generation; that will occupy me until Mei-yu comes back.
And there is unfinished work that I can't even start until
she's here."

The Lord Abbot considered for a moment, and then
said, "When your horse is tired, and Mei-yu not here to
distract you, there is the *I Ching* to keep you busy."

Chapter XXXV

		With Mei-yu's return, the final phase of jade-
craft began. During her absence, he had completed the
figures; and now the taskmistress drove him relentlessly
by her silent presence.

Tsao's features eluded the sculptor. However near Ju-
hai came to summarizing the man as an entirety, something was missing. The result was lifelike, but not living.
Ju-hai's memories combined with Yin-chu's confessions
regarding the plot against the Kwans gave a confusing
pattern of amiability, kindliness, craft, unwavering selfish-
ness, and not a trace of scruple. Nor was Ju-hai alone in
this estimate. Unprompted, the Old Man had declared
Tsao to be a compound of good and evil, ranging from
one extreme to the other; Tsao wholly sincere in whatever
the occasion required or permitted. Whether malignant or
benevolent, he was a serene entirety.

Persuasive—appealing—relentless—

As with the Old Man, so with Ju-hai; he had to stand

aside from his own feelings and remain aware of the man's merit. He had to see him as congenial, one who could be a friend, and also as one to be impaled on a bamboo stake.

Fury followed frustration, leaving Ju-hai's mind hopelessly bemuddled. And then, after Ju-hai knew not how many days of getting nowhere—

"*Now I know!*"

He shouted the words. He bounced to his feet. Turning from his work, he saw Mei-yu sitting on the Yarkand rug.

"You've been shrinking from wearing the jade away too much, even by a moonbeam's thickness, and spoiling something. Your mind was so puzzled by that man, you were thinking so much that you didn't ever give knowledge a chance. Now you know!

"Forget I'm here—" She saw his expression divide between question and doubt. "If you can't work with me watching you, I'll turn my back or I'll think of something else—but here's when I must not be away. My thinkings won't go toward you. For them, there's another direction."

"But you said that thinking is a shackle!"

"Ju-hai, darling, you really are not a literal-minded clod! You're just being what they taught you to be! Consistency is the destruction of blockheads! If only they could be so consistent they'd destroy themselves! All of them!"

He frowned. "Jade Lady, shall I go to the market and buy you a nice new whip? Or just go back to work?"

His allusion to the domineering wife made each try to outlaugh the other.

He got back to work so intently that he didn't know how long he'd been at it until there came a surprise—a feeling of total aloneness. He was so mortally lonesome that he risked an eye shift to see whether in her lunar fashion Mei-yu had quit the scene.

She was there, eyelids drooped, a Buddhist image in the lotus posture; the soles of her feet upturned, her hands arranged in one of her innumerable *mudras* which left Ju-hai confused whenever she tried to explain or discuss the symbology. If indeed she breathed, there was not a twinkle of gray silk tunic to indicate motion.

He reached for another of his instruments. Concentration became so complete that he no longer was aware of concentrating.

He made infinitesimal changes, using dainty touches with greased leather dipped in ruby dust. Tsao's face, though still short of perfection, became ever more real. The Old Man was menacing as a tiger centered on being a tiger.

The sculptures changed in the way that the characterless face of youth gradually matures. Ju-hai was doing nothing but brushing away the rubbish which had been concealing the image in the heart of the Stone of Heaven from the beginning.

Finally, that day, or several, or many days later, Ju-hai noticed the grayish mists. The suddenness of perception startled him. He blinked and focused his eyes again. They were not playing tricks. Those were wisps of mist, not illusion—fine wisps which rose like smoke from a joss stick until they twisted into spirals and loops, moving as if attracted by the jade figurines. The grayish-bluish twists gave Tsao's face a suggestion of mobility. Mist swirled about and enveloped the Old Man. Sometimes it seemed that Yu-tsun was inhaling the fumes. They spiralled, they formed a helix. Finally it was as if he drank the smoke, and that he was sharing it with Tsao.

Mei-yu had withdrawn so completely that it was an afterthought which made Ju-hai glance toward her. Neither posture nor expression had changed. An unwavering thread of bluish gray rose from the vee of her tunic, going slightly higher than her head, then leveling off toward the image-group.

The expression became ever more lifelike. Ju-hai wondered whether the abrasives were making those subtle changes, or whether the fumes nourished the jade, or turned into nephrite which became part of the heart-substance of the nugget.

Bit by bit, the fumes became ever more frail until none rose from her tunic.

She looked up, blinked, and smiled.

"That's all for now." Seeing his change of expression, she laughed happily. "You've learned! Like the boy who became a burglar—the story you told your brother."

Apparently she spent much of her spare time reading his memory.

Mei-yu flicked her closed fan. "Look again!"

"They *have* changed! I wasn't imagining it."

"Of course they have! You were flipping ruby dust and kitchen grease all over the place. It's everywhere except the ceiling and my dress. How you missed me, I can't imagine."

Ju-hai sniffed the air. He frowned and sniffed again.

"You're so funny, sometimes!"

"Now what?" Her amusement irritated him more than it should have. He was far more tense than she'd realized. "What's so funny?"

"You're wondering why you don't smell something burning. Do you think I'm one of those monks with twelve pinches of powdered incense on his shaven head, meditating so fiercely that he can't feel the smoldering stuff burn into his scalp? Nothing's afire."

"Well—after all—"

Then he laughed at himself, and she joined him.

"Ju-hai, darling, you've spent all your life insisting on understanding every little bit of every little bit."

"It might help with what I still have to do."

"It might, and I'll tell you as much as I can."

"Jade Lady, that smoke did make me wonder."

"I am surprised." She got to her feet, like water rising from a fountain, and smoothed her tunic. "Don't ask me where the smoke came from. I won't tell you, not a word, not until you know."

"Go ahead and have fun! If any female creature ever rated it, you do."

And then Mei-yu relented: he'd been driven by more than he realized. "I'd settle for a reasonable guess, even if it's not entirely correct. Provided you don't ask about lunar trade secrets."

"*Tai-tai*, if a man ever could make any sense out of female creatures, he'd love them, they'd be marvelous."

"*Aiieeyah!* What an idiot you can be at times! He'd look for something new and baffling and frustrating and fascinating."

Chapter XXXVI

Day after day, though there was little difference for them between day and night, Mei-yu sat by, and the grayish mist strands permeated the likenesses of oppressor and oppressed. In the evenings, Ju-hai speculated on vaporized moonlight, and whether it overlaid the original image, as gold leaf gilds but does not perceptibly increase the bulk of the thing overlaid—or whether the emanation was jade-vapor that was absorbed—or—

The answer was a mock-slash with her fan. "Wrong question!"

Once, at the end of a very long day when they had quit the shop, he got full sight of his face as Mei-yu set aside her makeup mirror, a pedestaled thing of bronze. And this reminded him of a question he'd discussed with the Old Man, but not with Jade Lady.

"I look like . . . not exactly somebody else, but I'm not me. I recognize myself, but that's because I know I'm not someone else."

"Surprised?" She glanced up and over her shoulder. "This is the home of always-now, but even so, there is always change, no matter what tricks time plays. Simple, not so?"

"Baiting me into another wine game answer? One of

these days, you'll get off to the wrong start, and I'll be calling the penalties."

She twisted about to face him. "The simplest way would be to give a right answer—you don't have to catch me in a wrong one."

"I'd always lose."

"Of course you always lose. Can you ever get ahead of *yin*?"

"Six is a changing line," he told her, triumphantly. "And *yin* becomes *yang*, and *yang* is always wrong! Penalty, six cups!"

Slipping into tunic and jacket, Mei-yu followed him into the library, where she set out the smallest cups, no more than thimble size. Reaching for the bronze jug, she said, "Old Master, it will be awfully dull watching me toss off six cups. For you, I'll get a bigger one. These are for elderly officials at a formal banquet, or a thousand-year-old Moon Person."

Ju-hai got back to the mirror image. "Whenever I thought I was getting to look different, I had a reasonable explanation for that notion. Even so, when I ran out of logic, it hit me suddenly and brought back everything I'd explained away. I couldn't dismiss it. What do you say?"

"I was wondering when you'd begin to notice. Yes, you're right, but don't interrupt me with penalties! Your long walk with the Old Man left marks, changes of expression, not just a few lines which would wear away. So did chanting *sutras*, learning *mantra* and *mudra*, and trying to understand the difference between sleeping with me and with a mortal woman. You've been here longer than you realize; of course you look like someone different—somewhat older, yes, but it's more than just the time. All that experience is enough to account for the change."

She allowed him a long silence for digesting what she'd said. Then Mei-yu caught him by the shoulders, and there was no more whimsy in voice or eyes, "Still stubborn? You still won't let me help when you go home to Kwan Village?"

"I made all of this problem. You've told me, over and over, that I didn't act out of malice or greed, or even out of bad stupidity. But the reasons make no difference. Until I clean things up, I'm not free from that *karma*."

Mei-yu's lips smiled, but her eyes did not. "Have you plans?"

"Planning too far ahead is confusion, not help; you get set, but things have been changing. For instance, this talk about my new appearance. If I'd had a plan, my new look would call for something different. Living with you makes me look old and mankilling, so I have to be different."

"Old Master, please do listen! You've never been a standard human—if you had been, I'd never have wanted you at all! So you don't have to be a blood drinker to live up to your new face."

He gave a lion-dancer's roar. "Meet the new Ju-hai! You're building up to another of your *yin* tricks."

"Of course I am! You've never been so fully alive as since you've got used to sleeping with my spirit-body. You can't tell *yang* from *yin*, and half the time you don't know whether I'm you or you're me. You had a good horse while I was gone, but I'm sure you didn't ride to Yotkan to play around with whores or sing-song girls!"

"*Tai-tai*, what are you leading up to? The next time I catch you in an earth body, you'll get more penalties, and they won't be measured in wine game cups."

"I'll bet I can take more penalties than you could enforce."

"*Hai!* Disrespect to Old Master. Woman, just tell me what's on your mind!"

"If you'd not been interrupting me so much, I'd have told you ages ago! You could become an Immortal, and that would profit you more than anything our nice friend, Lung Tzu, could figure out at the monastery."

She meant it. This was not *yin*-whimsy and not a game.

"Jade Lady, before I say anything stupid, wouldn't it be a good idea if I knew what I was talking about? Becoming, being an Immortal seems to mean something different for each one, except that they all live forever. The Eight Immortals, for instance: that picture of them riding in a little boat—the happy vagabond, the general, the scholar, the money bags, the impudent brat of a boy who looks more like a girl, and the Beautiful Lady, almost as elegant as you are. There's your Moon Goddess and there's Tien Hou, the Queen of Heaven. She doesn't wrangle with the Jade Emperor—"

"This gets confusing! See what I mean? Talking about it leaves me in a dizzy muddle—and now you're telling me I could become one! There are the humans-become-Immortal and the always-been-Immortals."

"*Aiieeyah!* Darling, it's not as complicated as you think. Lady Chang Wo and I, we'll be always-Immortals in the next cosmic cycle, which will be in about four hundred thirty-two billion years. Just as people die, so does the cosmos; and after it's rested up it reincarnates. There's nothing that never was not, and nothing that ever will not be. The names, the forms, the faces—they change from eye-wink to eye-wink."

"Hold it before I get confused!"

"Old Master!" The dark eyes glowed with the light of great revelation, and Mei-yu became beautiful beyond imagining. "Old Master, it is so simple! You already are an immortal, and you've always been one, only you didn't realize it."

"Once I get my jade work finished and I clean up that mess in Kwan Village, we'll talk about Immortals. You've given me a lot to think about."

More and more, Ju-hai realized that time indeed was deceptive. Now that he had completed the shaping of the jade, the final polishing progressed at unbelievable speed as he worked the pedals, spinning the flexible discs forward and back; and all the while, he turned and twisted the sculpture so that the abrasive-laden leather followed every curve. He worked alone. Mei-yu was away, attending to lunar duties. Neither her presence nor her probing mind stimulated or hampered.

She meant every word she had spoken on Immortality. Looking back at his farmer life, he had moments of amazement at the ease with which he could accept her views and her assurances. He began to suspect that their nonphysical relationship had effected a basic change; and while he was not alarmed, he had his moments of wondering whether the changes in his entire makeup were irreversible.

It was not entirely whimsical when he said to himself, "Some people—Master Lung Tzu, for instance—spend long lives learning how to become Immortals—it would be a funny business if I became one just from sleeping with Mei-yu, with no choice in the matter."

When the polishing was finally done, Ju-hai wrapped the figurine group in a scarf of silk, then devoted himself to books and calligraphy until Mei-yu returned from visiting all the lunar spirits of Turkistan. As before, she surprised him, stepping suddenly from behind a screen.

"I don't know any more now than when you left." He had a flash of wondering whether she suspected that he'd been considering the possibility of involuntary Immortality contracted from her—but he shifted his thought and carried on. "All I could do was talk in circles. If I don't get killed on the way home, or after I get there, then maybe the experiences will tell me about your wanting me to join the Immortality *tong*.

"But before I saddle up Wind Drinker, beat that camel into listening to me, and get packed up, I'd like to have you listen to me recite incantations, chant *sutras*, and watch me making *mudras*.

"All it will take, back in Kwan Village—" He ran the edge of his hand across his throat. "—is one mistake."

Mei-yu sighed, but there was not the wistfulness which he had expected, nor was there the sadness which depressed him. And the expression of her face was not what he had anticipated.

"Ju-hai, darling," she began, "I don't know what the Lord Abbot is going to give you as a final counseling, but I think you'll want to know a little more about what I arranged—what I wheedled out of the Moon Goddess."

He stood there, blinking like a toad in a hailstorm.

Mei-yu caught his hand. Her touch was amazingly solid.

"Lover, I brought a surprise! Remember, the first time I borrowed Hsi-feng's body—"

"Uh—um—you mean—"

"Idiot, try it and find out! It's all mine, and—"

He cupped his hand and slapped her backside. It was as rich in sound as a ripe melon from Turfan.

"Nice, isn't it?" she said with a touch of pride. "I designed it myself, all of it."

Chapter XXXVII

After welcoming Mei-yu, the Abbot said to her and Ju-hai, "Let's go to the Great Book room. You can plan your route all the way to Tun Huang, maybe even to your home village."

"Venerable sir—" Ju-hai pointed. "The *Book of Changes*—I am too stupid to question the *Book*."

The Jade Lady cut in, "It might impose a penalty, five cups."

The Abbot chuckled. "So you've been playing wine games? Carry on then, and I'll not look at a book or pick up a brush while you're here. Young Lord, the long road home will be no wine game!"

"Your Immortal Worship," Mei-yu said, "you're very kind. Could you possibly find time to spend with us? We need your advice in consulting the *I Ching*—and we'd love to have your company."

The Abbot's glance shifted to Ju-hai. "Young Master, the Mother of Jade is here. Asking me to consult the *I Ching* is . . . well . . . like the man who sat on the riverbank, selling water."

"Immortal Sage, and with all respect to Lady Mei-yu, I'd like to have you help me."

"Lord Abbot, he's quite right. I'm so much all-*yin* that I'm bitchy, biased, emotional and unable to see more than one side of any question. My own side, of course."

"Divinity, no one but Immortal *Yin* could speak and

mean any such words. Please imagine that I've kowtowed nine times." He clapped his hands.

"Would you eat here, or in my personal hovel?"

"*O mi to fu!* This room. I love those wraparound rugs and the way they go with the pillars and lacquer!"

"A gift from a novice who changed his mind about quitting the Red Earth."

As far as one could judge from the capitals of the two pillars about which the rugs had been wrapped, the weaver had designed the pattern so that it merged with the carving and the color of the exposed upper portion of the ceiling support.

"Spread out on the floor," Ju-hai observed, "that rug would be the oddest mess of mismatched parts!"

Lung Tzu chuckled. "A bit like the problem ahead of you. A confusing mess, with nothing fitting anything else. But set it on end, roll it the long way, and each dragon is wearing its own tail and its own head, and there's the picture!"

"So, we'll eat in the Great Book room," the Abbot said. "I'll tell the cook."

At the door, Lung Tzu paused as Mei-yu added a word: "This will be a real treat. I've lived on spirit food so long I've—" She sighed. "Well, I've forgotten what it's like, real food."

From the corner of her eye, she saw Ju-hai's questing glance trace her outline from embroidered Turki hood to her gilded shoes. "One quip out of you, and I'll impose a penalty you won't like!"

"The *I Ching* never imposes penalties."

"Old Master, you're too bright to believe *that*! Read the commentary on how to present a question and how to avoid meaningless ones."

"Please clarify. I'm dumber than you think."

She realized that he meant what he had said. "Very well—if you asked: *Will I go to Ch'ang-an?*—that's nonsense, stupidity insulting the source of wisdom. Unless you dropped dead, changed your mind, or were prevented by force and power, of course you'd go! You should perhaps ask: *Will it profit me if I go to Ch'ang-an to consult the shaman?"*

"That helps. There is more?"

"The *Book of Changes* predicts by telling you, in symbolic words, what forces and powers are acting at the time you toss the coins or divide the yarrow stalks into packets. The words would have a *meaning* that depends on the problem and what manner of person is going to act. Unless you have insight and wisdom, all you'll get is nonsense to match your stupidity. In that case, you'd better ask a *tao-shih* to get the solution."

"No problem now! Better let the Abbot get to work."

"Get the book! We can read the commentary, anyway."

As he got to his feet, she caught his sleeve. "Waiting on a female Immortal is not improper. Patting her backside would not leave the hand ceremonially unclean. But no matter what you're fondling or fingering, even if it's the rosary of one hundred and eight beads, the hands should be washed as a mark of respect before you touch even the wrappings of the *I Ching*. The washing is ritual—it has no reference to the state of your hands!"

He took a step and a second, then turned about and bowed deeply. "Jade Lady, never again will I be so presumptuous as to touch any of your new body without first washing the hands."

But she had no time to impose a penalty. The Abbot and the new novice stepped into the room. The latter, a lean, wiry little man whose friendly eyes suggested that he had seen everything and was on the alert for an encore, followed the Abbot. He carried an enormous tray. This he shifted to poise it on one hand as he cleared a table of writing gear, ink slabs, and brush-holders.

He was quite stooped and moved crabwise, but with amazing agility.

"Venerable sir—is this the *young* novice you mentioned?"

"Everything is relative. Chuan Tzu said that nothing is so small but what there is a smaller—nothing so great but what there is a larger. I am three times his age. He is probably three times your age. Jade Lady, on which do you impose a penalty?"

She made a mocking grimace. "I'm hungry—let's eat!"

Here was Mei-yu's opportunity.

There was shark fin soup with a bouquet which hinted that the novice had added an ingredient not ordinarily included, a plate of appetizers, hundred-year-old eggs with a pungent sauce of minced fresh ginger, minced scallion and wine with the juice of a lime, a *satay* of lamb-morsels with a Malay style sauce to match, pot stickers, pastry shells stuffed with minced pork and herbs . . .

Then came the more serious eatings: sea slugs with black mushrooms in a piquant sauce, deep-fried steamed duck, squabs stuffed with birds' nests . . .

The novice, relieved of his burden, bowed and smiled to expose a fairly complete set of teeth. "Venerable Master, the dessert soup will be served later—tree fungus in a sweet broth."

Ju-hai picked up his soup spoon. "Your novice is a magician. This is Taoist alchemy."

"On any other day, yes. But not in the presence of my guest who turns *yin* moonbeams into *yang* jade. That ultimate magic reminds me—when the tree fungus soup is served, I'll consult the *Book of Changes*, provided you pondered your question to the limit of your understanding."

"That I have done. Jade Lady told me a few things."

Finally, before the table was cleared, the novice brought bowls, a pitcher of warm water, and damp, steaming towels. He poured water over their hands, beginning with the Abbot's. And when this was done, Lung Tzu went to the tall, lacquered cabinet and took from its top the *I Ching*, all wrapped in silk. Taking it down, he turned to say to the novice, "Leave all that's left over and freshen the tea. After which, you needn't come back."

Then he turned to Ju-hai. "The *I Ching* on the table is for study. So many have handled it that the magnetism is confused and muddled; the spirits who attend the *Book* aren't able to do their best. The *Book* is a person, not a thing."

He turned to a small table on which sat two vases, in each of which was a peony; between them lay a censer and a jade holder filled with joss sticks. "For a hundred years, mine are the only hands that have touched the *Book*. Now, your question, Ju-hai?"

"I don't ask whether it will profit me to go to Kwan Village. It may kill me, it may put me on the outlaw's way, or it may get me the Kwan lands that belong to me. But I have to go. When I am there, whatever and whomsoever I face will do things that tell me what I must do next. Whether to kill, or to ride away if I can and must, I have no choice."

He drew a deep breath. "When my duty to living and dead is done, then I must make up my mind—" He flashed a glance at Mei-yu. "Concerning what view of life should be my view, whether that of the Red Earth or the kingdom of spirits, devils, and Immortals."

"You've been thinking earnestly?"

"To the limit of my wits."

"Ju-hai, will you toss the coins, or will you divide the yarrow stalks?"

"Let me toss the coins—or is it better with yarrow stalks?"

"Once you speak your choice, there's neither better nor worse."

The three stood shoulder to shoulder and kowtowed thrice.

Then Ju-hai said, "Exalted Book, this person begs leave to speak a question. When there is no obligation to hold me to Kwan Village, what way of action or view of life should guide me?"

Lung Tzu directed, "Take the three coins from the table and hold them with one hand or with both. And toss them against the Book."

Ju-hai did so. The blank face of two copper *cash* faced up. The third landed with its inscribed face upward. Lung Tzu said, "Seven, young *yang*," and drew a straight line.

The succeeding two throws gave a like showing, and Lung Tzu drew straight lines in accordance.

The fourth throw brought three blank faces up, at

which the *tao-shih* said, "Nine, Old *Yang*, and changing!
In the fourth place."

The fourth straight line up had at its midpoint a small
circle.

The fifth and the sixth lines were like the first three.
This completed the hexagram, thus:

"This is *Ch'ien*, the Creative. The forces of Heaven are
moving. He is unwearied, he builds up his strength. Success through perseverance. But a changing line gives a new
hexagram—thus—"

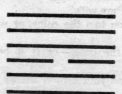

"And this," the Abbot continued, "is the operational
way which ought to take charge, after the forceful beginning. This is *Hsiao Ch'u*—the trigram *sun*, the gentle,
above the trigram *Ch'ien*, the power of dragons, the power
of heaven, working on the level of this world, its things, its
people. The keynote of the hexagram is this—the taming
power of the small."

He turned to Ju-hai. "Young Lord, here we meet *small*
and its opposite, great or large. But which is little and
which big? You remembered the words of the Master
Chuang Tzu, but under tension and pressure, will it be
easy to judge?"

After a pause, he resumed, "Nine in the fourth place,
Dragon in flight wavers over depths. This means, if you

complete your task, you win free choice. Whatever you choose, it will be right. You may choose to serve others, or you may withdraw from the earth. There is no fault, either way."

Ju-hai faced Mei-yu. In her eyes, now immeasurable dark depths, he could read nothing.

"The strong is for a while held in check by the weak. Only through the small can you succeed. The time is not yet for sweeping action. Be weak and small yourself. When you cannot be thus, let them serve you who can be so."

And this, Ju-hai knew, was all that he'd hear for the time.

Chapter XXXVIII

Mei-yu was all aglow and aflutter when they stepped into their apartment. "Ju-hai, darling, you were so blinking amazed when I told you and you couldn't believe me, not really, even after you slapped my behind and it sounded like the first time, when I borrowed Hsi-feng's body."

"I'm not asking you whose you borrowed for this time."

"Ju-hai, you're so thick-headed. This is a brand new one. I got a dispensation from the Goddess. I don't know how many billion moonbeams it took to shape it."

He set to work pinching out candles and tapers until she cried out, "Leave one or two—way over there—"

"We always got along nicely in the dark, *mei-met.*"

"But this is different! I didn't just build it, I *designed* it. That was when I was tending to lunar business."

She peeled out of her jacket and was twisting free of the long tunic when Ju-hai said, "The *I Ching* demands washed hands, even for me to have a look."

"Didn't I tell you, I had the cook bring in jugs of hot water and a tub?"

"You didn't tell me."

"I was too busy fidgeting and looking serene and virginal."

"You're superlative *yin*; you've changed the subject I forget how many times, and forgot what you set out to say. Penalty, three cups!"

There was warm wine and dim light. Then Ju-hai got into his tub, to be ceremonially proper for the wonder that rated just ahead of the *I Ching*. Mei-yu remembered the *finesse* of ritual.

"Old Master, it's all brand new, but not ceremonially washed. Do you mind if I take time?"

She plopped the new body into the tub. After interminable soaking and stretching, she reached up. "Give me a hand. The tub's awfully slippery, and I'm not used to myself in this body."

When Ju-hai turned from pinching out the remaining taper, she was in bed and in tears. Once her arms were about him, each sob was a cataclysm. Ju-hai felt that, from the beginning, he'd be right in fearing that no matter how long he lived, even if he became an Immortal, *yin*-creatures would remain riddles.

And finally, when her words were sufficiently coherent for him to understand, her clarification was the ultimate confusion; this was the first body she'd ever designed, and it would be awful if he didn't like it.

"And no use your pretending. I'd know the difference right away."

He finally got his chance when she had to pause for breath.

"Jade Lady, why not try it and find out?"

For once, logic prevailed, and *yin* approved.

When early sunlight reached the monastery, Ju-hai went to tend his horse and camel. When he returned, tea was steeping and wine was warming. Mei-yu had the curtains drawn back. She wore a long white shift with vertical lace panels and two lace spirals, appropriately placed.

"If I ever had a night's sleep like this, I can't remember

it." She gave a sigh that came from the hips; she'd found no more fault with the new body than had Ju-hai. "Old Master, your horse needs a rest after all your martial exercises! And I hate to think of your going up that horrible southern road. While I was doing some invisible prowling in the Khotan bazaar, I heard about how your army had fared."

Ju-hai's glance shifted from reddened toenails to shimmering black hair all disheveled. "I came out better than the whole dung-eating army! You said something about my animals. Yes, they do need a rest—I wish it could be till next year this time or longer, but Tsao has a grip on Kwan lands, and a private army to make it good."

She smoothed the fragile garment and drew it taut here and there. Probably she had a body more elegant than she'd had as a nun. Her eyes became dark and sad. "I'd hate to waste any of this. It's very much a special dispensation, and I'd not want Lady Chang Wo to think you hadn't appreciated it. The Goddess sees a fine future for you, unless you're killed by Tu Fans, or bandits, or disbanded soldiers along your road to fortune."

"What's this? Wasting it—You mean it won't last? It's only—"

"It's not illusion!" She sat straight up and flung back the veil of wavy hair that trailed to her hips. "It's as real as any human woman—or grain in the field—or peaches on a tree. It's form and substance, like everything lunar, everything *yin*."

For the first time, he got the full blast and majesty of *yin*. But, being super-*yin*, Mei-yu could not rest in the power of silence.

"Most of the lunar folk supervise creatures that have the awfulest *karma*, so they have to be dumpy, ugly, and clumsy. They have dispositions to match, and let's say nothing about their minds! When jade doesn't keep me busy, I supervise nature spirits, just a handful of them—there's millions of them. Animals don't have *karma* in the way humans have, so they're never as loathsome looking as so many humans. But when they're finally born into human forms—"

She shuddered, blinked, and caught him by the shoulders. "Just because I've been spending so much time with you doesn't mean that the Goddess or I or any of us loll around on our tails looking beautiful. You farmers follow ploughs, trot around emptying honey buckets to fertilize the gardens, and whine about hard work, little earnings, and high taxes; and you curse the government and the bureaucrats!"

She grimaced impishly and almost laughed. "Those honey buckets—they're incense for the invisibles who keep things going. So, Lady Chang Wo loves farmers more than other people."

"Hence you and me?" He didn't wait for comment. Mei-yu's presence was such a disturbance that it was never until too late that he recalled things he'd not asked. "How did you become Immortal—but first, the special dispensation—" He ran a sweeping gaze from breast to knee, skipping not an undulation. "What's going to happen?"

"It won't fall apart—nothing awful will happen. It won't be sudden, and I won't be caught by surprise. I'll know in time to leave before it—words are awkward—say, evaporates. *O mi to fu!* We'll be crazy-happy till you have to leave. Yes, and now I remember how I became a nun, or how I quit being one. I am getting scatter-witted! I was a cheap little imitation of Tien Hou, that Hakka girl who became Queen of Heaven. Anyway, I must have done nice things for people. But I couldn't have been more than moderately nice. Look at the job I have, sunrise to sunset, supervising all sorts of loathsome things—jade becomes almost a vacation!"

"*Mei-mei*, you sound bitter, cynical."

"You're the first one I've really felt I could talk to in a thousand years. So I'm swamping you with it while I have the chance—There is only one way you can stop me!"

"Why not eat first? It's a long time since we met such a good cook."

A single continuous move got her to her elegant, small feet, and she began warming leftovers and pouring hot wine.

"I accumulated so much good *karma* that I became

what I am now. You've been wondering about my very first body, my nun-body—well, I died, and the worms got that one. Now it's nice, making up for lost time!"

"Nothing like good *karma, tai-tai*. Does this body do more for you than . . . well, Hsi-feng's?"

"I can't speak for her, but if making love in it doesn't drive her crazy-wild, it's pure ignorance, and she ought to start studying her pillow book. One with pictures."

"What would a nun know about pillow books?"

"Improper question! Penalty, five cups."

"Improper answer! Penalty, five cups. With me leaving you so soon, nothing is an improper question except— when do we meet again?"

He took the chopsticks from her relaxed fingers. She quit the table before he could catch her hand.

"The pillow book," she said, as she drew the curtains of the alcove, "was in the nunnery . . . our book of hopes."

Chapter XXXIX

As the honeymoon neared its end, Lung Tzu spent more time with the lovers and learned of Mei-yu's moonbeam body. "Ju-hai and you, Minor Divinity, all this agrees with what I read from the *I Ching*. There are so many ways to become an Immortal—I've read, I've observed, but I've not lived long enough to know."

Mei-yu's mind turned from doctrine. "Ju-hai, Old Master, I've not made you younger. You look a lot older than when we met."

"No fault of hers," the *tao-shih* interpolated, "You've spent a bit over five years learning magic and jade-craft."

"Five years? You mean, right here? That's right, *you* wouldn't look any older!"

"Yes, five years," Mei-yu cut in. "I know it's hard to

realize that a place like this monastery has its own measures and dimensions."

Lung Tzu said soberly, "Young Master, the Empire is wearing out. What you heard about T'ang not being what it was in the old days was not the talk of disgruntled officials, or officers skipped when they rated promotion.

"Strong armies and good generals—these made T'ang great, and Ch'ang-an the richest, the most elegant, most cultured, finest city in the entire world. That barbarian Rome that used to buy our silks was once the greatest, but the citizens refused to fight and hired barbarians even lower to do what the Romans would not do. And so savages took the city and dictated the peace.

"Here in our land, intellectualists, bookworms and pacifists who spit on and despise the armies that protected them so they could sit on their fat arses and invite ruin are taking over. There'll be less and less law, more and more disorder."

He paused, and his face brightened. "There's just one hope left, or T'ang is finished, and chaos takes over."

"What's that, Lord Abbot?"

"About a thousand years ago, three kingdoms warred until one great captain beat and tied them together, to make an empire out of a mess. If one of our people does that again, we'll be great once more, and we'll beat off the barbarians and live our own true way of life. If not, foreign savages will rule and rob us."

He sighed and changed the subject. "Mei-yu, Jade Lady, you've done your beautiful best to persuade me to bait Juhai into retirement, even to search for Immortality. But until he goes to Kwan Village, meets his enemy, and destroys him or is himself destroyed, he doesn't have a choice.

"If he's destroyed, then whatever he may have done won't mean a thing. If he goes back, forgives those he can, and kills those he must, then comes the free choice, as the *I Ching* stated."

The time had come. Silently, they went to the clearing beyond the monastery gate and crossed the vegetable garden, to go beyond the millet patch. Mei-yu carried a basket in which was a bowl of live coals. They stopped a couple of paces short of Kwan Yu-tsun's grave. During the moment of silence which ensued when they halted, Lung Tzu's prediction for the Empire assured Ju-hai that in exacting a promise, and quitting the Red Earth, the Old Man had demonstrated his wisdom. He had spent his last years in summing up his life and then made way for one who had more energy and a hunger for the wisdom which comes only out of experience.

Ju-hai went to the grave and regarded the sculptured headstone with its inscription, the ideograms filled with black. He kowtowed thrice.

"Revered Father, I have taken long, but I am better prepared to heed your advice than I was the day you spoke it. I give you offerings in leave-taking. I go home then to send our enemy to be your coolie. I'll not dismember him or behead him and so make him useless. Doubtless you will flog him daily."

When he had done speaking, Mei-yu came up and set the basket at his feet, then stepped back. Ju-hai took out the bowl, fired three joss sticks, and thrust them into the ground. This he repeated until he had set out nine. Next he dipped out a tunic of red paper, on which was simulated embroidery. There was also a cap, trousers, and shoes. These he fed to the coals, a garment at a time. Finally, he burned pieces of heavy paper, painted with a metallic pigment to symbolize silver for the Old Man to spend in the spirit world.

Ju-hai set out mutton, cups of wine, bowls of rice, dried *lichis*, and green apricots in spiced syrup. Nothing was lacking except the firecrackers.

"Revered Father, I can't see how it will fare with our enemy. Either he will come to be your servant, or he'll send me to serve you."

He choked, brushed his eyes with the back of his hand, touched his sleeve to his nose, and backed off, bowing three times.

Upon their return, they followed the Abbot silently to eat with him in his quarters. They drank their tea, and he gave them permission to leave.

Sunrise interrupted the pillow talk which had taken most of their final evening. Ju-hai went with Mei-yu to the outer gate. There she stopped.

"No further, Ju-hai. If you came any closer to my refuge-cell, I couldn't let you leave. Whatever lies ahead of you, you have to cope with it yourself. This I've learned. You have a free choice—Nine in the fourth place—" She took a step, a second, then half turned, looked over her shoulder, and patted her backside. "I'll have a new one next time we meet—a nicer one, too!"

She made a choking sound and raced up the path. At the sharp twist, she turned, waved, and repeated the reminder.

He pantomimed, a caressing gesture that would have enclosed an hourglass figure; he'd accepted her promise, and he had only to live long enough to collect.

When Ju-hai went back to the second court, Lung Tzu was waiting for him. "Son, now that she's gone, let's have a bowl of *congee*. I couldn't ask her to stay—neither of you could have eaten." He ladled a bowl full for each. "Garlic sausages and dried shrimp, and who can guess what else that novice mixed in?"

Ju-hai dipped into his flowing sleeve and took out a small red envelope. "Please give this to your novice-cook. He wouldn't accept a gift. Serving me is serving you, he told me."

So they had rice gruel, solid enough to carry a man across mountain and desert from sunrise to sunset. Presently, the *tao-shih* handed Ju-hai a small purse, embroidered and very heavy for its size. "A long time ago, a guest gave me this. He arrived worried and left happy."

Ju-hai dropped the purse into his belt pouch.

In the library he put on his armor. The mail was dead black. The helmet now was copper red and matte. Its fine gold inlay had become black tracery.

"Moonlight won't reflect, starlight won't expose." When Ju-hai half-drew the curved scimitar, the Abbot checked him. "When you draw that one, let no man live to tell another what color it is."

"So deadly?"

"I read what a Persian smith inlaid in the steel. No, there's no magic; it's not charmed or enchanted."

"It was not—not for the man from whom I inherited it."

"It's most deadly, and many of its owners have had thanks and praise engraved and inlaid in its metal. See the pattern forged into the steel, like the rungs of a ladder— the *Ladder to Heaven*—except maybe among the barbarians of the islands eastward of the eastern coast, there was no sword ever forged like this."

Lung Tzu's smile proved his claim to vast age. "Remember, Ju-hai, with one arrow, you killed the great man who carried this sword. A prince on a sight-seeing, spying tour with two men as bodyguards. And you and an old farmer killed them and ate one of their horses!" When Ju-hai had absorbed that lesson and related it to the *I Ching* and Chuan Tzu's humor, which evoked laughter only from the simpleton of the cosmos, the common man, the Abbot said, "You're waiting for me to speak what I didn't wish to say in Mei-yu's presence, though she reads minds quicker than I ever read any book.

"Mei-yu is an honest female, which is to say, the kind that can cause more trouble than any conniving bitch! But with wisdom, you can keep her goodness ever from harming you. However much she wants you to become an Immortal, she would not—did not—try to trick or bait you with that beautiful body, the one she designed, knowing to the breadth of the finest hair on her body what you wanted most in a woman—she told you that you're already immortal—*that, like every other human and, for all I know, every animal, plant, or atom, you've always been immortal and always will be; you cannot ever cease to be!*

"My next point. The *Book* said that the small will overthrow the great. Remember this whenever you feel great. And don't forget this when you feel small."

After a frowning moment, Ju-hai recited, "There is nothing so small but that, in relation to something else, it is large. Nothing is so large that, in respect to something else, it is little."

Ju-hai knocked his forehead against the tiles, straightened up and remained kneeling. The *tao-shih* recited a short blessing, the fragment of a *sutra*. Standing again, Ju-hai snapped the cord about his neck, and released the archer's jade thumb ring. "I have another for the road. This is the one my father gave me for luck. Instead of being buried by drifting sand or yellow *loess*, he came here. We offer you his luck."

Ju-hai mounted the camel and led the haughty small stallion. Catching Lung Tzu's querying glance, he said, "With a long lead-rope, the stink of a camel won't annoy him. And with no rider, he'll be fresh and fierce when I deal with strangers riding weary mounts."

"To outrace?" the *tao-shih* asked with elaborate irony.

Ju-hai grinned. "To cut them down before they can escape."

He brandished his lance, cursed the camel, and rode down the Kara Kash toward the southernmost branch of the Silk Road which led to that Rome whose legions of men become clods, were beaten by fighting and warlike barbarians—who slept with the wives of pacifists, ate their bread, and, for games, used the heads of the unwarlike as balls for polo.

So Ju-hai rode alone, alert, wary, but without fear. After all, he wore the armor and the sword of a prince.

Chapter XL

Months after he put Khotan behind him, Ju-hai rode into the western market area of Ch'ang-an and made for the old familiar inn. He was tired, and so was the Bactrian camel. That revolting creature carried a burden considerably greater than he had when he set out from

Lung Tzu's monastery. He now carried the saddles, the gear and the arms of two bandits whose horses had outlived their riders. Ju-hai was inconvenienced by two Ferghana chargers, a pack animal and a well loaded donkey; and he was also burdened with experience.

His experiences on the trip began while he was riding Wind Drinker. The first of the lurkers along the South Road came from cover to tackle a lone rider encumbered with a baggage camel. He wore Tibetan armor of triple yak hide, each piece linked by brass rings to its companions. Despite the superlative edge of the curved sword, Ju-hai had a sweaty time of it, chopping the armor apart before he finished his man.

The armor, however, was good salvage, and so was the fellow's horse. "It would have been easier to get that turtle-brother with a lance," Ju-hai cogitated, as he rounded up his stampeded camel and resumed the march. Looking up, he saw two vultures circling.

"Eat hearty. Take my share, before it spoils."

Then, not far from the Lop Marshes, there was another encounter. Thanks to his vigilance and Wind Drinker's ability to scent distant animals, Ju-hai was not taken by surprise.

A rider with camel, lead horse, and donkey was worth any highwayman's effort. So the big man in armor reckoned. And the coat of mail and helmet was a temptation not to be resisted. No doubt such armor would turn the edge of all but the finest of blades.

The experienced warrior had just what the situation required: a mace, or "morning star," which would not, or need not, unduly damage the armor; the impact would finish the wearer or stun him so that he'd be easy meat.

Again, Ju-hai confronted a rider wearing a corselet of plates the peculiarities and construction of which even a militia man understood quite well.

"While I'm chopping off that bastard's jacket, he'll beat my brains out with his mace; and parrying is no good."

There came a war cry, the clatter of hooves, the scattering of gravel, and animals racing in every direction. Ju-hai wheeled Wind Drinker and sat his mount as if panic frozen. By presenting his offside to the charging raider, he masked his reaching for bow and arrow. These he plucked from case and quiver, continuing to look dumb.

The mace man twirled his heavy weapon. It looked all the more menacing that way. Since it was already in motion, there was no time lost in starting its deadly arc from a standstill. Ju-hai watched the arm swing. He caught the rhythm. He noted how the plates of armor separated in response to the man's continuing the gleaming arc of the mace.

Ju-hai whipped the bow over Wind Drinker's small ears and loosed an arrow. It struck where the plates gaped because of the twirling of the mace. The shaft sank home, and the rider lurched from the saddle.

Ju-hai dismounted and cut the man's throat, just to be sure.

He stripped the enemy, taking equipment and a handful of coins, and mounted to round up his animals and the lone rider's.

Hampered by loot, Ju-hai rode thereafter by night and lurked under cover by day. As a deserter, he was getting experience such as he'd never have gained during militia training. And being mess sergeant for the vultures was good for the soul.

Ju-hai had always been greatly thrilled, and half frightened by the great city of Ch'ang-an. Now it was almost like home as he greeted an innkeeper and arranged for the care of his animals. A bath, a night's rest, a heap of broiled mutton and bread at the Mongolian grille, and then he'd sleep himself to wakefulness.

Ch'ang-an was exceedingly important. Here he'd sell his loot, and consult Yatu, the shaman. He had to snoop and spy, learning whatever he could regarding Kwan Village, and testing his new identity as supply sergeant for hungry vultures.

His long ago friend, the jade artist who supervised half a dozen craftsmen, did not recognize him. It was not until he was back among the shops which supplied farmers and caravan masters that he tried out his story.

"I'm Hsiao-pao, surname Wong, wanting news of my army comrade, Ju-hai, surname Kwan from Kwan Village."

There had to be quips about his being quite too tall to be any small treasure—*hsiao pao*. Talk went in circles until the wrinkled old shopkeeper decided that he'd debated sufficiently the wisdom of telling what he knew.

"You said *army* comrade?"

"Yes, army comrade, maybe four or five or six years ago. Kwan Ju-hai was in the Hsien Ming Regiment. His father was a camel tender in the same regiment. The war was for punishing the people of Khotan for murdering the *amban*. Maybe you remember?"

"Yes, I remember plenty. What have you been doing after coming back from that punishment expedition?"

"When the Tu Fan people came from the mountains and broke up the siege, I was taken prisoner and sold to a good master, a caravan man trading with the western barbarians. Then he got Buddha religion very seriously and went to a monastery. He gave me freedom, one horse, and one purse of silver. So, I am looking for friend Ju-hai, for the news I can get."

The shopkeeper did not say whether the Kwans had or had not been posted as deserters. Ju-hai drifted to another familiar spot, where he told the same story. In due course, he heard that Old Man Kwan hadn't been in Ch'ang-an these past five or six years nor had his Number One Son—Number Two Son, Shou-chi, sometimes bought for the village and led the caravan, and sometimes he did not buy and did not sell.

Elsewhere he learned that General Tsao Ming-Hua led the caravan at times and lived luxuriously while the commander of his bodyguard, Captain Li, did the buying.

"Nobody likes him. Hard to deal with. Kwan Shou-chi, we like him."

"Next time you see him, tell him Wong Hsiao-pao saw his father, Kwan Yu-tsun and Kwan Ju-hai. They deserted before the army marched up the Khotan Darya. I don't know what happened to them."

"Which way do you go now?"

"Maybe I'll be staying here till I go west with a caravan. Maybe I'll go home to Szechuan."

Finally, Ju-hai went to the shop where he had fitted himself out as a student. There he pawed and picked until he had an outfit much like the one he had worn as a student.

In a bookstore, Ju-hai bought a scroll painting by one of the specialists who copied the work of old masters, offering these fine specimens of painting and calligraphy for what they were—the work of craftsmen who had practiced so long that each of his copies was as spontaneous as an original. For good measure, he also bought sticks of ink of high quality, well aged. He had not the least idea as to how aging made ink more desirable, but he had good authority.

Bundling up his purchases, he left them at the inn. He set out for the Mongol encampment, taking with him two jugs of *kao-liang*. Going to the *yurt* which had been Yatu's temporary home, Ju-hai learned that the shaman was asleep.

"What's he been drinking?"

"Whatever friends offer."

Ju-hai set out the jugs. "This is for the house. And this one is for Yatu. Please say I am Wong Hsiao-pao and will come back."

That night at the inn, he practiced calligraphy. There was a chance that being handy with a brush might pave the way for his detective work the following day.

Ju-hai readily found the home of Professor Wu, his one time instructor.

Ju-hai said to the gatekeeper, "Give this present to Professor Wu and say that Wong Hsiao-pao begs leave to knock his forehead on the tiles at that distinguished scholar's feet."

The learned man seemed no older than when Ju-hai first met him; the kindly eyes, the sensitive features, and the slender hands remained unchanged. Ju-hai regretted that he had not been able to share the scholar's achievements. After stylized courtesies, which were so natural in the Professor's presence, the old man inquired as to the happy circumstances to which he owed this unexpected pleasure.

"This fumbling person once had the privilege of drinking wine with one of your talented students. He imagined that I had done him a favor when I guided him about the markets and assisted him with his purchases. He was a stranger in Ch'ang-an, and I was only a little better acquainted. His personal name was Ju-hai, surname Kwan, the son of a landowner.

"I asked about his studies, having learned to write a little. My parents were tenant farmers in Szechuan. When they died, I made two desert crossings with a caravan. If he is still among your pupils I would like to renew my old acquaintance. With your tutoring, he should have done very well."

But first, Professor Wu had to thank his visitor and to express appreciation of the scroll painting and of the calligraphy of the verse which Ju-hai had brushed in one corner. Finally, however, the scholar got back to the question.

"I scarcely know what to say. Something unpleasant happened. Someone drugged him and his housekeeper with *afiyoun*. Housebreakers cut through the wall and got his expense money. There was drugged wine, and that's puzzling. The housekeeper nearly died. She would have, but for the healer who lived nearby. Young Master Ju-hai had taken only a little of the drug. He called the physician. Nobody knows where he went. He insisted on giving Doctor Hong his last silver." The old man sighed. "Sometimes, I've felt that he drowned or hanged himself from humiliation, despair—"

"This is sad," Ju-hai carried on. "He was like a brother to me. We met only twice, to share a bit of wine and some smoked duck and buns. But we were like old friends."

"This was three or four years ago, more likely closer to five," Professor Wu resumed. "I remember well and I remember that his father from Kwan Village, in the Tsinling Shan, never came to inquire. That is strange."

"Possibly Old Man Kwan was humiliated; perhaps grief killed him. He'd counted so much on his son's success."

Ju-hai's sadness was convincing and so were the tears

which gathered in his eyes as he thought back to his father's final days at the monastery; this evoked Professor Wu's sympathy. "I'm sure that you and my short-time pupil would have become sworn brothers if the acquaintance had continued. I thought that the housekeeper was a woman of a good family which had lost a fortune." After a groping pause, the Professor asked, "Where do you live?"

"Between caravan trips, I stay at the House of Auspicious Rest, in the west market. Maybe I could find this lady, before I go west again. Do you recall anything about her?"

The old scholar's face changed; despite his discipline in the Confucian tradition, he could not conceal annoyance, resentment or perhaps apprehension.

"Sir, forgive me. I have intruded. I beg of you, forget that I asked such a stupid question. How could a scholar remember the servants of other persons?"

Professor Wu clapped his hands. A servant appeared, awaiting orders. The master ordered tea. Ju-hai composed his features into the proper conventional form of equanimity. He'd drink his leave-taking tea, and make the most of what he'd got. There was more to Orchid than appeared on the face of things.

When the servant was gone, the scholar leaned forward and said in a low voice, "There is too much servant chatter. I don't know who the woman was. A certain distinguished Colonel Tsao—he is now a retired general—asked me to find her a household position. He said that he was a friend of her family. They had lost much of their land and their money. Do not quote me. Be careful when you look further."

He cut his remarks short. The servant came in with tea. When the master uncovered his cup, Ju-hai followed his example. They exchanged a few words on calligraphy, a few on the weather, and then the old man went to the door with his visitor.

"Be careful," he said, little above a whisper. And then, in his normal voice, "Carefulness, patience, and persistence in your calligraphy will be rewarding. You have my best wishes."

Ju-hai, going to the inn, called this a day well spent. Yet in view of the old man's warning, his prospects, three days cart ride from Ch'ang-an, were not as bright as they had been in the monastery on the Kara Kash, a few miles from Yotkan.

Chapter XLI

When Ju-hai completed his rounds of Ch'ang-an, he went to the Mongol camp where he found the shaman sober and none the worse for his binge. After greetings, the grimy Mongol eyed his visitor for a questioning moment, then grinned amiably.

"Took a long time to come back from the army! You found your Old Man?"

Yatu had not changed, though his Chinese had improved greatly. The narrow eyes, squinting from his flat face, were the only evidence of brightness sufficient to tell him to step into the *yurt* if snow began to fall. Immediate recognition troubled Ju-hai. He had spent little if any more time with the shaman than he had with Professor Wu; and there were shopkeepers with whom he had dealt twice a year, sometimes more frequently, during the several years before he'd led the wagon train from Kwan Village. None had recognized him.

"Nobody else recognized me."

"Nobody else will. For the eye, you look all different, somebody else—not a farm boy. You have lived a lifetime with your inside life showing through, you understand?"

"You talking, or your familiar spirit?"

"Me, I am talking. I see the buried self looking through the now-self. In a trance, I'm not there, my spirit friend talks, and people say my voice is somebody else's." He appeared to sense that Ju-hai still had doubts. "You are one people all the time. But—" He wagged an index finger. "You are many things, and new doings make a new face."

Ju-hai sketched his adventures; but to simplify the story, he left Mei-yu out of the narrative. The Mongol grinned and said, "This was not all desert crossings and feeding enemies to the vultures, and not all studying in a monastery. A woman has helped change your face. Don't worry too much about being picked up for a deserter. Get a new identity paper."

This encouraged Ju-hai and he changed the subject. "You must have had a good customer. When I came looking for you the first time, they said someone came in a red palanquin with four bearers and an escort of six soldiers. A mandarin?"

"A high-class whore; she weighed no more than maybe thirty-three *catties*." He made a gesture to outline a well shaped, slender female. "So you think you missed something? Not enough fancy bitches?"

"My teacher was upset and still is about the tricks my housekeeper played. The way he talked about it all, looked worried, and didn't want to say much, he must have felt that my housekeeper belonged to someone important. Your customer must have been an important man's lady. But I didn't come about that.

"Go and look at the animals and gear I have at the inn. I'll sell all except what you like for yourself. Buy a cart. You drive to Kwan Village and see how it looks and sounds to a stranger. Talk to people. Maybe someone will mention Hsi-feng, Lan-yin, or Chen Lao-yeh and his son. Don't ask about anyone by name, but do a lot of listening. I'll get a load of good wines, tree fungus, and other stuff they don't have in the village. When I get there, we'll eat at the cooked-food stand."

Yatu set out the following day. In addition to one of the

suits of armor, spoils of Ju-hai's encounters, there was
peddler's junk in the cart, including a few good things,
such as jade pendants and bracelets, and raisins from Turfan. And just in case haste was indicated, the shaman had
one of the Ferghana horses hitched to the cart.

"I'm a poor excuse for an archer," the Mongol said,
"but if a man comes at me with a lance, I can drive an
arrow through him before he can get at me."

"As long as your spirit doesn't tell you to rob the village
and race away with the loot, all's well."

Once the shaman set out, Ju-hai busied himself with
liquor and snacks and made the rounds of the *yurts*. The
stories offered by Yatu's neighbors agreed pretty much in
general pattern, and differences in detail were no more
than an expected inconvenience.

One who could read Chinese volunteered a detail not at
all surprising; the inscription, gilt on red, had stated that
the lady in the palanquin was a Prostitute of Supreme
Distinction. Ju-hai had never met anyone who had had
dealings even with a mere Prostitute First Class, who, regardless of the hour, was entitled to pass the sentries of
any quarter or city gate. Nor were these titles in any sense
advertising. Such a one was given a panel inscribed in gilt
lacquer which proclaimed her status so that she needed no
footmen with whips to gain unimpeded progress from her
home to whatever her destination, whether for shopping or
to the villa of a mandarin well out beyond the city walls.
For impeding her right of way, the penalty could vary
from a nearly fatal flogging to immediate beheading. It
depended on her client's status.

Why should such a person consult a grimy shaman? Ju-
hai felt that something about it all did concern him; but
nobody was able to guess what the shaman's familiar spirit
had told her. There had been too much whanging brass,
too many bellowing horns, whining flutes, and rumbling
drums . . . and the felt roofing of the *yurt* muddled and
soaked up the sound. Finally, no one in his right mind
would meddle in a shaman's business.

As he rode homeward after a quarter of a moon, prowling the capital, Ju-hai was certain of nothing regarding Orchid, except that he'd not heard the last of her.

With an early start, three day's cart travel was an easy jaunt for Wind Drinker, who had been hampered by the camel's pace and irritated by ignoble company. Now there was little doubt that he sensed Ju-hai's mood, sensed that they were heading into trouble, for which the horse was as ready as his rider.

Kwan Village had changed. Two soldiers in private livery lounged at the gate to exact *cumshaw* from every traveler who sought to enter. Ju-hai reined in, shifted Wind Drinker's posture, and regarded General Tsao's guardsmen as he had learned to regard all armed men: not mentioning names, but one false move and someone wouldn't be living much longer.

Very neatly, he flipped coins into horse dung, instead of into the clean dust, and he rode on, leaving the guardsmen to scramble for *cash* instead of demanding silver. Wind Drinker picked up and set down his hooves in the manner of a dancer and tossed his head, making forelock and mane ripple.

Long and dangerous days, fatal encounters, vulture feedings, and his association with a horse of noble ancestry had given Ju-hai a new ingredient, or brought a buried one to the surface; this Wind Drinker sensed. And with the gate behind them, man and horse knew that they faced the ultimate test.

Old Ah Hing, the innkeeper, bowed three times when Ju-hai rode into the court. A Ferghana stallion, three pack animals, one camel, and a cart which Ju-hai recognized, were in the area reserved for animals.

Ah Hing did not recognize the revenant.

Ju-hai dismounted and handed lance and reins to the friend of his childhood. "When you've taken care of my horse, get me a jug of *shao-hsing* and something to eat."

"Great Lord, which quarters do you prefer?"

"The less rubbish and vermin, the better."

Ah Hing shouted. An old woman hobbled from the house in the corner of the courtyard. Cells lined one wall of the enclosure. She hurried to the wine shop. Leading

Wind Drinker, Ah Hing went to a cell not far from where the shaman's cart was parked.

The place had been cleaned up. The smell of herbs indicated that vermin had been driven out—probably to other cells.

"Sir, the old woman will bring a chair."

"Thank you, and don't neglect my horse."

Ju-hai seated himself on the *kang* which would ordinarily be chair, table, and bed.

Half bent, the old woman picked her way in with heated wine.

"Your meal—I'll make it myself. Rice, yes, from the food shop. The Master takes his time, tending to a horse. When he has done with yours—that poor little animal, carrying you all day!—he'll ask you to look and see."

"Very good, Grandmother." While she poured wine, he fished a small red envelope from his belt pouch, put a coin into it, and gave it to her.

This was a gift, not a tip. Both ears and busy tongue would stay in action and she'd brief him. He knew Grandmother Ng from of old. And now farmers and their women and children were coming from the fields; familiar sounds told him what was going on.

Presently, Grandmother Ng brought a plate of chopped pork in spicy gravy and four very thin wheat flour *crêpes* —pork *mo-shu*. There was some red duck and a bowl of steamed rice.

Ju-hai had little more than done eating when Ah Hing led Wind Drinker to the door. Holding a lantern high, then low, he moved as Ju-hai shifted, squatted, and cocked his head. "I couldn't have done better myself. He looks good." Ju-hai produced another red envelope. "This is not payment. I offer you a present, with good luck wishes."

"The old woman has fed you? Do you leave in the morning?"

"I stay until it is time to go. I leave when it is time to depart."

Since the old woman had seen the book which he had taken from his saddlebag, she now came to the cell to bring a candle lantern. He decided against consulting the *I*

Ching or even glancing over pages of the commentary.
If he could not use the answer he had got at the monastery, further study would scarcely improve matters.

"Use the small, the weak, the unimportant."

But that was not as simple as it seemed. Along the road
from Khotan he had met those who seemed strong but
they had been no great problem; and of those looking
weak and unimportant, only a few of that majority could
be useful even to themselves.

He felt all manner of things crawling over his skin,
though there was no vermin in the cell; the crawlings came
from within. His horse would lose confidence in him . . .
and then he heard the scratching at the door, a most
discreet scratching.

Dagger drawn, he tiptoed and yanked the door open.

Candle flame, wavering despite the lantern's protection,
made the shaman's dish face, his sagging jowls, and his
enormous out-thrust ears change with each shift of
shadow cast. He wore a dozen faces, ironic, whimsical,
sinister—and friendly.

"I saw you ride in. But I decided to give you time to
eat."

Chapter XLII

The shaman reached for the bottle sitting between them, hefted it, sniffed it, and grimaced. "I forgot,"
he grumbled, and dug into his sheepskin jacket, from
which he took a small earthenware jug. He knocked the
wax from the stopper. "*Kao-liang*. Cuts the dust from
your throat." He slopped a dollop of the fiery stuff into the
wine cups. "You came in the right way. As if you were
going to buy the dog-loving place, if you happened to like

it. This is better than greetings and gossip with anyone at the hot-food stand."

Ju-hai nodded. "I still feel off balance. They've seen you before. They'd talk to you, and not waste wonderings about you. Before I forget it—have you heard anything about troubles in Szechuan?"

The Mongol gave him a blank look. "I remember you mentioned it before, I mean in Ch'ang-an, but what the point was, that's got away from me."

"I am supposed to be on my way to somewhere. And with the way I'm dressed, I'd be interested in military things."

"Now I remember—I was getting out of there; that was when the tiger clawed my leg and I beat the bastard's brains out. Well, there's always trouble down south; when there's no one else to fight with, those southern hotheads fight with each other. And a governor general that doesn't have a little private army is likely to get cut up before Imperial troops get around to help him."

Ju-hai nodded. "That makes sense any time; even when all is peaceful, there's likely to be trouble. So, if I get to talking to the General, I'll know what to say, and I can change the subject in case the talk gets too sticky. A soldier can always shut up quickly, because of real or imaginary confidential things—the only problem is not to say anything foolish.

"One more thing. No matter what kind of nonsense or falsehoods you've been spreading to kill time while waiting for me, you can always say that you didn't know what we'd be doing till I got here."

"I still don't know."

The pie-face looked blank and stupid, permanently so.

Ju-hai chuckled. "Pour us another drink. No human or animal can look as dumb as you can, when you feel like it. We are likely to be here until the Milky Way Festival."

Yatu remained looking very umbright.

"You probably have it in your language too. Anyway, there was a king and he had a beautiful daughter who didn't know how much longer she could stand keeping her chastity. And not a gentleman in the kingdom was going to risk taking care of her—not *that* king's daughter. She was his favorite. But there was a cow herder too dumb to be cautious and he and the girl got careless about it, and the king caught them at it."

The shaman made a cutting gesture.

"Almost that, but he was a just king; to be fair-minded, he knew he'd have to chop off his only daughter's head if he lopped off her lover's. So, he banished one to a star on one side of the Milky Way and the other to a star on the further side.

"His daughter said, 'Behead both of us, get it over, but don't be so cruel. The first thing I'll do when I get to that star is hang myself, and then you'll be sorry.'

"So the king relented. One whole day and all that night, once a year, the seventh day of the seventh moon, the lovers were allowed a honeymoon. And that day is a festival. I heard talk of it along the way, so we are going to dally around and see the fun."

"Now that you know the plan, what's the enemy doing here?"

"Collecting extra taxes that don't go into the Imperial treasury. Your brother works hard, all the time mourning for the Old Man and you, and that makes him no good for much."

"Tsao owns the land now?"

"Nobody but lawyers can answer that. It can be more profitable to own the owner, so maybe your brother owns the land and just takes orders."

Ju-hai cursed bitterly. "To protect the people?"

"He's a good boy, though everyone knows he isn't a quick thinker like the Old Man used to be. Your father would have tried doing something. You are going to do something. But brother Shou-chi is just another good farm boy."

"Captain Li—somewhere I heard he's commander of the bodyguard." Ju-hai's voice was remote. "With a hundred professional soldiers, give or take a squad or two."

More and more, it looked as if magic and nothing else could cope with the situation. He was thinking of the jade figurines rooted in a pedestal of jade, facing each other—

thinking of the fumes which had risen from the yoke of Mei-yu's jacket, to coil about and be absorbed by the figurines. Finally, there was the *mantra* to be chanted.

It was time to get away from metaphysical speculation. Abruptly Ju-hai demanded, "How's my brother really doing? You've seen him?"

"Seen, yes. Talked to, no. Nobody is happy. There's much hating that doesn't do anything." The shaman gulped a slug of *kao-liang*. "Your brother will see you soon."

He spoke as if he would command, and Shou-chi must obey.

And as the shaman stepped into the gloom of the courtyard, Ju-hai was sure that it would be, or already had been arranged. This was good. Younger Brother would do better for being prepared than blundering into a chance encounter.

Since rural communities went to bed an hour after darkness, whoever moved about thereafter would be conspicuous. On the other hand, being up well before dawn was commonplace. Accordingly, Ju-hai had been ready for Shou-chi's visit; and before the village was more than half awake, the brothers sat by lantern light.

"You've not changed enough to notice," Ju-hai said, after long groping for words.

Shou-chi poured hot wine he'd got at the food stall. He made a grimace of perplexity. "If the shaman hadn't told me, I'd never have known you. I saw you ride in, and my first thought was that another son of a bitch had come to rob us."

"That's encouraging, Younger Brother. So, I've really aged."

"No, it is something else." He passed his palms across his face, as if to wipe away perplexity. The hands were gnarled. "Your face is as smooth as when you left. It's your expression. The shaman said Father died. Maybe that's what left marks."

"Save the mourning till we can make it public."

"Killed in action?"

"We deserted. A patrol blundered into our camp."

"They got Dad?"

"Dad and I killed the three of them. That's where I got the armor. And there's other stuff I got from bandits I killed as I headed home alone." He sighed and shook his head. "I get tired of telling it over and over, but you should know what two farmers can do when they're hard pressed. You and I are two farmers. Understand?"

"There's more than three against us."

This discouraged Ju-hai, however right his brother was.

"The Old Man and I outwitted and outlasted the desert and got to a monastery. He got his strength back, but he didn't want to make the long march home. We were outlaws, and he was tired. Finally, we had a long talk, a couple days, with just catnaps at times, and a few drinks and a snack, and went at it again. At the end, he told me I was head of the house."

Shou-chi had followed the plough too long to be as quick as his brother. Ju-hai caught him by the arm before he could kowtow.

"None of that! Anyway, Dad gave me his blessing and then he died—in his sleep, I guess. A Taoist trick, walking out of your body the way you get out of a dirty robe, except you don't look for a new one. Did Yin-chu come back?"

Ju-hai had not given details of the desertion.

"Yes, Yin-chu came back and told us all about the war. Said you two just sort of faded out, missing."

"Accurate as could be."

"You said something about when we are in the clear, and taking care of the village."

"That's what I promised the Old Man. The General's bodyguard does complicate things a bit, I know that. And I'm no magician. How's the village militia?"

"General Tsao told us we'd have no more military training, and his guard would take our place, so in case of trouble, we'd not be mustered into the service."

"Sounds grand! But you don't look as happy about dodging drill and maneuvers as you used to."

"I didn't like it too much when they locked up the guard

arsenal. To make sure nobody stole the militia arms, they posted a couple of sentries."

"That was thoughtful. Nice people, yes?"

Shou-chi eyed Elder Brother, and decided that he had spoken satire.

"Then what?"

"There was quite a bit of rape, until the General got discipline back in line."

"What did he do? How many beheadings?"

Shou-chi gaped, trying to decide whether Elder Brother had lost his mind. "He strictly prohibited rape. You—meaning each of the guard company—pick yourself a girl and you do not touch anyone else's girl—or it's your head."

Ju-hai pounced to his feet. He got Younger Brother by the shoulder. "Who got Hsi-feng?"

"Nobody."

"*O mi to fu!* You mean—she's—dead?"

"She's crazy and nobody wants her. A crazy girl is hard luck."

Ju-hai sat down, a slow crumpling which just kept him from falling. Elbows on his knees, he held his head propped up, to keep it from drooping too low. Finally, he looked up and demanded, "What happened? Did she just get that way? She said she was pregnant that night I came back to find out about the Old Man. Was she really?"

Shou-chi nodded. "She had a miscarriage. And when the troops came back, with you and the Old Man missing, she went blank, looking and seeing nothing. She tends to housework, does it as if she was blind. She doesn't bump into things, but doesn't see where she's going."

"You said something about a Captain of the Guard. Is that the Li who commanded Dad's company?"

Shou-chi nodded. "He came back with the army."

"That's grand." Ju-hai was now smiling. "That's awfully nice."

"They say he's a dog-dung bastard."

"I didn't say he was not, Younger Brother." There was a moment of silence, broken only by the gurgle of wine from the jug. "How's our girl making it these days? I mean Lan-yin."

Shou-chi's voice was nearly a snarl. "I couldn't keep her in the family. Neither could her husband."

"What's wrong with—what's the matter?"

"General Tsao."

"General Tsao?"

Shou-chi nodded. "Tsao had his pick of the girls, but young concubines were too much for him. You can guess how women talk, and it must have embarrassed the old bastard. He sent to Ch'ang-an for stuff from the herb doctors and the doctor sent along a girl whose specialty was elderly officials. A Taoist doctor had taught her some of the Immortality promoting tricks and how to rejuvenate lovers."

"You mean like that woman in the *Prayer Mat of Flesh?*"

"I don't read much, but it's probably something like that. It worked fine and he wasted no time with farm girls."

"Where does Lan-yin come in?"

"The city concubine said she wouldn't live in any dump like this village."

"Talked that way to a general?"

"There were higher ranking generals waiting for her and she lost no time going back to town. To save face, he promoted our girl to be Number One Concubine."

"That son of a bitch! How long's that been going on?"

"Couple or three weeks before you showed up."

"How's it working out?"

"The General looks happy."

"Her son's pretty nearly your age. That doesn't add up, not a bit."

Shou-chi shook his head. "Our girl never gets old. These days, she's looking younger than you."

"While I was away, I used to wonder how long she'd manage to stay young . . . it begins to make sense."

Sunrise brought the crowing of poultry, early morning bird chirpings, and the mutter-grumble of buffalo and camel. Shou-chi got to his feet. "To keep things looking natural, I'd better show up where I usually am. What about you? You look as if you started thinking."

Ju-hai grinned, but not good-humoredly. "An idea was building up while you were talking. Maybe I can make something out of Tsao's taking her away from home and moving her in with him. Having her drop in for a night's fun and games, well, that's a tradition, and it's just a change of name and title. But by making it full time, the whole village loses face."

"Didn't take you long to figure that one! The way I saw it, she was kind of a member of the family. Turn and turn about, each of us figured her an honorary sister-in-law. But it was beyond my doing anything about it."

"Don't let that worry you. Let's find out ways of my having a talk with Chen Lao-yeh and their son. I'll get them to see that a tradition is one thing, but taking a married woman from her family is going too far. Younger Brother, you hustle away to work, and I'll do some thinking about details."

Chapter XLIII

Yatu, slouching carter or grimy shaman, had become a massive Mongol warrior, fully armed. As he rode with Ju-hai from Kwan Village and into the higher slopes, he explained, "I bought back some of the gear I sold for you in Ch'ang-an. Stowed it in the cart. A friend, he kept the horse at the edge of the settlement."

"Your spirit tell you something?"

"Common sense usually needs no spirits. Nobody in his right mind goes around unarmed. Be a good idea if we camped outside the village wall."

"You've been hearing things?"

"You Chinese are used to being screwed by the government. Back home, we don't get robbed. When the *khan* gets out of line, we kill the son of a bitch and elect a new one, and taxes drop right away. But the farmer clods aren't used to what's going on now, and they're good and sore. Until you people go killing crazy, you're not much good for anything but ploughing and wading in mud mixed with manure."

The shaman was too right, though Ju-hai could have given him interesting footnotes on history. "Meaning, practically no chance they'll break into the militia arsenal and massacre Tsao's bodyguard while they're asleep?"

Yatu muttered and mumbled, then got to articulate speech. "The buffalo pulls a plough all day and a kid rides him home for fun in the evening. That buffalo is nasty as a tiger and lots heavier. Only, try to get the clod to feel like a tiger. Now, you and your old man did well enough when you tackled something like three cavalrymen and killed them. That kept you feeling deadly, and before you reached Ch'ang-an, you got to be a good mankiller. But the two of us aren't enough for this mess.

"We might get Li and Tsao fighting each other."

The Mongol eyed him sharply. "I did hear that Captain Li is sore because he didn't get the promotion Tsao told him he was sure to get. Tsao getting boosted to general was what did it."

Ju-hai followed a trail which entered the wooded heights. Once it cleared the first ridge, it descended to a little valley. Here and there, gaps showed where woodcutters had been getting fuel.

"Good land," Yatu observed. "You ought to see what we put up with back home. Making our living's so hard that war's a vacation. This valley's good. Look at that creek." He pointed. "This bottom's nice land, only there are quite a few rocks."

"You sound as if you're going to settle here!" Ju-hai grumbled, as he reined in.

"Someone's going to want this land. The country's going to pieces. A hundred years and no wars, with not enough people getting killed off, so everything's crowded and getting worse. Not enough plagues, not enough famines, the climate's too nice, and there are too many people."

"You find fault with everything."

"Fact's a fact, no matter where you find it."

"Spirits again?"

"Common sense. Why did those Tu Fans come down out of Tibet and drive the army away from Khotan? Because Chinese armies are no good, not the way they used to be. The officers headed back to Ch'ang-an and pretended they won—and got promoted, so the bureaucrats wouldn't lose face. All nice until someone starts a revolt and what used to be the fighting T'ang will be running afoot, no horses left."

"No horses?"

"No horses—the Mongols or the Manchus will take them and the country, too. They got no bureaucrats. They'll climb over the Great Wall or knock it down, or buy their way in. I guess it won't be in your lifetime."

Ju-hai gestured and cocked his head. "Someone's chopping wood, quite a piece upgrade. Which is what I expected. Let's get to work. You keep the sun behind you—I have to get used to glare in my eyes again."

He wheeled Wind Drinker.

"Better take turns with the light. Where's your mace?" Yatu asked.

"Kept it out of sight—we're sticking to lance, sword, and bow."

The Mongol protested, "The way you nailed that mace man, you don't need arrow practice."

"I don't need mace work—I kept my arm in shape all the way home. Don't even talk about the mace. I'm keeping it hid. I don't want anyone to suspect I've got one."

He took off for his end of the boulder-cluttered valley.

They were using blunted heads on their lances. They had appropriated drill swords from the village militia armory. Each, however, had brought a combat blade and a combat lance.

At Ju-hai's shout, the lancers made for each other, weaving in and out among the boulders in a nasty pattern. Swaying in the saddle, Ju-hai prodded Yatu. Each wheeled and returned to renew the assault. This time, Ju-hai put his agile mount to the test. He pivoted Wind Drinker on the rear quarter and evaded the attack, with no attempt at countering. He did this over and over again, with each pass evading the rider on the larger horse; and each time, he was coming nearer. When they set to work with swords, Ju-hai evaded instead of parrying—and in passing, he clipped the shaman with a nearside *moulinet*.

The Mongol grumbled, "Neat work, but no force, I hardly felt that one."

"We have to try every way. With a curved blade, a drawing cut makes up for the light impact."

Despite Wind Drinker's agility, Ju-hai began to learn that the shaman was seeing through his tricks; Yatu was better than he looked.

"See what I mean?" He paused and they rested the horses. "I had to parry the last two. You were catching on—but when it's for business, the other fellow doesn't have time to learn. By the way, we'll use war arrows for the next course."

"You don't have to wear mail while you're testing it."

"What I'm testing is myself. See how close I can be, and still duck when I hear your bowstring."

"If you think I'm playing games like that for practice, you're crazy."

"I'll use drill arrows. But once, anyway, shoot a war arrow so you'll hit a boulder. Make it a near miss, just in case someone is watching our show."

Yatu frowned but said nothing.

Racing after Ju-hai, who wove in and out among boulders that were as high as his horse's withers, the Mongol loosed shaft after shaft. Ju-hai ducked at the twang of the bowstring. The arrow whisked past. The next shot, from longer range, he snatched in flight. Wheeling to charge at his partner, he repeated the trick; and he neatly deflected a shot with his shield.

Finally Ju-hai decided that they'd practiced sufficiently.

"We'll pick up the arrows," he said. "All except one war arrow. And don't leave a single one of the blunt ones."

Once the drill ground was clean, they rode back to the village.

"We'll be coming back tomorrow, and the next day. If anyone asks if we went hunting say that we are hunting for work with some provincial governor who wants a platoon or a company of guards, enough to stave off trouble till Imperial troops can restore order. And remember, we are heading south, where there's always trouble. If we find a good spot, we'll have to prove that we're good."

By lantern light, early in the morning, Ju-hai was busy twirling his mace until Younger Brother came into the room. He brought a pot of tea and a jug of *shao-hsing*.

"Was anyone chattering about weapons practice, in the rocky valley, yesterday? Yes? Did you offer any words? What did you say?"

"I said I guessed you were a professional looking for work, but if anyone wanted to know, all he had to do was ask you and you'd tell him. Anyone ask you, yesterday evening?" And after a pause, Shou-chi chuckled. "I was kind of sure nobody would risk it. How'd your piece of meditating turn out? I mean about the Chens and Lan-yin living with the General."

"It's going to take some neat talking, and you've got to do the most of it."

"Why me?" Younger Brother countered.

"Because I am a stranger and I hope to stay that way for a while. When people start itching to hear all about my plan for being commander of a governor's guard somewhere in Szechuan or Kweichau or Kwangsi—tell it different each time, and that will make them all the itchier to get the straight of it. Then you can invite a few of your better friends and tell them you fixed it up for snacks and drinks—with you buying them, naturally. But be sure you get Chen Lao-yeh and that young son of a bitch who tried to knock me off with an arrow. Unless you get the Chens, no party. That's the first move you've got to make."

"What's the next?"

"Again, your move. Chen's had all the militia drill the rest of us had, and I've always heard how he once went on a campaign and fought a couple of times, when he was about our age or younger. So you and other friends get him started on what a warlike fellow he used to be.

"I think I told you how they mocked Chen Yin-chu about his mother dying of lonesomeness with two thirds of the Kwans away from home. When I bounced up when he came to see if I were dead, he nearly died and he begun talking. He claimed Tsao had talked him into doing it. It was probably true, but I knew the mocking—you know what bastards soldiers and schoolboys can be—did get him in a murder mood, just to show them he was a tough character. He figured it would be easier to settle me than to tackle the whole dirty pack that was tormenting him.

"Anyhow, you start it. You've got to start it. You can say things that would get me mobbed or run out of town. I'd be insulting the town and that's what I can't afford to do."

"What are you figuring on saying?" Shou-chi challenged.

Ju-hai smiled sourly. "I'll say things that a stranger could say, not knowing he's stepping on the toes of home folks. I can say things because I am a stranger—the things you couldn't say, because you're a villager. That will take studying out."

"What are you planning to do?"

Ju-hai sighed. "You don't have any imagination, Younger Brother. If this works right, there's a chance of getting battle-seasoned Chen Lao-yeh challenging General Tsao for snatching Lan-yin and making her his Number One Concubine."

"*O mi to fu!*" Shou-chi shrank from the very idea. "You can't!"

"Younger Brother, *we* can! And if you and I cannot make that work, I'll figure out some other way of getting Captain Li killed in a duel—with luck, I'll be the new commander of the guard and I'll finally get at General Tsao."

The magnificence of the idea left Shou-chi dazed. He took a final gulp of *shao-hsing*, and went out to be a farmer again.

Chapter XLIV

     Now that the martial arts program was moving, Ju-hai undertook a more difficult and uncertain enterprise—getting an audience with General Tsao. It began with a present to the gatekeeper of what was now known as the *yamen*, a designation appropriate enough, but which infuriated Ju-hai because the governor's house, official residence, palace or whatever designation might apply, was where the Kwans had lived for three centuries; and of course it included the pavilion above the gatehouse, that overdone imitation of the gatehouse of Kaifeng. The grandiloquent ancestor had unwittingly built to accord with a couple of centuries of Kwan Village growth, and thus had designed it to be not too cramped for the usurper.

For the great man himself, once the secretary had been taken care of, there was an almost austere teapot and cups which Ju-hai had bought while prowling the jade workshops of Ch'ang-an. The unprettiness, the stark simplicity of the thing, and its dependence solely on contour, since it was devoid of floral gimcracks designed to conceal blemishes in the jade, made it a man's gift for a man, if of course that man were endowed from birth with good taste —that which a mandarin might lack, and which a farmer might have.

Ju-hai now had only to wait through each audience period, from sunrise until noon. During this time, overseers reported to Tsao. Clerks submitted reports, or brought their account books. At least once a day, a courier brought news from the capital. Although retired from the armed forces, Tsao remained subject to the Bureaucracy. To keep himself feeling at home, even in the foothills of

the Tsin-ling Shan, he had created a miniature Bureaucracy to complicate the life of Kwan Village.

For at least five consecutive days, Ju-hai sat in the outer-
most anteroom. He saw the same procession of steadies;
and always, there were one-time visitors, some of them
military men pausing for a bit of hospitality before moving
along to an eastern or a southern province. But there was
no monotony. Ju-hai sat in the posture of Taoist meditation.

When noon came, he ate and then rode with Yatu for
martial arts practice.

To maintain interest, he offered first the gatekeeper and
then the secretary an appropriate gift, to each according to
rank, and to each in coin.

His time was not wasted. Sometimes the posture of
meditation disguised the fact that he was cogitating on
lines he should speak when Younger Brother or any other
villager spoke such and such contemplated words, in response to words which Ju-hai would utter as he offered
wine and snacks to friendly villagers . . . such as Chen,
father and son. This went on and on.

Then came another return from martial arts practice; he
had scarcely taken off his helmet when the General's secretary came in haste and unstateliness to present respects:
"His Excellency, General Tsao, commands me to offer
expressions of esteem, and to say that he hopes you will
give him the pleasure of your distinguished presence. He is
especially interested in your martial exercises. He would
be honored to have you call on him at the *yamen*. Please
appear informally."

"How soon may I pay my respects?"

"At your earliest convenience."

"Tell his Excellency that I bow three times." And then,
as he watched the secretary clear the courtyard entrance-
way, he said to the shaman, "Mentioning our warlike
games makes it certain that something else touched him
off. He knew all about our practice from the start; you can
bet on it."

Yatu made an inarticulate sound intended as a question.
Ju-hai resumed, "This morning after the regular courier

came and went, there was a strange courier. He wore livery—riding for an important man."

"Maybe like the important whore who came to hear the spirit?"

"He wasn't wearing an identification plaque. Maybe he was too important to need one. His business didn't take long, and he mounted up right away and rode. I heard the hoofs, but not for long. He rode hard."

The Mongol tugged at the lobe of an out-flapping ear. "If the General talks about the courier business, you'll know what he wants to fix up is something else." So saying, he went to take care of the horses, and Ju-hai cleaned up and dressed for the informal interview with Number One Enemy.

The anteroom of the *yamen* was deserted. In the audience room, the secretary who had summoned Ju-hai was at his worktable, engrossed with a stack of papers. He was on his feet before the visitor had a chance to observe more than that a once-familiar room had been so refinished as to make it utterly strange.

"Honorable Wong Hsiao-pao, his Excellency will receive you at once." He made a bow and a gesture. "He is in the private conference room."

Ju-hai entered a study whose apparent size was reduced by bookcases and tall cabinets which lined two of the walls. A pair of three-leaf screens, folded back, withheld all but hints of Soaring Dragon and Dancing Phoenix, but gave a view of a court which had been much dressed up since Ju-hai had last seen it.

The old pool had been beautified by new and good rockwork and a red lacquered bridge. The latter crossed the far end of the tiny lake and descended to a walk which lost itself in willows.

During his ninety-degree bow, Ju-hai reminded himself that he must avoid betraying any awareness of how old familiar things had been changed.

"Your Excellency, Hsiao-pao, surname Wong, is flattered to have the opportunity of paying respects."

"Honorable Master Wong, forgive the abruptness of my invitation!"

There was that same old time affability of the kindly man who never did anyone an injury until he had a deputy to inflict it; however, five years or so had aged Tsao. He no longer carried himself as he had during his final months of active duty. Although by no means overweight, his jowls sagged and the front of his persimmon-colored tunic was not as sleek as it once had been. The clasp—it was mutton fat jade—of the girdle accented a bulge at the waistline. There were bags under the benevolent eyes, with their smile which seconded that of the broad, amiable mouth; but men even twenty years younger might be as puffy under the eyes.

Tsao's scrutiny of Ju-hai had been keen and it remained so, as he appraised his visitor and nodded approvingly. "Let's not waste time about the place of honor. We each know very well you can't escape it! Please be seated."

The General chuckled, gestured, and glanced about him and into the court. On a writing table almost free of papers was a brush holder, an ink slab, and sticks of exceptionally choice ink. A column of grayish lavender stone at least two inches square and half a foot tall rose from a receptacle sufficiently deep to hold it steadily in place. The upper end of this chop was shaped in the likeness of a lion's head, stylized to accommodate the palm of him who impressed the seal on painting or document. Right at hand was a sculptured stone receptacle little larger than the seal; it was filled with silk floss saturated with a red pigment whose purplish tinge made it nearly carmine, though it might without error still be called crimson. Wall spaces between bookcases were filled by scroll paintings. Each had been chopped by the same seal.

"Ah . . . your Excellency's paintings?" Then Ju-hai's glance shifted. "Hsi Wang Mu's mountain home?" Ju-hai had learned a good many things at the monastery, so he ventured another touch. "An unusual, striking treatment."

In front of the enshrined image of Kwang Ti, God of War, a joss stick was burning into its final third.

Ju-hai carried on, "Sir, nothing is lacking but retired comrades, practicing calligraphy, speaking of campaigns long past." He sighed, slumped comfortably. He was not amazed at his enjoying the company of this man whose doom had been planned well up the Kara Kash, in a monastery near Yotkan. He did not attempt to repel the sadness which took charge as he recalled his mission. "If ever I live long enough . . ."

Ju-hai recalled Nestorian missionaries in Ch'ang-an, competing with Allah-crazed Arabs who conquered whomsoever they attacked. The Nestorians, who seemed to be Buddhists whose brains had been beaten out or upset by drugs or drink, had spoken of a saint who declared that one should love one's enemies. This no longer seemed as insane as it once had seemed. He'd misunderstood . . . what they must have meant was, *Never blind yourself to the talent, the gifts that your enemy has. Don't let his goodness go to waste. Let him express it until you are obliged to kill him . . . Maybe that's why Tsao has a deputy to do his injuries to others. He and I, we have something in common.*

There was no sense of having lost time during his reverie. Tsao was saying, "The Way is better than the end of the Way, except when the Way is endless."

"Your Excellency sits on a windswept summit, at the same time reclining in a sheltered valley," Ju-hai submitted, offering paradox to cap a paradox; he had an instant of wondering when Mei-yu would intervene to impose a wine penalty on him and on his opponent.

Tsao reached for a brush, glanced sharply about, and replaced it. "If I were truly retired, I'd grind ink, and thank you for your words." He clapped his hands; when the secretary entered, he said, "Have someone bring us wine." And then he turned to his visitor. "The poem I visioned would relate to an old soldier sitting with a younger military man, drinking *shao-hsing* in a courtyard, looking into a court, perhaps, late of an afternoon. Thus:

> *"Each envies the other.*
> *One has fought his last war.*
> *The other has many to fight . . ."*

Ju-hai was thinking, *He's genuine—a genuine bastard, genuine poet, genuine companion.* And Ju-hai extemporized:

> "One with little past looks forward at hallucination.
> One with much past sees old achievement
> No longer shrinking from future error."

Each regarded the other appreciatively. Each bowed, the envier to the envied. If this were in the monastary on the Kara Kash, Ju-hai reflected, what would be the contribution of Lung Tzu, and on whom would Mei-yu impose a penalty, and for how many cups?

A servant came in with hot wine.

Tsao turned from long ago memories to the present he had quit for a little while.

"Your martial arts interested the woodcutters in the hills, and their stories interested me. May I ask what your rank is?"

Once the serving maid filled the cups and quit the room, Ju-hai answered, "I have no rank, and never had. I was a guard until bandits looted the caravan and included some of us with the plunder. This was on the southern route, somewhat east of Yarkand, where I and others were sold as slaves.

"The master was a Farsi trader who quit his native country to get away from the Allah-crazed Arabs and their *joss*. He traded several years and then converted to the Way of the Buddha—cut his hair, put on the yellow robe, and became a monk. He was old and tired, so he gave me my freedom, his weapons, and his horse. Riding alone, I got experience along the way."

Tsao nodded and smiled. "As did those you met—but didn't live to profit by it."

"Along the way, I heard that there are troublemakers in Kweichau and Kwangsi. Prefects and governors recruit bodyguards to keep things quiet until the Imperial forces can take a hand."

"You have a prospect?"

"I have no prospect and no promise of anything so far."

"You sent your card and asked for an interview."

"Your Excellency already had a guard company and a commander. All I hoped was that you'd be so kind as to offer suggestions. Or if you considered me competent, you might recommend me to some friend?"

"Before I go into rambling opinions—" Tsao indicated the agate-topped tabouret on which sat the teapot and cups which Ju-hai had left for the General when he first requested an interview. "I apologize for my delay in thanking you. The austere elegance is as impressive as your archery and horsemanship."

"I must beg leave to abstain from comment on my archery. And my horsemanship—sir, my horse gives me that—that which he inherited from a hundred generations, perhaps five hundred generations of noble ancestors. As for the teapot—I bought it before I had the slightest idea of offering it to a retired General. Your mention of it is embarrassing."

Tsao refilled the cups. "Before I give suggestions on events and people in the southern provinces, I must tell you that I called you to do me a service."

"This I cannot imagine! Please clarify."

"Possibly you could stay another ten days?"

Ju-hai got up and snapped to attention. "At your command, sir!" He resumed his chair. "In fact, I could stay until after the Milky Way Festival, at least a few days. How could I be of service?"

"His Highness, Prince Han Ta-yu, the Minister of War, will soon visit me, to wish me serene retirement. But for him I would have been retired as a colonel. This is my first opportunity to show my appreciation. I wish you to be one of the guests come to honor his Highness. All the local landowners and tenants will be invited to the banquet, so I should have a few military persons, other than my guard and commander."

"But this poverty-stricken person owns no land, has no rank."

"You need no rank to qualify as Honorary Aide-de-Camp to his Highness. You have presence and bearing."

"General, that's—that's impossible! I have no rank. For an aide-de-camp, he should have at least a colonel, perhaps a general officer."

"This is honorary. Rank is immaterial."

"But with so many local landowners, it would be inappropriate, your skipping them and appointing me, a nobody from nowhere."

"Young Master, no matter what landowner I appointed to be Honorary Aide-de-Camp, there would be resentment and jealousy. You don't realize how these rustic minds operate! Each clown would rather see you, an outsider, accorded the honor than see any of his neighbors get such a distinction."

"Sir, I begin to understand." Ju-hai frowned. "Now I remember! You have a captain of the guard, no doubt an outstanding soldier or you'd never have appointed him."

Tsao shook his head. "When one has a guest no more than two steps short of royalty, the commander of the guard must have his mind wholly on his duties, thinking only of security. Captain Li will not attend the banquet. If I commanded him to appear, he would not obey. He'd resign his position; he would not compromise his duty."

And then the simple, the self-evident thought finally came to Ju-hai. "I beg of you, spare me embarrassment! The first thing an officer of high rank asks when he meets an inconsequential person making the slightest pretension to having had military service is something to do with his regiment, his campaigns, the theaters of operation. I'd wallow in stupid falsehoods, giving absurd answers. I'd be most of all embarrassed because of embarrassing you."

Tsao pulled an exceedingly long face. "You sound as if you had met his Highness! The very things he always asks. And if you hadn't told me why you had no rank, I would have posed questions of the same kind."

"Your Excellency, there was some other mission you originally had in mind as your reason for asking me to call on you. Perhaps something suggested by your hearing of my archery or horsemanship?"

"The message from his Highness the Minister of War," Tsao temporized, "has scrambled details more than you realize. I'll bear it in mind and, once I've reviewed my plans for the banquet, we'll start all over. Your reminding me of the hazards of appointing a Honorary Aide-de-Camp suggests that I should be deliberate in my decisions on this banquet."

Ju-hai was now certain that Tsao's original task was related to the Minister's visit and that nothing had changed except that Tsao wished to review something which was not as complete and well detailed as he had believed. It was time to get away.

"Sir, before I beg leave to cease infringing on your time, there is a question. By now, half the village knows that I have had the honor of an interview. Already, a handful of villagers know that you will have a banquet in honor of his Highness, Prince Han. Be pleased to tell me what is to be said and what is not to be said. If I rely on my scattered wits, my attempts to evade questions are likely to embarrass you."

"You may say that when his Highness, the Minister of War, arrives there will be a banquet which will be attended by all landowners, all tenants, and by as many from nearby villages as wish to attend."

Chapter XLV

Before daybreak of the morning after Ju-hai's talk with Tsao, Younger Brother came to the inn for another briefing. Eagerly, he demanded, "What did he have to say?"

"Every landowner—and you're one, in theory—all the tenants—everyone is invited to a banquet for the Minister of War, his Highness, Prince Han. And that includes nearby villagers who feel like showing up. The General's obligated to the Minister, and the bigger the crowd, the better."

"This martial arts business you and the shaman have been practicing—that was supposed to give you an opening to try for a job as commander—well, vice-commander —second in command of Tsao's guard. Captain Li was to get suspicious and start making trouble so it would end in a quarrel and you'd settle him."

Ju-hai nodded. "That still is the plan, but I couldn't get at it, not yesterday. I did lead up to it, asking his advice for getting guard duty with some official in Kweichau, for instance, but the banquet business took over."

"And you're still interested in needling Lan-yin's husband to a fighting mood?"

"That's right."

Younger Brother threw up his hands. "I'm getting so confused by it all I don't know whether I'm the buffalo or the ploughboy. And now there's a banquet!"

"I didn't invite the Minister of War. But something about that visit got Tsao interested in me—something Tsao wants to use me for, wants me to do for him—probably against someone else. But the more I can stay mixed up with Tsao and his doings, the better my chances are."

"I still don't see why getting Chen Lao-yeh fighting mad is going to help."

"Nobody has got him that way yet. Maybe no one and nothing can get him that way. But if Chen speaks up at the right place and right time, and makes the matter public, it would embarrass Tsao. Chen's a landowner, and our girl wasn't a slave or a tenant's daughter. Remember how Tsao maneuvered to get our Old Man off the scene? He didn't want to risk doing it openly. Dad was a landowner."

"I begin to see what you mean—just become a pest and troublemaker, like a drought or a flood or locusts—and if enough landowners got excited, they might gang up on the guard?"

"He wouldn't have a guard unless he figured he needed one," Ju-hai said, and abruptly changed the subject. "The

Milky Way Festival looked like the best time. The Minister's visit just speeds things up a little. Let's get that wine party started as soon as you can get it moving, and news of the banquet will make everybody want to hear about who's invited.

"Chen always did like to talk about his war experiences and about what he did in two battles. Get him on that subject. A few nips of *kao-liang* will do it; and when he's built himself up as a fighting man—which he was—the next move's easy. A lot of good soldiers back down when there's battle at home. Chen's girl in the village a few miles from here is his answer to Lan-yin—nothing to do but get him talking war."

Two evenings later, Ju-hai had the dining room of the inn readied for landowners and whatever other local people his brother had invited. Ah Hing, the innkeeper, the Old Lady, and the keeper of the food stand had teamed up to supply broiled mutton, roasted duck, dumplings and buns stuffed with diced meat and herbs, and, for good measure, many of the snacks usually served at midday, as *dim sum*.

Ju-hai wore his plumed helmet and a scarlet jacket which revealed the shirt of mail beneath it, although the linked steel coif of his headgear would have sufficed. Shou-chi had told him, "Sure, they saw you ride in wearing your gear, or some of them did. Others heard about you and Yatu fencing and lancing and shooting. Those that didn't want to make sure it happened. A quick look, and then give them a fiesta!"

This sounded like good advice; and as the early arrivals came in, Ju-hai saw how well his brother had reckoned.

Shou-chi, of course, led the way; none had entered the dining space until he arrived. He took three steps forward, after a momentary halt, and then kowtowed. Ju-hai did not stop him until he'd knocked his forehead against the rammed-earth floor. As though he'd been distracted and caught off guard by early arrivals, Ju-hai started, turned from old Ah Hing, and sank to one knee, taking Shou-chi by the hands,

"Please don't! You're my guest! I was stupid—I'm the

guest of this town—" This was said as he rose, Younger Brother with him. "I was absentminded—still arranging things. It is written and it has been said, 'The Most Important Person is the one who is facing you.' "

This bit of Confucius, seconded by a peremptory gesture, kept the just-arrived Chen Lao-yeh and his son, Chen Yin-chu, from kowtowing. And thereafter, formality sank to each guest's clasping his own hands and bowing. Voices rose as ceremony tapered off with a crash.

Yatu, with soot and grease begrimed maroon cape over three-ply yakhide armor, plates linked together with brass rings, hovered a bit to the rear and to one side of the master, supplying Ju-hai with liquor somewhat diluted; after all, the host had to drink with each arrival, at the moment of arrival. Sometimes a line formed.

It was an oppressed village, taken over by a usurper under cover of legality; but since no one was being flogged and neither famine nor pestilence had taken charge, the unconquerable Chinese relished food and drink. The blessed moment was in command.

Shou-chi herded the Chens and his handful of confederates toward the corner where Ju-hai had stationed himself, once the gathering settled down to festivity. Despite the season, the elevation made the evening chilly. He had taken his post by the coals.

Time was becoming critical; once the guests had eaten and drunk, they'd disperse without warning, scattering as might a covey of quail. Except for urgent reasons with immediate demand on his attention, no sane farmer would lose too much sleep.

Shou-chi nudged one of his allies, a conspirator who didn't know why he conspired; but food, drink, and conspiracy are good, no matter where you find them.

"Sir, you must have done a lot of fighting in your life," the questioner led off, in response to Shou-chi's nudge.

Ju-hai chuckled happily. "Until the caravan was caught flat footed by Tu Fan tribesmen—this was somewhat east of Yarkand, on the southern branch of the Silk Road, you know. Yes, I did learn which end of a sword was sharp, but that was a bad day. I was a survivor and part of the plunder and was sold as a slave—sold to a Farsi officer who had quit his native country before the Allah-crazy Arabs cut off his escape. I think he must have been an *emir*, a sort of prince. He did nicely in our country. But he was getting old and tired, and he converted to Buddhism, cut his hair, put on a yellow robe, and retired to a monastery. And when I didn't want to cut my hair, he said, 'Son, then take my horse and things and go back home.' So I obeyed a good master."

"Where did you find your Mongol friend and your wagon, and where'd he get that awfully good big horse? Why didn't you get a big Ferghana horse like he's got?"

This was the substance of half a dozen questions, boiled down.

The festive bedlam had tapered off to the phlegmatic level which few Chinese ever reach.

"I started out alone, and my armor was bandit bait, or it may have been the horse. Instead of getting help, a road-robber tackled me single-handed. So I got his horse and armor and some silver he had with him. And at Lop Nor I met Yatu, and we bought a cart. A rider and a carter looked easy, but you'd be surprised, we got the cart loaded —with dead bandits' belongings. So we sold stuff we didn't like, and are having this party tonight."

Ju-hai had their attention. He glanced along the crescent of landowners. Some still stood; others sat on the floor; all leaned and swayed a little.

"You thought you'd hear from a soldier, and all you heard was a slave. I'm saying no more! Let me hear from a *soldier*, someone who met fighting men, not bandits looking for loot and slaves."

Someone nudged Chen Lao-yeh. "Tell Wong Hsiao-pao about real war, the time the militia cut up a division of Manchus."

Another mused, "*Hsiao-pao*—Little Treasure. But you came back from slavery with *lots* of treasure!"

Shou-chi turned from Chen Lao-yeh and faced Elder Brother. "If Ju-hai had come back with as much loot as you did, Lord Wong Hsiao-pao, we could pay off the loan secured by Kwan lands and get rid of that dog-fornicating General who bought the note."

Another confederate cut in. "Shou-chi, if I had the amount of that note right here, in silver, I'd bet it—I'd bet that if *you* had the money, you'd be a reckless idiot to try to pay off the loan. Something would happen to you—an accident, so called."

"If I were a fighting man like Wong Hsiao-pao, I'd pick a fight, challenge him to a duel. Tsao wouldn't be harder to handle than any bandit on the Silk Road. Easy!"

"Easy?" Chen Lao-yeh stroked his stringy beard. "What would be so easy? He's a professional soldier."

Ju-hai turned on his guest. "He wasn't any more fighting man than we caravan guards—we got clobbered about the same time he and his troops got beaten away from Khotan. He didn't do any more fighting than the traders and camel drivers. He'd be no problem—but don't bother; let him alone, he won't last long!"

He wagged his head and chuckled; his glance swept from face to face. Someone demanded, "What's going to happen?"

"Someone told me the other day that Tsao had a new concubine, a really hot piece, and she'll have him worn to a shadow in no time, and he'll die happy, too."

There was groping silence.

Ju-hai, the stranger who had blundered into forbidden territory, gaped and blinked. "Well, when I saw him, he looked kind of worn out and happy." He raised his voice. "Yatu, get another jug!" After a pause, he resumed, with a rueful grimace, "A stranger can be sure he is going to talk out of turn! I would as soon none of you quoted me, but if that's asking too much, do as you please about it!

"Speaking of loans again, he'd either take the money if I offered it, or he'd fight and I'd pay off his estate! Don't take my word for it. Ask the buzzards I fed all along the road! And before I forget it—if the General balked at meeting a no-name like me or you farmers, he'd lose face."

He didn't say what the subject of the duel would be, and there was no need. Yatu returned with a jug of wine and one of *kao-liang*. Cups were filled. They were emptied at a gulp. Chen Lao-yeh was grim and sweating. His son fidgeted and looked miserable.

Ju-hai got up. Things had gotten far enough. He turned on Younger Brother. "I don't know how much you owe him. See me when we can sit down and talk quietly. You people have been mighty nice; maybe I could lend you enough to make up what you're short."

He paused. He stood there, beaming. He took a stride, and clapped Shou-chi on the shoulder. "See that your neighbor's don't talk as loud as I just did. If I can raise some silver, and he balks, you challenge him. Then you get sick, or fall off your horse and hurt yourself, and appoint me to take your place."

The Chens, father and son, brightened perceptibly.

Chapter XLVI

The courier who had brought word that the Minister of War proposed visiting Kwan Village was overtaken by Tsao's aide-de-camp, who had an unlimited expense account and a corresponding opportunity for gaining rich *cumshaw* for the patronage he could offer. He was sent to order supplies for a banquet only one grade short of Imperial. In addition to wines, delicacies, and all the table luxuries that the world's most magnificent city could offer, there would be entertainers and musicians—the former certainly, and the latter probably; and by virtue of profession, whores, male or female. Whatever General Tsao kept of the revenues of Kwan Village for that year, he would still have to borrow to maintain his personal establishment.

Landowners and tenants, knowing who would ultimately pay for the festival, wasted no emotion and pulled
no long faces; they would face tough years if they lived
into the future, so they might as well enjoy the party.
After all, they had been robbed when there was no festival.

During the days which ensued, the population of Kwan
Village increased by a half. Retainers, servants, and all the
lower echelons of the great man's retinue came and found
lodging in the courts of what once had been the Kwan
residence; the lower ratings overflowed and crowded the
inn, or made camp in the plaza.

A few days after the first wave had settled down, field
music sounded off, and outriders came racing in to warn
that the guest would soon be in sight. Presently, the Minister's bodyguard cleared the gate. Drums thundered, saddle
drums pattered their beat like dainty dancers, gongs
clanged, and firecrackers rattled off, string after crackling
string.

Tsao's guard turned out, swordsmen, pikemen, and halberdiers.

Then came the Minister's elite, the personal guard.
There were neither footmen nor outriders with whips to
clear the way. Instead of such, there were troopers with
drawn swords, lancers, and archers, four at either flank.

The last-named were well known because of their orders; any bystander who failed to kowtow would be trans-
fixed by an arrow. Finally came Prince Han—in the saddle, not carried in a palanquin. If he'd worn blue shirt and
knee length pants and plodded barefooted down the pike,
he'd still have looked the soldier. Except where women
were concerned, he'd slept longer on the ground, in
bivouac, than had most men in bed.

His squarish face was angular, deeply lined, and would
have made him seem as tough as his guardsmen, except
for the lurking twitch at the corners of a mouth straight as
the edge of a sword and twice as hard. He was tougher
than any of his guard, and thus he could risk being natural, almost smiling—he couldn't remember when one of
his archers had shot an impolite spectator.

His Highness was one of the few survivors of a house

almost exterminated during the wars before T'ang became great.

Those seeing the red and gold palanquin from afar had observed that the curtains were drawn and that eight bearers carried it. But when it passed the spectators, they had their faces close to the road. Some might have imagined the elegance of the passenger, but they could not smell her perfume. This was masked by the sweat of many horses, and by manure recently dropped.

However, it was socially permissible to wonder how long the concealed lady had been a concubine, and whether she was an established lady, or one engaged for the trip. Many an upper-bracket lady balked at trips away from the city; hence, there were specialists who accompanied dignitaries into rural areas.

To appear without cap or appropriate tunic or proper trousers would be eccentric; to appear without a concubine would be unspeakable, indecent.

Once the Minister had accepted the salutes of Tsao's guard and had been welcomed by Tsao, the archers and others of his escort were relieved of duty, and gaping was in order. Ju-hai and Yatu got a good look at the red and gold palanquin as bearers—only two of them, now that the lady had alighted and entered the Kwan residence—carried it to park near the outer wall of the Kwan courtyard.

"That's the one that brought a lady to my *yurt*," the shaman declared. "Only, there's no reading on it. It's the one who had questions—the First Class Prostitute."

"You sure it's the same?"

The Mongol sighed and shook his head. "I can't be sure. But it looks like it."

"Whoever she is," Ju-hai conceded, "she could have been promoted to traveling concubine. That's the tough thing about being a shaman—not to know what the question is and what the spirit says."

"It may be tough for you," Yatu retorted, "but that's why a shaman lives longer than astrologers and so forth. Everybody knows he can't know what people ask and can't know what he answers."

"They ought to get into the great Bureaucracy and get rich in no time."

Yatu grumbled something about rather being a shaman than a dung-brained catamite, and would from that start have risen to eloquence and higher invective had not Juhai exclaimed and gestured.

"Tsao's Number One Girl! Look—"

"How many girls would that old bastard have?"

"That's not what I mean—she's herding six girls—"

"All dressed alike. Don't tell me he can take care of them all. I told you—"

"You and your dog-turd mind! Those girls are dressed up to be maids for some lady. They're Kwan Village girls, and don't tell me you've not been eying them! Never mind your guessings; I'll ask Peony—"

"Who's Peony?"

"The girl with the grocery basket, the one who's sleeping with the sergeant of the guard. I'll ask her the questions."

He got a quick briefing from Yatu before they intercepted Peony somewhat short of her new home. The sergeant of the guard, a big fellow as broad as a buffalo and a lot taller, was the best liked of all Tsao's men. After Peony's sixth raping, he suspected her of being a worthwhile woman. He said to someone, "A lot of these girls aren't worth a second whirl." And then he told the entire guard company, "I'm taking her home. What's done is done, and whatever is going to be done from now on, I'm doing it." He made a complex but very quick gesture; he did not bother to explain symbolism. He dismissed the company. Peony's popularity was no longer a menace to her. None of the guard fancied castration followed by beheading.

As the inviolable queen of Kwan peasantry Peony carried herself regally, thoroughly enjoying being a one-man woman. She'd learned that Wong Hsiao-pao was a gentleman, and that Yatu was crazy but harmless. She addressed the shaman.

"Mistress Lan-yin is showing the ladies-in-waiting around the General's mansion and telling them how to dress the bride and how to find things and places about the house."

"What bride?" Yatu wondered.

"Beautiful royalty is marrying General Tsao," she answered, then begged leave to move on.

"Is Lan-yin going to keep on being a concubine or does royalty bring her own choice of concubine?" Yatu wondered. "Does Tsao have to go without any concubine? With these royal bitches, you can't ever tell."

Ju-hai shook his head. "When you get to that level, you know as much as I do about Chinese custom." He recalled that he knew a lot about female Immortals, but royalty was something else. "If they pitched the Emperor's big tent over this town, it would be one elegant little insane asylum! See me after the banquet!"

Breasts bouncing with every bound, Peony came racing back. At middistance she called, impartially looking along a line midway between master and man, "I forgot to tell the great Lords, the bride is Lady Soong Ming-tien."

Peony did not wait for answer. She turned and raced homeward.

"Who is Lady Soong Ming-tien?" Yatu asked.

Ju-hai shrugged. "She could be close to royalty—the awfully rich important Soongs—or she could be of the dirt poor aristocratic Soongs. I guess there are some peasant Soongs and some that are low enough to be merchants."

But what most concerned Ju-hai was why General Tsao had seen fit to invite a stranger to a banquet, especially one probably intended to be the public announcement of a ceremony which would be most meticulously private, a contract linking two families, of no concern to the public at large.

Chapter XLVII

The banquet proved to be slightly pretentious.
At the head of the pavilion-hall, a dais was set up for
the Minister of War and the officers of his staff; with them
were General Tsao, his aide-de-camp, the commander of
the guard, and one secretary. These were seated. Standing
behind their chairs, the host and guest of honor each had
that most important retainer, a deputy drinker. The Minister, grim victor of many a hard fought field, however
advanced in years, did not appear to be the man to raise a
cup to his lips, pretend to taste, and pass it over his shoulder for a deputy to toss off.

The host, regardless of age, required a deputy; since he
had to respond to every drinking to the health or the
memory of every friend the host and guest had in common, living or dead, this was a sensible provision, quite
aside from the custom, sometimes optional, sometimes
mandatory, of going from table to table, drinking to each
guest, man to man.

Ju-hai, sitting with the landowners, had Yatu behind
him. As the nominal owner of the Kwan acres, Younger
Brother was on the dais. Ju-hai was wondering why Tsao,
after making such a point of wishing him to act as Honorary Aide-de-Camp, had not appointed Captain Li. That
officer had a place on the dais and he was not on duty. Ju-
hai's request for an interview had been ignored until Tsao
had got the Minister's message. It was as if he were being
entangled in an intangible network, constantly changing.

Chen Lao-yeh sat with the lesser landowners, among
those who might keep him in a combative mood.

Sweet-voiced cymbals and the boom of drums brought

lion dancers bounding out to caper, strut, roar, and posture their way about. It required two men to impersonate one lion, to keep the creature moving, jaws snapping, eyes rolling, and teeth menacing.

Having made the rounds of the hall, the creature descended to terrify villagers and guardsmen in the plaza.

After nine courses came an interlude for sword dancers and martial arts teams. They finally quit the scene, without anyone's having dismembered another performer.

Jugglers and acrobats gave well fed guests amusement and a chance to shake down what they'd eaten against better judgment. Servants moved about with basins of hot water and steaming towels, wrung dry, to refresh the diners.

All the while, Ju-hai had been giving more attention to Chen Lao-yeh than to chopstick work. As a matter of form, he picked a few morsels from each course. Yatu grumbled about the lack of deputy eaters. After a few cups of wine, Ju-hai passed the drinks over his shoulder to the shaman.

"Ease up, enjoy it," the Mongol urged. "Chen's just waiting for his minute, his mood. He *has* to challenge Tsao or else hang himself—he's got to do one or the other."

"What do you mean, he's *got* to?"

"If the new wife makes Tsao send Lan-yin back to her husband, that will make it insulting. But if Chen forces a fight and makes the old bastard give her back, he gains face."

Chen Lao-yeh's drinking kept Ju-hai on edge. Not enough, and he'd hold his peace; a bit too much, and his challenge would be laughed off as part of the entertainment. His moral supporters were eying him.

Now that the twenty-seventh course had been tucked home, servants were clearing the tables. There would be female dancers and singers before the final seven courses were served.

Chen got to his feet. He glanced back, wagged his head, and stroked his stringy black beard. He made for the dais, without even a glance at Ju-hai. Chen carried himself like a soldier. His tunic, apricot-colored, with purple embroidery and piping on the long sleeves gave him something akin to stateliness—or it might have been his gait and carriage.

Chen halted. Tsao raised a hand, making a restraining gesture to someone off stage. His glance shifted to Chen, and he smiled amiably. Ju-hai couldn't hear what he said, but he appeared to be inviting the landowner to propose a toast or to speak whatever else was on his mind. It was now high time for informality.

Chen bowed to the Guest of Honor. The Great Man's gracious inclination of the head and his amiability invited expression. Chen shifted sufficiently to face General Tsao. There was now no sound from the entrance from which lion dancers, acrobats, food servers, and jugglers had come. Chen bowed as deeply to the host as he had to the Minister of War.

"Sir, lavish host, this farmer begs leave to address your Exalted Presence on a personal matter, and with permission of the august Minister of War."

The Minister, his Highness, Prince Han, was all for hearing it. He caught Tsao's eye and nodded. The deep lines of his stubborn face came near shaping a smile. The narrow eyes were encouraging.

Chen said, his voice was resonant and steady, "I challenge your excellency to a duel, with whatever weapons you choose."

No one could possibly have failed to understand the words. And those words, coming from a farmer, were unusual. The ensuing silence was so deep that the rustle of silken garments was clearly heard. The Minister of War leaned forward. This was better than martial arts or female dancers—or a banquet, for that matter. This was novelty in a long life which had included much of the unusual.

Tsao's smooth face became more benevolent than wine and good will had made it. The lurking smile crept further from cover.

"A farmer," he replied, "one of those whom the Son of Heaven honors every spring time above soldiers and scholars, has more than a privilege. You have a right. No man from here or from otherwhere has challenged me since I have been protector of Kwan Village. Out of courtesy to our august Guest, be pleased to clarify."

Chen, grown greater than himself, had presence. "Your Excellency, this person has lost the respect of his fellow farmers ever since you took my wife, Lan-yin, to be your concubine. This was done in an abrupt mode and without proper negotiation."

"Chen Lao-yeh, I had been assured that you would have no objection, and that Kwan Yu-tsun and his sons, Kwan Ju-hai and Kwan Shou-chi, for years had Lady Lan-yin as a concubine in common."

"Your Excellency," Chen pointed out, "that was among neighbors. You or one acting for you made slighting references to this during your campaign against rebels in Khotan. Our son, Chen Yin-chu was embarrassed by the mockery of his comrades-at-arms. So was I, when I learned of the facts.

"I beg leave to represent that you have never been a friend nor a neighbor. Wherefore my challenge stands."

He shifted a little to regard the Minister, eye to eye. The latter was smiling. His eyes twinkled. He gave silent applause.

Tsao said, "Chen Lao-yeh, a landowner is entitled to meet any officer of any army, excepting his immediate superior. But, because of age and health, I must appoint a deputy." He smiled and gestured toward the man standing behind him. "Even for my drinking, I am represented by a younger man." He raised his voice. "Captain Li!"

The commander of the guard got to his feet. "*Ngo!*" he shouted. "At your command."

"Captain Li, I have been challenged by Chen Lao-yeh. Will you be so obliging as to be my deputy and appear in my behalf?"

Ju-hai would have got to his feet, but the shaman weighted him into place. "Sit down, you idiot, he has to speak!"

Chen Lao-yeh faced the captain. Lan-yin's husband seemed not at all drunk. He was exalted by wrath evoked by ultimate outrage. In the new and deeper silence, there was whispering as of bamboo stirred by a breeze. His Highness Prince Han no longer looked amused or entertained. An old hand, he scented death in the air.

Peasants, he recalled, with rural implements or even by hand, had dismembered Emperors. And this was Shensi Province, the cradle of the Chinese people, whose genius for many a century had centered in the ability to turn without warning from docility to homicidal mania.

A hundred guardsmen with sword and halberd would check the disorder—but not in time to save the lives of the men on the dais.

Shou-chi looked alarmed. Nor was he the only one.

Captain Li could have precipitated general manual dismemberment by saying, "General, I am your deputy." He said nothing, and it was not out of fear for himself. He was grim and old for his grade; he was wise.

Chen said, "General, I have fought in two campaigns, but I am no soldier. Captain Li is a professional and more worthy of being a general officer than are many of that rank. It is my right to have a deputy fight in my place!"

There was a gusty sigh. The Minister began to enjoy the party again. He was not alone in this. He chuckled, swallowed, bent double, and laughed aloud. He was a soldier, not a Confucian gentleman.

"Chen Lao-yeh, appoint your deputy! If no one else offers to serve, call on me!"

Ju-hai bounded up, made three long leaps, and slid to a halt. He bowed to no one. "Chen, let me redeem myself for being a liberated slave!"

Chen bowed. "General, Wong Hsiao-pao will fight in my place."

General Tsao addressed the Guest of Honor: "Your Highness, the days of your visit are dedicated to you alone. Do you grant permission for this duel during your stay?"

"*Permission?* General, it's not every day that one sees deputies fight it out while their principals sit on their tails, applauding! Captain Li, Honorable Wong, will you be sober enough tomorrow to fight, or would you like to relax for a day?"

"For me, a liberated slave, to meet a professional soldier of Captain Li's status is a chance to wipe out the stain of having killed nothing but bandits between Yarkand and Kwan Village. This is magnificent. Captain, if you've not drunk too much tonight, shall we meet an hour past midday?"

Each bowed three times to the other.

The Minister of War got to his feet. "Let each appear with weapons of his choice, each to be a surprise to the other, as it has been in every battle of my life, winning or losing. Whoever wins tomorrow, I have a gift for him." He addressed his host, "General, I've had a long day. If you don't mind, I'll skip the final courses—I'm sure your other guests won't miss me, and I know you'll urge them to stay until they fall on their faces."

"Your Highness, since you are leaving us, I'll give the two duelists permission to withdraw."

"Be pleased to tell them that I am no longer present."

Tsao raised his voice to battlefield volume. "Honorable guests, his Highness, Prince Han, Minister of War, has departed. Captain Li, commander of the guard, and Honorable Wong Hsiao-pao, our very distinguished visitor, are about to depart to prepare for combat tomorrow, an hour past noon.

"I remain with you for the entertainment and the remaining courses of the banquet—but first, I wish a few words in my study with Honorable Wong Hsiao-pao, after which I shall rejoin you."

Ju-hai said to the shaman, "I'll meet you at ground level." He turned to follow his host to the room where he had utilized some of the literary skills Mei-yu had taught him.

A swift-footed servant had fired joss sticks and lighted tapers. Tea was steeping in the elegant jade pot. "My good secretary anticipated our desires, at least mine. Please be seated," General Tsao said. "*Kwan Ju-hai*, I am sorely in need of your services."

"Your Excellency is mistaken."

Tsao smiled as affably as ever. "If you had done no more than present the Emperor's command to all commanders along your route that they facilitate your progress in overtaking your father's regiment, I'd have been impressed by your patriotism and your filial piety, yet might have forgotten your face. But Captain Li and I discussed you and we observed you until you and your father kidnapped Chen Lao-yeh's son—Lan-yin's son, of that much we are quite certain!—and made off with two camels. If it hadn't been for my intent observation, I'd not have recognized you. Captain Li still doesn't realize that he's met you before. If my former concubine, Lan-yin, recognized you, she gave no sign, never a hint. Harbor no suspicion—it would be unjust!" He poured tea. "Soldiers have been known to drink all night to prepare for battle at sunrise; sometimes they are right, and sometimes they don't survive. I'd advise tea. Yes, and before I forget it, your attempt was not foolhardy!"

"Indeed, sir? You leave me feeling very much a fool!"

"Ju-hai, I said that I was sorely in need of your services. I'd hardly wish to be served by a fool. You recall that the punitive expedition included several regiments. The man whose armor you wore when coming here was never one of my friends. He was a guest officer, going along for the adventure and enjoying such novelties as riding with a scouting party. If one of the horses of the three dead riders had not returned to the advance guard, we'd never have been interested in the circling of vultures. The armor of the two enlisted men identified the regiment; so we knew that the bones without armor were the remains of a gallant fellow who found more than the sport he had looked for.

"You wore that armor as if it had been designed for you, and whoever changed the color was a true artist, a great armorer! If you'd killed the third horse, we'd have ignored the vultures. Or if you'd ridden that animal up river, we'd have been saddened by the disappearance of our guest-officer, but—"

"Sir, I am to be of service to you? Please explain."

"When a boy and an elderly farmer kill an officer, two

professional soldiers, and two horses, considerable skill,
resourcefulness, and other of the finer military attributes
are indicated. Courage, a fighting heart, and great en-
durance, marching up that dry riverbed. How long did
your father last?"

"Until we came to Yotkan, where we found all that we
needed for recuperation. We made a quiet living, trading
westward toward Yarkand. And when we thought that,
after nearly five years, two deserters could risk returning,
the Old Man said he was too tired. He gave me his blessing and in a few days he died in his sleep."

"Then I wasn't the cause of your father's death!"

"He would be living now, if he'd wished to live. He died
in good health, because he had *lived*."

"No bond of honor or duty keeps you from serving
me?"

Ju-hai smiled cryptically as ever his enemy had. "It
depends on the nature of the service."

"Well said, well said! Some while before the banquet, I
married a lady of good family. Until our marriage, she
was the *protégée* of His Highness, Prince Han, his favorite
concubine. His Highness is loyal to each favorite as she in
her turn becomes a former favorite. My promotion for my
hand in staving off disaster at Khotan leaves me indebted
to the Minister of War. It would have been discourteous
for me not to marry the lady."

They sipped after-dinner tea—not the tea of formal
leave-taking.

As if startled, Tsao exclaimed, "I'm becoming too absentminded! You have a duel facing you. Whichever of
you is victor will be commander of my guard. And this
business, this need of your services—yes, it does relate to
my marriage." He made a wry grimace. "How complicated
life can be! I'd been so determined to convince you that
you and I could profit each other in more ways than you
might suppose—in ways relating to the Kwan lands . . .
But to discuss this before the duel! Ju-hai, you do need
rest."

He poured the tea of leave-taking. "But there's an advantage in our having had these words. There's no more

suspense, no more wonderings about remaining incognito; you'll remain so for the time, but not out of necessity. Each can serve the other."

Ju-hai went to meet the shaman, and General Tsao rejoined his guests.

Chapter XLVIII

When the trumpets sounded, Ju-hai mounted up and rode from the inn toward the village gateway. He met Captain Li riding from the guardhouse. The combatants-to-be pulled up and exchanged salutes.

"After you, Captain."

He followed his opponent onto the field. Like the valley where he and Yatu had practiced at arms, this uncultivated space was cluttered with boulders. Instead of taking stations, the duelists maneuvered, each trying to plot a course and find a promising line of attack while observing the other's picking his way about. With the sun so little past the meridian, neither could get the advantage as to lighting.

But there was no hurry. One of the two would spend the remainder of his life among the rocks. Ju-hai felt that loneliness, that total isolation, which had oppressed him each time he had turned from his animals to confront a marauder lurking along the way from Khotan. Here he faced the most dangerous enemy of his short career: like most of their kind, Li's predecessors had been less than impressive, or else they would have found good employment as men-at-arms. The Captain was a professional—a fact which carried far more weight at midday than it had at midnight.

Whether won in battle or purchased, Li's armor was

comparable to Ju-hai's. In either case, he had not worn it
on guard duty since Ju-hai's homecoming. He might have
borrowed it from one of the Minister's staff officers. Whatever the facts, it was beyond the means of any captain,
and there was about such armor something which impressed an opponent and made him feel that he was riding
in awkward nakedness into battle.

Then, as a flash of revelation, it came to Ju-hai. *I'm
wearing as good or better. I have no reason to be impressed.*

Like Ju-hai, Captain Li rested his lance in a leather
stirrup-bucket. Each had a quiver of arrows, but the case
in which Ju-hai usually had his bow contained a mace. He
had had the local smith shorten the pyramidal spikes
which rayed from the spherical head of it, and the distor-
tion of the case was not conspicuous.

When the duelists had done reconnoitering the field and
arrived at stations which each found acceptable, they
halted. Tsao's bodyguard were on the wall. The escort of
the Minister of War was formed in front of the gateway.
Tsao and the Minister sat in the pavilion above the gatehouse. In the manner of an army's wings, villagers
crowded each other to right and left of Tsao's guard—
men, women, children come to see in fact a spectacle so
often presented by traveling players at festival times.

A cluster of women sat well apart from Tsao and his
guests. Their tunics and headgear shimmered and twinkled,
brocade glinting. A few were veiled; and among these, Ju-
hai fancied there must be the General's newly wedded
wife, a lady for some reason associated in Tsao's mind
with his guard and its captain. As he sat his horse, waiting
for the heralds who were to officiate, Ju-hai saw all this as
a pageant for Lan-yin, set in motion for her, and by her.
Lan-yin should be there in the high place, but apart from
the General and apart from the other women.

Sitting the dappled bay, Ju-hai saw himself and the others as figures in a puppet show—except for Captain Li,
who was the shadow of a paper cutout.

Drums rolled. Two heralds—his Highness, Prince Han,
could never leave home without heralds—rode from the

gateway's shadow and reined in. They halted. They
wheeled so that their horses stood rump to rump. One
rider faced Captain Li, the other Ju-hai.

As one man, they sounded off the rules of combat, the
terms, the privileges, and the penalties. This was a finish
fight. If either quit the field while his opponent lived, soldiers would pursue that one to his death. Battle would
begin when the signal bomb exploded.

The heralds pivoted, moving toward the gateway.

The tall Manchurian sergeant of the guard came from
the shadows and two guardsmen followed. One carried a
bomb with a fuse. The other had a yard-long joss stick,
fired up and fuming.

The Guest of Honor gestured, the sergeant spoke, and
one guardsman set the bomb on the ground. The other
touched the joss stick to the fuse, and the signal detach-
ment faced about, to march through the gateway-tunnel.

The *boom* of the signal bomb set the combatants riding
at each other. Li had his steel gray well in hand and his
lance ready; he was appraising his opponent with the de-
liberation of self-assurance and experience. Ju-hai's Wind
Drinker wove among the upthrust rocks, making his approach a dance rather than a charge until the riders
emerged from the obstacle course and came into clearer
space and treacherous footing, with flat stretches like flagstones and nasty, glinting, sloping planes.

If a horse fell, the rider would fight afoot as best he
could.

In such a case, one arrow might finish the mounted
fighter's horse and level the odds.

Ju-hai swerved, crossing his opponent's line, wheeled,
and leveled his lance as if to drive home—as he could
have done, for Wind Drinker was agile, balanced like a
dancer. Instead, he reversed. As he pivoted again, he
evaded Li's lance and needled him with a backhanded
thrust. It had no force; it was only whimsy, showing con-
tempt and snagging the fine linked mail.

Li wheeled, and each came at the other again. Li's
charger, a large Ferghana horse, was powerful, durable,
but not designed for polo or tent pegging. Ju-hai wondered

whether that seasoned fighting man would succumb to mockery and to his own irritation.

If he and his enemy lived long enough, he would know. And Ju-hai knew well how expensive information could be. On the long road from Khotan he'd encountered men who had paid more than they could afford.

Now, without warning, Wind Drinker responded to rein and knee and became a tiger with wings. He evaded Li's lance by the thickness of a hand.

It was becoming a polo scrimmage, with nothing lacking now but a near-side backhand.

Distance again separated them, and each rider wheeled. For a long moment they gave their horses a breather which was needed. The dappled bay and the steel gray tossed their heads, snorted, spat foam, drooled, and showed their teeth. Each had wrath in his heart, as each responded to his rider's mood.

And it was as if Wind Drinker spoke to Ju-hai, saying that the time had come.

He hurled his lance far to his near side. It sank deep into the earth, and the bamboo shaft quivered; it was still quivering when Ju-hai drew the Persian sword with fatal histories inlaid in gold on the blade.

Instead of parrying or using a buckler, Ju-hai evaded Li's sweeping cut. The two opponents wheeled again, and then Ju-hai charged, low in the saddle, crouched, squatting like a Hun or Mongol.

But he swerved, and Li, though riding well, was handicapped by a mount too large for such work. In passing, Ju-hai's blade flamed wide of its mark and soared free, circling, to clang among the rocks.

Ju-hai, chest against the pommel of the saddle, came up with the mace he had dipped from the bowcase.

There was an instant during which Wind Drinker's shoulder cleared the cantle of the steel gray's saddle. The mace shot out in a near-side backhand stroke. With a sword, it would have been useless—but the orange-sized sphere of steel tapping the back of Li's head had all the force that was needed. The stubby spikes of the mace did not penetrate the fine steel of Li's plumed helmet. They did not even dent the metal. But whatever skullcap Li wore between his head and the steel of the helmet was meaningless. He crumpled and fell from the saddle, as limp as a bag of rice.

Ju-hai was afoot before dust ceased rising from the rocky earth. Wind Drinker stood by with reins trailing. The steel-gray horse had halted. Ju-hai knelt to unhelm his enemy. He waited, bending over, as if solicitous. There was not yet any sound from the spectators. The mace appearing from nowhere had stunned them as it had Captain Li.

Ju-hai waited patiently, but not long. He had grounded a stout soldier. Remembering, he took off his own helmet. Li was recovering, but his vision had not yet focused; he stared without seeing. It was not until his eyes saw more clearly that Ju-hai spoke.

"Try and remember me," Ju-hai said quietly. "I came to take my father's place in your company at Lop Nor." His voice was as smooth as Tsao's, as if mimicking the General. "That whip slash across my face . . . remember?" There was a flash of recognition, of memory. This had to suffice. "Once, you slashed the Old Man's face."

Li made a grasping move. Ju-hai pinned the wrist to the ground and struck with his dagger. Blood and air wheezing from a throat slashed ear to ear prevented whatever Li might have said.

Ju-hai said, "Dad, the bastard's on the way. Slash his face with a stable broom."

He sheathed his dagger after wiping it on Li's tunic. He retrieved the scimitar. Mounting up, he rode, twirling the mace; it was a good weapon for a fighter outclassed by a full dress professional.

Ju-hai sighed and said aloud, as he leaned forward to slap Wind Drinker's sweaty shoulder, "But don't try it unless you have an awfully good horse."

He reined in when he was close enough to the gatehouse pavilion to address Tsao and Prince Han without discourteously raising his voice. He rose in the stirrups.

"*Ngo!* Your Highness—your Excellency—out of respect to a fighting man much more skillful than I'll ever be, I did not take his head. I make no claim for his horse, his armor, or his weaponry."

And then he remembered that he should have dismounted and tried to do so. The Ministers' gesture checked him.

"Most interesting fighting I've seen in many a year. General Tsao has a good captain of the guard. He returned his concubine to her old home before the combat—a mark of respect, that she should not be the prize of a duel." The Minister bowed to Tsao. Then he continued. "To offer a present, as I promised, would belittle a superlative combat. Instead, if ever you weary of commanding a guard and fancy a military career, come to Ch'ang-an. I or my successor will appoint you to the grade of captain, perhaps higher, in the army of the Son of Heaven. I'll put this in writing. And now, you have permission to depart."

Chapter XLIX

Now that the Minister of War had gone with his retinue and Captain Li's funeral had been taken care of, Tsao and Ju-hai sat in the General's study to resume the conference which had been cut short because of Chen Lao-yeh's challenge. Tsao poured wine. "Ju-hai, I was happy when you turned down the Minister's offer of a commission in the Imperial army. I had given you little reason not to accept such an offer."

"Sir, you had spoken of great need for my services. Instead of keeping me awake until you explained, you let me get the rest I needed before I went out to meet Captain Li." Ju-hai drew a deep breath. He was still weary and depleted. "As it was, the arrangement was unfair to Captain Li. I had a chance to become commander of your guard. All he had was a chance to remain what he already was. And you didn't turn me in as a deserter coming home, wearing the armor of a guest officer of the Advance Guard of the Khotan Punitive Expedition. You mentioned need for my services—you mentioned your marriage—you referred to the Kwan lands. How are these related?"

"It's by no means complicated! If the Kwan lands are to earn enough to pay the interest on the mortgage, the management has to be good. If I had to take possession in default of interest, I'd lose—how could I manage matters? I'm a soldier. Soon *I* would be borrowing, and unable to make the interest. Then what?"

"Sir, there's my Younger Brother."

"It is Kwan Shou-chi I have in mind. Earnest, hardworking, but no manager. He's not like you. In the duel, you did everything Captain Li did not expect and nothing that he was looking for. You threw your sword away, making it seem as if you'd fumbled and dropped it. Your amazing horse was all that kept your enemy from killing you. And your near-side backhand stroke with the mace—that was masterly! Your Younger Brother would have fought bravely and died. You refused to fight, knowing you could not win against Captain Li, but here you are. You'd manage the Kwan acres to win!"

"While I'm captain of the guard?"

Tsao chuckled. "I'm sure you heard about the Manchurian sergeant and that well shaped girl, Peony. No one has raped her since the sergeant decided she was worth taking home. He'll do all the commanding that the guard needs. Except of course at ceremonies, such as paying respects to a visiting Prince."

"General, I begin to understand. But your marriage—someone said to Lady Soong Ming-tien, the daughter of a lordly house."

"Her parents live in Kaifeng. She has been away from home for some years. To be the concubine of his Highness, Prince Han, is a social distinction. An Imperial Concubine, of course, can go no higher—since there is no station higher than Imperial Consort, and this is a matter of State, not Imperial Preference. But Lady Soong was not an Imperial Concubine. And there is one step higher for her. Marriage—Number One Wife—*tai-tai*—even to one as lowly as a mere general."

"Sir, I begin to understand. It would be presumptuous of me to congratulate either party to this marriage. But to be of service in anything relating to your auspicious marriage . . . General, this dull-witted farmer is too perplexed to be of service."

"After her several years of—obscurity—she wishes to visit her parents. She wishes also to bring various gifts. Things of such value as to justify a bodyguard, an armed escort. You are to command Lady Soong's escort. News gets around. You have been favorably noted by his Highness, the Minister of War. You, your horse, your armor— each is distinctive, and will add to Lady Soong's homecoming.

"And then, a final distinction."

"Final distinction, your excellency?"

"Yes. The escort will consist of a platoon of Kwan Village militia—landowners or sons of landowners. When Chen Lao-yeh challenged me, you may have realized for the first time the standing of a landowning farmer."

"General, the truth never had real meaning until after the twenty-seventh course, when Chen Lao-yeh confronted your Excellency. Sir, I bow three times. But one thing I beg leave to request."

Tsao smiled benevolently. "You were reasonable with his Highness. Do as well by me, and it's granted."

"I beg leave to represent that Lady Soong should not set out for Kaifeng until after the Milky Way Festival. The festival should be as my ancestors developed it, year after year—a family tradition, with due respect to the Moon Goddess and to the Princess and her lover. These traditions have made for the successs of Kwan acres. And, may I ask one personal favor?"

"Please do so."

"You consider me commander of the guard. That I survived is my warrant. Ladies however well born do love a story that can be decorated and dressed up. If the guard and I were presented to each other late the night of the festival, it would be additional ceremony, adding to the importance of your bodyguard.

"And Lady Soong's escort should leave with formality. The escort might even wear armor and carry weapons of some of the professionals. Make a display of well-drilled landowners, looking like your bodyguard. And the company *guidon* would add a touch! Perhaps a few of the guard musicians—possibly a herald—if there's no herald, appoint one."

"Ju-hai, you go beyond my expectations. Lady Soong will bless you."

Ju-hai was too tactful to suggest that the scarlet and gold palanquin in which she'd arrived should be sharply checked for signs indicative of her one-time status as a traveling concubine. Others of the fraternity of bearers would note and be inclined to entertain the people of Kaifeng.

"One final detail," Ju-hai said, as he was about to quit the General. "While I was still thinking of going to Kwei-chau to look for employment, I had it in mind to offer a leave-taking gift. This gift could well be offered because I'm staying here. It might be worthy of Lady Soong's taking with her, as another gift to her family. The thing is a triviality, yet unusual: a piece of jade from Yotkan, a most unusual thing, with uncommon properties. A species of illusion, some would say. It could be offered after the guard and I are formally presented to each other.

"Until then, I had better avoid the guard until we meet after the festival. There would be less resentment because of the loss of their late commander and less intense grief."

Chapter L

Three nights after the duel, Yatu came to the door of Ju-hai's cell. "The General sent that concubine home while you were worrying about the battle. She wants to talk to you. I'll bet she knows who you are."

Ju-hai pondered a moment. "I wouldn't be surprised. The longer I am here, the more neighbors will recognize me. Where is she?"

The shaman jerked a thumb over his shoulder. "Waiting —and scared. She's half afraid you *will* see her."

"Bring her in. When you leave, close the door after you. She must know who I am or she wouldn't be worried."

The Mongol stepped back and reappeared a moment later, thrusting the visitor ahead of him. She was veiled, and a long cape concealed her figure. Her advance guard was that old familiar freshly bathed and ready for bed smell.

As the door closed, Ju-hai asked, "What's worrying you?"

"You had us fooled for a while but some of us—I'd be one of the first—to recognize—"

She choked, blinked, but after a gulp, her eyes met his and remained steadfast. Though Lan-yin was putting up a gallant fight, she could not keep it up. She was about to fall apart. The wrath which had helped sustain Ju-hai in his long ride home was beginning to fail. "What's worrying you?" he repeated, but gently this time. He reached out and drew her toward him. And as she clung to him, the old familiar feel of her body left him wondering what had happened to long-cherished hate.

He nudged her toward the *kang*. "Say it any way it comes."

"It would have been awful, facing you, even before the duel—" She choked and hunched over, burying her face in her palms. Then she spewed it out. "I'm so crawling ashamed! Things went further than we ever imagined. Chen and I did connive with Tsao—"

"I heard all that."

"But this you didn't hear. We didn't know opium was habit-forming, bad *joss*. We didn't know he was going to rob you of all your school money. We didn't have a big scheme, like the one he had."

Ju-hai didn't have the heart to say, "Because you're small scale people." He patted her shoulder. "I've seen enough of the whole business. I know it's truth you're telling. You and Chen got land hungry and you'd been the Kwan concubine, way back, starting with the Old Man."

She sat bolt-upright.

Ju-hai smiled, fondly and sadly. "Dad and I had a time of it after your son, who was perhaps my half-brother, left us afoot and took the camels. This was near the river, but when we had to move to a dry riverbed, we got into bad trouble. We had hard going. He was out of his head and I don't remember where my head was, or if I had one. He said a lot of things he would never have said when he was in his right mind. Anyway, you're one of the family, and young enough to be just right for that girl-craving old bastard, Tsao. I wonder that his Highness, the Minister, didn't take you back with him."

"*Aiieeyah!* Don't mock me."

"I'm not mocking you. How are you and Chen getting along?"

She caught him with both arms and kissed him until he was half drenched by her tears. "After all we'd done against you, you fought in Chen's place. He didn't suspect who you were, but he was afraid you wouldn't be his deputy after all. And with all his talking at that drinking party of yours, at the inn, he couldn't back down, so he challenged Tsao. If you hadn't done the way you did, I would have been sent home by Tsao's new wife; of course, she wouldn't allow me around the house. I would have been dumped out, and some of the village women would have been too happy for words."

"No wonder, the way you keep your face and shape! Anyway, you're back home. Things any different?"

She hesitated for a moment, wondering whether this was a query or a proposition. "Well—yes—I told Chen to bring his concubine to the village and she could move in with us. I was kind of nasty not making her welcome."

"Ease up, just a tiny bit." Ju-hai gained enough clearance to draw a deep breath. "You were saying?"

"About me and Chen—that will keep! Tell me about the Old Man. I'm awfully sorry. I never held it against him, taking that concubine and turning me loose to play with you and your brother."

"We outlasted the desert, got to a monastery, and he was as good as new finally."

He told her of the leave-taking, and of the Old Man's blessing. Without doubt, Lan-yin was one of the family. For a while they sat without words, remembering Kwan Yu-tsun, the man who knew when he had had enough, and who could quit the scene willingly, not kicking, screaming, or clawing for one more hour or one more acre . . . or one more of anything.

Abruptly, Ju-hai straightened up. "You and I did have a lot to say. But is there something else?"

"Yes. The General's wife wants to talk to you."

"That's asking for trouble! I have enough of that right now. I'm the new commander of the guard. The men liked Li. Sure, he was a military bastard, but they respected him. Even if they knew it was a grudge fight, and that I'd hated him from way back, I'd have trouble. What's this fancy bitch got in mind? I want none of her, not even if it's lined with gold leaf!"

"You ought to hear her."

"I've got enough problems without sneaking into the house that still belongs to me."

"I'll bring her here. It will be late. She'll have to wait till the wine takes hold."

"Wine or opium? You wenches are awfully confidential all of a sudden."

"Ju-hai, trust me, don't spoil it all."

"I don't know who was more of a fool about women, me or my Old Man. Go ahead, I'm good for one more gamble."

Lan-yin wrapped herself in darkness, and the shaman came in, bringing a jug from his cart.

"She left on her own feet," Yatu remarked, as he poured wine. "Good story, or just a good piece?"

"She's the go-between, acting for someone who has a story that I ought to know."

"How far do you go in believing either one?"

Ju-hai shrugged. "I'll listen and find out what they want me to believe. You know now how Lan-yin was one of the family. Too late now for her not to be. I think what she and Chen fixed up with Tsao went further than he or she reckoned. Tsao went so far beyond their farmer's imagination that I believe her side of it."

Yatu tugged his earlobe. "If you're wrong, we can ride."

"The Chens have settled one thing. His concubine is moving in." After giving the shaman an outline of Tsao's plan for the bride's visiting her family in Kaifeng, Ju-hai concluded, "What's wrong with that?"

"Nothing wrong. That is what makes me think twice."

"What do you say is *not* wrong?"

They took the whole business apart, piece by piece. They had to agree that a militia guard for Lady Soong was too perfectly logical, which made it the false note. They were still wrangling when the sentry's calling another watch told them that a good deal of time had elapsed. Maybe the women had run afoul of trouble.

"I'll get some sleep, or should we get another bottle of wine?"

The faint scratch-scrape at the door squelched that resolution.

Ju-hai said, "You get under cover, and stay watching, just in case someone followed them."

He opened the door, after putting out the light. Once Yatu slipped into the darkness, Ju-hai reached for flint and tinder. The taper flame revealed two women, each veiled. One was luxuriously perfumed to accord with the red and gold lacquer palanquin.

The door closed behind them, the women unveiled. One was Lan-yin, and the other was Orchid, Ju-hai's housekeeper in Ch'ang-an, now Lady Soong Ming-tien, the former concubine of the Minister of War—and finally, General Tsao's newly wedded wife, *tai-tai*, Supreme Lady of the Kwan acres.

"I didn't expect *you*, but I'm not surprised. Not even surprised that you're as beautiful as ever. We're not fighting. Let's sit."

Having been sleeping with quite a few of the most important men of the capital of the Empire, Lady Soong took charge of the situation. "I risked it, Ju-hai," she led off amiably. "After that lovely piece of dueling, you wouldn't be in a killing mood for a few days."

She was a fascinating bitch and, beyond doubt, born a lady. No upgraded slut could have learned such poise. She studied Ju-hai for a moment. "If Lan-yin hadn't told me you'd returned, I'd never have recognized you. No, I can't say how you look different—I don't think you really *look* different, except a lot older. But something's happened to you. An experience that went deep . . ." Then she smiled, in a meaningful way that made Ju-hai's ears redden a bit. "She must have been a most unusual woman. Anyway, we're partners again, you and I."

"It was arranged for us the first time. Is someone arranging it for us again? Or is this your thinking?"

"It's being arranged for us—by the same man. I thought you'd be interested."

"I am; if you were in my fix, you'd know how much I'm concerned! But I'm more interested in knowing who and what you are—even more than wondering how you manage not to look a day older than the last time we met. Me, I feel as if I've lived several lifetimes since I called the doctor and then got my horse."

"Who and what I am, or what I was? You're entitled to know! I am actually Ming-tien, surname Soong. Not noble, not wealthy, but not the lowest either, though I've had my wonderings at times. My branch of the family did lose quite too much. Instead of selling me, they arranged for Colonel Tsao to be my guardian. No doubt at all, he made the most of the situation."

"They may have been sensitive, good people," Ju-hai conceded. "But putting you into the hands of such a guardian . . . Well, he may have been . . . ah . . . unscrupulous in the face of great temptation."

"My prospects were quite good until my guardian got into an awful financial mess. So he sold me to a whorehouse keeper. It was a *good* house, one of the best."

"Providing temporary concubines for high officials when they travel in the provinces?"

She nodded. "I was young and very choice."

"You still are."

"I do believe you mean that! Anyway, I wasn't too happy about it all but I did meet some notable men. And since you were to be robbed, you'd be no more robbed if I got the money instead of my former guardian. So I bought out my contract."

"And in no time at all you were the Minister's favorite lady?"

"And for longer than I expected."

Ju-hai sighed and grimaced ruefully. "Lady Soong, since I've made peace with your husband, how can I wage war against you?"

"I thought you'd see it that way. In any event, his Highness is a darling! He did his best to make a good marriage for me. But Tsao was furious when he had to marry *me*, or be reduced to the rank of sergeant, captain, or something. There's a mystique about being a general. Being reduced would be worse than a death sentence. Now, it's your turn to tell *me* something."

"Lady Soong, until I hear the question, I'll not promise. I may not answer."

"You may not even know. Yes, I put opium into the wine, but never more than enough for sound sleeping and good lovemaking. So, how could I have got such a rugged overdose? Even if I had fumbled and got your cup by mistake, I never gave you such a heavy doping! An addict could have taken it easily, but I never used the stuff, and so it nearly killed me." She shuddered. "You saved my life!"

"*Tai-tai,* I'd never heard of the stuff until I woke up and you were blue-lipped. Ask me later—I think I can explain, but not now."

"Everything I did against you was done before I knew that I had a life that needed saving. Ju-hai, can I persuade you to save my life again?"

This was not female whimsy. Her eyes made that all too plain. There was no fear in their darknesses, but neither was there any glint of hope.

"Tell me more."

"If you'd not killed Captain Li—"

"He would have killed me."

"I mean, before the challenges were spoken. You were to command the escort to take me to Kaifeng. Captain Li was to have a party of disbanded soliders—"

"Meaning bandits."

"Of course! They were to sneak up on our road camp. The militia escort would be careless about security. As long as you and I were killed, the rest of the party wouldn't have to be wiped out. While I was being dressed for my wedding, one of the maids was late; she was busy hearing my ex-guardian, my soon-to-be husband, talking it over with Captain Li. A snoopy wench, bless her! She had a mystic feeling that something was going on and—anyway, that's the story."

Ju-hai frowned. "The whole business is crazy. Getting rid of me makes sense. But you? Is he afraid that you'll blackmail him with evidence that he'd been plotting against the Emperor? Or prove that it was his fault that the Tibetan tribesmen fouled up the siege of Khotan? Unless you're a menace that way, who'd be so crazy as to kill a woman like you?"

"You're sweet, but you don't see far enough. I'm one of the poor Soongs, and Tsao has a chance to marry into a wealthy family, a really important one. But he can't divorce me and he can't sell me."

Ju-hai regarded her from head to foot. "No daughter of

an important family would ever allow you around the house! You're too good-looking to live. But relax. You won't set out for Kaifeng until after the Milky Way Festival. If any of your maids learns anything about the route you and your escort will take to Kaifeng—"

Lady Soong got to her feet and caught Lan-yin's hand. The women pressed close to Ju-hai. Orchid whispered, "The three of us could outwit the trap. I might grab gold and other valuables—dope the guard for our getaway—"

"It's something to think about," Ju-hai conceded. "But it's a long time to the Milky Way Festival. Be sure you live till then."

Chapter LI

Ju-hai had concealed the jade figurines of his father and Tsao by taking a brick from the wall of his cell, chopping away enough of the inner face to make room for the little sculpture, and then replacing the face of the brick. Now that the Milky Way Festival was at hand and he had to test Mei-yu's magic and his own, he retrieved his jade work. The first sight of it surprised him, and this was followed by apprehension. He had assured Mei-yu that it was his duty to carry on alone, instead of relying on her; and such had indeed been his intent. What disturbed him was that Mei-yu had been at work, and without revealing herself to him.

His father's expression had changed. The Old Man's face was serene instead of desperately fierce. No longer suggesting a tiger about to pounce, the posture was that of one who had knocked his forehead against the tiles and was about to rise and receive a noble visitor. It was not so much, if indeed, at all, that the geometry of the figures or the facial planes had changed; but without any specific, *perceptible* alteration which Ju-hai could define, the effect of the sculpture was different from what it had been when he stowed it away to make sure there'd be no pilfering of a work he could not duplicate—even though Mei-yu would start anew, he had to act now, or fail forever; he had no second chance.

Tsao's smooth benevolence had the flavor of sincerity. What had happened to the vengeance, the curse, the death-and-doom which accompanied the gray vapor that he and Mei-yu had chanted into the jade?

He got into seven *catties* of Persian mail and took one of the felt skullcaps out of the helmet so that it would sit a bit lower, and the coif would drape differently. No guardsman was going to nail him with an arrow in the same way that he'd settled the former wearer. Finally he put on his scarlet cape.

Perplexed and alone, Ju-hai stalked across the plaza, his helmet plume jaunty, courting the breeze and the moonlight. He was scarcely aware of the crowd that had been jamming the plaza. But he smelled the fumes of broiling meat and heated wine; he heard the voices, the shouting, the cackling, and the chatter and laughter of women and children. Guardsmen prowled about. Those on duty were armed, awaiting their tour on post. The others, were festive; everyone was festive.

Except Ju-hai—and probably Lady Soong, who, according to plan, was to be butchered with her militia escort, some time a couple of nights hence.

Single-stringed fiddles wailed. Fish-head instruments went *tock-tock-tock*, holding their own against the small drums, and the great lion dancers capered about. Jugglers and acrobats were at it on the several lashed-bamboo stages.

He got a glimpse of Yatu, fraternizing with the natives and up to some shamanistic deviltry, no doubt, while planning escape routes, just in case something went wrong.

When Ju-hai entered the pavilion over the gatehouse,

the General was awaiting him, with an aide-de-camp and a couple of landowners, dignitaries from a not distant village. Tsao dismissed his aide-de-camp, knowing that neighboring and other villagers would depart with permission implied.

A glimpse of Ju-hai was all they needed. He'd killed a professional—and not having taken his enemy's head, he must be a kindly young man; but who'd want to fraternize with a tiger?

Although Ju-hai had never mastered levitation, it seemed that he walked on air, not on the floor of the pavilion-hall from whose railing he would accept the salute of the guard, when the General got around to have the guardsmen assembled. Ju-hai turned to the table set out in the pavilion space, far from the formal seats of honor.

"General, I beg of you, face south—you're not the Son of Heaven, but here you represent the Emperor! I'll turn my back to a plaza crowded with guardsmen not in ranks."

Tsao chuckled. "Now I know why you lived to return. That mail would stop any arrow."

"Having it, I wear it. But soldiers are philosophers— how else would they accept that death-dedicated profession? Since they knew I had no malice against Captain Li, I don't need mail tonight, but if I took it off before I received their salute, they'd be offended by my informality."

Ju-hai stepped to the chair facing north.

Servants brought wine and flaky pastries stuffed with minced meat and fried in a thick-bottomed pot heated so that, when cooked through, they had to be scraped loose. There were *satay* morsels and meat skewered on bamboo splinters and broiled. There would be no banquet—not with so much festivity and the shows of tradition.

When he could do so casually, Ju-hai said, "Sir, I mentioned a gift to honor my staying, rather than my departure. It seems more appropriate that I offer it before I am under your command and the guard under mine. Have I your permission?"

"Granted, and eagerly!"

Servants brought other trays of snacks and jugs of wine.

Ju-hai took the scarf-wrapped jade from his sleeve—the most flowing and most formal of sleeves, in the trailing fullness of which he might have concealed a cat or a small dog.

"Your Excellency, these images are of jade from Khotan. They have a curious quality, so the jade master told me. He said that if one recited the proper *mantra* and made the proper *mudra*, the images would communicate. One is the image of my late father. Perhaps you remember him?"

"How could I forget that fine old man." General Tsao sighed. "Now that I'm retired, his desertion and yours mean nothing any more! As a man, I understood then. As regimental commander, my understanding made my duty even more painful. Now, this communication—I'm sure you don't mean that his image addresses mine?"

"That would be strange indeed, sir! But I've noticed something odd. A peculiar quality of these figures has me puzzled."

"And in what manner could that be?"

"It's illusion, yet I've had the feeling that the expressions have changed. Originally, when the Old Man faced the image-maker, his expression was grim, resentful."

"It would be, it would be."

"But look closely now. He's still slightly on the stern side, yet there is a hint of the amiable. There has been a change, as if the good will between you and me—as if he were aware of the change in my attitude. He doesn't resent my serving you. I'd feared that he would not understand—that no matter how many sacrifices I offered, he'd resent my change. We were both hating you. But I've not had any threatening dreams—"

Tsao leaned forward, hunching a shoulder. "I'm still wondering how the sculptor got such a likeness of me. He never saw me."

Ju-hai regarded the General eye to eye and answered out of sincere conviction. "There was a strange woman involved in all this, and a *tao-shih*. Between them, they must have read my memories and the Old Man's. How between them and the jade master they could get an image that changed expression, I can't even guess."

"If only I'd seen these images when the artist completed them," the General mused.

"Then your judgment would confirm mine—I mean, if there really has been a change. The Stone of Heaven is strange. But you had personal problems, worrying about my brother's not being able to manage as my father did, and the way I might manage. As you said, if he didn't make the interest payments, you'd have to borrow and you'd be as bad off as ever."

There was a long pause. Ju-hai, still groping, nevertheless was gaining self-assurance. As he pondered, a thought came to him. "You and I came to agreement, bit by bit, and this relaxation shows. It's very subtle, but—look and see! You can't point it out, put it into words, but—"

Tsao nodded. "It does. That face does look the way I've come to feel about matters. I had been worried."

"When I fought Captain Li, that was my great unpaid debt to my father, offering him Li's life as a sacrifice. Li slashed him with a riding whip, perhaps because of the same sort of impertinent question as angered him at me."

"A good soldier, but difficult—yes, difficult . . . Did the jade master teach you the *mantra* and *mudra* to make these images communicate?"

"Sir, I've gone too far already. If I go further, I'll risk making a fool of myself; that weird woman and the sculptor may have been mocking me. The workmanship speaks for itself; please accept it as it is. If I attempted the test, and— well, any *mantra* is deceptive—the wrong tone . . ."

He hitched his chair back. He got to his feet. "Sir, let me be presented to the guard, and the guard presented to me."

Tsao snapped to his feet. He made a detaining gesture. "Please, Captain Kwan! I'll dismiss the servants. You can chant and recite not being disturbed by the curious and the gaping. I know that forcing one's memory is a strain." He wagged his head. "When I was a young officer and had to command a formal guard mount for the first time, it was like death by slicing slowly. I made not a mistake, but when I dismissed the guard, I went to my quarters and collapsed."

Tsao mopped his forehead with one of the warm towels that had come with the snacks and the wine.

Ju-hai made a gesture of resignation. "How can I balk?" After a pause, he said, "Sir, if you could withdraw your intentness, so that it would be as if I were alone, trying but without really *trying* to recall . . . This sounds absurd."

"It sounds," Tsao cut in smoothly, "as if you'd met a Taoist master, an unusual *tao-shih*. Is it a long *sutra?*"

"Not a *sutra*—a *mantra*, a *dharani* . . . that's what troubles me; I don't even know what I'm going to sound off about."

"Not long—then you can remember?"

Ju-hai sighed wearily. "It's monotonous, almost the same old stuff, over and over again. I practiced it a little. I didn't have anything else to do while the Old Man was recuperating."

"Try it. My patience has no limit; my curiosity has all the patience in the world," the enemy wheedled, gently, persuasively. "If there's even a slight change in the faces, the expressions . . . Don't strain. Forget I'm here. Pay no attention to the fun in the plaza. The guard will be here when you're ready. They won't assemble till we give the signal. You're commanding the guard, it's not commanding you."

Who's persuading whom? Ju-hai asked himself, uneasily, as he realized that the roles had been interchanged. But after an uncomfortable moment, reassurance took charge. He had baited Tsao and the enemy was responding.

Chapter LII

Ju-hai drew a deep breath, and slowly exhaled. The inhalation and exhalation he repeated until he was reassured, and presently, beyond the idea of assurance or of the opposite.

He began to chant, and he did not grope. The recital was not as monotonous as he had claimed; like Oriental music, it seemed at times repetitious because the variations were subtle, like a rug design in which a pattern seemed to repeat itself, yet actually never ceased varying. And he did not grope; it came to him as if he were again sitting with Mei-yu.

Ju-hai, though aware of Tsao, no longer took him into account, any more than he took into account the chairs in which they sat, or the table on which two figures emerged from their pedestal of jade. In achieving his fine balance, he had gone beyond straining and striving, beyond goal or purpose. The rhythm of his chanting was an end in itself. In this pose he understood, for the first time, what one of the masters had meant when he said, *Where the Buddha is not, hurry on . . . where the Buddha is, do not linger . . .*

And then it was as if Ju-hai's voice had become the echo of someone else, at once himself and *another* intoning. Although his voice should be coming out of his depths, the surge of sound which it had been during his hour after hours of rehearsal, he now could scarcely hear himself as himself. In the manner of a Mongolian shaman, he was becoming the vocalizer for *another*, one who had overwhelming power but lacked a body. And as *it* gained force, Ju-hai had ever less to do with what was going on, yet he was ever more a part of an entirety without losing awareness of individuality. There were time-stretches during which he was in a state akin to his mergings and blendings with Mei-yu when they had practiced jade magic and were at once one, yet separate individuals.

It startled Ju-hai when he became aware of seeing; there must have been long periods of not-seeing. And then, like a revelation, he saw the unwinding of what he and Mei-yu had built, hour after hour, day after day, with gray mists which perfected his jade-craft. The two figurines sat at an angle to the line of sight from Ju-hai to the General, so that the latter could see the faces of each image, somewhat between profile and three-quarter face. The mist emanating from Mei-yu had been absorbed by the jade figures. Now, in Kwan Village, by the light of a moon almost full, gray wisps spiralled like joss stick fumes from the Old Man's image. Whether the jade breathed or merely exuded was not clear, but whatever the mode, it emerged to rise and stretch out into layers, with other portions spiralling to make whirlpools.

These exhalations had energy in their own right and Ju-hai was reminded of the animation of horse-hairs in a trough or a pool of water; each hair, as boyhood talk had it, was alive and becoming a tiny serpent, animated by a life all its own.

Tsao attracted the gray streamers. They twined about him, except for those which became spindles, lingering in space, scarcely higher than the tabletop. These waxed and their gray-bluishness became phosphorescent. Whatever caused the glow, it was not transillumination by moonlight reaching into the open pavilion, a story above the plaza where the guard would form when the signal was given.

The multiplying spindles coalesced, becoming female figures, tiny dancers who grew moment by moment rather than the months and the years such growth would require in the Kwan world. They were elementals perhaps, or jade-spirits; and Ju-hai began to sense the direction of the enchantment which Mei-yu had taught him. Below, in the plaza, the drumming and the clanging brass of lion dancers and of all the other musicians became ever more distant, fading into silence. That echo-voice which had so disturbed him in the beginning was barely audible, and the voices of guardsmen, of villagers, and of all the travelers from neighboring settlement were—

And then they were not.

The wheeling figures became ever more solid and taller, though still short of full grown women. Whether Chinese, Turki, or barbarian, he could not decide, since faces and figures shimmered and changed, never solidifying into fixity. Apparently, Tsao was not aware of them. And this was reasonable, since they must be of a substance akin to Mei-yu's. Few humans could see her until she made herself visible. Although translucent, the mist, now becoming greenish, was denser than in the beginning. The lunar women circled about Tsao and grew in stature and opacity by coalescing, though they did not diminish in number, since those newly formed took their place.

Jade dancers! In pace and gesture, each moved in harmony with her sisters and now each was ever more jade-like in all but the flexibility of the dance.

And then Ju-hai knew that Tsao was aware of what was happening. His bland face became tense. His features were strained. His mouth worked, yet he made no sound. The man was chewing air, vainly. His hand labored and his fingers responded, but without meaning. His trunk shuddered as if he tried to get up but had not the power.

Solicitously, the dancers gestured, poised as if questioning and reassuring; their circle closed in. Finally Tsao moved. It was an awkward, unnatural move which left Ju-hai confused. He had never seen the like. Desperation and mortal determination strained his muscles, yet Tsao remained seated, gripping the table's edge, his hands and arms responding as might an image of stone if endowed with life and making its first effort.

The table tilted. It dropped, and the jade group thumped to the floor. It landed, sitting on its pedestal; fumes rose to merge with the spirals and the layers. And then Ju-hai began to understand. Now that the table no longer blocked his view, he could see that there had been a change of color. The white soles of Tsao's boots had become green and translucent; the felt now had a vitreous luster. The tunic was no longer apricot-colored. From hem almost to hip, the color was that of jade and so was the luster. And the greenness was creeping. The circle of dancers opened as though to give Ju-hai a better view of their work. Taller ones hovered near Tsao, gesturing, stroking his face, whispering in his ears to reassure him and comfort him.

Two knelt, adjusting his belt and buckle. One patted and tugged a bit at the shoulder of the robe. The silk yielded beneath the belt and a bit below—but only where the color was still that of apricot. Where the robe was green, there was no motion, no giving.

Ju-hai, not solidified into jade, yelled and leaped. He fell, stumbling over a leg of the tipped table. He clawed the floor. He was entirely himself now; there was no longer Ju-hai and *another*, and for moments he remained on all fours, groping for balance of body and balance of self and of mind.

It was as if he had been hurled from uttermost space back into his own world. He barely regained his feet, to stand unsteadily, weaving and wavering.

Then it was as if the entire evening of festive noise had been concentrated to explode in a tremendous blast of yelling, screeching screaming.

There was no music. No drums or cymbals sounded. There was nothing but voices blasting out of cracked throats. Something must have called the crowd's attention to what was happening in the pavilion—or what had happened.

Ju-hai turned about, without quite falling on his face. In the plaza, Younger Brother and the shaman were pointing toward the pavilion. Moonlight reached in, drowning the golden warmth of many tapers. Ju-hai, near the waist-high wall, steadied himself, and turned about. The few remaining dancers were becoming ever more misty. There was no longer a flow of mist from the image on the floor.

Tsao sat, perfectly posed, benevolent and serene, with not a trace of the consternation which he had battled until the jade dancers had reassured him and had smoothed his tunic. General Tsao was now wholly of fine jade from Khotan, the City of Jade—though a purist would insist that Yotkan was the actual origin. Appropriately, the chair in which he sat was of jade.

"I know it is unusual, such a mass of jade, so translucent. But you might say how you like *me*," a woman said.

Three lingering dancers stepped aside, revealing Mei-yu.

"What panicked the folks in the plaza," Mei-yu added, "was when I had my instant of absolute fire, to glaze the surface of the image. You were dazed and clawing the floor, divided between my world and yours. Yes, Tsao watches over Kwan Village."

He had so many questions that he did not know where to begin. And then he realized that he and Mei-yu had the pavilion to themselves. Clearly, the Kwan lands remained moon-ruled.

"I know it was rude of our daughters to leave without asking permission, but one has to—"

"Our—our—*which?*"

Her smile promised an interesting explanation, but had she attempted such, neither he nor she could have heard it. The sound which roared up from the plaza was different from any of its predecessors.

He would have caught her hand, but he remembered. He bounded to the railing, with Mei-yu after him.

Chapter LIII

Down in the plaza Ju-hai and Mei-yu saw the guard which he was to have commanded. Some were in livery, some were not, but all were too tightly packed to use such weapons as quite a few of them carried. Apparently they had been caught by surprise, in the way of unwary travelers when a flash flood catches them in a narrow ravine, with no chance for resistance, and escape an unrealistic hope.

The guardsmen were the center of a whirlpool which shifted slowly toward the gate. Villagers had taken the wall and from the parapet they hurled bricks, rocks, honey buckets, firewood, and whatever they could grab. Villagers came racing from the inn and from the food stand, carrying pots of steaming water or of coals and ashes. Others with lengths of wood from the hills were pursuing and clubbing guardsmen, armed or unarmed.

Ju-hai leaned against the rail, groping, gaping, still half stunned. He remembered his scimitar and had it half out of the scabbard before Mei-yu checked him.

She had no force, no substance, but her voice penetrated. "Let them have their fun—after these last four or five years, don't deny them. You've done your share. Ju-hai, don't you dare meddle or I won't tell you about our daughters!" When he slammed the sword home, took a stumbling step, and halted, Mei-yu's voice softened. "Lover, you're such a marvelous mankiller, must you be greedy? You'd share your food with your people; can't you let them take their share of killing?"

The howling mob, so tightly packed that it could no more butcher the enemy than the enemy could fight back, fell apart at the gate. Ju-hai muttered words about his being on the verge of disintegration, and she went with him to the chair he set right side up. Once she saw that he'd seated himself as he intended, and not on the floor, she knelt beside him.

"They—everyone—guards and villagers—saw more than you did; you were in a trance," Mei-yu began. "First what they called ghost-women, and then me—and the completing of the jade image."

"There was more to it than that," he said. "Whatever it was, it must have been a blend—you, me, and other things. Someone got into the militia armory. Those halberds and swords—"

Farmers were still racing for the gate. They had axes, scythes, flails, and kitchen choppers. Women were turning out with whatever household or farm equipment could inflict injury. Meanwhile, the mob voice receded and the silence that ensued made the cicada chirpings clear and crisp.

"They'll be lucky if they kill twenty of the guard; and the more that escape, the better."

Mei-yu's brows rose.

He went on, "The ones who escape will tell the story, and tax collectors will be very reasonable, with the story of the massacre getting bigger with every telling." He frowned. "Tsao—dead or *living* jade?"

Silence drenched in moonlight. Mei-yu finally said, "There were last minute variations. You didn't fumble, not really. You were on your own. I had no chance to brief you. Changing those faces—I mean the faces of the images—did make it better for you. It worried you, I know, and then you lived up to it, and I knew then and there that you were qualified. You held his attention from the start."

This reminded Ju-hai of the lad who was learning how to be a burglar.

"You've qualified," she repeated, "and you have a free choice."

Then his scattered wits coalesced a little more. He said, "Before we run out of time, there'll be no choice and no qualifying by anyone—not until you tell me what you meant about our daughters. Those dancing girls were mist and illusion vaporing out of the Old Man's image."

She gave him a grimace of amiable mockery; her eyes gleamed triumphantly. "So you still don't know where the grayish-bluish haze came from that was sinking into the jade you'd shaped? Ju-hai, Ju-hai, sometimes I think you'll never qualify! With all your jade-craft and other things, and magic and *mantra*, we did spend a lot of time in bed; and when *yang* and *yin* keep at their love makings long enough—three guesses, which one's likely to get pregnant?"

He made a collection of incoherent sounds and false starts at speech. "But—uh—what I mean— Listen, woman, you were on what you called a spirit plane or something—how—what I mean is—"

"My thick-witted darling, there's nothing in the cosmos that isn't either *yang* or *yin*, and something has to come into manifestation, so there's birth—mental things, the most dense and material on *that* plane. Thoughts are things, some sage or another said, and I was giving birth to the forms of our thinkings for Tsao and others. But especially thinkings for Tsao. I don't know how much or what kind of *karma* you and I stirred up and I'm not awfully worried."

She smiled in amusement. "Quit this invisible counting on your fingers and trying to reckon how many of our offspring appeared. Time and numbers are different on the spirit level. Now do you know where those vapors came from in the jade studio, upstream of the Kara Kash, in the Monastery of the Dancing Phoenix."

"Divinity, even this thick-witted mortal finally arrives at the only reasonable answer."

"Nice," Mei-yu contributed, after enjoying a moment of silence. "On that plane there are no labor pains. Which naturally means nothing to *yang*. Even so, you're qualified."

"Qualified for what, Divinity?"

"To go with me to my realm, to be a probationer, a provisional Immortal. Let Younger Brother be head of the Kwans. I'd love to have an artist-jade-lover with me; and with the vendetta out of your heart, I'd give birth to *nice* offspring."

On her feet now, she extended her hand. "It's a long, long way to Yotkan, if you mount Wind Drinker and ride. But mount the wind of heaven with me and we'll go to Yotkan, somewhat up from the Kara Kash, where the Old Man is buried. Sit here now in your armor and wait until Younger Brother comes back; the chase won't last long. Bless him before witnesses and take leave. I'll go frail-thin, so they won't know I'm here. They won't see you mounting the wind with me."

He had never seen her as lovely as at this moment. He was not beguiled by her sweetness; he recalled the deadliness lingering in her face when he had turned about and seen three of their daughters reveal her after she was done with Tsao. He knew well why the guard, looking into the pavilion, had been caught flat-footed by farmers. And he knew why they had fled in panic.

"Jade Lady, Divinity, for the first time I know beauty; and for the first time, I know what you and I had in the desert and monastery. I didn't know until now." After a long silence, he went on. "I'd be an Immortal of a sort, and we'd have our sleepings together, a *kalpa* of them, and I'd begin to learn your wonders. But these are my people. Soon they'll be coming back, tired, happy, and satisfied by the killings, and tomorrow, they'll want their festival undisturbed. I belong here. And the Old Man said something I have not forgotten."

"Tell me again, lover, what did Kwan Yu-tsun say?"

"He told me that he had lived his life and he was tired. He said that a man wanting to live too long is a fool; and if he does not become weary of the old self with which he's lived so long, he is stupid. He should die contentedly, having completed his mission; and whatever he has not done, it will be waiting for him in the next incarnation, when he'll have better equipment for meeting it."

He stopped short. "Jade Lady, thinking has never been more difficult, but these people—"

"I know." She sighed. "Hsi-feng—you've not seen her."

"Hsi-feng may stay crazy the rest of her life. Again, she may one day have sense enough to know that I came back. I can't quit what she and I started. She won't be the first Number One Lady to be crazy and revered. I've been a fool about women. Forget Lan-yin, and I won't bother to strangle Orchid. Now that Tsao is harmless, I'll send a militia guard to take her to Kaifeng. Or back to Ch'ang-an, to be a traveling concubine."

"Ju-hai, the *yin*-of-*yin* can't hate a man because he's a fool about women. With *yoni* on the brain, they do the silliest things, but . . ."

And then they heard voices in the distance, the chatter of farmers whose fury had cooled. Looking down into the plaza, Ju-hai saw his brother, contented and tired. He shouted, hailing him.

Then he said, "Jade Lady, the wonders you and I shared

I'll always remember. I can, but I don't want to quit Hsi-feng."

"Immortals live so long, which makes a loss everlasting. You will be sad only for a short lifetime."

Her sadness was not as convincing as it had been when their talk began. Also, she did not vanish in phosphorescent vapor.

A woman entered the pavilion. He smelled her before he heard her, and knew that, when he turned, he'd face Hsi-feng. Then he heard her.

"Old Master, I told Jade Lady I'd bet you'd say something as silly as you did. You're the most idiotic farmer a dizzy-slave girl ever imagined. I was bright enough to go crazy in time not to be included in the general raping. And Jade Lady visited me sometimes when you were away. We became friends, and that helped."

Ju-hai looked blank. Mei-yu laughed happily. "Old Master, I'll get you in another incarnation. Hsi-feng!"

"Yes, Divinity?"

"You promised to make me a promise."

"Divinity, what is the promise?"

"You are promising me that every moon you'll lend me your body, and I'll be Ju-hai's concubine."

Hsi-feng had scarcely promised, when Younger Brother came racing up the stairs and into the pavilion. "I remembered your story about the boy who learned to be a burglar. Yatu and I cut our way through the back of the armory. The sentry had a little wine with a little opium. Yatu said his spirit predicted trouble and so we got to work."

The shaman wore full armor, and carried a halberd red from recent use. Younger Brother added, "He was ready for this. All I had time for was to grab a helmet and a sword."

Yatu nodded. "Your chanting sounded like there'd be trouble so I got dressed for work."

Ju-hai said, "Younger Brother, you'll never be a soldier, turning out in improper uniform! I'll have to tell Mei-yu that I wasn't the only one who had to improvise tonight."

He and Hsi-feng turned. They saw no Jade Lady.

"She was here a second ago."

"She? Who do you mean?" Shou-chi demanded.

"Younger Brother, pay no attention to Hsi-feng. She thought she saw a woman up here with me. Just her jealous mind!"

"Jealous mind, my arse!" the shaman denied. "I saw women all around Tsao, till they faded out and only one stood talking to you."

This perplexed Shou-chi. "I must have missed something."

"All you missed is a look at my Number One Concubine. But get a good look at the new *tai-tai*. Hsi-feng can see invisibles. And from now on, the house is going to be run strictly; you can't fool her."

As if she'd not heard Ju-hai announce her promotion from slave girl to mistress of the Kwan Family, Hsi-feng said, "Old Master, I'll heat wine. You go down to your old study and listen to the fighting men tell you about the fun you missed."

"With fear and trembling." Ju-hai gestured to include Yatu. "Bring three jugs. Meat cutting is thirsty work."

"Make it four jugs," the shaman grumbled. "My spirit-devil gets thirsty; and if he's left out, he gets sore."

Ju-hai went with his brother and comrade to the apartment he had quit to go to school. At the threshold he paused, looked, and finally said, "There were times I thought I wouldn't see this again."

"*Tai-tai* must've known you'd be back," Younger Brother said, indicating the table and its litter of books. "Look—just the way you left it, only no dust."

Ju-hai cleared the table and took the chair which Younger Brother set out for him. "Sit down, both of you. While we're waiting, I'll give you the big problem. There is room in our family shrine for another guardian; or we can leave our friend General Tsao in the pavilion; we might even build a shrine for the guardian of Kwan Village out in the plaza." He raised a hand to check comment. "Think awhile, both of you. We've got urgent things to talk about right now."

The shaman hitched back his chair.

"Sit down, Yatu! You are the important matter we'll talk about. You're one of the family."

"I'm not Chinese," the Mongol objected. "I belong in that colony of my own people, outside the Jin Guang Men. Sure, it's good here—good people—but when there's a crowd of women around, well, they smell funny." He shrugged. "Though I suppose you can get used to anything."

"You hated to see our martial arts valley sitting there, not being cultivated."

"I remember. What of it?"

"Clear the ground and earn title to it."

The shaman grimaced and looked dumber than usual. "But I'm a foreigner and I couldn't get away with it. That flossy bitch said I didn't even smell Chinese."

Then Hsi-feng stepped in, breaking up the discussion. From twinkling toes to jade hairpins, she was mistress of the household. Ju-hai would not live long enough to estimate the woman-hours normally needed for the hairdo and dressing of the lady, after borrowing whatever accessories she might need. The entire scheme centered on the pectoral, the Dancing Phoenix which Ju-hai had shaped of jade as his farewell gift.

Hsi-feng carried a tray with one jug and one cup.

Three girls followed: Happy Springtime, with an enormous tray crowded edge to edge with snacks and centering on a large jug, which went to Shou-chi; Sunset Cloud set one jug and one cup in front of the shaman; finally, Lotus Bud put a jug and a cup well to the shaman's left.

At this, Yatu demanded, "What's the idea?"

Hsi-feng answered for the girl. "For your spirit-devil. He is one of us. Old Master, your guests are served. Now may I serve you?"

She set out a small jug and a small cup. Then the women quit the study room.

Saying nothing, Ju-hai eyed the shaman.

Finally Yatu said, "They smell funny. Your Number One Lady has good manners. My spirit-devil wouldn't give her a bad answer." He filled the cup at his left. "I'm his deputy—imagine he is drinking this one." After emptying the cup, Yatu grinned amiably. "That fancy bitch, the one that was Tsao's concubine, she was the one that said I smelled funny."

"You might get used to us?" Ju-hai suggested.

The shaman chuckled. "That's Chinese politeness! You might get used to me! But this business of my getting land—I can't swear any allegiance to your Emperor. There's a Great Khan beyond the Great Wall."

Ju-hai brushed that aside. "I told my Old Man about you, and he said if I ever lived through what was ahead of me, I should tell you he had adopted you as a son. So—no problem."

Yatu grinned happily. "When the Mongols take over the Empire, I'll go home to my people as I should. And when we take Ch'ang-an, I'll see there's no looting, no raping out here. I'll tell the Khan I own Kwan Village."

Finally, Shou-chi got his chance. "First, we have to find the silver the Old Man buried; and if we find the note that Tsao bought from the money lender, we'll burn the paper and the lender can sit in a tall tree and curse himself."

"Younger Brother, that's happy thinking. But there's something a lot more important. Our girl, Lan-yin—I'll not have time—"

"Sir, I won't either. The Manchu sergeant of the guard got killed this evening. Peony isn't a widow, never having been a wife. But, with your permission—"

"A fine figure of a woman," Ju-hai agreed. "But Lan-yin—"

"She can be my concubine."

When they filled their cups, Ju-hai said, "Permission granted. I drink to all that we've agreed on." They drank, and he added. "Stay until you fall on your faces. With your permission, I take leave. The new *tai-tai* is wide awake and waiting to tell me of the enemy occupation and the new discipline for all females of the Kwan Family."

Chapter LIV

In the Lunar Palace of Chang Wo, the Goddess poured tea and regarded Mei-yu. "Well?" she asked. "Did you tell him?"

"I told him he'd been accepted as a probationary Immortal," Mei-yu said. "He rejected the offer. He'd rather stay and take care of the people of Kwan Village." But she was smiling as she reported it.

Chang Wo nodded. "Ah. The final test—to refuse all rewards and choose instead to do good . . ."

"Well, not *all* rewards. He has Hsi-feng!"

"No matter." The Goddess chuckled. "She only seems submissive. He doesn't know that he's now truly an Immortal, does he?"

"I didn't tell him," Mei-yu answered. She drank tea thoughtfully. "After waiting a thousand years for a man, I can wait a century more, if needs be."

Chang Wo sat back, studying her guest. "You begin to develop wisdom, Mei-yu," she said approvingly. Then she leaned forward again. "And now—tell me all about it!"

ABOUT THE AUTHOR

E. HOFFMANN PRICE (1898–present) soldiered in the Philippines and France during World War I. At war's end he was appointed to the United States Military Academy, where he entered intercollegiate pistol and fencing competition. He was graduated in 1923 and commissioned in the Coast Artillery Corps. His first fiction sale was March 1924, to *Droll Stories*. By 1932, he was writing full time —fantasy, adventure, westerns, detective. When the pulps folded, he earned grog, gasoline and groceries by holding two jobs and by filming weddings and practicing astrology in his spare time. Thanks to his incessant motoring, he met and made enduring friendships with Farnsworth Wright, Hugh Rankin, Otis Adelbert Kline, H. P. Lovecraft, Howard, W. K. Mashburn, Clark Ashton Smith, Edmond Hamilton, Seabury Quinn, Jack Williamson, Robert Spencer Carr, Leigh Brackett, C. L. Moore, and a comparable number in the non-fantasy fields.

During the past sixteen years, Price has been known in San Francisco's Chinatown as Tao Fa, the *dharma* name conferred by Venerable Yen-Pei of Singapore, and he is mentioned in prayers every new moon and full moon in two Taoist-Buddhist temples. As a gourmet, he cooks shark fin soup, sautées *bêche-de-mer* with black mushrooms, and steams "tea-smoked" duck. He declares that in addition to silk, gunpowder, and the magnetic compass, beautiful women were invented in China. Doubters are invited to meet him at dawn, on horse or afoot, with sword or pistol.

Enchanting
fantasies
from

DEL
REY
BOOKS